THE MANGLE

Also by S. L. Stoner
in the
Sage Adair Historical Mystery Series
of the Pacific Northwest

Timber Beasts
Land Sharks
Dry Rot
Black Drop
Dead Line

THE MANGLE

A Sage Adair Historical Mystery
of the Pacific Northwest

S. L. Stoner

Yamhill Press
P. O. Box 42348
Portland, OR 97242
www.yamhillpress.net

The Mangle

A Sage Adair Historical Mystery of the Pacific Northwest

The Mangle is a work of fiction. Names, characters, places and incidents are the products of the author's imagination or are used fictitiously. Any resemblance to actual events, locales, or person, living or dead, is entirely coincidental unless specifically noted otherwise.

A Yamhill Press Book

Cover Design by Alec Icky Dunn

Interior Design by Slaven Kovačević/www.fiverr.com/slaven980

Edition ISBNs
Softcover   ISBN 978-0-9907509-2-5
Ebook   ISBN 978-0-9907509-3-2

Publisher's Cataloging-in-Publication *(Provided by Quality Books, Inc.)*

The Mangle / S.L. Stoner.

276 pages, 21.5 cm – (A Sage Adair historical mystery of the Pacific Northwest)
1. Northwest, Pacific--History--20th century--Fiction. 2. Labor unions--Fiction. 3. Women--Northwest, Pacific--History--20th century--Fiction. 4. Laundry, Steam--Fiction. 5. Martial arts fiction. 6. Detective and mystery fiction. 7. Action and adventure fiction. 8. Historical fiction. I. Title. II. Series: Stoner, S. L. Sage Adair historical mystery.

PS3619.T6857M36 2016   813'.6   QBI16-900019

In memory of

Helen Nickum
and
Sid White

Two people whose
unique, curious and kind spirits
bettered the lives of all
who knew them.

PROLOGUE

He didn't hear the scuff of boots nor the whispered conversation in the street outside. He was tired. A numbing ache pounded his shoulders, just as if they'd carried an oxen yoke all day. He smiled wryly. Truth be told, he'd rather carry a yoke than this weight upon his mind. When would it end? It wasn't just the expense. It was the unknown outcome. That's what kept him chained to this desk, locked inside this building, an hour past midnight. He should have been down at the beach, with Della and the kids. It would take months to recover the money they were losing every day. And, what did he gain? The women would hate him if he won. Even that win would be temporary. Any fool knew that the association was on the wrong side of history.

Eyelids heavy, he didn't notice the pen slipping from his fingers or the ink dribble landing too close to the white of his rolled up sleeve. The still warmth of late summer pressed around him, erasing the border between skin and air. Cheek on folded arms, his eyes settled on the framed photograph. They were worth it, worth all of it, he thought as peace rippled through him.

Neither the breaking window nor the muted whoosh woke him. It was the bang and roar and the falling, legs tangled in his chair. He lay on his side, a roaring pain in his temple where he'd hit the desk. As he drifted into unconsciousness a flare lit up the office and heat began searing his face and arms. Before he registered the pain his befuddled mind realized what had happened. The damn gasoline cans in the front room had exploded. He should have moved them upon delivery, he groggily mused before his dimming eyes fixed on the framed picture clutched in his hand.

It was all Sage could do not to run. Dawn was just hours away. They had so little time to find the two women. What inexplicable happenstance had drawn him into that saloon to stand next to those two sailors? Why had there been one of those lulls that let even a whisper be overheard?

They were complaining. They were supposed to have sailed the day before. But, there'd been a delay. Still, they'd be leaving soon. Come morning, their ship would steam away with the outgoing tide, down the Willamette, then the Columbia and into the Pacific. The sailors cussed the man who'd been tardy delivering the two passengers. Fine little ladies. Secret cargo. Passage money going into the captain's pocket instead of to the owners. These two would get some of it—enough to keep them quiet. And maybe there'd be fun with the women as well.

Ears pricked, Sage moved closer, hoping they were too drunk to notice his fear. "Howdy, fellows. Can I buy you a beer?" Sage asked. And, of course, they'd readily accepted.

"A coastal steamer," they'd told him. "Not safe enough to cross the ocean, mind you. Barely seaworthy riddled as it was with punk and sea worms. Just praying it floats long enough to reach 'Frisco. God willing, and no bad storm arises. Last time we'll sail on her," they'd both vowed. "Damn captain is a lying, thieving, drunk who can't steer a rowboat across a pond."

"What cargo are you carrying?" Sage asked, signaling for refills. He kept his face averted to conceal his burning interest.

"Mostly bits and pieces for those who want cheap and don't mind slow. No regular freight. And two passengers, this time." The two sailors exchanged exaggerated winks. "Ladies of the night," explained one, responding to the look of polite curiosity on Sage's face.

"I would think they'd travel by train", Sage prodded.

"Aye, a train does make more sense," agreed one. "But, it can be tricky keeping someone on a train from running off. Captain says a certain gentleman is paying to have them sent back. He has a prior claim. A matter of money owed," they reckoned.

Her dish dropped and shattered on the floor when the policemen stormed the hall soon after it opened. Alarmed shrieks and cries of "Mommy!" filled the room. Chairs crashed, tables upended as people rushed about. The police separated the women from the few men in the hall, herding them into separate corners.

A policeman stepped forward, his brass buttons shining, gold badge glinting and black baton holstered. Standing tall and solid before his men, his blue eyes swept the room. His smooth German face was serious but unthreatening. His gaze stalled, snagging momentarily on her face, before he continued his survey.

His attention returned to Caroline. "My name is Sergeant Hanke. We are here for your union president," he said in an official voice. "Is he here?"

There was stiffening in the women around her. Caroline needed to take charge, measure up to Mae's faith in her. Stepping forward she swallowed and took a steadying breath so that she could say, calmly, "Why? What is the problem, Sergeant?" she asked, her steady eyes willing him to answer.

His quick glance around carried unease. Though they numbered at least ten, the police were confronting thirty or more people in the hall. Hanke removed his beehive helmet, signaling courtesy as well as his intent to avoid confrontation. His words to Caroline were polite, matching her calm. "Well, ma'am, your president is needed for our inquiries."

"Your 'inquiries'?" Caroline prompted, her fingers tightening on the dish towel she held.

"We are investigating the death," Hanke said, "of a steam laundry owner. He was murdered last night."

Twenty one days earlier

ONE

Portland, Oregon Early August, 1903

Hearing creaks and clops, he peered around the corner. Just a big-wheeled wagon rolling up the dirt street, a drooping horse between its shafts. Water dribbled from the huge tank on the wagon bed. After rainless weeks, street watering damped down the dust about as well as pissing on a rock—especially in this heat.

He snorted and leaned back against the building, grateful for the shade. Probably, some councilman's relative won the watering contract. That's how things worked here in Portland, Oregon. Not like Chicago where they spread out the jobs to keep their butts in office. There, hands were always out. It was expected. No pretending to be holier-than-thou, like around here. He knew what was holy. More than most folks. It sure wasn't the well-dressed society folks who took advantage all week long and then sat in the Sunday pews exuding piety. That's one reason why he left the God business. That and the money.

"No point in thinking about such things," he told himself. He'd ambled too far down the path. Damn, he wanted to be done with this job. Three nights he'd wasted, hanging about, waiting for a chance to get her. So far, no luck. If she'd been an ordinary doxy he would have had her the first night. He knew the patter, knew how to spot the ones tired of being tired and how to trick the ones who weren't as smart as they thought. But no, this one was special. They'd warned him that she'd never fall for patter or tricks. He'd have to do a snatch. He fingered the bottle in his coat pocket. One whiff and she'd be his.

So far, there'd been no opportunity. Sure, it was dark enough, barely a glow in the western sky by the time she came out the door. But always there were too many people. It being summer sundown, the streets were crowded with folks getting off work at nearby canneries and other factories. They might be dead tired but they'd still leap to stop him. Besides, she was savvy. On the way home, she kept away from gaps between buildings and never used the deserted alley even though it would have shortened her walk.

He took off his hat and wiped the sweat from his brow before once more peering around the corner. The laundry's door remained shut. Maybe tonight, she would vary her routine, stray into an isolated spot. That's all he needed. Just one opportunity and he'd have her. He pulled a readymade from his box and lit it. They were paying him so much, four times the usual. Afterward, he'd stay away from the pipe, he promised himself even as he felt his inner demon smirk.

Around him, the dusk deepened and the shadows spread. The musky marsh smell drifted up from the river, filling the space between the tin-sided warehouses and carrying mosquitoes. Slapping at their buzz, he drew deep on his cigarette, exhaling smoky clouds to chase them away.

Patience would soon deliver her into his hands. Eventually, he'd get her, one way or another. After all, everyone said that the man from Chicago was an expert in the business.

Sage's hired cab picked her up, just a few blocks from the laundry. After mumbling hello, Mae closed her eyes and slept. He cursed softly whenever the cab jostled into and out of the paving's grooves, gaps and holes but she didn't waken. The city officials' cronyism explained the deplorable condition of streets paved in a hodgepodge of cobble, woodblock, asphalt and dirt—most in disrepair.

As they rolled to a stop before Mozart's Table she awoke, climbed down from the cab, pushed open the restaurant door and headed upstairs, too tired to even glance toward the dining room. She climbed slowly, as if carrying a hundred pound miner's pack on her back.

Once inside, Sage paused to confirm all was well in the restaurant before following her upstairs. This assignment was taking a huge toll on her. "Just how long do you think you can keep this up? You're not a spring chicken anymore," he said as he entered her third floor room. Though his words were teasing, they carried worry's bite.

For once, she didn't bristle. "I'm asking myself the same question," she said, her words muffled because she sat at the table, forehead resting on her folded arms. Raising a face that glimmered white with sweaty exhaustion she said, "It's that god awful heat. The work isn't that hard. He has me working the "old lady" job, hand ironing ruffles, laces and frills. Lordy, though, I do wish Cobb would give us stools. Ten hours is too long to stand in one spot—especially in the heat." She straightened and with a groan, bent to unlace her sturdy boots.

His gaze sharpened. Mae Clemens usually gave as good as she get. That was one of the things he liked about working with her. But tonight, she'd barked no comeback to his gentle tease. His mother was only in her mid fifties but, still, he'd rarely seen her so tired. How much longer could she last? It had been over a week already.

He collected the tray Fong had left on her dresser and carried it to the table. She toed off her boots with a sigh of relief before dully examining the sandwich and milk he put before her.

"I'm so pooped my appetite's already gone to bed," she said, poking the sandwich with a finger. "I can't imagine how those poor women manage to go home and cook dinner for their kids after a day like today. I feel as bad as I did after eleven hours separating coal ore. Except, back then, I was thirty years younger. I could recover."

Her words triggered his memory of the mine shed. It was a memory sharp as the coal that scarred their hands. They'd both worked year around in the sheet metal shed, in sweltering heat and freezing cold. Beginning at age seven, he'd crawled atop the conveyor belt to toss aside the ore chunks the women sorters, like his mother, couldn't reach. That job ended when he was nine and they sent him to work down in the mine. After wriggling into slits dug beneath the coal faces, he'd hand-drilled holes for the dynamite and shoved it in.

Day after day, he rode the rattling cage down into that hot, dark hell until fate intervened. There'd been an explosion. Even now, his body twitched. There'd been choking dust, sweat burning his lacerated back, his arms and legs white-hot with pain as he inched up the air shaft, the mine owner's grandson clinging to his chest like a terrified monkey. Only the two of them had survived.

His mother cleared her throat, her face apologetic. "Oh, son, sorry I brought that up. I'm so darn tired that I can't keep my tongue leashed."

He laughed. "Well now, that there's a real change of pace," he teased as he hugged her shoulders gently. She had to be sore.

She lifted a hand, as if to give his arm her customary slap, but then let it drop. "I'm too tired to keep you in line. So, you just go ahead and abuse your poor tired mother."

"Tell me about your day," he urged, to remind her that her suffering was in the aid of important work. St. Alban wanted their report. The national labor leader had assigned them to help Portland's steam laundry workers who were negotiating with the laundry owners. They were asking for so very little: To work six days a week for nine hours a day rather than the ten they now worked. And, they wanted a few cents more than the ten cents an hour they were currently making.

Usually, it was Sage who acted as St. Alban's primary undercover operative in Portland. But, this time, there'd been no job openings for men at the Sparta Laundry. And, it had to be the Sparta, rather than one of the six other steam laundries, because its manager, Thaddeus Cobb, was the ringleader of the laundry owners' association. Cobb's single-minded intent kept all the other owners in line.

Mae had been the one to get the laundry job because women did most of the laundry work. She was watching Cobb and tracking the progress of the workers' efforts even as she ironed.

Her work-reddened hand kneaded her aching shoulders as she said, "One of the girls was nearly hurt bad tonight. She was feeding sheets into a mangle that has no safety guard. Her fingers got tangled in the sheet. It nearly pulled her arm between the rollers. Scared the poor gal so bad that she just yanked off her apron and walked out the door."

Mae looked at him, her face sad. "It's the god awful heat and noise. By that last hour we're all dizzy, barely able to keep upright. When the outside thermometer reads 100 degrees, just imagine how hot all that steam and equipment makes it inside. Two ladies fainted right where they stood. Anyways, the feeder girls were moving fast, trying to get done so they wouldn't have to work overtime. The light was failing. After ten hours in that heat no one can think right." Mae drank milk and bit the sandwich before adding, "Those poor women."

In his role of restaurateur, John Adair, Sage toured the Sparta Laundry the day before so he knew exactly what she meant. He'd told Cobb he wanted to determine whether the facility could adequately clean his restaurant's linens. Since Mozart's Table was Portland's second most exclusive restaurant, Cobb had been eager to prove the Sparta's modernity to its owner. Escorting Sage through the plant, he'd emphasized the laundry's efficient equipment while Sage hid his reaction to the hellish working conditions. His head started to pound as Cobb yelled his sales pitch over a deafening cacophony of belt snaps, metal clanks, engine chugs, steam hiss, steel wheel rattles and sloshing water. The air stank of chemicals, starch and soiled clothing. Underfoot, scummy water slicked the floorboards. Every worker wore heavy boots.

About five males worked in the wash tub area. Clad in sweat-soaked sleeveless undershirts they dumped clothes and linens into the cylindrical wash tubs, mixed in chemicals, hauled out the washed clothes and dropped them into whirling extractors to centrifuge the water out. After that, they piled the cloth onto hand trucks for delivery to the women.

The lion's share of the work fell to the women. There were about sixty of them. They worked steadily as sweat drenched their dresses and dripped from their pinned up hair. Some sorted and marked the incoming soiled clothes, others shook the wet fabric loose and carried it over to the women who fed it into a variety of mangles, releasing steam clouds into the air. Some of the women were repetitiously stomping machine pedals to press cuffs, collars, shirts and who knew what else. An overhead clutter of vibrating belts, wires and pulleys powered the specially-designed machinery.

He'd immediately removed his suit coat, noting that Cobb had left his own coat behind in the office. Between the heat outside beating down on the roof and the stinking steam that billowed from every piece of equipment, it felt like a steam bath, the thick air clinging to everything it touched. Overhead, two open skylights did nothing to relieve the heat. There were no exhaust fans.

Mae interrupted his recollections, saying, "At lunch Rachel Levy told us about the morning's meeting with the bosses. She said the union's dropped the wage increase demand. Now, they're only asking for a nine-hour day. Cobb promised to give them the association's answer tomorrow." Defeat deadened her words.

"Jeez, I hate to hear that. How can those women possibly live on six dollars a week? Especially, those with kids and no working husband?" Sage hated that they'd dropped the wage demand but understood how fearful they'd be of striking. No one could build up savings when earning only six dollars a week.

Mae was shaking her head. "I know, I know. Most are single mothers or single women without any outside support. I feel the same as you do but I kept my mouth shut. Just did what I'm supposed to do—'observe, support and now, report'. Though, I surely did want to say something."

Sage grinned, "I'll just bet you did. No wonder you've had a hard day. Bet you nearly bit your tongue off keeping your opinion to yourself."

This time she delivered a blow to his shoulder. But it was a feeble blow. She really was tired. "Finish eating," he said. "Then to bed. Are you going to work again tomorrow?"

His question kindled fire in her eyes and she snapped, "Well, really, Sage. Surely you know me well enough to know I don't give up that easily!"

He grinned at her. "That's more like it!" he said, artfully dodging the swift hand she shot in his direction.

TWO

"You said you'd bring her three days ago! I can't keep that room empty forever. I'm losing money on it!" The slack skin on her jowls quivered with feigned outrage even as her faded blue eyes glittered with calculation. She was trying to milk more money from him.

He made a show of studying the grimy kitchen—sending the message that this was the bottom of the barrel when it came to whorehouses. These days, she entertained few customers and those paid little for her wares. He leaned across the table to grab her wrist, squeezing and twisting until her hand darkened and she squealed from the pain.

"I've paid you all you're going to get, so quit your whining," he said before releasing her. She quickly dropped both hands beneath the table.

He sat back, sipped his whiskey and swallowed hard—watered rotgut. He hardened his face to keep the upper hand. People like her slithered their way around others, especially if they saw an opening. If caught, she'd act surprised and whine.

"So, is the room ready? Are the window boards nailed up? Is there a padlock on the outside? You've got the drops, right? And, you remember I said that she's special? Not meant for your business?" He peppered her with questions, despite knowing the preparations had been in place for the last three days. She nodded silently, cowed by his sudden aggression. Not his style really, but a drunk like her wasn't susceptible to civil persuasion. Fear's what kept her in line.

"You'll only have her for a few days," he reminded her. "Just until I can get her shipped out. She's going far away, so far that she won't find her way back."

The house madam nodded, continued to watch him warily and stayed silent. He knew she needed his money because she liked to party right along with her customers, plowing her piddling profits into drink instead of repairing her ramshackle house. Obviously, her business was on its last legs. All that was just fine for his purposes—just so long as she kept the door padlocked until he was ready to move the girl out. The house's location was perfect, there on the fringes of the North End, near the river and amongst other similar houses squatting alongside the railroad tracks.

"Just how far away will she be going? I don't like the thought of an American girl being sold to them slant-eyes over there in Shanghai, China," she said.

Her objection gave him pause. He'd taken her for someone lacking any scruples. He shook his head. "Naw, she isn't going to Shanghai. She'll go from San Francisco to Panama. There's going to be lots of single men down there digging on that canal now that the U.S. is taking it over."

She frowned. Still, she suppressed whatever comment she might have made and instead asked, "How are you going to get her from Portland to Frisco?"

He raised a cautionary finger, narrowed his eyes and blanked his face. She swallowed, looked away at the peeling walls and then at the bottle between them, "So, how's about another drink?" she mumbled as she pushed the bottle toward him.

Trailing Cobb and the other man was easy because they never looked back. Since he couldn't get a job at the Sparta, Sage decided to learn what he could about its manager. Who knew? Maybe he'd stumble on one of Cobb's secrets. Something he could use as leverage later on. The wealthy always had secrets. Sometimes they hid criminal secrets—more often, socially embarrassing ones. Either kind worked when it came to leverage.

In the past, they'd used those rich man's secrets to further social justice. He didn't always feel good about doing it, but his need to better lives was stronger than his reluctance to acquire another smudge on his conscience.

And, it was Cobb who needed investigating because his brain and resolve powered the Portland Laundryman's Association. He'd founded it as soon as the city's laundry workers joined the Shirt Waist and Laundry Workers' Union. Cobb knew that the current dispute was critical because the outcome would establish work hours for every city laundry, not just the Sparta. Even the two laundries not in the association would adopt whatever terms the union won. They'd have no choice since laundry worker turnover was extremely high. And, no wonder. People quit the brutal job the minute they chanced upon a better situation.

So here he was, wearing his John Miner disguise. Looking like an itinerant workman as he trailed the two men. To his surprise they walked the fifteen blocks between the Sparta, at East Burnside and Water Avenue, and the United States Laundry on Grand and Salmon. Cobb strode with the ease of a well-conditioned athlete. Not so his companion who struggled to keep up. By the time they reached their destination, the pudgy fellow was mopping his brow with a big, white handkerchief.

The two men mounted the two steps and entered the wood frame building. Now, why do you suppose they'd visit one of the two laundries that had refused to join their association? Sage silently asked himself. He paused outside, before deciding he didn't know enough to answer that question. After contemplating the closed door, he decided to chance it and take a stab at getting more information.

Usually his John Miner disguise, with its shabby clothes, battered hat and drooping mustache, worked well. Those who customarily saw him as John Adair, the urbane owner of Portland's fancy restaurant, never considered that he might mingle with the "lower classes" crowding Portland's streets.

He set his hat low and kept his face down as he slowly opened the door. Inside, he found an empty anteroom. No receptionist sat at the desk. Quietly shutting the door, he surveyed the room. Two doors opened off it. One door was wide with a steam-covered window in its top half. It obviously opened into the washroom area. The second door seemed to lead into a smaller office. Voices sounded from beyond that door. Cobb's was one of those voices.

Wooden chairs, intended for waiting customers, sat against the wall beside the office door. He slid onto the chair nearest the door. Quietly he opened the folded newspaper in his pocket and raised it before his face, making sure it was right side up. Then he listened.

"Look Finley, your laundry is undercutting the bargaining position of every member of the association," said Cobb.

An unknown voice, doubtless Finley's, protested, "Look here Thaddeus. I'm doing what I think is right. I haven't recognized the union. I promised you I wouldn't and I haven't."

"Don't try to play stupid, James. You might not have signed an agreement but you are dancing to that damn union's tune. It's bad enough that they pushed through the ten-hour legislation last March. That cutback from eleven to ten hours cost us plenty."

"Look," Finley's voice was entreating, "my girls, many of them have families. Ten hours, especially during the hot summer we're having, is just too long to work in that steam. Since we've switched to nine-hour days, accidents have gone down. So has my turnover. And, the girls work faster."

Another voice, this one angry, interrupted, "Of course your turnover has gone down. Hell, you probably have a waiting list of gals since you are undercutting the rest of us. Why would a girl work ten hours when she can get the same pay for nine?"

There was a scrape of chairs, signaling that Finley's visitors were about to depart. Sage moved quickly down the row of chairs until he was sitting in the one farthest from the office, his nose buried in the newspaper.

Despite the increased distance, Cobb's final words were perfectly audible. "Finley, I give you fair warning. The United States Laundry either joins the association and increases work hours back to ten, or you and your investors are going to be very, very sorry."

"But Thaddeus, why can't we just keep going as we are? I can't hire any more girls away from you fellows. I have a full complement, right now."

"Because," Cobb said, his voice biting and cold. "We're about to up the game and you need to be on our team. There's no middle ground here, Finley. You try straddling the line and we're going to plow you so deep into the dirt that you and this laundry will never crawl out."

There was a scuff of shoes as Cobb and his companion exited the office. Without a glance in Sage's direction, the two men were quickly out the door and on the sidewalk. Sage didn't bother to follow.

No sound came from Finley's office. After a beat, Sage walked to the office door. Inside, Finley sat, elbows on his desk, head propped in his hands. Then he sighed, straightened and reached for the black crank telephone on the wall beside him. As he did so, he saw Sage standing there, hat in hand.

"What do you want?" he demanded, his voice belligerent. Instantly, Finley seemed to regret his sharpness because he added, "Sorry to snap, Mister. But, if you need a job, we're full up right now."

Sage meekly ducked his head and said, "Thank you, sir. Maybe I'll come back another day, just in case."

"You do that. Good workers are always welcome when there's an opening," Finley responded with a smile.

After again dipping his head respectfully, Sage turned and left the office. Once on the wooden sidewalk, he paused to mull over Cobb's last words. "We're about to up the game." What the heck did that mean?

Rachel entered the washroom a few minutes late. Her lips were a thin straight line. She shook her head as she made her way to her position at a mangle. Everyone's eyes followed her as she crossed the wet floor. She was young, slender and nearing thirty, with dark curling hair pinned atop her head like all the others. While not beautiful, her strong, vivacious face was attractive. Even in what was clearly defeat, she projected a calm, kind, nature which was probably why the laundry workers had chosen her as their spokeswoman.

Like everyone else, Mae felt disappointed upon seeing that head shake. Her co-workers' discouraged faces and slumping shoulders mirrored exactly what she felt. It didn't matter that she'd only been working little more than a week in this steaming hell or that she didn't have to work here at all. Her dismay might not be as sharp as the others' but it still stabbed.

Sliding the hot iron carefully over lace flounces, Mae swore she felt her feet swelling within her soggy boots. On her other end, her eyes burned and her nose ran from the chemicals her iron steamed out. Setting down the iron, she gazed about, lifting one foot and then the other to gain some relief. Steam billowed upward from the washing and pressing machines. Water dripped from her raised boots. She could tell that, outside, the heat was rising to make it another scorching day. If there was a worst time to start working in a steam laundry, she'd sure like to know when.

She did all she could to be cooler like everyone else. Beneath her bib apron, her dress was unbuttoned and pulled loose from around her neck and she'd rolled her sleeves up above her elbows. Still, sweat ran down her back, under her arms, and off her forehead. Since everyone else was just as sweat stained, no one noticed.

Mae rubbed the small of her back and studied the new girl working at the shake table. There the women snapped and flattened the cloth taken from the water extractors. Shaking was the laundry's starter job. It weeded out those who couldn't tolerate heat, aching repetition or standing for ten hours a day. Her first three days, she'd worked at the shaking table. Her shoulders still remembered the fiery burning at that first day's end. One of the women advised her to stoop her shoulders as she lifted and snapped the wet cloth loose. That had helped but little and seemed to leave her curled in a stoop after the day's end. Her current job, ironing delicates, was easier.

Yup, she'd made it through those grueling first days and it looked like the new girl would too. She guessed the girl was about twenty-two. A smile accompanied her every word as did a twinkle in her deep brown eyes. As Mae watched, the girl shook out a piece of clothing, then held it up for the others to see, her mouth forming a dramatic "O" before she collapsed into laughter. It was a pair of men's long johns that someone had decorated with appliquéd hearts—probably his wife. The other women joined in the young girl's laughter.

Maybe those other women weren't worried, but Mae clung to her suspicions. Certainly, the timing was one problem. Anyone hired once labor troubles began was suspect. Management always hired spies and troublemakers. So, who was this girl, really? She called herself, "Caroline Stark". "I'm probably just chasing ghosts up the holler," Mae chided herself before adding, "Still, something about her isn't ringing true."

Grabbing a new item to iron, a flat piece needing little attention, Mae continued to study the new girl. Caroline worked quickly and did her share. Yet, even from this distance Mae saw that the young woman's pale hands were smooth. Nothing like the reddened claws of the other woman. Still, maybe this Caroline person was new to hard times. It wouldn't be fair to call her a phony without some kind of proof.

Suspicion had become her second nature. Mae wasn't proud of it but suspicious she was. She hadn't been born into the world carrying that frame of mind. Sure, life in the Appalachian mine fields was hard but it was hard for everyone. That was just how things were. They, none of them, knew any different life.

No, her suspicious nature had been a treacherous husband's parting gift to her character. "You deal straight and honest with friends and family and they'll look after you," is what her pa taught her.

Sage's daddy, John Acair, Sr., had proved Mae's pa wrong. In an ambush of her own husband's making, both her father and brother were murdered. Greed and ambition turned him into a Judas who'd betrayed them to the mine owner's thugs.

His vile act triggered a landslide of changes. She wanted to kill him, except the coward skedaddled before she caught him. Later she was grateful that he'd fled because she had her baby, John Sagacity . . . Sage, to bring up. Even when he was a babe, she'd called him, "Sage." Never John or Johnny.

Nine years, she'd raised the boy. Together, she, her child and her remaining brother lived in a company shack while she worked in the mine's sorting shed. And, at seven, Sage had joined her there, just as all the children did. No choice about that. It was how mining families made the rent and paid off their store debt. School was out of the question, leastways regular schooling. Still, she'd taught him to read at an early age, just like her pa had taught her.

Everything changed once again when methane in the mine exploded, killing a number of men, including her only brother and the mine owner's son. By quirk of fate, Sage saved the mine owner's grandson. A proud man of German heritage, the mine owner rewarded Sage by giving him a good home and education. She'd had no choice. She'd agreed to let him go and hadn't seen her son again for nearly eighteen years.

Her eyes stung and watered until she had to pull a rag from her apron pocket to wipe them. To distract herself, she focused once again on the new girl. And then she saw it. Saw what had tweaked her suspicion all morning. Even as her hands snapped the wet cloth, Caroline's deep brown eyes calmly assessed her surroundings but not with the wide-eyed curiosity of being in a strange, new place. When no one was looking, those brown eyes were too calculating—exactly like someone measuring a situation, looking for an advantage.

The lunch whistle interrupted Mae's speculations. The mangles silenced, the steam stopped hissing and everyone trooped into the cooler air outside where they gathered beneath the shade of an ancient willow tree standing in the empty lot next door. Rachel stood with her back resting against the huge tree trunk. The other women sprawled on the ground around her, taking advantage of the shade offered by the tree's hanging fronds. Mae pressed in close to hear Rachel speak about the morning's negotiations.

Rachel didn't horse around. She came right to the point, saying, "Cobb won't respond to our settlement offer of a nine-hour day with no raise."

Sharp cries burst from the group. One woman protested, "But, Cobb promised yesterday that he'd give the answer today!"

Rachel nodded. "Yes, he did. But this morning he claimed that he hadn't had the chance to confer with the other laundry owners."

"He's just stalling. He doesn't want a strike so he's leading us on, hoping we'll give up," declared another woman, sending murmurs of agreement rippling through the group.

At that comment, Rachel raised a cautionary hand, "I agree," she said. "It's clear that everyone in their little business association follows Cobb's lead. He didn't need to talk to them. So, yes, he's stalling. But, that may be to our advantage."

"What do you mean, Rachel?" asked a woman standing near the front.

"I can't go into the specifics but our union and the local labor council are putting some things together that might help us and they need more time. In fact, we're not ready to deadlock on the negotiations for awhile yet. We're not prepared."

"What? What are they putting together? What preparation?" called another voice.

Mae held her breath, hoping that Rachel stayed silent on the particulars. It wasn't safe to trust everyone with their plans. She searched the faces around her until she spotted that new girl. Caroline. She sat at the edge of the group, her attention riveted on Rachel. Although her face was blank, her body craned forward like a hungry dog's waiting for a crumb to drop.

THREE

THE STINK OF SEWAGE, ROTTEN fish and garbage wafted from the river at the end of another hot and windless day. Sweat still soaked his hat band even though the sun had dipped below the western ridge. It was heat like Chicago's in August but without the humidity. On the eastern horizon a mountain's snowy slopes shimmered against a near white sky. Soon they would glow orange in the sunset.

Bet the wind's blowing cool and clean up there at the snowline, he thought. Hell of a lot better place to be than on this dirty wharf. His kick of frustration sent a cabbage, one that had missed the boat, flying into the river. He couldn't believe he'd failed to grab her yet again. It was almost as though, somehow, she sensed her stalker, just like deer could sense the hunter. But, that couldn't be the case. He was careful to stay out of sight or blend in.

Footsteps on the wharf planks halted his silent grumbling. The captain had arrived. After shaking hands, the man said, "I believe that I fully comprehend your proposal, sir. The terms are satisfactory. When did you wish to deliver the cargo to my ship? I don't want her aboard until I am completely loaded and the stevedores are long gone."

Pretentious words, spoken as if this fellow captained a fine sailing ship, instead of a rotting scow that even seagulls shunned. No matter. As long as the fellow did as asked, who cared?

"I won't be delivering her until the night before you sail. When is that going to be?" he asked.

The man squinted at the sky as if the wispy clouds displayed the ship's departure date. Despite the early evening dusk, the habitual drunk's puffiness that ringed the captain's eyes was unmistakable.

He thought about knocking the pompous ass down a peg or two but couldn't. He needed this sorry excuse of a sea captain. He just hoped the ship stayed afloat long enough to deliver the girl to San Francisco. Thoughts of a white face covered by sea water flicked through his mind but he pushed them away. Once aboard ship, her fate will be in God's hands, not mine, he told himself.

"Depending on the weather, we should be raising anchor early morning, fourteen days from tomorrow. Is that date agreeable?"

It was. It had to be. His boss was getting irritated. What originally looked like a one-day job had already taken three with still no success. The fellow footing the bill was getting his knickers in a twist over the delay. Too bad, he thought with a rebellious flash. The job was crap, anyway. If they could find someone else to do the snatch, let them. He'd procured women in St. Louis, Chicago, and in countless Midwestern plough towns. He knew how to make a snatch without creating a ruckus. And, that's what they said was most important. "No ruckus."

"Yup, that'll do. I'll let you know if there's going to be a delay," he told the captain. After handing over the advance to seal the deal he left, moving at a fast clip and without a backward glance. He needed to cross the river before her workday ended. Otherwise, he'd miss her. He'd grab her tonight.

It hadn't cooled overnight which was a rarity in western Oregon. Even this early in the day, the sun blazed in a pale sky. Marginally cooler pre-dawn air, lingering in the shade behind the willow fronds, offered little relief from the rising heat. Sage sat with his back against the ancient bark already feeling the sweat rising. Cobb was still inside the laundry. Sage didn't know what Cobb was up to, but it was surely something. Until he found out, he'd stick to the laundry manager like "burrs on a bunny," as his mother would say.

Sure enough, Cobb left the building as the laundry's equipment began to hiss and clank. The man headed south, strolling along Water Street toward the Morrison Bridge. Sighing, Sage stood up, parted the fronds and followed. Soon the two of them were crossing the river, keeping abreast of the street trolley rattling over the bridge planks alongside them.

Cobb entered a small restaurant at the bridge's end. Sage waited outside on a shaded doorstep. Fifteen minutes later, Cobb exited the restaurant accompanied by the managers of three other steam laundries. Obviously, they formed a delegation of some sort.

The men didn't converse as they strode northward. Within a few blocks, they entered the front office of a riverside warehouse. Sage ambled past to read the building sign. It said, "City Chemical Supply." He puzzled over that until he recalled the chemical stink rising from the laundry's washtubs and ironing equipment.

Sage sat on a nearby empty hand cart and considered the building. It made sense that one of them would visit a chemical supply house now and again. But, why would all four of them do so at the same time?

Mae doubted she'd survive the final hour. Steam clouded the washroom making the air the most stifling it had ever been. Glancing around, she saw that the other women were in the same shape. Everyone's face was shiny with sweat, pale with fatigue and all were moving slowly. Three women had run to throw up in the single toilet. The only drinking water came from the dirty faucet over the filthy sink where they rinsed the burning chemicals off their skin. The water coming from that faucet tasted nasty, like it mingled with the chemicals. Chemicals that turned your skin raw couldn't be good for your innards, she thought. Like the other women, Mae avoided drinking from that faucet but she'd long ago emptied the water jug she'd brought from home.

Just as she started ironing yet another lace-trimmed blouse, a terrified scream pierced the steam, followed by frantic yips of alarm. Startled, Mae's head flew up to search for the commotion's source. A mangle's leather conveyor belt had stopped moving. Everyone was running toward it, Rachel in the lead. A door banged as the foreman rushed from the office.

Iron safely stowed, Mae joined the other women at the mangle but, upon reaching it, she wished she'd stayed behind. Two girls worked the machine, feeding bed linen through two heavy, canvas-wrapped, steel rollers. One girl's face was dead white as she whimpered in pain and fear. The two rollers had her hand trapped up to her wrist. The foreman was frantically wrenching a bolt, trying to free the top roller.

The washroom stilled except for the soft hissing of idling machines and the swish of the unattended washtubs in the far corner. The women and the few washtub men stood in a silent semi-circle around the mangle. Rachel's murmurs of assurance and the clink of wrench on the steel bolt seemed loud. The girl was being kept upright and steady by Rachel and the girl's sister. When the roller was finally freed, the girl looked at her hand and fainted.

That was probably best, the calm part of Mae's brain said—even as she found herself recoiling in horror from the sight of that bloody, burnt hand.

Within minutes, a closed laundry van was taking the unconscious girl to the hospital, her sister and the foreman sitting on her either side, the horse running at top speed. Muttering began even before the vehicle turned the corner. "She's going to lose that hand," one of the women said glumly.

"Aye," agreed a soft Irish brogue. "It's never they're keeping it, once it's been mangled."

Mae poked her head inside the washroom to see the wall clock. Thirty-five minutes to go. She looked back at the workers who remained outside after witnessing the girl's departure. She rejoined them.

"Cobb's so greedy that he won't spend a few dollars on a safety guard. Lots of other laundries have them. We've asked and asked him," someone said.

The other young woman who'd been working the mangle sat snuffling on the building's stoop. "Debbie was so tired," she said in a voice thick with tears. "She's been up half the night with her little one all week long. But, she had to come to work or they wouldn't have food to eat." She covered her head with her apron and sobbed.

A close by rustle made Mae turn to see Rachel remove her apron and fold it carefully. She looked at the others and said calmly. "I will not work another minute today. And, tomorrow, I intend to arrive two hours late. I ask that you join me in this protest against these unsafe conditions and the treatment we receive in this laundry."

People nodded and spines straightened like alder treetops in a wind's lull. As they returned to the washroom, the women were loosening their apron strings.

Mae noticed that Caroline stayed behind on the outside stoop, her arms around the sobbing girl. She felt her eyebrows rise at the sight. Maybe that newcomer was alright. Could a calculating and, up-to-no-good management spy, fake tears? Mae hoped not. But then, that familiar bitterness came back. She'd bedded with a traitor and never once suspected him.

Raised voices sounded outside. Joining everyone else, Mae stepped out of the building to find Rachel standing feet spread and hands on hips, almost nose to nose with one of the laundry's delivery drivers.

"You mean to tell me that you refuse to support the people who have to work in this hellhole?" The words were loud enough that all could hear.

"My men have families to feed. If they refuse to work tomorrow, they might lose their jobs."

"Two hours, that's all we're asking. Your jobs are the safest of all. You know the delivery routes and have customer loyalty. Cobb won't fire you." Rachel's tone had softened but only slightly. "Look, tonight a young mother is going to lose her hand. Tomorrow, that same thing could happen to one of us." She swept her hand in an arc that encompassed all her co-workers who were now encircling them.

"I can't ask my drivers to lose their wages or their jobs. They can't afford it." The delivery driver licked his lips nervously but held his position.

"Your drivers," the words coming from Rachel dripped scorn, "make $15 a week plus bonuses. We. . . ," here again she swept her arm to include her co-workers, "make an average of $6 per week. So, don't you dare talk about risk or say you can't 'afford' to do the moral thing."

A smattering of applause and hear, hears! came from the group. The delivery driver backed toward his wagon, clearly intimidated by the scowling people who surrounded him.

His chin jutting he said, "I've given you my answer." Turning on his heel, he scrambled onto his seat beneath the cab roof, snapped the horse's reins and, seconds later, the closed delivery wagon was rumbling down the rutted dirt street.

Mae considered the faces around her, hoping the uncooperative delivery driver hadn't dampened their enthusiasm. There was disgust but no resignation on their faces. Gathering around Rachel, they patted her on the back.

"Ha!" spat one of the women. "If we don't clean the damn clothes, that old so-and-so won't have nothing to deliver. That'll burn holes in his pockets!"

Mae's eyes stung for the second time that day. This time, it wasn't the chemicals. Clearing her throat she asked, "Who was that fellow, anyway?"

"L.D. 'the traitor' Warder. He's president of the so-called delivery drivers' union," came the disgusted answer.

FOUR

"YOU RECEIVED MY NOTE?" HE asked, hoping the reminder would lessen his boss's outrage over yet another night of failure.

His boss silently puffed cigar smoke in his direction before swallowing more whiskey. Even though they were alone in the hotel room, there'd been no offer of a companionable drink. His boss finally spoke, "Yes, I got it and passed the information on immediately. Don't know yet if it is accurate. If it isn't, he's going to be even madder. He's already in a tizzy because you've yet to deliver. It'll be worse if we've given him false information. He'll fire us and hire someone else."

He relaxed. It sounded like the note would buy him a little more time to grab the girl. He knew his information was accurate because he'd made friends with one of the laundry women. Romance was on her mind which, of course, he encouraged. He'd easily sweet-talked her into joining him for beers at a local saloon. While they sat in a quiet corner, she'd told him that she could stay for a drink because the ladies were going to report for work two hours late the next day. Some girl had hurt her hand and the women planned to withhold their labor in protest.

Despite her tentative hints, he'd not taken her back to his room. He didn't want anyone to know where he stayed. Besides, he had a note to write and have delivered. His boss needed to know the women planned a two-hour strike for the next morning. So, acting the regretful gentleman, he'd escorted the disappointed girl to her boarding house's front door before he hurried off to find a messenger.

Tracing a wet ring on the varnished table top he said, "Actually, I checked. I was outside the laundry at 8:00 a.m. this morning. None of them had shown up for work. There were only delivery drivers milling around, waiting to load up."

His boss nodded. "Well, well, then. But you still haven't delivered the girl. Our client is becoming quite upset. I promised him you were the best and he paid your train fare all the way from Chicago. He's expecting results. Besides, what with your fancy education and all, you're supposed to be the smart one. She's just a dumb washerwoman. What's your excuse for failing last night, anyway?"

"They were upset over the girl getting hurt. The whole crew walked off the job early and they left as a group. People surrounded her. I knew they'd walk her home so it was a waste of time to follow her. I took my gal out for a beer instead."

"Your gal?"

"Well, that's what she thinks she is. We know better," he added unnecessarily. As if he'd care about some steam laundry drab. Besides, she was too cow-eyed trusting. She should have stayed on the farm. He liked his women sassy, tough and a touch sophisticated.

"So, when are you going to grab the Levy woman?"

"I'm going to go there at noontime, just in case she goes out on her own. Otherwise, I'll be waiting tonight when she gets off. This time, unless she has company, I'm going to poke a knife in her ribs. She'll come along. One way or another, she'll be in my hands and locked away by tonight's end."

"Why didn't you try that knife gambit sooner?"

He couldn't believe his boss lacked the imagination to answer that question for himself. But the man was paying, so he kept his tone respectful. "Because, she could scream or fight and there's a lot of folks down there close to the river. The steam laundry isn't the only workplace shutting down at dusk. People might come to her rescue and create that 'ruckus' you said our client didn't want. You said he wants people to think she just walked away—deserted them and their little fight. That way, the police won't put much effort into finding her."

His boss stabbed his cigar into the ashtray. "Well, at this point, I guess we have to risk whatever it takes. Try to get her without anyone seeing but if you can't, then get it done any way you can. And, no more excuses," he commanded.

"No more excuses, no more excuses," the man from Chicago repeated in a mocking chant—but only after he was back out on the street.

❀   ❀   ❀

Sage stepped inside the red brick Davis Building. Home to a number of unions, its meeting halls were empty first thing in the morning though he was sure the various union offices were up and running. Climbing to the second floor, he entered the Carpenters' office. Only Leo Lockwood was there.

"Leo, thanks for meeting me this morning. You're not going to get in trouble for leaving the job are you?" he asked, noting that the union president was fully recovered from the both the strike and his own false imprisonment for murder the previous autumn. The stocky man's smile was wide and easy with real affection lighting his eyes. Sage and his friends had straightened everything out, settling the strike and winning Leo's freedom by finding the real killer.

The two men clasped hands before sitting down on the wooden chairs. The Carpenters' Union president grinned and waved a dismissive hand as he answered Sage's question, "Naw. Ever since Earl Mackey learned I didn't kill his dad and we settled the strike, he's been darn friendly. I swear that whole to-do changed the man. He's turning into a pretty good boss."

Sage smiled and said, "Sometimes that can happen. I'm glad to hear it, Leo." Then he sobered. "Leo, I need to ask you where the Federated Trades Council stands on the laundry workers' nine-hour day demand." Since he wasn't a card-carrying union man, Sage couldn't attend the Council's meetings to find out for himself. As a Council member, Leo was in a good position to keep Sage apprised of how the group was reacting to the laundry workers' labor dispute. Leo wouldn't hesitate to share that information because he was the only Portland labor leader who knew that Sage secretly worked for the labor hero, Vincent St. Alban.

Leo rubbed his chin thoughtfully as he said, "The Council feels bad that the state federation of unions only got the legislature to pass a ten-hour workday bill for all women but not the nine hours the steam laundry girls needed. We all know that's an awful job."

Sage had closely followed the Portland Council's efforts in the legislature that prior spring. It had lobbied hard to get nine-hour days for the laundry women but, in the end, the state labor union federation judged a three-hour reduction in the workday would be a step too far for the legislature. They decided to try for a two-hour reduction instead.

Leo too, was familiar with the reasoning behind the shorter reduction request because he said, "As you know, the state federation decided we had to get the camel's nose under the tent. First get ten hours for women, then get nine hours for everyone—men and women—in a subsequent session. They believed asking for nine hours, for men and women, right off the bat, would stir up too much political opposition since the standard at that time was twelve hours."

He chuckled ruefully and looked Sage in the eye. "All of which is a long way of saying the Council has unanimously voted to support the laundry gals in their nine-hour demand."

"Well, that's good news. Did they vote on any action?"

That question lit Leo's face with another grin, "Matter of fact, they did. They are going to do two things right off the bat. The first is to raise every union member's monthly dues a penny for a strike fund. Now, we know the gals don't want to strike. But who knows what Cobb and his buddies will do?

"And," here Leo paused for dramatic effect—clearly he had something monumental to impart, "it looks like they're going to sell shares so they can start their own cooperative laundry."

"Wow, that's a clever idea. Who thought of it?" Sage asked.

The red flush flooding Leo's face answered that question. "Well," he said, "Some of us have been talking about how hard that work is and we thought maybe we could make it easier on the ladies and still turn a fair profit. So, if Cobb locks them out, there'll be work for them at the cooperative laundry."

"And, the Council's going to do it? Start a laundry?"

Leo nodded. "They're taking it back to their unions and going to get authorization to buy shares. We figure that we can count on union households to use the union laundry. So, that's a ready market."

"Heck, I'll buy into that," Sage said.

This time Leo's response was a shake of his head. "Nope, they decided that only unions and union members can buy shares. Even then, they are going to limit just how many shares can be bought by any one person or union."

"Sounds like it was an involved discussion," Sage mused. He'd heard of union cooperatives before but, still, it was a new idea for Portland.

It would certainly raise the laundry women's spirits when they heard of the plan.

"One other thing," he said to Leo, "Would you let the Council know that the president of the laundry delivery drivers' union has refused to support the women?"

Leo's face turned grim. "That L.D. Warder is a pain in everybody's backside. He's nothing more than the bosses' mouthpiece all down the line. He makes every driver negotiate a separate contract with his boss. 'Course that butt-kissing means that Warder can guarantee that his favorite buddies will get the best pay and routes. I'm not surprised he won't cooperate. I'll be sure and let the Council know.

"Well, I better get back to work," Leo said, standing up and slapping his cap onto his head, "Don't want to discourage Mackey's newfound good nature."

Just as Sage turned toward the door, Leo stopped him with a call, "Say, Adair, I almost forgot. Someone I trust says that Laundryman's Association brought in a New York City fellow, name of James Farley. Says Farley hires strike breaking scabs and sends them around the country. Summons them to new jobs using telegrams. Since the bosses will pay double wages to scabs, he always finds plenty of takers. If Farley is in town, you and your friends better watch your step. He's not fussy about what kind of animal he hires. Leastways, that's what my friend told me."

Someone must have warned Cobb about the women's two-hour protest because, when Mae arrived at the steam laundry two hours late, she and the others found the doors locked. The few delivery men still around said that Cobb had been there early so they could load up the finished laundry and get on with their deliveries. That done, he'd locked himself inside the building.

Mae eyed the group of women, particularly the new girl, Caroline. If someone warned Cobb, it was likely her. Even now the girl was coolly observant rather than upset like the other women. Once again, suspicion flared white hot. Just who was this young woman?

Half an hour later, the foreman exited the locked washroom and stood on the stoop. He wasn't a bad sort for a foreman. He took no obvious pleasure in hectoring the women to work faster. In fact, he spent most of his time looking apologetic and lending an awkward hand wherever he could. This morning, he looked grim.

"Ladies and gentlemen," he said, "Mr. Cobb has instructed me to inform you that the laundry will remain closed for another hour." That pronouncement made, he turned to go back inside.

"Why is he keeping us out?" called one of the women.

The man looked embarrassed when he turned around to answer, "He said that's your 'punishment' for abandoning your jobs last night and this morning. Says he's docking your pay five hours."

"They amputated my sister's hand last night!" shouted Debbie's sister. "Does Cobb know that?"

The foreman's voice was soft as he said, "Sadie, I was there with you at the hospital. Of course, he knows. I told him."

"Doesn't he even care?" asked another woman.

The foreman removed his cap and ran his fingers through a thatch of graying hair. "Gloria, I really can't say," came his honest answer. Mae pitied his dilemma.

They milled around in the empty lot near the willow tree, waiting for the laundry door to open so they could return to work. For a long time, nothing happened then the door opened once again and the foreman stepped out. This time he carried his metal lunch bucket.

"Where you going, Harry?" called one of the girls.

"I just quit," he responded and strode off down the street, his step jaunty—like he was heading off to a party.

They looked at each other, dumbfounded. Before anyone could speak, the washroom door banged open. Cobb stood in the doorway in his shirt sleeves, hands on his hips. "Anyone planning to work today better get themselves in here, this minute. Otherwise, this door is getting locked and you're out of a job."

Wordlessly they all filed into the washroom and donned their aprons.

FIVE

He stood and stared. The lunch bell hadn't rung. But, there she was, coming straight toward him. It was Saturday. The laundry would run all day long. So why was she out on the street late morning and dressed like that? Normally, she wore faded gingham dresses with hemlines a good two inches above heavy work boots. Not today. Today it was a neat, dark blue outfit like clerks wore in department stores—a long skirt and a high-necked white blouse covered by a short jacket the same color as the skirt. She'd tied a jaunty red scarf around her neck, shiny walking shoes covered her feet, and a yellow straw hat perched atop her curly black hair.

He stepped toward a shop entrance, turning his back, aware his surprised reaction might draw attention—especially from her. One couldn't stand on the boardwalk, gawping at strange women and go unnoticed. That was the last thing he wanted, today in particular. He quickly stepped inside the rundown hardware store. Sunlight streaming through the filthy windows dimly lit its interior. An eager clerk approached him, asking "May I assist, sir?"

"Umm, ah, I was needing a wrench," he said, his eyes flicking toward the window. She would pass by any second.

"Certainly. Our wrenches are right back here. We have some fine ones in stock. Did you desire a pipe or a buggy wrench?" the clerk asked, turning to bustle away toward the rear of the store. When he glanced back, to make further conversation, all he saw was the outer door closing behind his would-be customer.

Once back outside, the man from Chicago followed her down the boardwalk. He'd never seen her out of her drab working clothes and heavy boots. For the first time, he realized that she had a trim little figure and, while her features were too strong to call her pretty, she was far from ugly. Handsome was the word. A little bit of face paint and she'd be striking. She had the kind of face you'd notice first in a room full of pretty women—an iris among the tulips.

She'll be good little earner—wherever she ends up, he mused. That thought gave way to image he tried to ignore, that of a dingy whorehouse servicing the Panama Canal's construction crews amid the heat and swarms of mosquitoes.

In God's hands, he reassured himself. Just like they'd told him. All in God's hands, not his.

Half a block ahead, she paused to speak with the slow man selling pencils from a corner packing box stand. The man from Chicago halted, pretending to study a warehouse window, as if reading something posted there. There were so many homeless job seekers flooding the street he could play at being just one more.

The pencil peddler and the woman exchanged words and smiles before she walked on. Holding his breath, he followed. Maybe, for the first time, she'd go down the alley to reach her boarding house. It was, after all, broad daylight.

She paused at the alley's opening to peer down its length. He again turned aside, just in case she looked back. She didn't. Instead, his sidewise glance caught her shrug just before she boldly stepped into the opening. He fingered the bottle in his coat pocket. If he acted fast, that shortcut would be her last act on Portland's streets. He sped up.

Sage paused in the dining room entrance admiring, not for the first time, the tall straight figure of Angus Solomon. The Portland Hotel's maitre'd stood at his podium like a benevolent ruler surveying his troops, And, in a way, he was exactly that. This dining room was the most exclusive one in the city, even more so than Mozart's Table. Certainly, it offered the city's most skilled wait staff. The black waiters, recruited from the Carolinas, were an attribute the hotel used to justify advertising itself as the most elegant establishment on the west coast. Solomon himself had been enticed away from service in a Carolinian governor's mansion to oversee the new dining room.

When Solomon spied Sage standing at the back of the line he nodded toward the room's least desirable table—one next to the kitchen and behind a drooping palm. Sage stepped out of line, seated himself and ordered coffee from the waiter who appeared at his shoulder. It would be a while before Solomon would be free to talk. So, Sage settled back in his customary seat and mentally replayed the discussion he'd had earlier in the day with three of his fellow conspirators.

They'd delayed their meeting until early Sunday afternoon because Mae needed to sleep after six days working in the laundry. Once she was 'up on her pins' as she liked to say, they'd gathered in his third floor room above Mozart's. It had been just the four of them around the alcove table: Herman Eich the ragpicker, Fong Kam Tong, Mozart's ostensible houseman who was also Sage's teacher and Mae Clemens.

Sage started off by addressing his mother. "So, nothing happened yesterday? Like Cobb giving the women his response to their nine-hour day demand?"

"He told Rachel that he still hadn't had a chance to 'confer' with the other laundry owners." Contempt coated her words.

"Well, that's a lie. I saw him with at least three of the other laundry managers yesterday morning. They had every opportunity to 'confer'" Sage said.

She nodded glumly, "Yes, that's what we figured. He's just stalling" She told them about the foreman quitting, adding, "They tell me that Cobb spent more time on the shop floor yesterday, than he did all the whole month before."

"The question is, why is Cobb stalling?" Sage wondered aloud. "We know he's got something planned that he said will 'up the game'. He mentioned it to Finley."

Mae knew about Cobb's visit to Finley at the United States Laundry and what Sage had overheard, but Fong and Eich didn't so Sage filled them in. As he did so, he studied the two men.

Fong was short, slender and, although raised in Canton, his was the narrow, angular face of a northern Chinese. When he'd arrived at Mozart's kitchen door, he'd wanted an opportunity to work in the restaurant so he could learn how to run one of his own. He discarded that idea once he discovered Mae and Sage's undercover work for St. Alban. Fong had joined in their missions and been crucial to their success. He was also teaching Sage the deadly Asian fighting art he called the "snake and crane."

Herman Eich was just as unlikely a comrade as Fong. Yet, he too, had proven himself invaluable. Tall, where Fong was short, Eich was an oft seen figure on Portland's streets, pulling his creaky, two-wheeled cart from dust bin to dust bin, collecting discarded items to fix up and sell to those of small means. The ragpicker liked to quote poetry, his or someone else's. Lately, he'd turned sweet on Mae and Sage suspected the feeling was mutual. He dare not ask. His mother could be surly as a mother bear when it came to her personal business.

"If I may give a summation of our understanding at this point?" Eich asked, before continuing at everyone's nod. "The laundry workers are waiting for Cobb to accept or reject their nine-hour day proposal—he appears to be deliberately withholding that response. Cobb has threatened another laundry owner with retribution should that laundry not join the association's position. Cobb has also indicated that he has something up his sleeve but we know not what. There appears to be a man in town, name of Farley, who might be a union buster working for the laundry association. If he is here, there is every chance he has or, will, import other miscreants as well. Finally, the city's unions appear to be rallying behind the laundry workers' cause and taking steps to assist. The only exception is the union that represents the laundries' delivery drivers. There is also a new laundry worker, Caroline, whose behavior seems suspicious. Oh, and the decent washroom foreman has quit his job."

"Good summation, Herman," Sage said. "It underscores that there is still much we don't know."

Fong, who'd stayed silent, moved to add more tea to everyone's cup. As he poured, he said, "They will attack fast like viper. Maybe many vipers at same time. We must learn all about vipers. "

Fong's analysis and strategy, as always, was both sobering and accurate. There was nothing more to add.

"Tell me, Mae, is there any one woman whose absence would wound the laundry workers' efforts, discourage them from pursuing their goals?"

Eich's question brought a vigorous nod from Mae. "Rachel Levy is their chosen leader. She's brave, outspoken, smart, humble and kind. I think they'd follow her anywhere. If she were gone, I can't say they wouldn't give up. But then, I haven't been looking around to see if there is anyone who can fill her shoes."

Eich ran gnarled fingers through his beard, his brow furrowed in thought. "Perhaps, Mae, you might start looking for Rachel's understudy and get to know more about that Caroline woman? If everyone's agreeable, I'll appoint myself Rachel's invisible guardian and general observer of the laundry building. That way, if she or the others appear in any danger, I can intercede and sound the alarm."

"Her boarding house is about ten blocks from the laundry. It stands on pilings in the ravine that runs along Southeast Eighth. She'll be leaving there tomorrow morning about six. That's a tad early to haul your cart all the way across town." Mae said. Eich lived in a lean-to alongside the Marquam ravine, south of downtown, on the west side of the Willamette River.

"Ah, but that is the beauty of these hot summer days. I can bed down in one of the fields on the eastside, not far from her boarding house. As long as I stay away from the mosquitoes infesting the river marshes, I will be quite comfortable," he assured her.

"My cousins and I will look for Farley's strike-breakers. Some cousins who work in hotels may know of other newcomers." Fong's offer was welcome because the efforts of "cousins" proved invaluable many times in the past. These men were not Fong's blood relatives but, instead, were members of his fraternal organization, what the Chinese called a "tong." The cousins were effective informers because they performed Portland's lowest paid work in rich people's homes and in hotels, restaurants, bordellos and drinking establishments. In their lowly servant roles, they went unnoticed by the whites.

Sage heaved a sigh. "Okay, then. I'll take on Cobb and the other association members. I'll keep tailing Cobb when he leaves the laundry. And, I will also try to find that union-buster boss from New York. I suspect he likes to travel high on the hog, especially since he has some boss paying his expenses. That means a visit to Angus Solomon," he said, as though that prospect was onerous.

His theatrical gambit didn't get past Mae. "Ha, poor you. Fong's going to creep around town, risking a thump on the head. Herman's going to rest his weary bones in a field, I'm going to continue slaving in that sweatshop of a laundry and you, poor Sage, will be forced to sit and stuff your face in the luxurious Portland Hotel dining room."

They'd all laughed—appreciating that humor ended the meeting

So, here I am, Sage thought as he gazed around the "luxurious" dining room. Mae wasn't wrong in her use of the word. Linen cloths, heavy silver cutlery, crystal glasses, carpeted floor and plenty of light streaming through the tall glass doors from the hotel's covered veranda made for an elegant scene. Belt-driven overhead fans caught and whirled the air flowing in through the open doors. This was a much cooler place to dine than Mozart's these days. Not for the first time, Sage questioned whether his opposition to electrifying the restaurant wasn't but a simple case of stubbornness. It looked as though electrification was here to stay.

Solomon was still graciously greeting guests so Sage signaled a waiter and ordered lunch. May as well prove his mother right—she'd like that. Around him, the room was nearly full. In one corner, a demanding group of men kept the waiters hustling. It would be a while before Solomon could break free.

It was Monday morning and Mae was trying not to be alarmed when she saw that Rachel was absent from her cuff and collar mangle. Cobb probably called for a negotiation meeting, she assured herself. That assurance flew out the window when Cobb charged into the washroom with a stranger in tow.

Cobb looked like he was prancing on his toes, glee elevating him above the floor. He gave the bell hanging by the office door a vigorous clang—signaling that they should quiet all machines and gather around. Next to him stood a well-groomed fellow with brown hair, narrow in the hips and too darn poker-faced to be trustworthy.

"This gentleman here," said Cobb, "is your new foreman. His name is 'Mr. Sinclair'. I expect that you will show him respect and do exactly as he instructs. No back talk. He's not a weak-kneed softy like the last fellow."

None of the women smiled a welcome. Mae understood. They had little hope that Cobb's handpicked foreman was anything other than a toady and probably a bully as well. "Birds of a feather," Mae muttered under her breath. The woman standing beside her nodded.

An awkward silence followed the introduction until Cobb said, "Well, I told Mr. Sinclair that there's to be no union talk during working hours. Keep your minds on your work, instead of on making trouble," he said before scooting back into his office, no doubt relieved to escape the stares of his unhappy workers.

The new foreman took a few minutes to gaze about him, looking like a duck who found himself in a chicken coop. As the women returned to work, Sinclair began wandering around the washroom, pausing beside each work station but saying nothing. The faces of the workers he observed stayed blank except for a grim clamping of their lips.

When the foreman reached the shaking table, Mae paused to watch. She wanted to see if he exchanged any special looks with the new laundry worker, Caroline. There was nothing. In fact, it seemed as if Caroline deliberately averted her gaze. Well, even that could be a sign they knew each other.

Mae sighed and went back to ironing her ruffles and laces. Another new face at a bad time, she thought. But that concern was quickly replaced by a sharper one. Where was Rachel? Did she quit? Was she fired? Or, had something worse happened to her?

SIX

"Easy as shooting a duck in a barrel," he told himself, one side of his mouth lifting in a smirk that he quickly suppressed. He narrowed his eyes and studied the laundry workers. A few were females who, with clean-up and paint, could definitely be little moneymakers. Like that gal now locked in the whorehouse. Not that a lock was needed. The laudanum guaranteed she'd give no trouble.

The boss and the client were happy. He patted the roll of bills in his pocket. He'd made his report Saturday night and, right away, Farley handed over the $300. That's why he liked working for the man—no dickering. You do your part, he delivers on his.

"Say, Sinclair," Farley had said, "You have any interest in earning a few more dollars before you hop the train back to Chicago?"

When he said, "Yes," his boss laid out the new plan that had him working as a foreman in the Sparta Laundry, reporting directly to the client. So here he was, shop foreman, the man in charge. Sinclair gazed around the washroom, the steam coating his neck before trickling down his spine. Damn good thing he wouldn't be working here all that long. This must be what hell feels like, he thought as he wiped his neck with a clean handkerchief.

Sure enough, he'd be seeing hell if the creaky old prior's predictions were right. But what did that old man know, locked away with his moldy old books behind six foot high walls? Not the real world. Not Paul Sinclair's world, that was for sure.

He stepped closer to a table where the women stood snapping wrinkles out of wet clothes. He remembered to spread his lips in a smile only to have it freeze when not a one of them returned it. He let the smile slide away. *You'll be sorry, you stupid cows,* he thought to himself. *I'll be writing down every one of your names. That's what Cobb wants. A list of enemies.*

He stepped over to one of the machines that pressed shirts. The woman at that machine looked up at him and smiled. "Don't work so fast," he said as he patted her shoulder, winked and moved on. He'd made her promise to keep their friendship secret, saying Cobb wouldn't stand for his new foreman being close friends with a union member.

That should keep the silly girl happy, he thought. *Let her keep thinking that, because she told me the foreman quit, she's the reason I got this job.* He glanced back over his shoulder. Maybe he should rescue her from this hell hole. For sure, he could talk her into going back to Chicago. She'd jump at the chance to elope with him, believe any story he told. They always did. Every damn time. At least in a whorehouse she wouldn't be working so many hours in the sweltering heat. That work took place in the night. Besides, if she did fall for it, he'd get even more money in his pocket.

Sage leaned back in his chair, his stomach pleasantly full. He was sipping his second cup of coffee when Angus Solomon came to stand beside his table. It was one of their customary meeting places—the single table next to the kitchen door and screened from the other diners by a tall palm. The location allowed Solomon to stand with his back to the dining room while they talked. He always remained standing. It would never do for the hotel's black maitre'd to actually sit down with a patron. Instead, his demeanor always made it look as if he were merely engaged in polite small talk. As far as they knew, the nature of their actual relationship remained a secret from all except Solomon's wait staff. Sage had seen their sharp eyes glance in their direction more than once.

"Mr. Adair, it is always pleasant to see you. Has business or happenstance brought you here to grace us with your presence?" Solomon said in a soft Carolinian drawl.

From the sparkle in those brown eyes, he could tell Solomon was ready for their next joint adventure. They had worked together since the beginning, the elegant Carolinian and Mozart's owner. Solomon, operated a hotel for black train porters at the same time he managed the dining room of the city's most exclusive hotel. Both jobs put him in an ideal position to discover information about newcomers to the city. While this was a whites-only hotel when it came to the patrons, it made a point of hiring blacks to perform the establishment's menial tasks as well as provide high-toned service in the dining room. This segregation benefitted their missions because the hotel's guests and bosses rarely noticed the "help," while the help noticed everything.

"We are in need of your assistance once again, Mr. Solomon. We've received information that there is an undesirable visitor in the city. His name is James Farley and he is supposedly from New York. We think it likely that he is staying here at the hotel. Do you think you could find out?"

Solomon smiled broadly. "Why Mister Adair, if that fellow is registered under his own name, confirming the information will be easy. But, since you have his name, even you could inquire at the front desk as to his presence here in the hotel."

Sage nodded. "That's right, I could. But it might get back to him. And we can't have him knowing that we are interested in his activities just yet. We think he's in town to help the owners in a labor dispute that's brewing. And, we're almost positive he won't be here alone. He hires spies and thugs—both men and women—to do dirty work on behalf of the bosses, including getting rid of union leaders, one way or another. He also imports scabs to cross picket lines to take the workers' places. All and all, he's an unsavory character," Sage said repeating the additional information Leo Lockwood had sent by messenger earlier that day.

Solomon understood because even as he nodded agreement, his lips tightened in disgust. Sage continued, "So, we need to confirm he's here, as well as discover who else is working with him. His toughs won't be staying at this hotel because they'd stick out like sore thumbs. But I bet they'll sneak down the hallways in order to meet secretly with him in his room. They're the ones we need to identify and follow. And we have to do it without Farley learning what we're doing."

Solomon wasn't surprised at the request. It wasn't the first time the Portland Hotel's workers had gathered such information. In fact, their help had been invaluable more than once.

"May I ask which labor dispute our investigation would specifically aid?" Solomon asked.

"You know about the laundry workers wanting a nine-hour day?" he asked and, at Solomon's nod, he continued, "We think the laundry bosses have brought Farley and his pals to town. Plus, we know they plan to act soon because their leader, Cobb, has said so. It's our thought that we'll be better prepared to respond if we know in advance exactly who they are and what they are planning."

"I know about the steam laundries," Solomon said. "A few of us, have obtained employment running the laundry washtubs. They are very brutal places to work. From what I've heard, even nine hours are too many hours to work in that environment. I am thinking my colleagues will feel privileged to ascertain the information you seek, provided such information is available."

"If you do find something out, please send a message to Fong at Mozart's. He'll come see you at your hotel. He has men who will follow Farley's little helpers."

That request brought a grin to Solomon's face. For some reason, the tall black man and the small Chinese man had formed a strong friendship. No doubt, Angus Solomon looked forward to working with Fong Kam Tong again.

He'd glided away. Sage thought about Solomon saying that black men worked in the city's steam laundries. It was rare for black men to work alongside white men performing the same job. The fact that they did, was an indication of the undesirability of running wash tubs. Only that could explain such an exception to the customary workplace segregation.

Rachel Levy was still missing when the noon whistle sounded and the women filed out the door. Mae thought about the morning. The oddly cheerful Cobb had never returned to the washroom. The new foreman had continued his rounds, saying nothing but stopping at every machine to observe and show his teeth like a hungry shark. Mae didn't trust him or his phony smiles.

The women ate their meager lunches in the adjoining empty lot beneath the willow's shade. It was hot and no whiff of air cooled the sweat on their backs and brows.

Mae didn't wait for everyone to settle before she raised the question that had nagged her the entire morning. "Where's Rachel today?" she asked the union representative's closest friend. "Is she sick? Or, did Cobb fire her?"

Everyone paused in their fussing to wait for the answer. "I don't know," said the woman, Beatrice, "I waited for her this morning as long as I could. We meet every work morning on the same corner but she never showed up. The last time I saw her was on Saturday." Worry creased the woman's brow. The other women murmured in dismay.

"She would tell you if she was fired, wouldn't she?" Mae pressed, trying to figure out if there was any explanation for Rachel's absence. As she asked the question, fear prickled her backbone.

"Sure she would," responded Beatrice. "We've always expected Cobb would fire her. Especially after she told off that delivery driver, L.D. Warder. But even if Cobb fired her, she still would have met me and told me so I could tell everyone else. Her plan was to ask the Trade Council for money to live on so she could keep working on our negotiating team and start meeting more regular with the workers from the other laundries. She's been told that the Council would agree to pay her."

The woman took a deep breath and said, "There is absolutely no way Rachel Levy would walk away from us." That declaration triggered vigorous nods of agreement from the other women. They believed in the woman they had elected to represent them. They were certain that she would not let them down.

Mae's sense of foreboding strengthened. She knew their faith in Rachel was not misplaced. As she chewed her simple sandwich of bread, cheese and ham, Mae looked around for the familiar figure of the ragpicker. He was nowhere in sight. Maybe he was following Rachel. Maybe he knew where she was and what she was doing. She tried to hope, though she feared it was more likely Herman was still trying to find the missing woman. She fought the urge to run off to find Eich and Sage, to sound the alert, to start the search for the missing woman. She forced herself to stay put, despite knowing that it would be hours before she could get word to her partners that Rachel was missing.

Lunch was mostly a silent affair, though they briefly discussed the new foreman, with the general agreement being that he was "smarmy" and couldn't be trusted. The only dissent came from Chrissy, the young girl who ran one of the shirt mangles. She timidly said she thought Sinclair "very handsome" but stayed silent when one of the older women warned her to stay away from the man until they knew him better.

During this discussion, Mae noticed that the new girl, Caroline, said nothing. But, as usual, her dark eyes were sharply observant. She was obviously taking in every word that was said. And, likely noting who was saying those words.

When one of the women suggested they all pray for Rachel's safety, Mae noticed that Caroline was quick to duck her head and tightly clasp her hands in prayer. Whether her show of piety was sincere or an act, Mae couldn't tell. Her musings can to an abrupt end when the shrill steam whistle summoned them back to work.

SEVEN

She heard the groan before she felt it rasp her throat. Next came the realization that her thoughts were dragging, as if wading though deep water. And, her head ached with a steady throb. After that, the itching started, she raised an arm but saw no bites or insects. Still her skin needed scratching. Suddenly realizing she was near naked, clothed only in a thin cotton sleeveless shift, she yanked the tattered blanket to her chin despite the hot and stifling air.

The room she was in was dark except for the dim blades of light forcing their way through the curtain. It hung inside boards nailed across the single window. Why would someone nail boards over a curtain? An ordinary door was set in one wall. With a groan, she forced herself to slide her feet to the floor and sit up. Nausea swooped through her and her aching head turned dizzy. She gritted her teeth, rose on wobbly legs and made it to the door. When she got there, the door knob turned but the door wouldn't open. She'd been locked in. Why was she locked in?

Making her way back to the iron cot, she eyed the meager furnishings—a narrow woven wire cot, a scarred wooden fruit box, and chipped ceramic chamber pot in the corner. Her blouse, skirt and shoes were nowhere in sight. Only her jacket, with its enameled rose lapel pin, was on the chair. She slipped it on despite the heat.

Sitting on the cot, she fought to remember how she'd ended up in this place. It was like she was telling herself a story with pieces missing.

She remembered leaving the laundry. It had been so hot. She'd been looking forward sitting on the shaded porch tacked onto the back of the boarding house. Because it stood on stilts over the ravine, it was a few degrees cooler than their room. She thought that maybe she'd sit in the wicker chair and read a little before drifting off to sleep. It was such a luxury to be lazy on her free afternoon.

She never made it to the boarding house. She was certain of that. What happened after she dropped Rachel's lunch off at the laundry? A recollection of Danny's face brightening with pleasure upon seeing her meant she'd walked as far as the pencil stand. She always stopped to speak to him because he reminded her of her cousin Bennie—simple but sweet to the core, incapable of deceit. After that, she'd walked on, wanting to get out of the beating sun, to get home. She remembered the alley. The two-story building on its south side had cast it into deep shade that was a welcome relief.

She tried to remember what came next. There'd been hurrying foot-steps, the jolt of being yanked back against someone's body, something wet, cold, stinky covering her face, smothering her as she gasped for air. Then nothing. Now she was here. Someone had brought her here.

A tin pitcher of water sat on the fruit box beside a tin cup. She poured the water into the glass. Even in the dim light, she could see it was murky. Still, her tongue felt sore and dry, like cotton coated it. She was so thirsty. Against her better judgment, she drank the brackish water before lying back to ponder her situation.

Just before her thoughts stilled, a terrifying thought knifed through her headache. What happened to her, everything, from being grabbed off the streets and jailed in a room with her clothes missing, all of it exactly matched the newspaper stories she'd read. Cautionary tales they been, warning about the dangers of falling victim to white slavers. Had they stolen her in order to turn her into a prostitute? A strange lassitude overtook her limbs and her thoughts drifted into such vivid dreams that she no longer cared about the answer.

Sage stood at Mozart's podium, smiling graciously at the cus-tomers arriving for the noon hour dinner when the street door opened slowly and an intense Chinese face peeked in. Once the man saw Sage notice him, he closed the door. It was one of Fong's cousins with an urgent message. Urgent because, otherwise, the messenger would have knocked on the kitchen door and waited for Sage to be fetched.

Sage signaled for Homer, Mozart's head waiter, to take Sage's place at the podium. By now, Homer was accustomed to these abrupt and inexplicable departures and willingly stepped in to perform Sage's role without a hitch. Casting a final glance at the elegant dining room, Sage grabbed his homburg and made his apologies to the waiting patrons.

Once outside, he saw the Chinese man again. This time, peeking at Sage from the alley. When Sage reached him, the man wasted no time, "Mr. Adair. Mr. Fong say hurry quick to Portland Hotel. Man you want, eating there right now."

That was enough. Sage dropped a few coins into the man's hand and headed toward the hotel at a near run. When he got there, Solomon's eyes lit up and he tilted his head in the direction of a table near the window. Sure enough, there was Thaddeus Cobb sitting with a stranger. They were leaning toward each other over empty plates, obviously engaged in an earnest conversation.

"Oh, what the hell," Sage told himself and he strolled in their direction. Upon seeing him approach, Cobb raised a palm before the other man who abruptly stopped talking. Cobb smiled widely as he stood to greet Sage, his hand outstretched. The other man also rose, expecting an introduction to someone Cobb clearly considered important.

"Mr. Adair, how nice to see you! This is my business associate, James Farley. He's traveled here from New York," Cobb said as he shook Sage's hand. While Farley and Sage shook, Cobb explained Sage's status to Farley, "Mr. Adair is the owner of the city's most exclusive restaurant, Mozart's Table. I will have to take you there before you leave town. We hope to acquire his future business for our laundry."

Farley was a rotund man, with small stony blue eyes sunk deep beneath bristling gray brows. He had a button nose and a rosebud mouth that flashed an insincere smile. From the smile, Sage gathered his was an unwelcome interruption.

Cobb, however, didn't seem to mind, because he snapped his fingers at a waiter and motioned to an empty chair at a neighboring table. The waiter carried the chair to their table and Cobb gestured for Sage to take a seat, saying, "Please, sit with us. Unfortunately, we have finished our luncheon but would love to have you join us for coffee."

Sage would have liked the conversation to reveal Farley's purpose for being in Portland, but Cobb had other ideas. "Look here, Adair. Have you had anymore thoughts about moving Mozart's laundry business to the Sparta? I understand you are still using that Chinese laundry down on Second. Surely, they can't get your linens as clean or sharply pressed as our steam laundry. "

Somewhat taken aback by the knowledge that Cobb was so familiar with Mozart's business, Sage hesitated before answering, "Well, I've been using that laundry on Second for three years and they've never let me down. Always done a fine job. So, I do have some loyalty to them."

That comment brought a snort from Farley who said, "You have loyalty to a Chink. Ha! That's a new one!"

Cobb glowered at his companion before turning to Sage. "Yet, you did request a tour of the Sparta. Surely that means you are contemplating making a change?"

"Yes, the owner of the laundry informed me that it is likely that he will close up shop and move out to Hillsboro to take over his cousin's washhouse. He says the rents are getting too high here in the city and that the steam laundries are taking too much of his business."

That answer brought a fleeting smile of satisfaction to Cobb's face but he said nothing. The waiter brought Sage's coffee and refilled the other men's cups during the ensuing silence. Once he'd departed, Sage turned toward Farley, "So, Mr. Farley, what brings you to our fair city?"

For a moment Farley was speechless, clearly flailing for an acceptable answer. Sage was aware that Cobb was holding his breath as if concerned that Farley might say the wrong thing. After taking a hurried swallow of coffee to stall for time, Farley said, "I had heard that there are some business opportunities here. I have some funds to invest and thought I'd see what I could find."

Sage felt Cobb relax at his side and decided to play along, "Oh, yes. Portland has been growing by leaps and bounds. And, now the city fathers are planning a Lewis and Clark Exposition for 1905. The business community is certain that event will attract hordes of people who will remain in the city." Both men eagerly nodded, happy to have dodged the uncomfortable question about Farley's presence.

Sage decided to goad them a bit. "Though, I am sure that Mr. Cobb has informed you that this is a highly unionized town. Labor carries a big club here. Isn't that right, Cobb?"

Cobb cautiously nodded. Farley waved a dismissive hand in the air. "Oh, those damn unions can be handled. Fellow just has to know how to put them in their place."

"What place is that?" Sage couldn't help asking. He could tell that Cobb had gone rigid, likely fearing that Farley's arrogance would lead him to slip.

"Why, in the ground or jail, if possible. If not, at least in a place that leaves them toothless. Either way, I've lots of experience in that regard, so I'm not worried."

Sage hid the clenching of his own teeth behind the edge of the delicate china cup. We'll just have to see about that, he thought to himself.

Exiting the laundry, Mae paused to look around for Eich or Sage. Neither was in sight. She'd have to walk to the trolley and ride it home. She'd gotten soft working in Mozart's because she found herself dreading the trip. Far better to snooze in the cab whilst Sage dealt with the driver.

She started the six block walk to the trolley stop but soon paused to think. If she went home, without knowing what had happened to Rachel, tomorrow would bring that same uncertainty. Besides, the women needed to know where their union representative had gone. Nothing could hurt their spirits more than Rachel's continued absence. That thought brought an involuntary shiver at odds with the still pressing heat of what had been another unbearably hot day.

Her decision made, Mae turned east, away from the river. Rachel had told everyone where she lived. Finding the boarding house should be easy because there were few on the east side of the river. Mostly it was still farmland although the areas between the villages of Buckman, Sunnyside and Mt. Villa were rapidly filling with houses. Two things were at work to make that happen. First, was that a trolley now rattled its way between the little settlements. And secondly, union activity in the city had raised people's wages. For the first time, regular working people could afford to buy their own homes. Small builders flocked to take advantage of these eager new homeowners, often constructing pattern houses from Sears and Roebuck. So many family homes were being built that folks had taken to calling the area "Union Town." That idea made her smile until she noticed passersby looking at her like the heat had stupefied her head.

The boarding house was easy to spot despite the deepening night. It was a two-story clapboard building with wide verandas front and back. As she advanced, she saw that most of the building sat upon stilts anchored in the sides and bottom of a ravine. Streams, ravines and swamps riddled the eastside. Now that the city had annexed it, the developers and landowners were hoping to exploit the area. Men were encasing streams in pipes while fill dirt was eradicating the ravines and swamps. She tried to imagine what the area would look like in another twenty-five years and couldn't. She'd miss seeing the farmland climbing up the gentle slopes of Mt. Tabor to the east and the milk cows meandering along the dirt roads.

Her thoughts screeched to a halt at the familiar sight of the rag-picker's cart parked across the street from the boarding house. Her eyes sought Herman and a momentary pang of fear grabbed at her heart. He wouldn't just abandon his cart. Then, a relieved gasp escaped her. There he was, sitting on the porch. And, next to him, sat Rachel her hands clenched tightly in her lap. The strained look on the young woman's face said that something was very wrong.

EIGHT

"I'M EXPECTING TWO OF MY best operatives to arrive in the next few days. As you know, I already have one in place," Farley told the assembled group of laundry owners.

"James, perhaps you should wait until our coffee has been replenished," interrupted Cobb while nodding at the white jacket waiter silently moving around the table pouring from a silver coffee pot. To the waiter he said, "Once you have finished pouring the coffee, you may leave the room and close the door behind you."

The fellow nodded, finished serving and, closing the door firmly behind him, departed. Cobb addressed the group. "Thank you all for coming tonight. We have had a pleasant visit but now we must discuss our plans. So far, we are exactly on track. We have just struck the enemy and weakened him. We have warned the namby-pambies that we will no longer tolerate their neutrality. Next comes our boldest step of all."

"Are you certain that it won't backfire on us? The unions are making a big to-do over working conditions in our laundries. They keep yammering on about the laundry women being the weaker sex, in need of protection."

Cobb was nodding patiently, as if he'd anticipated this question and answered easily, "There is always a danger that the public will turn against us. That's why we have to control the time line and have our defense prepared. Offense, actually," he added, correcting himself.

"What about the Chinese laundries? They'll steal our customers."

Cobb's hand waved that concern away, "The Chinese laundries can't do as good or as quick a job as a steam laundry because they don't have the equipment. They'll be overwhelmed with orders which will make them slower than usual. So yes, in the short term, they will benefit. And, believe me, they will take advantage. I'll bet their prices will soar. But, that's all good. In the end, once we're back in business, our customers will return."

"I fail to see how losing business to the Chinks is going to help my laundry," said one of the men who, up to that point, had been scowling down at the tablecloth.

Cobb was dismissive of the man's concern. "As the cost and the soiled laundry piles up, who will your customers blame? And how long will the women be able to hold out? It's the laundry women who matter in this fight since they do most of the work."

"I don't see why the girls have to raise a fuss. They should be grateful for the work. There aren't that many businesses hiring women. I tell 'em, if they don't like the work, go find another job. That's what I'd do," said yet another of the men. Around him, there were nods of agreement.

"Yes, but in the meantime they cause problems, don't they? And every time we hire another one she runs to the union and cries that she's worked too hard and paid too little. There's another thing in our favor. They don't make enough to save. So, I ask you again, 'how long can they hold out?' How long can their so-called 'union brothers and sisters,'" scorn dripped off Cobb's words, "afford to support them all? How long will they be willing to support them all?"

One of the men shifted uncomfortably in his chair. "That may be true but I don't know how long I can hold out, myself. I just bought two new extractors and still owe on them," he said worriedly.

"Not a problem," Cobb assured him. "We've already agreed that, if any one of us falls short of funds, the rest will help out with a low cost loan. Right fellows?" Cobb's piercing eyes raked across their faces, as if daring them to disagree. He got unanimous nods of agreement. He turned to Farley saying, "Okay James, let's fill everyone in on what happened today and what we have planned."

"Two times in one day, Solomon?" Sage asked as he slipped inside the Portland Hotel's closed dining room. There were no patrons, just the waiters snapping fresh linens out over tabletops and carefully positioning cutlery. A clattering came from the kitchen as the help washed, stacked and put away the dishes. Soon all would be set and ready for tomorrow's breakfast crowd. Sage was glad Mozart's didn't serve breakfast because by the end of the night, most everyone was too tired to set up for the next day. Usually, they sent the waiters home to rest and, first thing in the morning, he and Mae readied the dining room for its first customers of the day. Of course, that all changed when he and Mae were on a mission for St. Alban. Then their head waiter, Homer, took over running the restaurant.

Solomon smiled, and gestured at a nearby table where Sage promptly sat. Solomon joined him and signaled to a waiter. The fellow laid down his handful of cutlery and made his way over to them. Despite what must have been a tiring evening, the fellow acted bright-eyed and vigorous. He was younger than the other waiters and, Sage couldn't remember ever having seen the young man before. His smooth, nut brown face was handsome by any standard, with high cheekbones that bespoke a mixed Indian and African heritage. Sage cast a questioning glance at Solomon whose face looked remarkably similar.

"I'd like to introduce my nephew, Nathan, who just arrived here from the Carolinas to make his fortune," said Solomon. Sage rose to shake hands. After they took their seats, Solomon said, "Our private dining room is currently being used by Thaddeus Cobb and the other laundry owners for a meeting. I asked Nathan to serve as their waiter in the hope he would overhear something." Pride was in Solomon's voice indicating he believed his nephew smart and discreet enough to carry out such a sensitive and secret task.

"They are here right now?"

Solomon nodded and turned to Nathan. "Suppose you tell Mister Adair what you overheard?"

"They are exceedingly cautious not to be overheard," began the young man, his well-spoken words mirroring his uncle's refined way of speaking. "But one of them, the man who currently resides here in the hotel, did say that he has one operative in place and expects two more to arrive any day now. 'Operative' was his word, not mine," Nathan said.

It struck Sage that perhaps Solomon's entire family was highly educated but he only said, "That is all you were able to overhear?" rushing to add, "Not to say it isn't valuable. It means we now know exactly how many people Farley and Cobb have working behind the scenes. We didn't know that before."

Nathan smiled. "It was all I could overhear but, they complained that the room was too hot. So, I opened the outside door onto the terrace. I was thinking that someone standing on the terrace might be able to overhear more. I can't do it because they'd notice and so would the hotel's manager. But perhaps someone who appeared to be a guest, such as yourself, might want to enjoy a breath of fresh air before going to bed."

Sage was already rising before the sentence had ended. "Great idea. I could do with some fresh air. Thank you very, very much Nathan," he added before hurrying off.

"Shh. Let's let Sage sleep a bit longer before we wake him up." Mae cautioned Eich as she unlocked the door to let them into Mozart's kitchen. It was close to midnight and the cook stove was cool to the touch. It was too much trouble to boil water for tea or coffee. After pulling the string to light the restaurant's only electric bulb, she asked. "How about some wine, Herman?" She wasn't ready to be alone just yet. And she wasn't ready to face Sage and add yet another worry onto his shoulders. Right now, she needed peace and a chance to rest her thoughts. Herman understood. He'd held her when she finally gave into her fear and despair at the end of their fruitless search.

They took seats at Ida's plank table, wine glasses before them. The single light bulb dangling overhead cast harsh shadows. Still it was better than gas jets spewing even more heat into an already too warm room. Poor Herman, he looked exhausted. Probably no more than she did, she told herself glumly. After a day in the steam laundry and hours roaming the street she was sick with worry. If they ever reached the end of this escapade she was going to sleep for three days straight.

She bent to unlace her boots, saying, "Herman, if I don't get these clod hoppers off, I swear my feet will swell too big to get them off." As she straightened and wriggled her freed toes with a relieved sigh, she heard footsteps hurrying across the restaurant. Damn. Sage, it had to be him. It was still too early for Ida's pie baking to start.

Sure enough, the doors burst open as her beloved son strode into the room, a scowl darkening his face as soon as he saw her. She raised a hand. "Don't start," she cautioned.

Of course, he ignored her. "Where the hell have you been? Do you realize that you are almost three hours late getting home?"

She looked up at him, letting her face sag into its weary lines. "Oh hush up, Sage. I can't count the number of times I've waited for you to come home from one of your jaunts," she said tiredly.

A throat cleared and Sage started. He hadn't realized they weren't alone. Eich was walking toward the table, holding an empty wine glass. "I am happy to see you down here, Sage. Your mother was going to send me up those stairs to fetch you. Glad I don't have to climb them. It's been an extraordinarily long day," the ragpicker said with a warm smile. "For both of us," he added, nodding toward Mae, his eyes commanding Sage to back off his attack.

Sage's face lost its anger. He quietly took a seat and accepted the wine from Herman. He still shot her a stern look but she responded with a deliberate eye roll to let him know his look had no effect.

"If you are done bellowing like a lost calf," she said, "we've been hunting for a missing woman."

"Missing? Who is missing?" he asked.

"Rachel Levy didn't come to work today. Eich caught up with her outside her boarding house first thing in this morning. He thought he was going to follow her to work but instead, she was wandering all over the eastside, looking into nooks and crannies, abandoned buildings and old sheds." She looked at Eich, saying, "Herman, you tell him the rest. I'm so darn tired, it hurts to talk."

The ragpicker patted her hand, his deep brown eyes affectionate. He turned to Sage. "After awhile, I realized that the poor woman was frantic. I couldn't watch anymore without trying to help her, whatever it was she was doing. So I approached and asked if I could assist.

"She just dissolved into tears. It was only after she calmed down that she was able to tell me what had happened. It seems that two days ago, on Saturday, her sister Rebecca stopped by the laundry to drop lunch off for Rachel. Rebecca works as a sales girl in the Olds and King department store. Apparently, the owner has decided to work his sales clerks only five and one half days a week. He lets them take a half day off on Saturday."

"Yes, I saw his ad in the *Labor Press*. He's asking folks not to shop in any store past 6 p.m. on Saturdays. He closes his store then so his sales girls only work a half day. He's asking that the other merchants follow suit," Sage said.

"Humph," Mae commented, silently adding "and hogs will fly" as she sipped her wine and said nothing. Eich continued his explanation, "Yes, well, Rebecca works the Saturday morning shift at the department store. When she gets off work, she picks up something special for Rachel's lunch and drops it off. Then she goes home to the boarding house where they both live.

"Rachel's lucky to have a sister. So many of the girls have to make it on their own when they come to Portland," observed Mae.

"Well, it sounds like she was lucky until Saturday, anyway," Sage noted.

Eich heaved a sigh and said, "Yes, until Saturday. You see, Rebecca never made it home to the boarding house. No one saw her once she left the laundry after dropping off Rachel's lunch."

"Is that what Rachel was doing today? Searching for her sister?" Sage asked.

"Yes, she started Saturday night when she got home from the laundry. She searched that night and all day Sunday. She went to the police but found no help there. In fact, they managed to both offend her and scare her," Eich said.

Mae stirred to say, "They waved off her concerns. Told her that Rebecca probably ran off with some fellow she met in a saloon. Told her that Rebecca was a grown woman and unless she was taken by white slavers, her sister didn't get to tell her what to do. Poor Rachel didn't get any further than the officer on the desk!" Mae still felt the burn of outrage over the pain the police officer's callous words must have caused the frantic Rachel. When she saw Sergeant Hanke she was going to tell him a thing or two.

"Is it likely she took off with some man?" Sage asked.

Mae shook her head emphatically. "I am sure she did not. First of all, Rebecca doesn't drink. And, according to Rachel, her sister would never step foot inside a saloon. She says they are close and Rebecca never hides anything from her. I believe her. Rachel is a smart gal. Nothing much gets by her," Mae said.

Eich's tone was firm as he said, "Well, one thing for sure. Rebecca's not in any abandoned shed nor building nor field nor eastside alley. Rachel looked everywhere all day Sunday. Then I looked with her all day today and Mae and I helped her look a second time tonight. Someone has taken that young woman and hidden her from sight. I don't think she's anywhere on the east side. They somehow moved her over here from across the river."

Mae watched Sage ponder this troubling turn of events. It was a disaster. Not just for the girl, Rebecca. But also for their mission because her sister, Rachel, was the Sparta workers' chosen leader. If Rebecca's absence distracted Rachel, she'd be a poor leader right when she was needed the most. Maybe that's what the kidnappers wanted. Still, there could be some other reason the girl was missing.

Sage told them what little he'd been able to overhear while standing on the Portland Hotel's veranda. "I arrived too late to hear much, since Cobb's meeting was winding down. Still, I overheard Cobb saying, "And we need to thank Farley here. It took awhile but he finally managed to chop the head off the snake."

He rubbed his face as if to stir himself. He was weary too. "At the time, Cobb's comment made no sense. Actually, it still doesn't. How would kidnapping the union rep's sister be like chopping off a snake's head? Did they hope to distract Rachel by kidnapping her sister? Nah, that couldn't be it. Far easier and more effective to just grab Rachel herself."

He looked at Mae and Eich. "Well, I guess this means we better add the finding of Rebecca Levy to our tasks," he said.

Mae nodded. "Yup, I told Rachel my friend John Miner would find her sister come hail or high water." She got up and set her empty wine glass in the sink. "Sage, don't make me a liar. The laundry workers need Rachel and she needs her sister," she told him before squeezing Herman's shoulders, dropping a kiss on Sage's forehead and exiting out the kitchen doors.

NINE

"My mistress requires these table linens by tomorrow afternoon. Will that be possible?" the maid asked with her hand firmly atop a laundry bundle. Sinclair could tell, by the way she keep a firm grip on the bundle's twine, that she wasn't about to let it go until she obtained that promise. After the counter clerk assured her that the laundry would be ready for pick up the next afternoon, the maid relinquished her hold and scooted out the door.

It was after nine in the morning and the laundry business was well underway. By now, the delivery trucks were rattling up and down the city streets, each man on his assigned route, dropping off and picking up laundry. Sinclair glanced into the office but it was empty. Good Cobb was gone. Not that he would have complained about Sinclair's late arrival. Cobb couldn't complain. After all, Sinclair knew nothing of running a steam laundry. He wasn't there for that. He was supposed to watch the women for suspicious activity and provide a list of the troublemakers.

Besides, he'd had to stop and check on the girl. He'd found her lying on the cot, her heavy breathing evidence that the laudanum was doing its job. As he'd stood in the darkened room, gazing at her face he told himself, just nine more days and she'd be on her way south. Soon she'd be someone else's problem. Even if she managed to make passage back from Panama, so much time would have passed that she'd only be a vague memory to her kin. Most important, the laundry workers' squabble would be long over.

This morning he was ready to act the role of laundry foreman. He wasn't looking forward to it. Already, the temperature outside, coupled with the washroom steam, would be enough to make a snake sweat. He removed his suit coat and hung it on Cobb's coat tree.

Upon entering the main plant he stopped at the sorting alcove where the women were pulling apart bundles of dirty laundry, sorting the items and inking laundry codes on collars and elsewhere. This area wasn't as hot as the main washroom but he wanted to pinch his nose shut against the stink of unwashed clothes and linens. God knew what diseases and other disgusting filth lurked in those folds.

He held his breath and passed quickly into the main washroom. There, a wet heat rolled against him, enveloped him and, for an instant, paralyzed him with its grip. Damp instantly stuck his freshly laundered shirt to his back making him silently vow that there was no way he'd hang around in this steam bath all day. He'd just pass through, look the women over and then leave after coming up with some excuse.

First he eyed the washtub area, watching the men busily stir the tubs, add chemicals, toss the wet stuff into whirling water extractors and pile it onto hand carts. Sweat plastered their thin, sleeveless undershirts against the men's wiry torsos. He shook his head. Not work he'd ever want to do. Pandering was definitely easier on the body, if not the conscience.

Casting a glance around the entire area he saw that everyone was working as they should. The shake table women were vigorously snapping the clothes free of wrinkles. He knew from watching yesterday that their vigor would dwindle come late afternoon and evening.

Idly he cast his eye over the women working the mangles. Chrissy caught him looking and sent him a shy smile but he didn't respond. He couldn't, because the sight of the woman working the mangle next to Chrissy paralyzed him.

Rachel. It was that woman Rachel. Despite the heat, dread shivered up his back. Had she escaped? His mind flailed. Even if she had escaped, there was no way she could have made it to the Sparta Laundry before him. It just wasn't possible. My god, maybe she'll recognize me. Panic jolted through him but he fought to control it while his mind frantically sought a solution. He could snatch her when she left the building. Surely she would leave once she saw him. She'd for sure run for the police. Hell, maybe she wouldn't recognize him. He'd grabbed her from behind. She'd been barely conscious when he'd walked her to the whorehouse, staggering under her weight, acting the part of one drunk escorting another. Calm yourself, Paulie, he cautioned himself. There's got to be an explanation.

His heart thumping, Sinclair forced himself to make a leisurely circuit of the washroom, stopping at every work station, smiling at the workers even though few smiled in return. Today, he didn't care. His focus was solely on that one woman calmly feeding cloth into the mangle. When he reached her station he looked directly at her, tensing, expecting her to cry out in recognition when she raised her eyes to his face. But there was nothing—just a calm, cool gaze quickly averted so she could pay attention to her machine.

He stood unmoving, his mind flailing for an answer. It wasn't making sense. He'd talk to Chrissy, he thought. That's what he'd do. She was a ninny but she was the only one who might tell him something. Sidling up next to her, he murmured, "Noon, Water Street Lunch Counter." She heard him over the steam hiss of her mangle and gave a small nod, the corner of her mouth quirking upward.

He moved away, his shoulder blades tight. Was that Rachel woman watching him, calculating how she was going to expose him in the most damaging way? After one more glance around, he hurried outside into the hot, dry air. Standing in the roasting sun's glare, he debated what to do next. Cobb obviously didn't know Rachel was back at work because Farley would have been screaming about it first thing this morning. Farley—boy, was Farley going to be angry. Probably demand the money back. He didn't have it all, having spent some of it on a few celebratory pipes the night before. What a mess, what a damn mess. He'd better come up with a good explanation and fast.

Wheels rattling across wooden street pavers, three stories below, snapped Sage fully awake after a restless night's sleep. A soft thump sounded overhead. He turned from the window. He had much to do. He needed to talk to Fong and it was Fong up there in the attic. Quickly he slipped on loose pants and a baggy shirt and headed for the attic stairs. Reaching the top, he paused in the threshold, watching Fong's body flow through a set program of moves, his bamboo stick whirling overhead, jabbing low, sideways, backwards or down. It was a stick form that Fong said he would teach him, once Sage was "ready"

Whatever that meant. Stepping into the room, Sage lowered himself onto the polished fir floor, sitting with his legs folded, once again the humble student acknowledging the master.

One final jab and Fong was crossing his arms, his stick motionless at last. After a moment of absolute rest, Fong turned to him. "Ah, lazy student finally raise eyelids to greet day," he observed, a broad smile blunting the criticism.

"Hey, I was up late," Sage protested.

"You ready to practice?" Fong asked before turning away to assume the beginning stance. Sage uncoiled his legs, which were already cramping, and copied Fong. For the next half hour the two of them moved through the 108 movements. They did the same movements every time but, yet, they were not the same. It was odd Sage thought, how each time the experience was somehow different from beginning to end.

Once he'd asked Fong why every time, the same series of movements, felt different. His teacher gave his customary indirect answer.

"Each time is a new journey," was Fong's answer.

"But a new journey to where?" Sage had pressed. Instead of answering, Fong had silently touched his belly, then his heart, then his head before turning away to begin moving through the form once again.

Today, Sage asked no questions. His body followed Fong's movements even as his mind flitted around the problems confronting them. How were they going to find the girl? What did Cobb have planned?

Of course, Fong noticed his distraction. Once they reached the end position, Fong was all business. "Your body move like sideshow automaton. Your chi flowing in fits and starts. What is on your mind?" he asked, his tone kindly rather than chiding.

"I was up late because Mae came home way late from the laundry. That's because she and Herman spent most of last night hunting for a missing girl. She's the sister of the woman who is the union representative at the Sparta Laundry."

"They find girl?" Fong asked, his forehead puckered with unease.

Sage shook his head. They both knew that the city's streets were dangerous places for all the young women pouring in from the countryside. The newspapers carried stories about white slavers—the men and women who tricked or kidnapped young women to sell into prostitution.

"Mae promised Rachel that we would find her sister. The girl's name is Rebecca. Do you think the cousins would help?"

"Yes, of course," Fong said quickly, before adding, "I know of bad Chinese who sell women. They use opium and drink to make them obedient. Cousins can check underground and the few Chinese sporting houses. Also, we better ask Mr. Solomon to do same with his people. Not sure it will be much help. Other than few cooks, Chinese and black men not usually in sporting houses selling white women."

Sage's lips twisted at Fong's use of term "sporting house" the polite term for a whorehouse. Damn, maybe he'd have to ask Lucinda to help in the search. As the madam of the city's most exclusive "sporting house", she might know where someone could hide a young woman.

"You maybe ask Miss Lucinda to help?" Fong suggested, eerily echoing Sage's thoughts.

Sage heaved a sigh. "Yah, I suppose I'll eventually have to."

Fong's eyes warmed sympathetically, "You have fight with Miss Lucinda over there in Prineville?"

That question caused Sage's heart to thud painfully. His friend was referring to Sage's brief encounter with an almost-range war on the east side of the Cascades. It had been the first time in a year that he'd set eyes on Lucinda. She'd been there nursing smallpox victims in Prineville's whorehouse-turned-hospital. Because of a stupid misunderstanding on his part, they never really talked. But, once he learned of the misunderstanding, he'd been hopeful as he rode the train back to Portland. He foresaw a grand reunion, the warmth of her smiles and their pleasure at knowing all misunderstandings were at last behind them.

Well, that hope was soon squashed flat as horse plop on a city street. He'd gone to see her, thinking they could finally straighten things out between them. Just as he'd rounded the corner, though, he'd spotted her standing on the front stoop of her park side mansion. She'd been smiling, but not at him. She didn't even see him. Instead, she stood in the arms of the same man with whom she'd moved to Chicago the year before. Sage didn't need to see more to know that there was no hope. Turning on his heel, he'd tossed the flowers he carried into a nearby trash barrel and slunk back to Mozart's, like a dog with his tail tucked.

"Nah, nothing like that, Mr. Fong. I guess the time's never right for me and Lucinda. I may have to ask her to help but before I bother her, I'd like to try to find Rebecca myself. We have to find her. Otherwise her sister, who is vital to the success of the labor dispute, will be too distracted to function."

"You think this Rebecca taken to cause union sister worry?"

Sage shook his head. "Maybe. But, that doesn't make sense. If they wanted to weaken the laundry workers' resolve, they would have snatched Rachel herself. I think it was just a coincidence. This town is dangerous for girls living 'adrift,'" he said.

It was a new use of the word for Fong because he asked, "'Adrift', why do you use that word?"

"Oh, that new science, called 'social work,' uses that term to mean women living on their own, apart from their families. Not sure why they started using it. Probably because more and more single women are moving to the cities, trying to make new lives on their own," Sage answered.

Fong nodded as he mulled over the idea. Then his forehead wrinkled with a new thought. "Newspapers say stolen girls end up in strange towns, not in town where they are taken."

Damn, he hadn't really considered that problem. Fong was right, they had to find the girl and find her fast. Who knew how long white slavers would keep her in Portland. Dread wiggled into his mind. Maybe Rebecca was already on her way somewhere else. He'd better find out.

❁　❁　❁

Mae felt relief at seeing Rachel working her mangle first thing that morning. The night before, it had taken her and Eich quite of bit of talking to convince the young woman that she would never find her sister all on her own. Lord knows why someone would snatch a sales clerk. Well actually, she reminded herself, both the Lord and the Devil, probably did know the answer.

For sure, the three of them searched everywhere on the eastside where a body could be hidden with no luck. That meant someone was hiding her sister elsewhere. It also meant, she reassured Rachel, that her sister was probably still alive.

"The women at the laundry need you," Mae told the distraught young woman. "You'll never find her on your own. If she's alive, and I truly believe she is, then someone is keeping her out of sight. All your running here and there will do, is put own yourself in danger. Believe me, I know people who can find her. They have spies everywhere in this city. I promise you that they will find and return your sister."

Rachel grabbed hold of her fears and straightened her spine. Looking Mae in the eye she said, "You are sure? You promise me that your friends will find her?"

Mae grasped her hands and pulled the young woman close in a hug. "I, for certain sure, promise. It may take some time but they will find her."

Rachel turned toward Eich, "Mr. Eich, do you know these people Mae is talking about? Can they find my sister?"

He backed Mae up with adamant vigor. "Absolutely, if anyone can find Rebecca, they can. Like she says, it may take a few days but your sister will be found and returned to you."

With that Rachel's chin raised. "All right then. I am placing my sister's safety in your hands. I'll get on with the union work. I will go back to the laundry. We have a nine hour day to win from those scalawags. I refuse to let them win."

Clearly, Rachel's determination had lasted through the night. When she'd arrived and explained her absence of the day before, the women clustered around her murmuring encouragement, doing their best to sound hopeful. This attention couldn't erase the dark shadows beneath Rachel's worried eyes but she calmly went to her station and began her work.

By late morning, the stink and heat of the steam had become nearly unbearable. That new foreman, a fellow who seemed to know nothing about running a laundry and to care even less about it, had briefly showed up and then skedaddled like his tail was afire. Shortly after his departure, two women fainted at the mangles. The washmen carried them outside only to have them stagger back to work once they'd revived. At least that foreman wasn't around to dock their pay for their lapse into unconsciousness, Mae thought grimly.

As the day's heat intensified outside, it grew even hotter inside. Finally, Mae began feeling weak, dizzy and sick to her stomach. She set down the iron and stumbled over to the dreadful sink. Cupping her hands, she drank thirstily; glad there was no foreman to hurry her back to work. She decided to stretch the break by pretending to use the toilet though she'd swear her body was dry as burnt toast.

Opening the door to the single toilet, she was startled to find someone already inside. Mumbling her apologies, Mae backed out and hurried to her ironing board. She could have waited but was afraid to. Afraid that the woman inside, that new girl Caroline, would read the suspicion that had to be written across her face. And, Lordy, she sure was getting even more suspicious since she'd seen that girl quickly shove something beneath her apron. It had looked like a notebook though Mae couldn't be sure because she'd only caught a glimpse. She cast about for an explanation. Just what the heck was that Caroline person, if that was her real name, writing down?

Unions were learning hard lessons about union busting. It was a growing and lucrative business that provided management with spies for every labor dispute. Now it was beginning to look like Caroline was one such spy, in league with management and gathering information harmful to her co-workers.

"We'll just see about that, missy," Mae muttered to herself as she slammed the iron down hard on a defenseless piece of lace. She'd be keeping an even closer eye on Miss Caroline. And, first chance she got, she'd jab a stick between that gal's spokes.

TEN

"Gentlemen, this is no time to turn faint of heart." Cobb' voice was mildly accusatory. He flashed them a satisfied smile and added, "Everything is in place."

The four men around the table leaned forward, intent on learning more. Strain showed on every face although that hadn't stopped a one of them from finishing his breakfast.

"Thaddeus, what exactly is the plan you claim to have in place? You've been so secretive. It's like you don't trust us!" There was a tremble in the accusation, as if speaker were overcoming fear. Still, the man swallowed and continued, "I have to say, one more time, that I'm not sure a work stoppage is good for business. We're going to lose customers. Why, with my laundry shut down, I'll probably lose more money than if I just agreed to a nine-hour day. We got them to drop their demand for a wage increase. Why don't we congratulate ourselves and give way on that one little thing?" He looked around the table. No one nodded in agreement. Rather, their faces were blank masks, as if they were children fearful of how their stern father would react to a sibling's challenge.

Cobb's lips thinned momentarily as he wrestled his frustration under control. "Ryland, we've been over this before. Sure, maybe you could afford the loss of one hour a day. But how long would that be enough for them? Next month, next year, they'd come right back at us. And, next time, they'll be even greedier. They'll remember they won the first round and that will give them even more courage the second time. And what if they decide we can't hire or fire who we want, when we want? Or, maybe they'll demand a say in what kind of equipment we can buy. I've already had them hollering about the mangles. What happens if it's the extractor next or the chemicals we add to the wash water? You've all heard rumblings like that," he said to nods all around. "It all comes down to whether you or your workers will control your business. The real issue is control. Every demand they make will cost you money. We have to nip this rebellion in the bud and fast." Again, there were nods and even a muted "hear, hear".

Still, Ryland wasn't finished voicing his concerns. "Cobb, it's easy for you to talk about sacrificing today for tomorrow's gains. But that sacrifice is not going to be hitting your pocket. You're just a manager. I own my laundry. My family works there. If we halt operations, our family's income stops."

This time, Cobb's face flushed and the men around the table stiffened, as if bracing for a blow. It didn't come. Cobb maintained control. "Lewis, Henry and I might be managers, but our continued employment depends on our success. We wouldn't be advocating resistance without the agreement of the owners. They are willing to make the sacrifice. Besides," he added, his jutting chin reinforcing his point, "I have informed the owner that I plan to forego my salary for the duration of the shut down."

His declaration eased the tension and the others shifted in their chairs. Ryland, however, made one more attempt so feeble that it signaled capitulation, "I don't have the resources, they do. If we do this thing, I'll stick with it as long as I can but I can't promise I'll stick with it for a long time."

Cobb nodded his understanding. "We understand Ry. I am confident that the union won't be able to hold out very long." Cobb smiled widely without showing his teeth. Rubbing his hands together as he said, "Okay, men, let me fill you in on what will be happening."

The others were instantly alert. After all, Cobb's proposition would determine the future course of events.

"First, I've got a side deal going with the drivers' union president. They'll go back to work just as soon as we hire replacement workers for the washrooms. His cooperation is not even going to cost us all that much.

"Second, in another day or so, I'll have the names of the most trou-
blesome agitators. One of them is already out of the picture. You men
were supposed to be making the same kind of lists. Do you have your
lists in hand?"

There were nods all around.

"Okay, then. We have agreed to fire every single person on those
lists the night before we lockout. We'll let them work all day and then
give them the boot once the work day is done."

"I don't understand," Ryland interjected. "If we are going to lock
them out the next morning, why fire those on the list the day before?
They'll be gone the next day anyway. Everyone's going to be fired when
they come to work the next morning and find the doors locked."

"To cause dissention, to weaken them. Come on man, think about
it. If we fire them the night before it means the big mouths won't be
around in the morning. They'll be off meeting with the union president about us firing them, planning their strategy. That means, the
next morning, the locked out workers won't have anyone to lead them

Cobb's face twisted with disgust. "Mostly it's the damn women who
are causing all the trouble. What's their average weekly wage? Six dollars,
right?"

Ryland and the others nodded in agreement and Cobb continued,
"So, we lock them out and all that time they're sitting there they'll need
to pay for food and rent. How long before they run out of whatever
piddling savings they have? How long before they start thinking of just
themselves or their squalling kids? How long before the idea of coming
back to work on our terms starts to look good? And remember, the
more we discredit their leaders, take them off the playing field, the easier it will be for their followers to cross the picket line. Simple human
nature at work." Cobb sat back, confident in his analysis.

"Yes, I guess you're right. Some of my gals work little Sunday jobs
but for sure, most of them are living hand to mouth." Ryland said re-
luctantly before his forehead wrinkled, as if he'd just realized something. Cobb saw it and jumped in to distract him.

Cobb looked at each man closely to make sure they caught his next
words firmly. "Okay, then. We'll fire the leaders the night before and the rest
of them will come to work the next morning and find the doors locked."

For the first time Lewis Gillibrand, manager of the inaptly named
"Union Laundry" spoke up. "What about that Rachel woman who
works for you? She's their elected representative. Even the women

working for me seem to really like her. She's got the gift of gab and then some. You fire her, she won't give up. She'll just have more time to stir up support from other unions and stir up our workers all the more."

This time, Cobb's smile was thin-lipped. "We've taken care of that little missy. She'll not be bothering us any longer." His declaration sent a chill across the other men because their eyes widened and they exchanged uneasy glances. In the ensuing silence, they seemed to conclude that it was best to leave some questions unasked because not one of them opened his mouth to speak.

Finally, Gillibrand cleared his throat to say, "What about the newspapers? The *Labor Press* will definitely attack us with both barrels. And, Johnston, over at the *Journal* is pretty cozy with the unions as well."

Cobb raised a cautionary finger in the air. "Who reads that *Labor Press* rag? Just union people and we already know they'll be against us . . . except for our own drivers' union." He allowed himself a satisfied smirk.

"Some of my drivers are sympathetic to the women. They might not follow their union president," said Ryland, his former fire now an ineffective sputtering.

"A few drivers might, but most won't want to lose their jobs. You know how it is. There are plenty of hungry men more than eager to fill their shoes if given a chance. And, they know it."

"Anyway," Cobb said dismissively, "The *Gazette's* firmly in our pocket. The day of our lockout, the *Gazette* will so inform the public by painting us in the most favorable light. It's all arranged."

Their plans finalized, the men filed out—all but Cobb and the man who'd been sitting quietly in the corner. That man stood and walked to the table.

"Mr. Cobb, I must apologize deeply," said Farley.

Cobb looked up at him, his face puzzled, verging on irritation. "What do you mean, man? What's wrong?" he snapped.

"Sinclair came to see me here at the hotel, just before this meeting. He told me something disturbing."

This time, Cobb's irritation was unmistakable. "Damn it. Spit it out. I haven't got time for this. I need to get back to the laundry."

Farley took a deep breath and said quickly, "Sinclair didn't grab Rachel. He took her sister instead."

"What?" The single word cracked like a pistol shot.

"They look alike. She came out of the laundry. He thought he got the right one. When he got to work this morning, there Rachel was, working at her mangle."

"You're telling me that we have imprisoned a girl who has absolutely nothing to do with anything?"

"Well, she is the sister. That's got to slow the Rachel woman down."

"I expect a refund," Cobb said. "And, I expect your incompetent dunce to complete his mission. He was supposed to take care of her before the lockout but he can do it after."

"What about the sister? The one he took?"

"I don't give a damn what you do with the sister. Just don't let her loose right now. We need to keep the pressure on. Remember, the name of the game is to weaken them any way we can."

Farley nodded, put his hat on his head and prepared to leave the Portland Hotel's private dining room. As he reached the door he turned and said, "In all my years of helping management wage these fights, I've never seen a manager give up his salary during a labor dispute. That is a real effective tactic. It shut that Ryland fellow right up."

"You fool," Cobb said without heat as he slapped on a fawn colored fedora that perfectly matched his summer cutaway suit. Looking at Farley he said gave his mirthless smile and said, "I lied."

The cab dropped Sage off in front of the New Era hotel just as the streets began slowing down after the raucous rattle of early morning commerce. All around, the stoop sleepers had stirred awake and vacated their nests to forage for food and work. The North End was home for itinerant workers with its day-job hiring halls and various nooks and crannies for sleeping.

The air on his skin felt cooler this morning, maybe the heat wave was going to break. He hoped so. He'd had enough of sweating and muddle-headedness. The summer of 1903 would definitely go down in the record books as a hot one. That triggered his persistent worry. It was too hot for his mother to spend ten hours a day in that steam laundry. There's a consolation if there's a strike or lockout. At least she'd be done with working there.

Inside the hotel lobby, an electric ceiling fan was already whirling at top speed. There was a line of black railroad porters who were patiently waiting to check out. Most sent curious looks in his direction. The busy desk clerk saw him and pointed toward the hotel's dining room. There he found Solomon sitting at a single table, an open account book before him. When he saw Sage he slapped the book shut and gestured at the chair across from him.

"Why, John. How nice to see you. It's not often you bless us with your presence so early in the day. Usually your habits are those of the owl's rather than the meadow lark's."

"Hey, I get up early," Sage protested, before conceding with a grin, "But only when I have to."

"Ah, from that response I perceive that your visit is more in the nature of business rather than the pleasures of socializing?"

"Afraid so, Angus. And I mean that. I wish I were here just to visit." Sage said before mouthing a "thank you" to the waiter who had materialized at his side with a cup of hot coffee.

Solomon peered quizzically into his face before asking, "Are you here to learn whether we've found the other two union buster operatives? Sorry to say, we haven't, though Farley did inquire about tomorrow's train schedule."

"Well, that could be when they're arriving," Sage mused then he straightened, saying, "But now we've got another problem."

"Ah," Solomon said and then waited for further explanation.

"A young woman has disappeared. Her name is Rebecca Levy. She's the sister of the union representative for the laundry workers."

"Do you think her disappearance is connected to the labor dispute?"

Sage shrugged his shoulders saying, "I'm thinking not. If they really wanted to take the wind out of the workers' sails they would have snatched the union representative herself. Mae says she's a real firecracker. Still, having her sister missing will slow her down though she says it's not going to stop her—so long as we're out hunting for her sister."

Solomon's eyelids dropped low over his bright eyes while he considered the situation. "So, you are thinking that perhaps the girl was taken out of town on a train?"

"That's one thing that could have happened. She could also be here in town, locked up in some room."

"So, how are we going to find her?" Solomon asked and Sage breathed a mental sigh of relief. Solomon was a busy man. Besides working long days in the Portland Hotel's exclusive dining room, he also ran his New

Era Hotel. The latter gave Solomon access to the railway workers which meant he might be able to find out whether someone had already taken the girl out of the city by train. He knew other local men, living in the area, who might have seen her taken aboard a ship.

Sage said, "Thank you very much, Angus for your offer of help. As always, your assistance is most appreciated. My understanding is that the girl has dark hair and eyes, is about twenty-eight years old and comely, though not pretty or beautiful. When last seen, she was wearing a sale's clerk's dark blue skirt and jacket with a white blouse."

'So, she's a sales clerk?"

"Yes, she works for the Olds and King department store. Last Saturday she left work at noon. She dropped her sister's lunch at the Sparta Laundry. She said she was going home to the boarding house where the two girls share a room. She never got there and no one has seen her since."

"The idea is that we ask whether anyone saw a young woman who appeared to be under duress, accompanied by a man who seemed a stranger to her or of whom she appeared afraid?"

"That's the idea, all right," Sage said. "Mr. Fong's people are searching the underground, asking around the docks and at the few Chinese houses of ill repute. So far, no one has seen her. Maybe you can ask your people to look around the docks."

Sage's hands scrubbed his face as if to wipe away the tired. "Still, if she's aboard a ship, how could we possibly find her? We can't search every ship in the harbor and they sail downriver twice a day. There's just too many and I can't think of any excuse we could use to search them. Not to mention we don't have enough men. Our only hope is that someone saw a woman matching her description on a wharf or hustled aboard a particular ship. Much as I hate to say it, we have to find her before they put her on a ship or she's lost to us. And, we're just going to have to trust she's not already aboard one."

Solomon shoved back his chair. "Well, then, I had better take my leave from you. Some of the porters are still in the lobby. The sooner I ask them about the girl, the fresher their memory will be and the faster they'll be on the lookout. I'll also send word out to neighborhood men to keep a lookout on the streets and down near the docks." Solomon shook Sage's hand before quickly crossing the room and entering the lobby.

Sage drained his coffee cup and headed into the kitchen. None of the kitchen workers paid him any mind. They were used to him leaving by the back door.

❋ ❋ ❋

"I imagine you and Rebecca found it hard to live in the big city after growing up in the country," Mae commented to the young woman walking beside her. It was a lovely evening with a temperature lower than it had been for days. Even the washroom had been cooler that day. For the first time, Mae's limbs weren't limp noodles by day's end. Maybe she was getting used to the hard work she mused, before rejecting that idea.

The young woman grabbed Mae's wrist, bringing her to a halt. She looked earnestly into the older woman's face, saying, "You know, you don't have to stay with me tonight. I mean, I appreciate it. In fact, I welcome it. But, I'd be alright on my own."

"Rachel, I never had a sister but I know, sure as God made green apples, I'd want someone with me while I waited for news of her. Besides, my friend, John Miner, is going to drop by tonight to talk to you. He's one of the people looking for Rebecca. I want to be there to introduce you." She smiled wryly, "I kinda like to throw my two cents into the pot. He says I do that every time, whether it's wanted or not."

"It sounds like you two are good friends," Rachel said before she turned and started walking up the street once again.

"I like to think so," Mae responded, hiding her small smile from the other woman.

ELEVEN

Unlocking the padlock, Sinclair freed the hasp and eased opened the door. He lifted the kerosene lantern to light the still figure stretched out on the cot. Downstairs, drunken shouts erupted, driving him further into the room and away from the noise. He closed the door behind him and listened. The girl's breath was steady but faint.

Lifting a flimsy ladder-back chair with one hand, he positioned it beside the cot. Setting the lantern down on the small table, next to the water pitcher, he quietly lowered himself onto the chair. No need to take the risk of waking her even though the drugs meant that was unlikely to happen.

She lay on her back, her face relaxed. Damp tendrils of curly black hair trailed across her wide brow. Jutting cheekbones beside a somewhat long nose gave her face an angular look. A wide, full-lipped mouth looked like it would transform her whole face when she smiled. He gave his head a shake, stirring himself from his reverie. He couldn't remember the last time he'd studied the face of a sleeping woman.

He picked up the tin pitcher and saw that it held a goodly amount of doctored water. He brought it to his lips. A little pick-me-up would be good. But he arrested his motion and put it down. He had to meet Farley soon. It wouldn't do to display dilated pupils and a dreamy air. Especially since Farley was unhappy that he'd failed again.

There'd been no chance tonight. Rachel hadn't left the laundry by herself. That older woman who ironed lace stuck to the girl's side the whole way back to the boarding house. He'd stood across the street watching them enter the building. The older woman never came back out. Apparently she was staying at the same place.

It wasn't a place that he could sneak into. Two stories tall, covered with weathered gray clapboard, its sole entrance opened directly onto the boardwalk. There were so many ravines in Portland that they'd taken to erecting buildings on stilts. This was one of them. There was a rickety set of wooden stairs up the back of the building but those stairs passed by a number of open windows. Someone would see him. Besides, he had no way of knowing which room was hers.

Sinclair shifted on his chair beside the bed, deliberately relaxing his clenched jaw. Damn, he was beginning to hate this sweltering town. One problem after another. That's not how he worked. He had a system. It relied on flirting, cheerful patter, lies and false promises. All this drugging and imprisoning—that was the job of the whorehouse owners once he'd turned the women over. His job was to catch the girls and deliver them, light and easy. It was their job to keep them.

Loud shouts erupted below causing him to glance toward her. She hadn't moved but her eyes were open. Her gaze sharpened as the dilated pupils in her dark brown eyes contracted. He quickly reached for the pitcher, shoved his arm beneath her head, raising it so she could drink. She swallowed, her eyes never leaving his face.

He turned away to break that connection—making a show of carefully setting the pitcher back down. When he looked at her again, he breathed a sigh of satisfaction. Her eyes were already fluttering. She was dropping off to sleep, moving back down that long dark velvet tunnel. After his day's frustrations, he envied her.

The large dark eyes opened and skewered him with an intensity that froze all thought. Her lips parted and one, soft word reached his ears. "Why?" she breathed before closing her eyes.

"Well howdy do. Where've you been keeping yourself, John Miner?" said a boozy voice as soon as he sat down at an empty corner table.

Sage looked up from beneath his battered hat, "Hey there, Ivy. You know how it is. A man's got to work wherever he can. I've been out in the woods dodging logs." After a few more such pleasantries she left to fetch his beer. Taking a sip, he couldn't stop from making a face. It was far below the standard set by the rural breweries. He didn't care. He was too tired to drink it anyway. Damn it had been a long day. Much longer than expected.

The visit with Solomon had gone well enough. He was confident that the railway porters were now on the alert for Rebecca Levy. If anyone had seen her on the streets, down near the docks or taken away on a train, Solomon would learn of it.

The day had stretched into an endless trudge. Noontime found Sage at Mozart's Table where he donned his host attire and manned his podium, a genial smile plastered across his face. It was a busy noon dinner hour, the tables full and turning over fast. Their restaurant was a favorite of upper crust idlers as well as downtown's wealthy merchants. The décor was gilt framed copies of old masters, dark walnut wainscoting, pale green plaster walls and crystal chandeliers. Evenings added a string quartet playing classical music on the small balcony above the diners. Everything about the restaurant pandered to the city elites' perception of themselves as superior to Portland's commoners. He wasn't always comfortable with the ruse but the access it gave him to the doings of the city's wealthy yielded valuable information inaccessible by any other means.

The dinner hour over, he made his way to the kitchen. Sergeant Hanke's broad back was his first sight when he entered through the swinging doors. The policeman sat at the small table before a heaping plate of Ida's leftovers. As usual, between bites, the big policeman was praising Mozart's cook.

"Miz Ida, I have to tell you that never have I had such tender pot roast. It practically floats right into my mouth," he was saying.

"Oh pshaw," she said, waving a dish rag at him. "You said the exact same thing last week." Despite the dismissal, her round cheeks colored.

Ida Knutson was an excellent cook and fine human being Sage thought, not for the first time. She, her husband Ike and her nephew Mathew lived in Mozart's second floor apartment, right below the floor occupied by Sage, Mae and Fong. Ike Knutson worked long hours in a shingle factory. There he fed wood shake bolts into twin saw blades—a terrifyingly dangerous job requiring unrelenting concentration.

Hanke's large jaws chewed calmly, like a full cow in a big grass pasture. The sergeant was both tall and sturdy, his placid Germanic face topped by thick sandy hair. His shambling gait, mild blue eyes and somewhat bovine countenance were misleading. In critical situations he proved to be quick thinking, brave and capable. And, despite taking regular advantage of Mozart's leftovers, his first loyalty was always to the law. Sage could get him to bend on the finer points of implementation but he knew better than to push the big policeman's integrity any further.

"But Miz Ida," Hanke protested once he'd swallowed, "That's the whole point. Every meal you cook, the food gets better. Eventually, I'll turn up one day and find a band of angels sitting at this table, forks at the ready."

That compliment left the cook speechless. She shook her head and turned toward the sinks. "Good heavens, he's turned Irish on me what with all his blarney," she muttered loud enough for Hanke to hear.

Sage took the chair opposite the policeman. Hanke smiled but didn't slow his shoveling.

"Sergeant, you're just the man I was hoping to see."

Those words made the big jaws stop working and the blue eyes sharpen. Hanke swallowed and said, "Oh-oh. What law are you wanting me to break this time?"

"Nary a single one," Sage assured him. "I need you to educate me about the business of white slavery."

Hanke grimaced, put down his fork and wiped his mouth. "Actually, I've been learning about that trade my own self. Some local ladies formed a branch of the Society for Social Hygiene. One of them has made it her job to make sure I am up to snuff concerning that business." The roll of his eyes said that he'd heard more than he wanted.

"Well, what about it?" Sage prodded.

"It exists," the sergeant said before opening his maw and filling it with whipped potatoes.

"Come on, you should be happy I'm only asking you to talk. Usually, my requests require more effort on your part. In fact you, as an officer of the law, should be falling all over yourself to enlighten me."

Hanke sighed heavily. "Well, then, since you put it that way." He dabbed at his lips with the napkin, swallowed some water and said, "As you know, 'white slavery' is the name given the practice of forcing women into prostitution. They're not all white, either. The 'slavery' part comes from the fact that they keep the women behind locked doors and beat them if they don't cooperate. Or, they're given so much opium that they become enslaved to it and don't want to leave. Once the panderer has sold them to a slaver, the women are told they must go with men to pay off the slaver's expense of capturing them and clothing them in gaudy clothes."

Sage leaned forward, asking, "Where do these women usually come from and how are they captured?"

"Mostly they come from farms and small towns. Some of them are lured here by newspaper ads," here Hanke's big finger tapped the newspaper that lay atop the table. He picked it up, snapped it open and read:

> Wanted: Lady partner for vaudeville sketch—one who can
> sing and play piano preferred. Must have good appearance.
> Will furnish wardrobe for stage and street.

Tossing the paper down, Hanke said, "That's a perfect example. A gal reads that ad and hops a stagecoach or train all excited about starting a new life. She gets to town all starry-eyed and a slick-tongued panderer immediately latches on to her. Or else, the panderer travels into the countryside to woo some ignorant girl with promises of a job or marriage. She jumps on the train with him and next thing she knows, she's a prisoner in one of the whorehouses."

"So, if a girl taken by a panderer is still in the city, we'd find her locked up in a whorehouse?"

Hanke nodded. "That's where I'd look. Some places, like Miss Lucinda's, the women want to be there," The policeman screwed up his lips before continuing, "For a white slave gal, though, you'd want to look in the cribs attached to the saloons or those crummy houses catering to men without much money."

Pearl-gray light washed across the eastern sky, heralding another day. Neither Mae nor Rachel smiled at the sight. Both women were tired and still sleepy as they walked toward another ten hours of work in sweltering heat.

"Thank you for keeping me company, Mae. I don't think I could have spent another night alone in that room. I miss her so. I'm sorry my yakking kept you up so late," Rachel said.

Mae took the other woman's hand and squeezed it. "You'd do the same for me if the positions were reversed. Besides, we had to hear what Mr. Miner had to say."

"Yes, thank you for him too. Now that I know so many people are looking for Becky, I have some hope." She sighed and changed the subject. "It was nice of him to bring your clothes." That comment was heavy with an unspoken question.

Mae chuckled, "Yes, he can be a right helpful fellow when he's got a mind to be."

A bit later Mae cleared her throat and said, "I have to ask, Rachel. Are you sure you want to keep on doing this union work?" She hurried to add, "We'd all understand if you are too upset over Rebecca."

For a few minutes, Rachel walked in silence without responding, the morning croak of frogs in the swamp along the river the only sound. When she finally spoke, the words were calm and measured. "The women and men we work with are good people doing the best they can to stand on their own two feet. They deserve better. My father taught us that greed is a goal with no end, the very evil that brought about the Sodomites' downfall. If my sister . . . ," here she faltered, swallowed and finished, "If my sister were here, she'd say I should keep fighting."

Mae glanced at the young woman's determined profile that was strong and sculpted as a granite statue. "Well, back home, my pa used to say that the only way to clear a cornfield is one rock at a time. Guess you and I will be hauling us a wagonload of rocks in the days ahead."

"Your father was a farmer?"

Mae laughed. "Not exactly. He planted a little bit of corn all right but mostly he added to his miner's wages by cooking it up in small batches of moonshine. There were six of us kids."

"Is your father still alive?"

That question always brought such a stab of pain. It had been years, but still the wound was raw. "He's dead. Killed by the mine owner's thugs because he fought for a union in the mines," Mae said.

Down by the river, the sawmill's whistle tooted. Both women stepped up their pace. Neither looked behind so, neither woman saw Paul Sinclair slinking after them.

TWELVE

"The notice is written and will be submitted for publication the day after tomorrow. And, tomorrow night, the troublemakers will get the boot and we're locking the rest of them out the next morning. We'll see how rebellious they feel after a few days of no income." Cobb swallowed some coffee and smacking his lips, added, "I love the coffee in this hotel."

"You said you have a meeting with the union today? Any chance of reaching a settlement?"

"No, Farley, there's no chance because we intend to make an offer they'll have to refuse. If they were to accept it, their own members would give them the boot." Seeing Farley's questioning glance, Cobb continued, "We've already made them drop the wage increase. The only thing left is their nine-hour workday proposal. We're going to tell them they have to drop that demand as well. That leaves them with nothing. And, if they agree to take nothing, the workers will be so angry that they'll vote to go non-union." Cobb rubbed his hands together, a smile on his lips. "We're going to have them trapped between the Devil and the deep blue sea, as the saying goes."

Both men paused while a white-coated waiter approached their table with a coffee pot. "Just leave the pot, we'll refill the cups ourselves." Cobb instructed. Once the waiter was gone, Cobb leaned forward, his voice lowered. "Tell me, how are your operatives doing? I haven't seen much of Sinclair."

"Hmm, yes, well. Sinclair's been trying to get at that Rachel woman but apparently she is now escorted everywhere by another of the women," Farley said.

"Well, that shouldn't stop him. Surely he can figure out how to separate them or else put the other woman out of commission so he can grab Levy." Cobb twisted his lips in frustration, "I thought you said Sinclair could do the job. Up to now, he's failed completely."

"Well, not completely. He has the sister. By the way, he's asked if he can let her go since she's the wrong one."

"Hell, no! Having her sister missing must pray on Levy's mind. We need to do everything we can to throw her off her stride."

"He says he can't hide her in the whorehouse much longer, the woman there is unstable and ornery."

"He's already arranged for ship passage to San Francisco. Tell him to put both Levys on the damn ship."

Farley didn't respond right away to that idea. Clearly he had something on his mind and was trying to figure out how to say it. When his words came, they were tentative, "Sinclair is considered the slickest procurer in Chicago. But he's always relied on his patter and charm. Most of his girls step willingly into his traps. They're looking for excitement and an opportunity to experience the life of the city. This situation is different. This gal's a reputable sales clerk. She's got nothing to do with the union."

"Jesus, man, are you telling me you were so stupid as to hire a panderer with scruples or a conscience?" Outrage laced Cobb's hissed words.

"No, no. Well, maybe. He spent almost four years in a religious seminary before he abandoned it for the sporting life and opium pipe. I've been noticing that there seems to be some reluctance on his part." Seeing the scowl on Cobb's face, Farley hastened to reassure. "It's probably nothing. He hasn't refused to do anything I've asked him to do and I am sure he won't. He's gone too far and is in this too deep. Besides, he needs money for that opium he likes to smoke now and again."

"You damn bet he's in too deep. If he balks, we'll deal with him in ways he won't like. You let him know that," Cobb said. "What about the other two? Now that they're here are they having second thoughts as well?"

Farley shook his head. "No, they are exactly on track and making progress. Everything is going as planned and they'll be ready for the lockout the day after tomorrow."

"They've made sure Warder's still on board?"

"Oh yes, one hundred percent. No worries there."

"All right then, everything is ready. Tomorrow it starts." Cobb's grin was a mix of satisfied and wolfish. Then it vanished and his features hardened. "The girl stays locked up and Sinclair snatches the other one. You make sure he toes the line or else you take care of him, you hear me?"

"Well, ladies," Sage said, his voice muffled by the arms and bodices pressed tight against him in grateful hugs. "I regret that you had to spend the early morning hours in the cells. It took me awhile to raise the cash."

"Oh Mr. Miner, sweetheart, we're just delighted you thought of us at all since that bugger of a saloon owner decided to let us rot instead of bailing us out. And, after all the money we've made him," replied a blowsy woman well past her prime. She obviously spoke for the six other women who gave vigorous nods in agreement.

"There is a price," Sage warned them. As one, they giggled, pursing their lips and making a show of twitching their hips. Their antics attracted the attention of the desk officer who made no pretence of ignoring them. The officers entering the building to start their morning shift added a few catcalls to the scene.

Sage spread his arms to gently herd them out of the police station. "Come on ladies, let me buy you breakfast. I have something I need to ask you."

It was a jolly breakfast, the women seemingly no worse for wear after spending a few hours in the hoosegow. He waited until their plates were empty and their coffee refilled before telling them about the missing girl. "I was hoping you might have an idea of where they are keeping her," he concluded.

The women exchanged looks. In the morning light, their faces were pale, paint smeared and tiredly garish. But sympathy softened their expressions. One of the more restrained of them spoke quietly, "That's what happened to me. It took me ages to work off my debt. Once I did, it was too late to go back home. I've written my folks more than once but they never answer." Her eyes filled with tears and she looked down the table.

Her words killed the group's merriment and all fell silent. It was as if each woman was recalling her time of innocence—before her fall from grace. Sage wondered how many of these women would leave prostitution if they could. Life was hard for single women, for women cast adrift, all alone. He studied their faces, some of them ravaged by alcohol and opium addiction.

Another woman at last piped up, "They won't lock her in a room above a saloon. Too public, too many people and too expensive. Those rooms are for making money with plenty of customers wanting to use them. So, I'd look in one of the crappy sporting houses." The other women nodded in agreement.

"You could even narrow it down. Unless they have her locked in a cellar, she'll be kept in a room with a boarded up window. That's where they kept me at first. Maybe you could look for something like that," a small woman with a baby doll face offered hesitantly.

Everyone else nodded grimly. Sage nodded too, giving her a smile before asking the group, "How many crappy sporting houses are there?"

"That's the ticket, sweetie. Our Lucy girl has it right. You don't need to look for her in the fancy sporting houses 'cause they don't do that kind of thing Just look in them run-down places that can't keep all their rooms busy. I guess there'd be about thirty or so of them houses this side of town," answered the oldest looking woman of the group.

Sage let his breath whoosh out. Thirty. Too many to search all by himself. He needed to meet with Solomon, Fong and Eich. It was too late to arrange a meeting this afternoon, but maybe late tonight or to-morrow morning would work.

His stomach clenched. There wasn't enough time. If her kidnappers were going to move Rebecca Levy out of Portland, he needed to find her fast. Even a day's delay might be too much. Frustration momentar-ily twanged. His hunt for her sure was distracting him from St. Alban's mission. He should be sniffing around the steam laundries, getting to know the drivers and following Thaddeus Cobb. Because for certain, Cobb had something up his sleeve and it wasn't good.

Sage and the women exited the restaurant. After obtaining their promise to keep a lookout for the missing dark-haired, dark-eyed young woman, Sage received their hugs and admired their backsides as the entire group sashayed down the street. Raucous laughter floated behind them with one of the women tossing him a saucy wink over her shoulder. He sent silent good wishes after them.

Mae sat against the wall, facing the table. Walking across the luxurious Portland Hotel lobby in her laundry worker dress and boots had made her feel drab and self-conscious. No doubt that had been Cobb's intent when he insisted that they agree to conduct the bargaining in one of the hotel's meeting rooms. She studied the men across the table. Although there were nine men in the association, only these four sat on the association's bargaining team. Thaddeus Cobb was a trim fellow who obviously took pride in a well-turned out appearance. At a distance, he might seem good-looking but close up his eyes were too sunken and near each other, his lips too narrow and bloodless.

Beside Cobb sat Lewis Gillibrand, manager of the ironically named Union Laundry. The two men couldn't be more different. Gillibrand wore a grubby waistcoat sprinkled with the spots of food that had dribbled from his rubbery lips. The man was nervous because his tongue kept flicking out to wet those lips.

Mae moved her gaze to the third man of the four. This was Joseph Cook, manager of the Pacific Laundry. Rachel said his workers hated him for driving them too hard on antiquated machines and for having a cold heart untouched by kindness. The man flashed gold every way he could—as a stick pin, heavy rings, sparkling watch chain. Even his rectangular slit of a smile flashed a couple gold teeth. It was a smile that looked more like a snarl and never reached his dead fish eyes.

That left the fourth man, Ryland McCarthy. He sat a bit distant from the other three as if he couldn't bring himself to be in the same corral with the rest of them. Mae narrowed her eyes as she watched him. He was twitchy as a cat with fleas. First shifting in his seat, next fiddling with a pencil, then glancing at his watch. He owned the American Laundry and was the only owner in the room. The other three were managers doing the dirty work of the owners. She noticed that of the four, only McCarthy had the rough, red hands of a man who actually worked in the laundry. She decided he was the only one of the four worth knowing.

Early that morning Rachel had surprised her with the request. "Mae, I need someone there who can watch what goes on and tell me if we're missing something. Doing something wrong. We have tried everything and it's still like we're talking to brick walls."

So, Mae was here at the bargaining session as an observer, sitting in her chair against the wall. The union bargaining team filed into the room to take seats across the table from the management team. The laundry union president was there as the lead negotiator, sitting in the middle with Rachel at his side. There were three other members on their team—two women and one man. Like Rachel and Mae, the other two women wore faded work dresses and heavy boots. The man was also shabbily dressed, obviously someone who minded the washtubs and extractors at his laundry.

The management team looked well fed and rested. The workers on the union team were thin, pale and haggard of face.

The laundry union president was the first to speak. "Mr. Cobb, I remind you that we have dropped our request for a wage increase. We have been awaiting your answer on our nine-hour day proposal for some time now. Surely, you men have had a chance to talk about it. We would appreciate your answer, sir."

Cobb's smile was smug as he said, "Our answer is: we reject the union's offer."

There was a collective gasp from the union side. They hadn't expected such a summary dismissal of their compromise offer.

Cobb held up a finger. "We do, however, have a counter. One you can take back to your members to make them think you weren't a complete failure." There was a snide implication in the emphasis he put on the word "complete," which said that, in fact, the union had completely failed. Cobb made his offer: "We are willing to extend the lunch break from twenty minutes to thirty minutes."

The union team members looked at each other, dismay sagging their faces.

In a sugary, helpful voice, Cobb suggested, "Maybe you would like to confer with your team about our offer. In the hallway." This time his look was so smug that Mae itched to slap his face. She looked at the other three. Two, Gillibrand and Cook also looked smug as two cats who just licked the butter churn clean. McCarthy was gazing into the corner as if he wished he were somewhere else.

With dignity the union president rose, looked at his team and nodded in the direction of the door. They all filed out to stand together in the hallway. Mae stood with them.

"He didn't give us shit," exclaimed the man. The others' stormy faces showed their agreement.

"We've already given up all of our demands except for the nine hours. I don't think I could face my people if we accepted management's offer," Rachel said. Her words were met with vigorous nods.

Rachel turned to Mae, "What do you think? Are they going to move toward us or is this the end?"

Put on the spot, Mae quickly gathered her thoughts and then spoke, "I think they walked in knowing you would reject the offer. They were counting on you to reject the offer. That's why McCarthy can't look at any of us. Of the four, only he feels shame for what they are doing."

"But why don't they want labor peace. If we strike them, they'll lose money. Why won't they meet us part way?" asked one of the other women.

"Because Cobb thinks he can break us. He wants to teach us to stay in our place, that's why," responded the president.

Mae cleared her throat, aware she was going to sound a bit preachy but deciding to speak anyway, "For them it's more than money. It's about power and control. That's what they fear losing. Because if they lose their power, they might have to admit they are no smarter, no more deserving to be in charge than any one of us. That would tip them right onto the slippery slope—one where they'll have to ask themselves why they have so much when the rest of us have so little. So, they must win. Otherwise, the walls around their consciences just might collapse. And that's what scares them. They'd have to look at what they're doing to other people."

There was a beat of silence as the others absorbed her words. It was finally broken by the union president who said, "Well, I guess it's unanimous. We reject their offer and tell them we will stand on ours until we've had a chance to talk to our members."

"What's going to happen next?" asked the wash man. His face was grim with worry but Mae noted that he stood with his chin raised and his shoulders back.

"We'll call a meeting of our folks. We'll them what's happened and see what they want us to do." was the president's answer.

THIRTEEN

RACHEL AND THAT OTHER WOMAN, Mae something, walked into work around one in the afternoon. Both looked pretty grim. Sinclair was there because he'd been ordered to "mind the shop" while Cobb was in bargaining. Sinclair watched as the Levy woman paused to speak to some women who, in turn, spoke to others. Word spread among the employees like a breeze blowing through long grasses. Most nodded assent upon receiving Rachel's word. If negotiations had gone as Cobb planned, Levy was telling them that there'd be a meeting after work. He might as well check.

He began to walk among them, pausing here and there to give a quiet compliment. He didn't have to make one up. These were hard working people. He got nods in acknowledgement but no smiles nor speech. He couldn't take offense. After all, he was the boss's representative. When he reached Chrissy she smiled, though even her smile was subdued.

"Hey, there girl. You want to meet me at our usual place after work? I'd like to buy you supper."

This time her smile was bright but then it dimmed. "I can't. We're all meeting after work to talk about the negotiations."

"Oh yah, how are those going anyway? Cobb's been real closed mouthed about them whenever he bothers to show up. I don't think he trusts me."

"Not good, I guess." She stiffened, "We better stop talking. Everybody says I'm not to blab to you."

"Ah, Chrissy gal, I understand. But, remember, they have no way of knowing that you knew me before I even started working here. Or, that you're the reason I got this job in the first place. You know that even though I'm taking Cobb's pay, I have no reason to be loyal to him. He treats you gals terrible."

She brightened. "That's right. I am the one who told you about the job opening." She situated the shirt collar in the mangle and pushed on the pedal to lower the pressing board before saying, "Well, maybe we could visit a bit after the union meeting? It shouldn't last but an hour or so. Folks are pretty tired. That's why we usually meet on Sundays instead of after work."

He gave her his warmest smile, making sure his eyes twinkled, "Okay, that's what we'll do. I'll be waiting for you at that saloon near your boarding house," he said, as he gave her shoulder a squeeze and moved on. As he did so, he glanced at Rachel who appeared oblivious to their conversation. Probably has her mind on her sister. The urge to reassure her pulled at him but he turned away instead.

Heading for the cool of the office, he didn't notice that two pair of eyes had been watching his every move—one pair calculating, the other pair narrowed in suspicion.

Sitting in Solomon's well-appointed apartment sipping iced lemonade, Sage felt a pang of guilt thinking of Mae at her ironing board in the midst of noise, stink and steam heat. Although she claimed ironing delicates was the easiest job, he hadn't missed her grimaces when she pulled off her soggy boots nor the tiredness deepening the lines of her face and draining all color from it.

It was late afternoon. Fong, Eich and Sage were sitting around a polished mahogany table, waiting for Solomon to arrive. Solomon's home was on the ground floor, tucked behind the New Era Hotel's lobby desk. A wide range of books filled elegant bookcases, family portraits hung on flocked wallpaper and comfortable couches and chairs sat atop ruby-red oriental rugs. It was the luxurious setting of a well-off and learned man.

Solomon entered, wearing a wide smile on his face. "Sorry, gentlemen, for the delay," he said. "A little mix up in the Portland's dining room delayed my departure."

"That's okay. We thank you Angus for taking the time away from your job. I trust your absence won't cause problems for you." At Solomon's head shake, Sage continued, "I take it no porter has seen our girl Rebecca leaving on a train? And nothing about a dark-haired woman being taken onto a ship in the harbor?"

Solomon poured coffee into their cups from a silver coffee urn sitting in the middle of the table as he said, "During the past few days, I have managed to query every porter on every line coming into and leaving the city. I did learn two things. The first is that two men, acting a bit secretive and unfriendly, arrived in town a day ago. I have not been able to ascertain where they are staying. I speculate that they are staying in a boarding house. They are below the standards of the Portland Hotel's customary clientele but interestingly a housemaid reported seeing two men fitting their description in the corridor outside Farley's room."

"That must be the two operatives Farley was expecting to arrive by train. Do you have a good description of them?"

"I think I have better than that. The housemaid told me about the two men as soon as she saw them. So, I sent my nephew to linger about in the corridor until they came out. Then he followed them. They went over to the union hall. After they left there; they met with a third man in a coffee shop. Unfortunately, my nephew couldn't go inside. 'No Negros Allowed,'" he added with a wry twist of his lips. "Anyway, since they went to the union hall it suggests they will pass themselves off as union men."

"Probably. I suspect they'll work the delivery driver angle. Help Farley keep the drivers in line," Sage said.

"Would your nephew recognize third man from the cafe if he saw him again?" asked Fong. "Cousins can keep under watch if he is pointed out to them."

"Undoubtedly, he could. If you want to meet me here later tonight, I'll have my nephew here for you to talk to him," Solomon said before continuing, "But, I have news of the girl as well. Not quite as good but maybe you'll find it helpful."

Eich leaned forward, dark brown eyes intent in his bearded face, "Did they see where she's being kept?"

Solomon gave a rueful shake of his head. "Sorry. One of the men working here at the hotel, said he saw a drunken girl with dark curly hair being half-carried along the street late Saturday afternoon."

"Where?" asked Eich and Sage simultaneously.

"He says they were down near the rail yards, close to where he lives in one of the few houses left standing after they built Union Station," he said, adding, "The station was built on top of my people's houses, forcing most of them to move across the river into Albina. Anyway, he says he saw the couple just a few blocks from his house."

Sage leaned back in his chair, looked at his friends and said, "Well, his sighting tallies with the prostitutes' information. They said if some-one's holding the girl captive, it will likely be inside a rundown sport-ing house like those near the rail yard. I don't suppose your man can describe the fellow walking with the girl?" Sage asked.

At Solomon's negative shake of the head, Sage turned toward Fong. "Have the cousins heard of any imprisoned girls?"

Fong said, "Sorry, cousins say she is not in any Chinese sporting house or with any Chinese pimp. And, they also ask every China man they see. No one saw white girl a prisoner in any white sporting house."

That didn't surprise Sage. Few Chinese cooked or cleaned in the white sporting houses. And, although the Chinese traveled Portland's streets in the day time, they tended to stay away from places where they might encounter drunken white men. Ignorance, poverty and drink often brought out the bully in white men who enjoyed terroriz-ing people who were smaller and looked different than them.

"Well, Mister Fong," Sage said, "I did acquire a bit of information from some sporting ladies that might assist the cousins in their search. Is there any chance they could snoop around the whorehouses near the rail yard for boards nailed across a window? That's what the girls said we should look for."

"Just how you meet these prostitutes?" Fong asked.

"I talked with Hanke while he was having his usual noon meal in Mozart's kitchen. I asked him what he knew about white slavery in Portland. He knows a lot, it turns out. Anyway, he and Chief Hunt were planning prostitution raids that very night. He thought, and correctly it turns out, that not all of the girls' pimps would bail them out. I hung around one of the saloons they raided and bailed out some of the ladies afterward. In exchange, they gave me ideas on how to look for Rebecca.

"I'm thinking that if we can find that boarded up window, Hanke will cooperate and raid the place. He told me that his chief is frustrated so many cops are on the take. To conduct last night's raid, they had to summon the officers at the last moment, while keeping the purpose secret, just so the raids would be a surprise. We'll have to be just as careful if we mount a raid to rescue Rebecca."

"Ah, that means cousins better make hatchets sharp enough to split hair," Fong said, with a smile.

Eich shifted in his seat. "What about Mae? Do you think she's in any danger?" he asked, his wide forehead creased with worry.

Sage shook his head but added, "The real danger is that she is going to collapse. She's working all day in that damn heat, then going home with Rachel, Rebecca's sister, and not getting enough rest."

"Still, someone did most definitely kidnap Rebecca. What if he comes back for Rachel?" Eich persisted.

"Why would they? I'm convinced that Rebecca's kidnapping has nothing to do with the labor dispute. She was in the wrong place at the wrong time, that's all. From what Hanke told me, more white slavery goes on than we think. Most of the adrift women the white slavers grab have no friends or family living close enough to raise a hue and cry. I think a white slaver maybe saw an opportunity and grabbed Rebecca, not knowing she had a sister around to raise a fuss," said Sage.

Sage saw, from the expression on Eich's face that Mae and Eich had probably discussed this point and reached a different conclusion. Mae was convinced that Rachel was in danger. That's why she insisted on going everywhere with the woman. Sage and Mae had a whispered quarrel on the boarding house veranda the night before.

"It's silly for you to sleep here when you could be so much more comfortable at home," he'd insisted.

"I am not that uncomfortable here. Besides, it's easier on you if you don't have to fetch me to and fro every day."

"I don't mind. At least that way, I know you're staying out of trouble," he said, realizing as soon as the words left his lips that he'd said exactly the wrong thing.

Mae pointed her finger at his face. "I am telling you for the last time, John Sagacity Adair, you are not in charge of me and you will not tell me what to do! You don't browbeat Fong and Eich about their safety, so don't browbeat me." Though there was only a quarter moon lighting the night sky, it was bright enough to see her eyes shooting fire in his direction.

"Okay, stay here. But when you finally collapse from exhaustion, I'm carting you back home and I won't want to hear another thing about it."

Instead of responding, she shot him another glare before turning around, opening the door and stepping back into the boarding house. She shut the door firmly enough that it rattled the window next to it.

He looked up from his empty coffee cup and found Eich studying him with kind eyes and a teasing smile. "You tried to boss her around, didn't you?" the ragpicker asked, his grin parting beard from mustache, "Even I've learned that is a losing proposition."

Before Sage could answer, Eich continued, "I am afraid I don't share your certainty that she and Rachel are in no danger. I'm concerned. So, since there is so much open land on the eastside, I've found me a little camp site near Rachel's boarding house. I hope you will forgive me if I focus on watching over Mae, instead of looking for Rebecca. Though I will do that too, once I know they are both safely inside either the boarding house or the laundry." He gazed around the table to see the other three nodding their agreement.

Despite their exhaustion, the laundry workers trudged across the Morrison Bridge to the union building's meeting hall. Mae counted noses—all but ten of the forty Sparta Laundry workers made the trek and those ten were women with small children at home. The majority of workers from the other laundries were also there, filling the hall's wooden benches to overflowing. The union president got right down to business.

"Thank you for coming. The Association flat out rejected our nine-hour proposal. They countered with an offer to extend our twenty minute lunch by ten minutes for a total of one-half hour."

Angry, derisive shouts exploded throughout the room. "Cobb takes four hour lunches!" "They don't care if they kill us!" "My sister lost her hand to those criminals!"

The last shout to ring out, "To hell with their damn job!" inspired cheers.

Once the tumult died down the president said, "We told Cobb that we would allow you all to vote on whether to accept or reject their offer. That's one of the things we need to do tonight."

"If we reject it, what happens next?" asked a woman in the front row. The question turned the room pin-drop silent.

"Well, the parties could decide to stay in negotiations. Or, we could vote to strike," Mae noticed this last comment caused many to shift uneasily atop the benches. "Or, management could decide to lock us out."

"What do you think we ought to do?" came the question.

"I think that we should stay at the bargaining table. Though, if management decides to lock us out, there's not much we can do in return."

"How likely is a lockout?" asked the worried voice of a Sparta Laundry wash tub man.

"I won't lie to you. I think the likelihood is high," the president responded honestly. "Rachel Levy, who you all know, has been planning for that happening. Rachel, can you please tell them what's planned?"

Rachel rose to her feet, letting her eyes rest on every face before she said, "As you know, I've been working with our president and some others to make plans in case the managers do lock us out. We have a number of things in the works. First, we are going to start a commissary in this very building. Other unions and their members will contribute food, clothing and other necessities. There will also be a jobs desk. We need volunteers to help gather and distribute the donations and other volunteers to identify and solicit temporary jobs."

A number of women's hands shot into the air, causing Rachel to laugh. "Thank you, ladies. Please give me your names at the end of the meeting.

"Additionally, the local labor council has said it will be contributing funds. These are for the rent, utilities and doctor's bills of those who need the help. Fortunately or unfortunately for us, our wages are so puny that keeping us going won't be all that costly. We're champions at making do with boiled bones and paper-stuffed shoes." Her observation brought the first laughter of the night.

A smiling Rachel held up a hand to quell the laughter. "There are two other things in the works. The first is that we have applied to the Shirtwaist and Laundry Workers International Union for strike fund money. That means every person who walks the picket line at a laundry will get paid for that day's work."

She took a deep breath, clearly excited about her next piece of information, "I am also pleased to announce that the labor council intends to purchase and run a cooperative steam laundry. It is their intent to provide jobs for all good union members."

There was a momentary cessation of all sound and then the room erupted in handclaps and cheers.

Mae looked at the hopeful faces around her, wishing with all her heart that their good spirits would last through the trying days ahead. She'd been in strikes before. She knew how hard it was to stay hopeful when the larder was empty—especially when children were going hungry.

She scanned the faces once again until her eye caught on the figure of a woman slipping out the door at the rear of the hall. She quickly searched the room for the Caroline woman. She was nowhere to be seen.

FOURTEEN

Sinclair knocked on the peeling and warped door. It was early. Dawn light had just rimmed the distant mountain, but this was the only time he could check on the gal, Rebecca. It was no wonder he'd mistook her for her sister. Farley finally understood that. But Farley still insisted Sinclair keep her locked up. Said that's what Cobb wanted.

The house's madam flung open the door, ready to let loose on whoever stood outside. Her war paint from the prior night blotched around her faded eyes. When she saw him, her pale lips slackened with surprise. At last finding her wits, she said, "Well now. What the hell are you doing on my stoop this god awful early in the morning? You said you'd be stopping by this evening."

Sinclair brushed past her, heading for the stairs. Her voice trailed after him, "Now I haven't had a chance to take care of her yet today. Besides, she's a little minx that one."

The key was in the padlock and he soon had the door open. Enough light filtered through the curtain and between the boards to see the dark shape lying on the cot. She stirred at his entrance so he quickly shut the door behind him even as he heard the madam's heavy steps climbing to the second floor. He needed a moment's peace from that screechy voice.

The room stank. He peered at the chamber pot in the corner and found it full. They must not have emptied it since he was last here. Rustling drew his attention back to the bed. Rebecca was sitting up, her hands clutching the cot rails to hold her steady.

"Who are you?" she rasped. "Why are you doing this to me? Do I know you?"

Before he could answer the door swung open and the madam entered the room, her slippers shuffling across the uneven plank floor. When she reached his side she shook a finger at the girl. "Don't you trust this one. She threw the water pitcher at my head when I brung her dinner."

"Is that before or after you decided not to empty the damn chamber pot?" he asked."I told you she was to be kept healthy. And why is she tied to the cot? I told you not to do that." He didn't try to hide the contempt he felt for the woman.

He noticed Rebecca watching the exchange, confusion in her face. "Why am I to be kept healthy? Why would you care?" In the dim light he saw the glitter of silent tears trickle down her face as hopelessness collapsed her shoulders. She lay down, curled onto her side, her back to the room.

He turned toward the madam. "Get that pot emptied." The woman turned toward the door saying, "I'll tell Amy…" only to stop when he snapped out, "You pick it up and haul it yourself, right now. And when you come back, I want to see you bring fresh water and a decent meal."

She reddened, opened her mouth to protest and then had second thoughts because she clamped her lips shut before leaning down to lift the overfull chamber pot, grunting with the effort to prevent it spilling.

After she'd thumped back downstairs he moved the chair near the bed and sat. For some minutes he silently stared at the unmoving figure on the bed. How had he come to be in this situation? Sure he'd been a rambunctious kid more clever than his sisters. "Always busy as a bee," his mother used to say. But she said it with love and a smile. She may have cuffed him about the ears to "get his attention," but she'd often praised him, too. When, at sixteen, he'd returned from his two-years as a runaway, she'd cried with joy. When he'd declared his intention to attend the seminary she puffed up like a strutting hen.

But, he wasn't the son she thought he was. Those two years working in a Chicago whorehouse, with the madam as his first girlfriend, changed him forever. And, he'd discovered opium, his first love. He'd returned home as someone else. Someone his mother never knew.

The door behind him opened and the woman shuffled in carrying a tin pitcher and cup in one hand and a plate of bread, cheese and meat in the other. She banged everything down on the fruit box beside the bed. "She throws any damn water at me again," she declared, "and she can die of thirst for all I care!" That said, the woman stomped from the room, grumbling about fetching the slop jar.

Once the door had closed, he turned back to the girl. She rolled over to face him. He could only see a glimmer of eyes sunk deep in the hollows above her cheekbones. She's lost weight, he thought to himself. For just a second, he remembered her easy smile as she'd talked to the pencil seller and her jaunty walk down the boardwalk when she'd moved on. Innocent, sweet and alluring all at the same time.

That recollection stabbed him in a way he hadn't felt for a long time. He shrugged away the feeling and reached for the tin cup the madam had just delivered. Pouring water into the cup, he passed it to the girl who hesitated, then took it and drank greedily.

She handed the cup to him and sank back on the bed. Eyelids fluttering, she managed just one more word. "Why?" she asked again in a whisper.

He'd left once he was sure the laudanum had done its work and after the madam delivered a clean chamber pot. Carefully snapping shut the padlock he paused, staring at the door, visualizing the sleeping girl, curled atop the cot. Shaking himself loose of that image he ran down the stairs. When he reached the front stoop, he paused again, this time to stare unseeing toward the street's end where parched weeds covered a field alongside the railroad tracks.

"Damned if I know," he muttered, finally answering her question as he stepped into the street.

Mid-morning sun slanted down through the skylight's clean glass. Fong's weekly cleaning ritual ensured dirt never blurred the light. Given the excessive heat of the past few weeks, Sage would have welcomed even that miniscule lessening of light. Fong, however, merely adjusted their training schedule so that the two of them practiced the form either in the early, cooler, morning hours or late in the evening.

Once, when he'd complained of the heat, Fong sent him an unsympathetic look, saying, "Snake and Crane practiced in climate much hotter than this. Sweat is good." That had been the last time Sage voiced that particular complaint.

They moved through air warm as their skin. After awhile, it felt like his skin and the air merged, all borders gone. Following that routine they began the two person exercise Fong called "push hands." When Sage'd first performed this exercise, it had seemed silly to so slowly block each other's thrusts and kicks. No longer, though. When he'd used this training out in the world, he'd found himself able to block, parry, kick and hit with lightning speed.

Fong breaking into a relaxed stance signaled the exercise session's end. As usual, his teacher looked cool even as Sage panted and swiped away the sweat dripping off his face.

"My men not find boarded window," Fong told him, once they were sitting on the polished wood floor.

Sage heaved a sigh, "Well, it was a long shot. They probably have a curtain hanging between the boards and the window.

"If this about laundry problem, it odd that union leader sister get taken and not leader," Fong mused aloud.

"Yah, well, I'm not sure that her kidnapping has anything to do with the union. According to Hanke, white slavery is a growing problem in Portland. She was walking alone. Easy pickings. Still, that's what Ma and Eich are sure it's about the laundry fight."

Sage clambered to his feet, rubbing the small of his back. "I am not sure I'll ever get used to floor sitting cross legged on the floor. Maybe a person has to start doing that as a child."

"True. Start as child, floor sitting no problem. All children can sit on floor. You must keep practicing," Fong said before standing up with the undulating grace of curling smoke. "It takes much work to be child again."

"I should have known you weren't going to make it easy on me," Sage said without rancor. "Well, guess I better be off to visit the ladies."

"Scarlet ladies from yesterday?" Fong asked.

"I wish. No, these are the ladies who are trying to eradicate the scarlet ladies' profession," Sage said.

Fong's face softened with sympathy as he said, "Ah, I see. May your visit be short and soft as a falling plum blossom."

"Very funny. Besides, I doubt they'll get angry." Sage said.

"Not ladies. You," Fong responded as he flashed his toothiest smile.

Sage went downstairs to don his proper man-about-town attire. He had visited with the city's only police matron while he waited for the prostitutes' release. Before he left, she gave him the address of the Society for Social Hygiene. That's where he was going this morning.

When he reached the downtown building housing the Society, half an hour later, he found two other organizations' names on the door's frosted glass: the Temperance Union and the Oregon Suffrage Association. He noticed he was somewhat nervous as he turned the door knob and entered what surely had to be a hothouse of feminine passion.

Inside, all was clean and calm. The waiting room was empty but the tinkling bell above the outer door quickly summoned a no-nonsense woman. Her light eyes widened in surprise when she saw him though her voice was composed as she asked, "May I assist you, sir?"

He cleared his throat, "I was hoping to speak to someone with the Society for Social Hygiene."

The woman's look sharpened but she merely tilted her head, studied him momentarily, though not long enough to make her scrutiny awkward, and said, "I will check to see if Mrs. Nathan Harris is available to speak with you." She turned and disappeared down a short hallway leading from the waiting room.

Sage looked at the wooden chairs and decided to remain standing. A collection of wall posters competed with each other in terms of message and color. He had time to swiftly peruse a few declaring pointed messages like, "Equality for the Mothers of Men;" "Lips that Touch Liquor Will Never Touch Ours;" and "Stamp Out Syphilis-Every Baby Entitled to be Born Healthy," before a dignified woman, encased in a black, high-necked, bombazine gown, entered the waiting room. Her face was kindly though she didn't extend her hand. Instead, she said, "Hello, my name is Mary Harris," before continuing, "I am very sorry, sir. But if you have medical concerns I must direct you to your personal physician for a social examination and specific treatment information."

Sage's foot took an involuntary step backwards as heat reddened his face. Raising his palms to stop her words, he protested, "No, no. I don't have a medical problem. I'm here to talk to you about something else."

The woman's eyebrow rose skeptically as she said, "I suppose you've come here to discuss a 'friend's' problem?"

"Yes," he said before quickly adding, "No, no. Not in that way" when he saw her lips twitch at his initial "Yes." He took a deep breath. "Look, can we go in your office to talk about this?"

She hesitated and then gestured down the hall. When they reached her tidy, sparsely furnished office she indicated he should take a chair. He did so while noticing that she left her office door propped open.

He quickly explained about the missing Rebecca, ending with a request, "I was hoping that you might know the names of local procurers and the location of the likely sporting houses where she might be imprisoned." Seeing that eyebrow arch again, he quickly clarified, "Of course, I thought you'd know because of the Society's efforts to steer women away from prostitution."

"Yes, of course," she echoed dryly. She thought a moment and then sat forward, "I have heard rumors that there is a new procurer in town. I wish I could tell you more but, I'm not the one who has regular exchanges with the unfortunate women. Let me see if I can find out more. How can I reach you?"

Mentally, Sage kicked himself. He should have realized that would be a problem. He didn't really want his name bandied about in group of very vocal, energetic, middle-class women. Then he hit upon it, "Please send a note to Attorney Philander Gray. Tell him you have information for John Miner. He'll let me know and I will personally come see you again."

As he passed out through the waiting room his decision to remain incognito was reinforced. A bright-eyed young woman stopped him, a piece of paper in her hands. "I am collecting names of men who support women's suffrage," she said as she thrust paper and pen in his direction.

"I've already signed it elsewhere," he lied and slipped out the door before she could say more.

"I will sign it," he told himself once he was in the hallway. "Just cant sign it now." Of course he'd sign it. He smiled to himself, adding, "Mae and Lucinda won't give me peace until I do.

Late morning the new foreman, Sinclair, left the washroom when Cobb poked his head around the door and gestured with his hand. Sinclair exited rapidly, though Mae couldn't say whether his prompt response came from obedience or relief at being able to vacate the stifling heat of the washroom. Not that they needed him. Like most places she'd worked, supervisors were about as useful as teeth on a turkey. The people who did the work were the ones who knew best how to do it. Good supervisors knew this and tried to assist workers—good ones like that foreman who quit. Bad ones, well, back to turkeys, she thought ruefully. Bad ones strutted about with puffed up chests, gobbling nonsense.

Her eye was caught by the sight of Rachel leaving her mangle and striding swiftly into the wash tub area. There she approached one of the men and they conferred, heads bent toward each other, both of them sending nervous glances toward the closed door into the office area. The man nodded and raised his hand to his forehead in a salute to Rachel. She was smiling as she walked back to her mangle, stopping to talk with two women; one at a mangle, the other at the starch table. They each gave her nods of agreement and she left the women smiling.

Mae could only shake her head in admiration. The gal had clearly come up with something. Rachel was still raising folks' spirits even though Mae knew she was growing ever more disheartened. Mae had heard her crying quietly in the night over her missing sister. "Oh, well," Mae told herself, "I expect I'll find out at noontime what our Rachel's up to."

And so she did. As soon as everyone was seated beneath the willow Rachel stood up, a wide smile lighting her face. "Ladies and gentlemen, we will now listen to first hand reports from the Cobb Laundry Detective Squad. "Burdett," she called turning to the wash tub man she'd spoken to earlier, "do tell us the results of your sleuthing."

Burdett stood up, dusted dry bits off his rump and gave them all a lopsided grin. He clearly was reveling in the moment. "Wahl," he drawled, "Rachel here asked me to find out whether our new foreman was a laundryman or a management spy."

"And?" someone urged from the edge of the group.

He smiled and said, "Wahl, I told him I was getting pesky little soap spots on the clothes and asked should I boil the clothes."

No one said anything, letting Burdett enjoy stretching out the suspense. "Wahl, he told me to go ahead and give 'em a boil!" he cackled, slapping his leg for emphasis.

As one the group laughed aloud, one person crowing, "That Sinclair's a spy for double darn sure!"

Only one person didn't join in. She, instead, looked perplexed. Once the laughter quieted, Caroline spoke up, her voice hesitant at the thought she was revealing her ignorance about the laundry profession, "Why is it funny that he told you to boil the clothes?"

One of the women threw an arm around Caroline shoulders and gave them a squeeze. Still, she answered the girl loud enough for all to hear, "Why child. Boiling causes the spots. Someone who knew the laundry business would have told Burdett to dump in some caustic soda. That's what prevents those spots."

Rachel's team of detectives also included the two women she'd spoken to earlier. They offered further evidence that their new foreman was ignorant of steam laundry procedures. One discovered he didn't know how to tighten a mangle roller. The second said, "I asked him if it was alright for me to do the starching on the wood table instead of the zinc covered one. And he said, 'Yes.' Any fool knows starch sucks the wood resin up into the cloth. That's why we use the zinc topped table," she told Caroline.

Rachel spoke next, "So, to sum it up, our Mr. Sinclair is a steam laundry foreman who knows nothing whatsoever about the job. What does that make him, folks?"

"A spy," they called in unison.

"No, no," protested a thin voice, "He didn't know anything about the Sparta or our fight. He just got into town from Chicago. He said he worked as a foreman in the laundry there. That's why Cobb hired him . . . ." Her protest died out as she evidently realized Sinclair had told her at least one lie. She'd just heard proof that he knew nothing about laundries.

All eyes turned in her direction. Rachel voice was sad as she said, "Oh, Chrissy. What have you done?"

FIFTEEN

The workers cast sly glances at him as they trooped back in following their twenty-minute lunch. Well, that was to be expected. By the third time one of them asked him for assistance, he'd realized they were testing him. Their reactions told him he'd failed each test.

Meandering around the room, Sinclair eventually made his way to Chrissy's mangle. "How's it going Chrissy?" he asked, putting a light hand on her shoulder.

Even before she responded he knew that she had changed. Beneath his fingers her thin shoulder felt rigid as a stick. She didn't shrug off his hand, but her movements as she kept working the collar mangle were abrupt and faster than normal. Her response was equally abrupt as she snapped out the single word, "Fine." She didn't even look at him.

When he turned to move on, he saw more than one pair of watching eyes. Maybe, when she was out from under their scrutiny, she'd be more likely to talk to him, he told himself. He'd try again after work.

Cobb appeared at the office door and gestured for Sinclair. As he made his way across the washroom, Sinclair realized that Cobb never walked through the washroom. Instead, he seemed to remain in the front office, whenever he was there at all. Sinclair gave a mental shrug. What did he care? Lots of bosses are afraid of their workers and lots of bosses kept themselves looking busy doing everything but productive work.

Cobb got right to the point once they were inside the office with the door shut. "Sinclair, this is the day we start the ball really rolling. So, once the end whistle sounds, I want you to hand these out to the seven people who are named at the top of each notice," he said, thrusting sheets of paper toward Sinclair.

Sinclair took the papers and read the top sheet. It was a simple statement:

> Your services with Sparta Laundry are hereby terminated as of this date. Your final check will be available for pick-up from the office on the regular payday, Friday of next week. You are not otherwise permitted on Sparta Laundry property. Should you violate this directive, you will be arrested for trespassing.
>
> Thaddeus Cobb
> Manager, Sparta Laundry

Sinclair said nothing, thinking only about how cold the brief words seemed and about how the people who received the notices would feel when they discovered their livelihood abruptly cut off. He tried another mental shrug, telling himself once again that what happened in this laundry had nothing to do with him. "Why not hand them out now?"

"Good Lord no!" Cobb responded sharply. "You do it now, who knows what those union hooligans will do. They might break my machinery or walk off the job. We can't have that. They need to finish this last load of laundry. In fact, if they haven't finished by quitting time, I want you to keep them working until they do.

Sinclair felt his forehead wrinkle as he pondered Cobb's directive. He asked, "So, exactly how do you want me to hand out this notice," giving the papers a little shake.

"When all the work is done and people are leaving, I want you to stand outside the door. As they exit the building, I want you to hand the notice to the seven people. That way, only those already outside will know we've fired their leaders. Later today, two of Farley's men will be here. They'll stand inside the washroom to make sure no one comes back in. And, they'll be guarding the place overnight.

"Where will you be?" Sinclair had to ask.

Cobb made a theatrical show of astonishment. "Why home, of course. I don't stay late, you know that. It will be up to you and the guards to lock the place up."

"Does this mean I can stop trying to grab Rachel Levy?" Sinclair asked.

Cobb shook his head vigorously, "Absolutely not. Just firing her isn't going to extract that particular thorn from our side."

Apparently, thought of the Levy woman triggered another sore subject for Cobb because he said, "I don't know what has happened to women today. All their yammering about the right to vote is ridiculous. Hell, half of them are idiots and a womanly woman doesn't want the vote. She wants to take care of her husband, children and home in that order. The last thing we need are women like Rachel Levy getting the vote, women like her are too passionate and ignorant when it comes to politics. Look at those Temperance gals. Women are sticking their nose into everything and I'm damn tired of it."

Sinclair could only nod but he was wondering, "Just when could a woman working in Cobb's laundry find the time to play "womanly" woman? He paged through the papers, noting each showed a woman's name. Yes, he'd given Cobb the names of the most outspoken union supporters. They were all here.

"Are any of these women supporting children?" he had to ask.

Momentary vexation pressed Cobb's lips into a thin line and furrowed his brow before he said, "Sinclair, I don't know and I don't care if any of them have brats. And, neither should you. I am paying you to do a job. Now, do it."

Sage greeted Mozart's guests and, when not doing that, filled in for Mae, making sure the waiters had water to pour, clean glasses and dishes and every other niggling task needed to make things run smoothly. He could tell from the harried faces of the waiters he wasn't particularly good at filling his mother's shoes.

Customers lingered well past the noontime dinner hour. Finally, at two thirty, he ushered the last patrons out the front door and flipped the sign to 'closed'. There would be two-and-one-half hours before the start of the supper trade. Gazing around the empty dining room, he couldn't but admire it yet again. It was an elegant setting and perfect for drawing in Portland's elite—exactly as intended. The opening of the kitchen's swinging doors stopped his ruminating. Herman Eich stepped into the elegant room, an incongruous sight in his slouch hat, baggy britches and scuffed boots.

Sage strode toward him. "Herman, is something wrong?" At the ragpicker's negative shake of the head, Sage asked, "Can I get you some lunch or coffee?"

"No, I just wanted to stop and talk with you while I am on this side of the river. Your mother is fine. I followed the two of them to work, and they're both safe inside. I've spent a few days now, talking to folks. Seeing if I can find anyone who saw Rebecca Levy the day she was taken," Eich said.

"Any luck?" Sage asked.

"Well, maybe. There's a young fellow who sells pencils along the route. He's a bit slow grasping things. But, it seems he might have been the last person to see her on Saturday. He says he saw her step into the alley that leads to her boarding house. So, I'm thinking she might have been jumped there and taken out the alley's other end. You might want to talk to him. Maybe you can get more details. He's a nice fellow, just a bit hard to get information from," Eich said.

"Are you still spending most of your time on the eastside of the river?"

"Yes. Since Mae works such long hours, I have plenty of time to explore. I am ranging far and wide. There's enough houses that I can fill my cart with usable discards. I even met an old fellow who remembers hunting cougar and bear on Mt. Tabor. Imagine that."

Sage tried to imagine wild animals roaming the gently rounded dormant volcano but couldn't. Not now, with most of its timber felled and new houses crawling up its sides. There was even a steam train and a trolley servicing the folks living there and in the farther town of Mt. Villa beyond its eastern slope.

"So, where do I find the pencil-selling fellow?"

"He's there on Grand Avenue between Belmont and Morrison. He's got a little blue flag flying above a wooden packing crate."

Eich soon headed out, saying he had to check on his home base and retrieve more objects to sell. Sage thought about Eich's one-room lean-to attached to a small house. It was a snug little place, one he and Mae visited often. Although Eich could have succeeded at anything he tried, he chose to write his poems and earn his living selling usable items foraged from dust bins and damaged ceramics he restored. Despite his hand to mouth existence, Eich was one of the most contented people Sage had ever known.

After Eich and his cart rolled away down the alley behind Mozart's, Sage climbed to the third floor. There he carefully hung his hosting outfit and donned his John Miner disguise. As he changed his clothes he realized he was grumpy. A few minutes later, he finally figured out the reason. Usually, he drove the missions. This time he was somewhat sidelined. Everyone else was out doing.

Well, he'd change that. He'd go talk to the pencil seller and then maybe try to locate the two men Solomon's man had followed from the Portland Hotel to the cafe. It was a good bet that these were Farley's two operatives. Maybe he'd also wander past the U.S. Laundry. See if Cobb and his associates had delivered on Cobb's threat. Now that he had purpose, Sage's mood lightened a bit. But still, he felt a vague sense of worried anticipation, like the guy in the tenement bedroom waiting for the fellow overhead to drop his other shoe with a great big thud.

The hours lumbered through late afternoon and into the evening. The foreman made them stay late to finish up all the laundry. When the quit whistle shrilled, Mae was picturing herself sitting on the boarding house's back balcony, her feet freed from her soggy torture and resting on a rattan ottoman. She quickly untied her apron strings, rolled down her sleeves, buttoned up her dress front and considered how the afternoon had gone.

Despite the lunchtime laughter, she'd watched as uneasiness spread among her co-workers. They had to be wondering how they would feed their kids, pay their rent—survive—if they were locked out. There were only so many jobs for women in Portland. Steam laundries, at six dollars a week, were still at least a dollar a week more than what women could make working as a sales clerk, housemaid, cook or cannery worker. According to the help wanted ads, those were the only jobs available to women. Even then, most ads requested a "girl." Folks with money probably didn't like bossing a mature woman around. Mae considered the faces around her, noting that few could be called a "girl." These were women, hardworking women regardless of age, who were skilled at steam laundry work but little else.

Mid afternoon the phony foreman, Sinclair, stepped through the door from the office holding a sheaf of papers in his hand. He stood by the door, gazing around the room, scowling before his expression turned stony. He was a good looking man, she supposed. Neatly barbered brown hair topped an open face that made him look friendly. He had tidy eyebrows, a regular nose and long mouth above a slightly squared chin. The few times she'd heard him speak, he'd sounded educated. He looked more like a bank teller or finance clerk than a laundry foreman. Still, it was no wonder Chrissy succumbed. Good looks, a kind demeanor, intelligence and flattering attention—what country girl wet behind her ears could resist that devil's mix? Mae hadn't. A similar scoundrel had fooled her.

Sinclair left his post by the office door, making a show of meandering among the mangles while following a fairly straight path to Chrissy's side. Chrissy flashed him no smile and kept her eyes on her work, obviously ignoring his presence. Sinclair quickly moved away.

After seeing that exchange, Mae turned her mind and hands to ironing. When she looked up, Sinclair was gone. At least, he'd spent little time parading about like a benevolent overseer. He'd abandoned that act right quick once he realized they were on to him. He had to know that, by now, everyone knew he was Cobb's spy.

Mae had later spent some time wondering from whom, besides Chrissy, the Association might be getting its information. She narrowed her eyes in the direction of that Caroline girl just as she looked up and caught Mae staring. At first, the young woman's face looked confused before being transformed by a tentative smile.

Keeping a poker face, Mae merely gazed back. It was time to make the girl uneasy. See which way she'd jump once she realized not everyone trusted her. That little tussle over, Mae had returned to her task, wielding the iron with a vigor driven by worry and frustration.

But she could finally set down her iron, the workday was done. Laying her apron across the ironing board, Mae sighed with relief. The weather had broken a bit cooler that morning. Probably never got past seventy-five degrees outside—making it over ninety degrees inside the washroom. Downright unbearable but still a sight better than when the heat wave raised it to at least one hundred and ten steamy degrees inside.

Done readying for the walk to Rachel's boarding house, Mae headed for the outer door and heard raised voices coming from outside the building. Exiting behind another woman, who was one of the more vocal union members, Mae saw Sinclair waiting just outside—as though in ambush. He gave a sheet of paper to the woman just ahead of her. When Mae paused to receive her own paper, Sinclair shook his head and gestured for her to keep moving. Once outside, she saw that only a few of the women held one of Sinclair's papers.

The others stood bunched around these women and their voices raised in anger. Whatever that paper said was riling them up. Mae hustled over to the group. Glancing back over her shoulder, she saw Sinclair nip inside and slam the door shut.

SIXTEEN

Careful not to touch the filthy walls or step in urine, Sinclair climbed to the door at the top of the stairs. Faint murmuring came from inside but no one answered his knock, so he opened the door to see people lying about on stained, bare mattresses, eyes closed or turned inward. The only furniture in the room was the mattresses scattered across the floor. A candle on the floor flickered but barely lit the dark. No one stirred at his entrance.

Opium smoke layered the air, clogging his nose and heightening his anticipation. Finally, the nearest man lifted a limp hand to gesture at a small black lacquer tray beside his mattress. It held small brown balls of opium, a pipe and matches. As Sinclair reached toward the tray a nearby man rolled onto his side to vomit on the floor before rolling onto his back again without bothering to wipe the vomit from his chin. Sinclair wasn't appalled. Nausea was opium's sidekick. Yet a formless thought stilled Sinclair's hand, leaving it to hover above the tray.

Then Sinclair's stomach roiled, he straightened and backed away from the tray. Seconds later he was out the door and charging down the stairs. Once outside on the sidewalk he gulped air, trying to rinse away the smell. "What the hell is happening to me?" he asked himself as he stumbled down the street trying to grapple with the change. He'd smoked opium in many such dens over the years. So, why had this one sent him fleeing?

When he walked into the saloon he saw few late night patrons. Only one fellow stood at the bar, a glass of liquor before him. The noise of glassware clanking came from a small alcove. He eased up beside the solitary man who glanced at him then looked away.

The barkeep entered and Sinclair ordered. Beer in hand, he turned to the other customer. "Hello, there. I am Paul Sinclair from Chicago. Only been in town a few weeks," he said, offering his hand. The other man shook and smiled, saying, "My name's Brice Copeland. Nice to meet you, I'm also new to Portland."

"You plan on staying here or are you just passing through?" Sinclair asked.

"Only passing through. I'm just up from Panama."

That sent a jolt across Sinclair's shoulders. He'd always had a hard time believing in simple coincidence without the benefit of divine intervention. The seminary lessons were hard to leave behind. "Panama, huh? What were you doing in Panama?"

"Working as a structural engineer for the French on the canal," Copeland said, reaching for his glass. As he carried it to his mouth, the man's hand trembled. As Sinclair watched, the shaking worsened and involved more than Copeland's hand. Copeland carefully sat the glass down and pressed both palms onto the polished bar.

"I was well-paid but my health's ruined."

"What do you mean?"

"Panama is nothing but malaria and yellow fever. Over 34,000 men have already died from disease while working on the railroad or the canal. Eighty percent of the workers have gotten malaria. That place isn't fit for man or beast." Copeland held up a hand that still jumped around. "Me, I've the malaria. I can't seem to shake it even though I take quinine every day."

"Is that why you left Panama?"

Copeland shook his head. "Nope. Once you get malaria, it doesn't go away no matter where you live. I left because things are getting dangerous down there."

"What do you mean?"

Well, the French are hoping the United States gets the treaty with Columbia so it can take over building the canal. The U.S. Congress has authorized forty million dollars to buy it. But if Columbia refuses to give the U.S. sovereignty over the canal and a ninety-nine year lease, I'm afraid the folks in the area are going to rebel. Civil war, encouraged by the U.S., in other words. I didn't want to be down there for that. Besides, the French have pretty much stopped work."

"I saw in the newspaper this morning that the Columbian congress rejected the treaty," Sinclair said.

That brought a glum nod from Copeland. "Yup," was all he said.

"So what brings you to Portland?"

"The railroad trust has hired me to lobby Oregon's congressmen."

Sinclair wrinkled his forehead, trying to make the connection. "What do the railroads have to do with the canal?" he asked.

"Well, they spent a lot of money bribing Columbian congressmen in an effort to stop the treaty from going through. Now that they were successful there with their bribing, they want to focus on stopping a proposed canal through Nicaragua. The reason for their opposition is simple. If there's a canal, it will mean far fewer goods shipped over U.S. railroads. Instead, ships will do the hauling. They sent me here to be a walking, talking example to Oregon's congressmen of just how dangerous plague-ridden Central America really is."

"So, you've decided a canal is a bad idea?"

Copeland shook his head as he held up his shaking hand, "If they can get rid of the plague it's a great idea. But, I ask you. Who's going to hire a structural engineer who shakes worse than aspens in a thunderstorm? I've got two kids and a wife to support. So, I'm grateful for any work, no matter what it is."

"Your family was with you in Panama?" If so, maybe Panama won't be all that bad a place for Rebecca Levy, Sinclair told himself.

"Hell no! They stayed back in the U.S. That place is a hellhole. An absolute death sentence for a woman."

"Surely there are women there?"

"Yes, of course. There are local women there but European and North American women don't last long. It's sweltering hot, humid and mold grows on everything. And, it's unsanitary. Folks drink out of rain barrels swarming with hatching mosquitoes. There's no water system to speak of. North American women can't handle it physically or mentally," Copeland said, adding, "Actually, I wouldn't send my worst enemy to that place."

Sage crumpled the newspaper and tossed it onto the kitchen table. What a crappy way to start the day. At least he now knew what Cobb had planned besides firing the union leaders. The front page, Sunday newspaper announcement was succinct:

> Notice: Owing to our inability to guarantee to our patrons prompt delivery of work entrusted to us, we decided to close our plants effective today, for an indefinite time. (signed) Sparta Steam Laundry, City Steam Laundry, Portland Steam Laundry, American Steam Laundry, Star Steam Laundry, Oregon Steam Laundry, Union Steam Laundry, Opera-House Steam Laundry, Pacific Steam Laundry.

A few choice curses slipped out before he caught Ida casting admonishing glances in his direction. Mozart's cook didn't tolerate swearing in her kitchen. "Sorry" he mouthed at her as he stood up. Yesterday's firing of the steam laundries' union leaders had been bad enough. A total lockout would be tough on the workers, their families and their union. From what Mae had said, the unions weren't quite ready.

Sage noticed that the U.S. Laundry wasn't on the list of those laundries locking out their workers. Neither was the Albina Laundry. He wondered what that meant about Cobb's threat. Maybe he backed off. "Guess I'll have to go take a look tomorrow," he told himself. "But first, I better head over to the union hall for the workers' meeting."

The night before, he'd been waiting outside the Sparta Laundry when it shut down for the night. His mother had introduced him as a friend, John Miner. He listened to the workers talk about Cobb firing Rachel Levy and six other women. Runners headed off to warn the union leaders at the other laundries. It was no surprise when the women sent to the nearest laundry quickly returned with the news that the manager had fired the outspoken union members at that laundry as well. From that piece of information people concluded that the firings were a concerted action by the Laundrymen Association's nine member laundries. Right then, the workers agreed to meet the next day, Sunday, to discuss strategy.

Dressed in his John Miner duds, Sage made his way down from Mozart's third floor and into the basement tunnel. It being early, most passersby were too sleepy to notice a man climbing out of the ground in the alley beside the restaurant. Dusting his hands on his canvas trousers, Sage set off for the eastside of town. He needed to find the pencil seller. It being a Sunday, maybe the fellow wouldn't be at his stand. He'd already missed him the evening before when all Sage found was an empty wooden crate.

Sage was surprised to find the eastside's boardwalks crowded with church goers and folks just enjoying a stroll in the cool Sunday morning. Fishing holes at Hawthorne Springs and Sullivan's Gulch explained the fishing poles jauntily carried on a number of shoulders. The huge Hawthorne Park covered blocks starting at 9th and Hawthorne. It was the favored site for union picnics. Today, the park was riotous with running children, many of them probably coming from nearby union households. Folks called the area, "Union Town". He liked that.

Ahead, he spotted a young man standing behind a wooden shipping crate. Sage stepped up his pace. It looked like he was in luck. The fellow leaned against the brick of a warehouse. Painted a bright red, the crate had a calico cloth of blue and yellow draped across its front. Pencils, topped with rubber eraser plugs, filled glass vases. Behind this colorful stand stood a young fellow of about twenty, his face smooth with the widely spaced sleepy eyes and small nose frequently seen in those who thought a bit slower than other folks. Pausing before the stand, Sage was welcomed with a wide smile and sparkling eyes. The fellow spoke carefully, his words a bit halting and blurred, "May I help you select a fine pencil, sir?"

"You certainly may, I need five of them," Sage responded.

After the two of them had fingered enough pencils, Sage selected five whereupon the fellow moved to his next item for sale. "Would you be interested in an ivory handled Faber pencil sharpening knife, sir? Those pencils will need to be kept sharpened." Sage had to smile. This fellow had his sales routine down. He added the Faber pencil knife to the five pencils.

Transaction concluded, Sage moved cautiously into his real reason for being there. "Do you know Miss Rebecca Levy?"

His question triggered a wide smile that the young man quickly damped down. "Why do you ask about her?" he wanted to know, his lips pursing with suspicion.

"I am a friend of her sister, Rachel. We can't find Rebecca. She's missing."

"Yes. Miss Rachel told me Miss Rebecca is gone."

"Do you remember the day she went missing? It was a week ago yesterday. It was Saturday."

"I saw her that day. I remember."

"You saw her then?" Sage repeated.

"She stopped. Told me 'hello' and asked me how my day was going. She always tells me 'hello' and asks me that. She's a very nice lady. I like her."

"Did you see where she went after she stopped to visit with you?"

"I saw her go into that alley right over there," he said pointing to an opening halfway down the block.

Sage took a deep breath, slowing his words because this was the most important question of all. "After she went into the alley did anyone else go into the alley after her?"

That question caused an eye squint as the fellow searched his memory. Then his face cleared and he nodded emphatically. "Yes, a man. He wore a nice suit, not scruffy like you."

That honest answer made Sage smile. He asked, "Did the man come back out?"

The fellow shook his head vigorously, confident of his answer. "No, he did not come back out."

Sage tried to get a better description but the pencil seller had nothing to add other than the man in question had no beard or mustache and wore a 'bowl" hat.

"Well, thank you very much for talking to me," Sage said and turned away, discouraged. Half the men in Portland wore suits and bowler hats. He'd gone about five feet, when the fellow added a single, riveting comment, "The man always wears that hat."

Sage whipped back around. "You've seen him before?"

That question brought a solemn nod. "Many times since that day. First sister comes, then man comes."

"What? You mean Rachel Levy walks by and then the same man comes by after her?"

This question turned the nod vigorous. "Yup. Not just Miss Rachel. He also walks behind an older lady who is with Miss Rachel. Maybe he is following that lady too."

"When was the last time you saw the man in the bowler hat?" Sage asked. A jolt of hope, mingled with fear, stopped his breath.

The pencil seller scrunched up his face in thought. "I saw man in the bowl hat last night. Doing the same thing. Following the two ladies.

❀　❀　❀

Mae saw Sage sidle into the hall while the union president was in the middle of his speech. Rachel Levy saw him too because she quickly rose from her chair and walked over to him where they conferred in whispers. Even from across the room she saw Rachel's face fall and shortly after saw the woman quickly swipe tears from beneath her eyes. Mae didn't know how she did it. Sleeping in the same room, Rachel's restlessness and soft crying often stirred her awake. How the young woman missed her sister. But, Rachel hid her sorrow well. Most of the women in this hall didn't even know Rebecca was missing. Certainly they wouldn't be able to tell it from Rachel's appearance or actions.

Mae came alert when the union president mentioned Rachel's name. The young woman immediately left Sage's side to mount the stage at the front of the room. For a moment, she gazed at the crowd of over three hundred people, mostly women, her eyes searching their faces. Then she took a deep breath and her clear voice rang out. "Are we asking for too much?" she asked in a near shout. "No!" came the answering shout. "Are our bodies giving too much?" she asked in an even louder voice. A "Yes!" came back with equal vigor.

Rachel laughed before raising her hands to pat down the noise. She said in a calmer voice, "Every one of us in this room has suffered mightily standing for hours on end in the steam and the heat. Felt our skin shrivel and break and our muscles and fingers and feet ache to the point that sleep is impossible. We've seen our co-workers collapse at the mangles or, worse, lose their fingers and hands to one."

"Hear, hear," someone shouted, and others repeated that cry until it swirled throughout the room.

"We know from today's newspaper that tomorrow we will be faithfully standing before the doors of the steam laundries, ready to subject ourselves to suffering, trying to earn that tiny bit of our employers' profits they are willing to share. We will be there because we believe that reason and talk is how people should solve problems."

Rachel shook her head slowly. "That loyalty, that faithfulness resides not in the hearts of our employers. We will stand there in the morning but the doors will be locked." The crowd was now somber.

Rachel took a deep breath, then said, "So, my dear sisters and brothers we must pull together as a family. We must work together to help ourselves weather this downturn in our incomes, this strain on our families. While our union leaders reach out to our employers, we must reach out to each other. This adversity can break us, or it can make us stronger, bring us closer."

Again Rachel searched their faces. "As our president just told you, we will have help from the city's unions. We are grateful that our brothers and sisters in other unions are already stepping up to assist us with strike funds, food, clothing, and even pooling their money to buy a steam laundry. It will be a union-operated laundry where we can work in a healthful place, in a place that recognizes our worth and treats us with dignity. But, my dear sisters and brothers, we must do our part as well. We must walk the picket lines before every steam laundry and staff the union hall dining room, the job search table and do other things to help ourselves and each others' families."

Rachel paused until silence cloaked the room before leaning forward to say firmly, "Remember what the Greeks and our own country's founding fathers told us, 'United we stand, divided we fall.'" As she shouted the motto, she raised a clenched fist to pound the air.

The noise was deafening as everyone leapt to their feet to raise their voices and fists in return. Mae joined in even though she had seen it all before and feared how it might end.

SEVENTEEN

"You know, at this point, I'm just letting the current carry me along," he told the unconscious woman on the bed. Feeling an awkwardness akin to shame, Sinclair studied the strong features, the bold brows, the dark lashes against the smooth cheeks. There was nobility in that face. Perhaps it was her race. Jews survived and lived to triumph despite centuries of persecution. Panama. Could she survive even that? Illness would make a fine bone structure like hers first sharper then skeletal.

"Stop it," he told himself. He shifted on the chair, wanting to get up and leave the room. To descend downstairs where, even though it was just early afternoon, liquor-fueled riotousness seemed to have erupted. He looked at her again, thinking how little she must know about the way of life taking place right outside her prison.

"I've been following your sister, Rachel," he told her, feeling a trifle silly talking to an unconscious woman. "She hasn't given up her union work, you know. We thought she would, but she hasn't. And things are getting tougher for her. Cobb's fired her. He's locking the rest of them out tomorrow morning."

Sinclair gazed at the rough boards across the window. Outside, the streets echoed with drunken shouts and the clatter of fast moving cabs and carriages. The North End was a rowdy place for men who possessed little other than hope. He wondered what it must be like for her, hearing people beyond the window but prevented from catching their notice.

He turned back to tell her, "You will soon be out of here and on a ship, you know. It's important that, once you're aboard, that you obey the captain. I thought I'd pay him extra, just to make sure the men leave you alone. It's a rough ship. Not suitable for a lady, I'm afraid. When you reach San Francisco, someone will be waiting for you. After that . . ."

Sinclair's monologue trailed off as shame speared his throat, killing his words. He stared down at the unconscious girl. How much alike, in character, were the two sisters? It was strange, sitting here looking at the still form of one sister while remembering the on-going liveliness of the other. *Too lively. She's causing me problems.* For certain, even when he finally managed to capture Rachel, she'd be a fighter. That was her nature.

Besides, now there was that other woman, Mae something, from the laundry. She looked to be older than him by nearly two decades but his gut told him that didn't matter. She'd be a fighter as well. A blue-eyed hawk she was. And tough, he could tell that about her. Some women emitted a fiery confidence that warned a man to take care. She was one of those. She was wary, too. She barely let Rachel out of her sight once they were on the street. Because of her, he'd been forced to drop much farther behind whenever he trailed the pair of them.

Sinclair looked down to see his hands rapidly turning his hat brim. *Damn, he was nervous.* He hated this job. Why was he bothering these women? They wanted nothing more than they deserved. Besides, he hated Cobb's smug confidence and little twists of cruelty. *And Cobb is a coward who can't do the dirty work himself. No, instead he hires men to do it.* That's why it was him, Paul Sinclair, who had to stand at the laundry door and hand out that spiteful letter and watch those exhausted faces turn angry and alarmed.

For some reason he thought again of that stupid needle and too big camel. Maybe it wasn't wealth in itself that blocked a rich man's progress into heaven. Maybe it was what he did to get that wealth. A string of words—ruthless, devious, greedy, cruel and inhumane—came to mind.

"What do you think, girl?" he asked the still figure. She said nothing. Faced with her continued silence, he heaved a sigh and left the room, snapping the padlock shut behind him.

The madam waited for him at the bottom of the stairs. "You're still going to take her out of here in four days?" she asked before rushing to assure, "It's not that I don't appreciate the money but, it is extra work and, well, business has picked up. We could use that extra room."

His smile felt like a grimace but he answered readily enough as he clapped the bowler onto his head, "Yes, we are still on schedule. She should be out of your hair in four days. I'll let you know if that changes but I don't expect that it will."

It was the ninth day since Rebecca Levy had gone missing. Early morning gusts drove welcome rain against the windows. In a few more months, everyone would be tired of the drizzle but, after days of searing heat, people would celebrate this wetting. Except maybe others like himself, Sage thought to himself. That was because he had to drag himself out from between his dry sheets, don his John Miner outfit and hit the wet streets. On the brink of feeling sorry for himself, he remembered that the laundry workers would also be out in force, standing in the rain before the locked doors with their newly-made picket signs.

He'd escorted his mother and Rachel Levy back to the boarding house, warning them that the pencil fellow said someone had been following them. Perhaps it was the man who'd taken Rebecca.

Mae was unsurprised at the news, saying, "I figured as much. My shoulders kept feeling the so-and-so's beady eyes on us. I talked to Mr. Eich about it. He said he'd glimpsed someone a time or two but it wasn't enough for him to be sure. With all the factories around here there's plenty of folks on the street just before and after work."

This further alarmed Sage so he went to find Fong to make plans. One of Fong's cousins would follow in addition to Eich. That way, if the two women separated, Fong's man would follow one while Eich stuck with the other. Fong immediately set off to make the arrangement. More than once Fong had drawn on his cousins' skills—sometimes at the loss of their own life. Maybe their willingness to assist was because of Fong's reputation as a tong conciliator or it was simply the habit of mutual aid they relied on to survive in the hostile white world. Something else played a part too. Fong once told him that the Chinese also yearned to see economic and social justice in their adopted country. These were the thoughts running through Sage's mind as he dressed and again exited through the tunnel into the cooler but wet day.

Fortunately, the rain had ceased and he merely had to navigate his way around puddles. Once across the river, he avoided walking dirt streets churned into muddy morasses by early morning wagon wheels. Sure enough, about forty people, mostly women, stood before the Sparta Laundry, holding aloft hand-painted placards. "Unfair to Workers," said one. "Women Laundry Workers Are Being Abused," said another. "Women's Health Not Profits," declared a third. Someone started a rousing union song and all joined in.

Sage was relieved to see Eich's cart parked nearby. That meant the ragpicker was somewhere close and so was Mae Clemens. Twitching willow fronds high up in the willow tree drew Sage's gaze upward where he saw the features of a grinning Chinese face. It was one of Fong's regulars. What an agile fellow, he thought as he smiled back. For now, Rachel and Mae were safe.

No longer worried, Sage turned and strolled away south. As he hoped, the United States Laundry was open and operating with steam billowing from its high, open windows. He entered the waiting room and found a woman clerk standing behind the counter. He asked her if he could speak to the manager.

"I am sorry but Mr. Finley is not here at present," she said, before adding apologetically, "He's asked me to tell folks that he, regretfully, has no open positions at present. We know the other laundries have locked out and wish we could hire their workers. But, we just can't."

"Mr. Finley intends to stay open?" he probed.

The woman's answering nod was hesitant. "If he can." Then in a rush, she let her outrage spill forth, "He thinks those scamps from the laundry association have threatened our supplier. The supplier should have delivered new chemicals to us on Saturday. When Mr. Finley sent word, asking where the chemicals were, the supplier wrote back that it had run into difficulties. That's where he is now, across the river at the chemical company."

"What will Mr. Finley do if the supplier doesn't deliver the chemicals?" Sage asked, remembering that he'd watched Cobb's entourage call upon a chemical business the week prior. To verify his suspicion he asked, "Would that be the City Chemical Supply Company?"

The woman nodded glumly. "That's the only place in town that sells steam laundry chemicals. If they won't sell to us, then we can't continue doing laundry—plain and simple. Mr. Finley will have to close us down." Sage saw the worry in the woman's eyes. He wished he could reassure her but suspected the chemical company had bowed to Cobb's demands. It wasn't a novel tactic. When the majority of its regular customers threatened to withdraw future business unless a supplier complied with their wishes, the supplier inevitably complied. There'd been a recent news story in *The Daily Journal* about a discrimination lawsuit making its way through the courts. In that case, anti-union lumber mills were refusing to provide a unionized construction company with lumber. They hoped to turn the construction company against its own workers.

Sage could think of nothing to say. The United States Laundry was in a dire situation. So was this woman, since a closed laundry meant unemployment for all its workers. She must have seen sympathy in his face, however, because she smiled faintly and said, "I expect Mr. Finley will think of something."

When a second downpour let loose, Rachel declared the picketing over. She asked that everyone head toward the union hall across the river. Mae wandered over to stand beside Eich who was sheltering in a nearby doorway. "You go on and find yourself some place to dry off, Herman. Rachel and I will go over to the union hall with the whole group," she told him.

"There'll be plenty of folks around so we'll be in no danger. Also," she nodded toward the upper branches of the willow tree, "thanks to Mr. Fong, we are being watched over by our Asian angel. So, you needn't worry."

For once, Eich didn't object. She could tell by the deep lines and slight pallor of his face, that he was good and tired. His guard duty had to be cutting into his sleep. Even though his lean-to was crude, its cot was still much more comfortable than bedding down on the ground. The heavy rains last night probably meant he'd slept curled up in some doorway.

"Alright, Mae," Eich said, but raised a cautionary finger, "But, I do so only because I am trusting that you will stay with the group and wait at the hall until I am outside to escort you two back here across the river."

She'd given Eich those assurances and set off with the others for the union hall. It was already crowded when they arrived. In the far corner, a huge pot of soup simmered on the cook stove. People lined up to receive full bowls, hunks of bread and a sympathetic smile from the volunteers drawn from the ranks of other unions. Mae looked around and saw the Caroline woman washing bowls while engaged in lively conversation with the woman drying them. For a new gal, that Caroline sure does have a way of wiggling right into the middle of things, Mae thought sourly before Rachel beckoned her to join a group of women. Soon after, Mae stopped thinking of the newcomer all together.

About an hour later there was a disturbance at the door as four women swept in. They were uniformly dressed, wearing well-tailored walking suits, their skirts grazing the tops of shiny dress boots. Mae had seen these women before. They frequented Mozart's during the lunch and tea hours. She had filled their water glasses and overheard their conversations often enough to know why they were here. These were some of the city's well-off suffragette leaders. She watched them approach the union president and engage him in discussion. Soon faces flared red and voices rose. The president gestured for Rachel to join him and she, in turn, grabbed Mae's hand, tugging her along.

Mae couldn't pull away. It would cause a scene. The four women would for sure notice her. At the same time, if she got too close they'd remember her face from Mozart's Table. She just hoped that her rain bedraggled hair, shabby clothes and averted face wouldn't trigger their recollection of the restaurant hostess who'd sometimes seated and served them.

She took care to stand a bit behind Rachel but soon realized she needn't have worried. The four women were too incensed to even notice her. One of them shook with anger as she shrilled, "We women must insist that you drop this campaign for a nine-hour day."

The union president responded in a tight, overly patient tone that signaled he was repeating himself—probably not for the first time, "The working conditions are brutal, these women need to get relief however they can."

"You are undercutting our campaign for equal rights," cried another of the suffragettes. "You are basing your whole nine hour campaign on the claim that women are the 'weaker' sex and deserve 'special' protection." She practically spat the words, "weaker" and "special."

Another one of the four added, in a more measured tone, "You can't possibly believe that these women," here her sweeping hand indicated the laundry workers gathered around the uproar, "are in any way less capable, strong or enduring than men."

The president shook his head. "As I keep telling you, you are missing the point. We don't think any human, man or woman, should have to work sixty hour weeks. But we have to start somewhere. This is how we begin to chip away—by focusing on the laundry women. Their job is the hardest, most brutal. And if that means we must pander to ignorant men by calling these women 'the weaker sex' then so be it!" The president was bristling as he began to lose his temper, sending a dull red creeping up his face.

His words had no impact because the four women jumped in, repeating their protests, even stepping on each other's points.

Rachel moved to face the women. "You are correct. Some of us believe that not only are women not the weaker sex, but that many of us are stronger physically, mentally and morally than men. But, that is not the point. The point is that the steam laundry job is killing, maiming and brutalizing mostly women. Whatever it takes, we are going to stop that."

One of the women sniffed, "Hah! All I see before me is a traitor to her sex."

Before Rachel could defend herself, the newcomer Caroline stepped forward, one hand briefly touching the small cross at her neck. "Ma'am," she said politely, "I notice the four of you are wearing gloves, may I ask that you please remove them so that we may look at your hands?"

That request took the women completely by surprise, so much so that they began removing their gloves before they thought to question the reason. Soon eight hands were bare. Everyone could see that at least three of them displayed the pale fingers and unblemished hands of those who used hired help to keep their households.

Caroline turned to her co-workers and raised an eyebrow. Some of the women understood immediately and stepped forward, their bare hands extended. Soon red, cracked, and scarred hands appeared next to those smooth white ones. It was a sharp contrast. As if two different species were involved: so much so that the suffragettes' hands vanished behind their skirts.

Caroline, her tone calm and eyes kind, quietly drove home the point, "These women suffer daily. Yes, you are absolutely right. Women need equal treatment and your fight is a noble one. But, you must recognize that our fight is also noble. We fight to relieve our suffering now, today. And to relieve the suffering of our families, now, today. We are not abstract human beings. We cannot sacrifice our families' health and happiness; we cannot ignore our pain and suffering, in order to obtain some future goal for some unknown future people. We are here today. We must fight for ourselves, today."

There was such entreaty in the young woman's face that, on one hand, Mae felt her suspicions weaken. On the other hand, she wondered why such an obviously educated woman was working in a steam laundry.

These thoughts took place even as quiet nods rippled through the surrounding crowd. One of the four suffragettes seemed to understand because her eyes filled with tears and her gaze dropped to the reddened hands still extended toward her.

Silence settled over the group until harrumphing in irritation, the most hectoring of the four turned and headed toward the door. The others followed, though the teary one cast an apologetic look over her shoulder as she exited.

EIGHTEEN

"Where's the big fellow?" Farley asked the waiter as he nodded toward the podium at the entrance.

The waiter paused, glanced at the podium and said, "Oh, you mean Mr. Solomon. He does not work the breakfast setting, only lunch and dinner."

Farley saw Cobb enter the restaurant and gestured for the waiter to fill the empty cup across from him. "My guest may also want to order breakfast. Please bring a second menu."

The frown on Cobb's face telegraphed that the Sparta Laundry manager was in a foul mood. Sure enough, the first words out his mouth were, "Fine kettle of damn rotten fish!" He grabbed the just-delivered menu and snapped it open, even as he flicked a dismissive hand at the waiter.

"What's happened?" Farley asked, frantically trying to anticipate what he or one of his three operatives had done wrong. Sinclair was a problem because that Rachel woman was still on the loose and stirring up trouble. But, the other two operatives were right where they were supposed to be.

"That damn trade union council plans to open up its own steam laundry. That's what's wrong," Cobb said.

Farley repressed a sigh of relief and showed what he hoped was a sympathetic face. "Surely, that will take some time. They can't do it overnight. We can go ahead with our plan. Everything should be over and done with by the time they can get a new steam laundry operational."

Cobb scowled, clearly not appreciating Farley's optimism. "That would be true if they started from scratch. But I have reason to believe they are secretly negotiating for an already existing steam laundry. If that's true, they can start operating the minute the ink dries on the sales contract."

"Which laundry's thinking of selling? Did you find that out?" Farley asked.

The waiter appeared and Cobb barked, "Scrambled eggs, toast and jam."

Farley looked up and said in a much milder tone, "The same, please," before leaning forward to ask again, "Who, do you know who?"

Cobb's lips twisted. "I don't know who, damn it. But it has to be a member of the association. The two other laundries, the U.S. and the Albina, are going to make a boatload of money as long we've got our operations locked down. No way either one would sell right now. So, it has to be someone in the association."

Farley leaned back, put a thumb to the side of his chin and absent-mindedly stroked while he thought. As he did so, he noticed that Cobb was twitching in his chair. The laundry manager might hide his fear from the others in the association but Farley knew the meaning of Cobb's twitching and bluster. The man was scared.

Farley leaned forward. "Okay, then. The first step is to figure out who is thinking of selling to the unions."

"And, the second step?"

"Ah," said Farley, "The second step is to take whatever action we must to stop the sale."

"So, how are we going to accomplish that first step?" Cobb's voice was tight with anxiety, the strain in his face willing Farley to come up with a solution. At that moment, Farley became aware that the waiter was standing at their elbows. At Farley's nod the black man silently slipped two dishes before them, filled their cups and departed.

How long was he standing there? Farley wondered but said nothing. Instead he smiled widely, "We're in luck. My operatives are in a good position to make that very inquiry."

Mary Harris sent word through Sage's lawyer friend, Philander Gray, that "John Miner" should call at the Society for Social Hygiene's offices first thing that morning. Donning his businessman's duds, Sage was soon on his way. Yesterday's rain had washed away the dust, turning every tree lushly green. Telling himself he only wanted to walk beneath the trees, Sage detoured to the Park Blocks. There he strolled down the middle of the long green stretch, slowing only when he reached a point across from Lucinda's house. She was nowhere in sight so he didn't pause. Walking on, disappointment and relief warred inside him. If he'd encountered her, he didn't know what he would have done. Still, he admitted ruefully to himself, a part of him yearned to see her.

The offices of the women activists were abuzz when he got there. Four women bustled in right behind him and immediately closeted themselves inside an inner office with the door shut.

He soon forgot them because Mary Harris quickly arrived on the heels of the receptionist who'd gone to tell her of his arrival. She was still dignified and still wearing her dead-black, high-necked bombazine dress but her smile was sunny as she said, "Mr. Miner, I do believe I have a little bit of news for you. Come back to my office."

As they walked toward her office, Sage heard a loud argument break out. He thought it came from the room the four women had entered. Mrs. Harris caught sight of the curiosity on his face and said, unapologetically. "The suffragettes are quite a lively bunch. Their work is a credit to us all. I understand they suffered a setback yesterday afternoon and are meeting about it." Sage merely nodded.

Entering her office, Mrs. Harris directed him to a chair. This time she closed the door behind them. That was progress of some sort. She sat down in her own chair and cleared her throat. For some reason she had a little smile on her lips as she asked, "I don't suppose you would be interested in joining our little foray tonight? The Reverend Doggett is going to lead a parade through the vice district, entreating the prostitutes to abandon that life."

Sage's eyebrows rose. He'd seen such parades and heard the hymn singing. "No," he said quickly. "Besides, does that even work?" Mostly he'd seen rotten vegetables thrown from second story windows pelting similar parade participants.

Her smile was brief, as if acknowledging the futility of such efforts. "Our colleagues in Chicago tell us that once and a while it works. They say it makes those in the parade feel like, just for a moment, the good people of the city have reclaimed the worst of the streets. I figured you'd say 'no' but I felt obligated to ask.

"Now, I don't have a specific name for you," she said, swiftly changing direction. "But, there is definitely a new procurer in town from Chicago. My source," here she seemed to be trying the journalistic word on for size, "says the strange part is that he doesn't seem to be procuring any girls."

Sage wrinkled his forehead. "If he's not doing business, how do they even know he's a procurer?"

Mary Harris tapped the edge of a rubber eraser on her desk, her face thoughtful as she said, "That's what is most interesting. He went to the bars where prostitutes and procurers hang out. At every one he asked whether anyone knew of a madam who was hard up for money. Of course, none of them would tell him anything until he produced his bona fides."

"Bona fides?" Sage echoed.

"He had to give them the name of a well-known Chicago madam. They telegraphed her to receive confirmation that he was who he said he was."

"Sounds like they were being cautious."

She smiled sweetly as she gave him the jolt. "Yes, Mr. John Adair, it seems they were better aware than I that a fellow might fib when it comes to saying who he really is."

Surprise spurred Sage into speech, "How did . . . ."

She didn't let him finish. "I knew I had seen you somewhere. Last night, I remembered. You were lunching at the Portland hotel and my friend pointed you out as the owner of that very fancy restaurant, Mozart's Table. This morning, I asked around and got your name." She leaned forward to confide, "Really, Mr. Adair, you aren't the kind of man a lady forgets any time soon. Especially, with that white blaze at your temple."

Sage's face flushed hot and he struggled to keep his voice calm as he said, "I am afraid you've caught me red-handed. I do apologize for misleading you, Mrs. Harris. It's just that white slavery is unsavory. Not a subject for polite society. I thought it better people didn't know that I was in any way associated. Bad for business, you know."

She relaxed in her chair. "I figured as much. And, I won't reveal your secret or your involvement in this quest. I'll do everything I can to help you find the girl." At this she straightened once again and said, "I do have a bit more information."

"What?" Sage asked, glad to see the conversation move onto safer ground. He didn't want to dwell on who or what he really was because it inevitably led to him telling even more lies. With some people, he didn't mind lying. But with people like this woman, guilt always crept in.

"The stranger apparently found an answer to his question because the next time my source saw him, he was telling everyone that he'd solved his problem," she told him.

"I don't suppose your source got the name of this fellow?" Sage asked.

She shook her head regretfully. "No, he tried. But he has to be careful or folks will get suspicious. He did give me a description." She picked up a piece of paper and read from it. "Dark hair and eyes. In his thirties. Well-groomed. Always wears a bowler hat."

Sage tried to swallow his disappointment but knew it weighed down his words, "Darn, that sounds like half the men in Portland."

She nodded sympathetically. "I know. My friend is trying to get more specifics but that Chicago fellow isn't coming around anymore."

"Do you think he's left town?" As he spoke the question, fear snaked through him. If the procurer left town that would mean Rebecca was gone as well.

"I sincerely hope not," she replied, showing that she too understood the implication.

Sage left the Society's office with a muddled mind. Was it be possible that they'd already moved Rebecca Levy out of Portland? Then hope surged as he realized that there was one important thing about that Chicago-based procurer—he wore a bowler hat. And the pencil fellow was sure that a man with a bowler hat was still following Rebecca's sister, Rachel. The fear he'd felt in Mary Harris's office eased a bit as he let certainty take hold. Sure a lot of men wore bowler hats but it was still too coincidental. The Chicago man, with his odd inquiry and failure to make an effort to procure women, had to be the same man following Rachel Levy. So, that meant he just had to find the bowler-wearing man, follow him and liberate Rebecca from whatever locked room they held her in. He picked up his pace. It was time to find Mr. Fong.

Mae sidled up to Caroline, grabbed up a cloth and began drying the soup bowls Caroline was washing. It was the second day of the lockout. Every time she looked, the young woman was helping to sort donated clothes, stirring the soup or otherwise making sure she remained in the midst of things. "A real paragon of helpfulness," Mae grumbled to herself before deciding she needed to learn more about the young woman.

"I notice you wear a cross around your neck. Are you religious?" Mae asked.

Caroline smiled and nodded. "Yes, I was raised Catholic."

"Did you attend school at St. Mary's Academy?" Mae probed.

"No," Caroline answered before quickly changing the subject, "I never thought the Association would lock us out. Did you?"

"I suspected they would. Once we got down to the one issue of the nine-hour day, there wasn't much else they could do. Either control the timing and scare folks with a lockout or wait for a strike, not knowing when it was going to come," Mae told her.

The woman's brown eyes studied her appraisingly. "It sounds like this isn't your first labor dispute?" she said, her tone rising into a question at the sentence's end.

Mae had the uncomfortable feeling that the tables had turned and now she was the one being interrogated. "No, it's not the first. How about you?" she asked to deflect further questions.

Caroline's eyes widened innocently. "Oh, this is my very first union fight. I'm afraid it's all new to me."

"I take it you've never worked in a laundry before," Mae pushed, not wanting to lose her advantage.

This comment triggered a shy smile before Caroline responded, "You've got me there, I'm afraid. I know very little about steam laundries. Though, I have to say, this past month has done a lot to educate me."

Her answers are slippery, Mae thought. It didn't seem like the woman was lying but neither did she think Caroline was entirely forthcoming. "So, are you intending to stay working in laundries or has this experience soured you?" she asked.

This time, there was a hesitation before Caroline responded, "I guess I'll need to see what comes of this," here she waved to encompass the room full of women. "I may stay working in laundries or maybe turn my hand to something else."

Mae looked down at those hands, noted the woman had a writer's bump on her right, middle finger. It took a lot of writing to make a bump that big. This woman was no stranger to schooling. She decided to take the plunge, asking, "Why would an educated woman like you be doing laundry work?" She asked knowing her tone was too blunt to sound friendly. She was tired of chicken-stepping around.

Her question rattled the girl, because Caroline suddenly looked around and said in a high pitched, excited voice, "Oh, there's Gertrude,

I've been looking for her ever so long. I have to catch her before she leaves." Seconds later she'd turned and was moving across the room, leaving Mae's question unanswered.

Mae watched her greet another woman and so caught the furtive look Caroline cast back in Mae's direction. Mae pretended she didn't see that look, glancing away as she raised her hands to fuss with the bun at the nape of her neck. Even as she engaged in the ruse, Mae was thinking, "Well, little Missy with the cross around your neck. You might be slippery as a wet frog but I'm that falcon overhead and both of my beady eyes are going to stay fixed squarely on you."

NINETEEN

IT WAS DARK BUT STILL noisy in the saloon's rear corner. The late evening light outside didn't compete with the few electric bulbs overhead. Sinclair gave a mental smirk when he saw Farley twitch uneasily at the rowdiness around them. Sinclair had spent countless hours in such places. Heck, at age fourteen, he'd run one like it—soon after its owner, the madam of the adjoining brothel, had taken him into her bed.

So, it was with a practiced eye he tallied how many men had reached the point of being susceptible to the come hither looks of the saloon's whores and how many others needed more boozing to reach that state.

At least that was his first analysis. But then he started seeing the scene differently. First, he noticed that this saloon could make some claim to cleanliness. Once you looked past the tobacco-stained floor, the scarred tables looked clean and the glasses lined up behind the bar lacked greasy smears. And, the customers weren't the hop-headed wastrels, petty thieves and confidence men of Chicago's Near West Side.

Mostly they looked like lonely men who belonged to distant families. The women also seemed less hard. Beneath the face paint, he saw hopeless young faces with tired, world-weary eyes. Sinclair reached forward, grabbed his nearly full shot glass and gulped it empty. He reached for the whiskey bottle Farley had bought.

Farley shifted uncomfortably and said, "Hey now, I don't need you drunk for this meeting. In fact, you better be sharp as a tack because we have to make plans." Once Sinclair nodded his agreement, Farley leaned forward so he wouldn't have to shout above the piano's tinny notes and the rough voices now raised in song. "I'm glad you arrived a bit early. I have to tell you, the two men we're meeting are a bit short on character though you might not realize it looking at them.

"Still they do their job. I've used them before. They know how to blend in. More than one owner has tried to hire them permanently once we've won the battle. I always tell them, "Oh no, sir. You don't want to bring these creatures into your nest. They succeed at what they do because they crave the excitement of lying, cheating and thumping. That is what they like best—not holding down a full time job."

Sinclair had never worked in the management spy business before. Sure he knew about hired thugs, large numbers of them frequented the saloons and bawdy houses. He had to agree with Farley's assessment of their character. But, Farley was a businessman, out to make money. "Seems like you could earn a finder's fee if they hired them," Sinclair commented.

Farley grinned wolfishly as he said, "Ah, but you see, my goal is to convince the owner to put one of my better operatives permanently into his plant or business. I promise him that, for a small monthly fee, my operative will alert me if an organizer comes around and tell me which workers are disgruntled so the owner can fire them before they can cause trouble. The beauty of the setup is that I just start someone working there who's willing to snitch off his co-workers for a bit of extra cash each month."

Sinclair's nose wrinkled in disgust before he could suppress it. Farley noticed, saying, "Oh come now, as long as men have worked together, at least one of them will tattle to the boss. They want to get favorable treatment or power over others or even a pat on their head. Bosses discover right quick the fellow who is willing to betray his co-workers. You can bet they've always rewarded that willingness. Besides, what's better? Having the tattler be someone with a grudge or who wants your job to go to a friend? Or, do you think you'd get fairer treatment from an outsider who is being paid for accuracy? Me, I'd choose the latter."

Sinclair wasn't sure that someone who needed to justify their continued pay would act more fairly than a garden variety traitor. But, hell, snitching even happened in whorehouses. Before he could respond, two men entered the saloon and looked around. Spotting Farley, they sauntered over. "Hey, there Mr. Farley," said the blond one. Sinclair studied them, trying to see the venality that had to dwell within their souls. He saw nothing of it. They looked like ordinary men stopping in for a beer after work. Shabby clothes but clean. Hair trimmed even if not expertly styled.

Farley gestured them into seats at the table and poured each a whiskey, his manner as gracious as a wealthy man playing host. Each man grabbed a glass, raised it and drank. When Sinclair looked into their faces he saw both had eyes hard as pebbles.

"This gentleman here is Paul," Farley said and then turned to Sinclair to say, "And this is Bill and Tom. Leastwise, that's what we're calling them today." Everyone mumbled acknowledgements and fell silent until a disturbance at the door snapped their attention in that direction. A highly agitated drunk plunged in off the street and began hollering, "The goddamned whorehouse is on fire! It's gonna burn up!"

His yells sent chairs scraping across the floorboards as people leapt to their feet. One man shouted back, "What goddamned whorehouse, you fool? We got one on every corner!"

"It's that wood house, down there by the rail yards," the drunk shouted back. His words hit Sinclair's gut like a fist. She flashed into his mind's eye, surrounded by leaping flames—drugged, tied and trapped behind the nailed boards. Already on his feet, he glanced in Farley's direction before heading toward the exit.

By the time he slammed through the batwing doors, he was moving at a fast clip. Since he hadn't thought to look beneath the doors for feet coming in, he nearly bowled over a fellow who was entering. Only the man's swift side step prevented the collision.

Despite his panic, Sinclair's early training in good manners made him throw the man an apology without slowing. That other man said nothing. But the fleeting glimpse Sinclair caught of his face showed the man's concern rather than any anger. Once in the street, Sinclair began running. As he did so, he looked ahead to the east. Sure enough, the orange glow of conflagration was rising in a twilight blue sky. Fire bells clanged to life at a nearby fire station. Only then did Sinclair realize he'd left his bowler hat behind. When he'd jumped up, the hat had tumbled from his lap and rolled beneath the table.

Sage just missed getting knocked to the ground when the frantic man exited the saloon. That mishap surely would have made his entrance remarkable, which was the very last thing he wanted. When shadowing people you wanted to blend in and not be at all noteworthy. "Be the dark within the dark," Fong would say. Well, the collision hadn't happened, he was still upright. Besides, the folks inside the saloon were too riled up at the news being shouted by the drunk Sage had just seen stagger into the saloon. Apparently there was a fire somewhere.

He slid past the crowd around the drunk and found a seat beside the wall. From there, he could observe most of the saloon. He was careful to appear uninterested in the three men who were just retaking seats at their table. Even so, he shifted so that he could watch them from the corner of his eye. Unfortunately, none wore a bowler hat. But, he told himself not to fret. Solomon's nephew had overhead Farley tell Cobo that there were three operatives. So far, they'd only found two. Maybe it was Farley's third operative who wore the bowler.

Sage ordered his beer and started sipping. He'd had worse. At least it wasn't dirty water with a smidgen of beer. If he'd had any doubts about the ability of Fong's cousins to find and follow the right men, those doubts vanished the second he spotted Farley sitting with the two fellows he'd followed from a boarding house in Northwest Portland.

Although Sage was turned away, his ears were straining to hear like a frightened rabbit's. It was a wonder they didn't raise his hat. He desperately wanted to hear what these management spies were planning to do for the Laundrymen's Association.

At first the conversation was too low to hear over the uproar about the fire. Once that calmed down, bits and pieces floated to him.

Farley's low rumble was the hardest to hear though Sage's ear caught him saying the word "drivers." One of Farley's companions complained about having to drive horses. The other complained about Portland's lack of what he called "sensible plotting." Their complaints stirred a vague sympathy in Sage who was skittish around horses and who had, more than once, gotten lost trying to find his way around the city's crumpled landscape.

He kept his face averted. Farley might recognize him from the Portland Hotel. And, as for the other two, he'd memorized their faces while following them. Those faces made him sad. They both looked like decent men who earned barely enough to keep their clothes clean, food in their stomachs, a roof over their heads and a beer in their hands once the workday was over. It was their unremarkable looks that made him sad because it was so easy for them to pose as union brothers. It was dishonest men like these who betrayed the strikers and caused people to get arrested or sometimes killed. He knew because his father was a man like these two. His mother hadn't given him the details but he knew his father had fit in, just like these men. And like with them, betrayal came easy to John Adair, Sr.

He shook loose from those thoughts and again tried to hear. This time his reward was Farley's voice sounding clearly, "Cobb wants the deal stopped. I've got the one angle covered, but you men need to do your part. You nose around, lift up a few rocks and discover who it is. You do that and you'll get a bonus."

Find out who it is? Who what is? And, what angle? Sage took a big swallow of his beer, trying to wash down the frustration he felt hearing these snippets of sentences.

By this time, the fire outside had been forgotten. The lull inspired the piano player to pound the keys into a rousing march—one that everyone felt obliged to sing with lusty vigor. The men at the next table might as well have moved into another room. As long that the piano was making noise, Sage would hear nothing more. He forced himself to unclench his jaw. As Ma would say, "Don't try to carry water in a holey bucket." Fong, on the other hand, would advise him to "breathe deep, relax belly." So, he stopped trying to eavesdrop and followed Fong's advice.

When the men at the neighboring table began to stir, as if readying to leave, Sage stood and exited out the door ahead of them.

"I don't believe it. She's been working her heart out. The women like her. I've seen nothing but compassion from her."

They'd been having the heated discussion all the way across the bridge. Rachel wasn't giving an inch.

"Look, I'm not saying we take her behind the outhouse and thump her. I'm only saying we need to be cautious where Caroline Stark's concerned," Mae said in a patient voice.

"Mae, that's not how I work. I'm about building unity, not about turning on folks who've done nothing but try to help." Rachel's voice was less strident, almost as if she were convincing her own self of what she was saying.

Poor girl, Mae thought to herself. Grief and worry about her sister, losing her job and now shouldering the responsibility for her suddenly unemployed co-workers had the gal hanging on by her fingernails. Mae pondered the strength of the young woman at her side. On one hand she was too young to carry such burdens. On the other hand, her youthful energy and optimism might help her jump hurdles that would slow down an older person. Mae grabbed the other woman's arm and gently tugged her to a halt.

"I'm just asking that you move slow and careful where Miss Caroline Stark is concerned. Don't take her to your bosom just yet. Don't give her access to all of your information. Something about her isn't right."

Rachel's face grew stormy, "Darn it Mae, you keep saying "something's not right" about Caroline but you can't tell me anything more. I am not going to turn down help from such a capable person on the basis of that. It's not fair. It's not right." Rachel turned and resumed walking, Mae still at her side.

"Rachel, have you ever felt little prickles on your neck and then turned to find someone watching you?"

"No. I can't say that I have."

Mae knew this was an honest answer because the girl was a strider. She'd stomp toward her goals and woe to anyone getting in her way. If Rachel thought about it at all, she'd probably figure there was no sense worrying about something before it happened.

They reached the end of the trestle road that ran from the bridge end across the riverside marshland to dry land. A few blocks south, sparks shot to the darkening sky from beneath the wire netting of a lumber yard burner. Boat traffic on the river had ceased for the night. On the river's west bank sailing ships gently tugged against their mooring ropes. The docks alongside were empty and still. For the first time, Mae became aware that very few people walked the eastside streets this late in the day and that the light was fading fast. Mae glanced behind and saw that their Chinese shadow. Funny how reassured she felt at seeing him.

"Rachel, I used to be like you. I believed in people who were helpful, friendly, and smart. I too wanted to think the best of people. But I learned, in the hardest way possible, that I also need to trust that little seed of doubt I sometimes have about folks." Mae stopped there, not wanting to say anymore about her husband's and others' betrayals.

"Are you saying you think Caroline has something to do with Rebecca's disappearance?" Rachel asked in an incredulous voice.

"No. Absolutely not. But I am saying her presence in the laundry just doesn't make sense."

"So what if she seems to be educated? People fall on hard times. Shoot, Rebecca and I were going to be teachers until our mother and father died in that railway accident. We still hope to be," she added softly.

Then her voice became stronger as she said, "Don't you see Mae? Caroline does everything I ask her to do and better than anyone else could. The other women, they're wonderful but they have kids to care for and most of them, bless their hearts, can barely read. I need someone like Caroline to head up the job-finding committee, to go talk to prospective employers in a way that represents us well." Here she looked at Mae and said in a tone that was both chiding and joking, "And, you've refused to take that task on."

Mae sighed, "I have other responsibilities. Besides, someone has to keep an eye on you since you refuse to show any sense when it comes to your own safety."

"I don't have the time to worry about myself. I am too worried about Rebecca and the women at the laundry. I don't know how much longer I can go on." Fear caught at Rachel's voice.

Mae glanced sidewise at the young woman and saw that her eyes were full and her lips trembled. Softly, she made a concession, "Okay, how about this. How about you ask Caroline to compile a list of potential businesses that would hire our folks but you don't send her out to talk to them on behalf of the union? And," here she let her voice get stronger, "you don't let her into your inner circle. You don't let her know all of your plans, or help you make them?"

Rachel trudged along in silence, mulling over that suggestion. Finally, she nodded saying, "Okay, we'll start like that but I can't keep that up indefinitely. She's going to realize pretty quickly she's being shut out. We run the risk of losing her when that happens. This business is hard enough on everyone without them finding themselves under suspicion by the people they are trying so very hard to help."

"Three days," Mae said, "Give me three days."

Rachel laughed, "Okay Mae Clemens, you have three days in which to discover the secrets of the mysterious Caroline Stark."

TWENTY

Sinclair rounded the corner and nearly crashed into the crowd gathered to watch the fire. He looked at the whorehouse but couldn't see any flames, although smoke shrouded its faded clapboard front. "Where's the fire, where's the fire?" he shouted.

"Yeow, Mister. You just blasted my ear drum to smithereens," came an Irish brogue next to him. "The fire's in that yon corner house," the man said, pointing at an equally run down building two doors away from where Rebecca was being held.

Though relief washed through Sinclair, he continued to push forward. If sparks settled on nearby roofs, the whole block might explode in flames. Most of the structures were dry wood. He struggled closer, just in case.

As Sinclair reached the front of the crowd, a fire wagon clanged up the block and halted, its two horses skittering sideways on the cobblestones. Hoses were unfurled and soon water gushed out. One of the firemen climbed an outside staircase, lugging the hose nozzle. Sinclair shivered despite the warmth in the air. He'd seen more than one tenement fire in Chicago. In his opinion, they didn't pay firemen enough to risk their lives like they did. He'd seen more than one fireman vanish beneath a building's fiery collapse. And more than one electrocuted by dangling wires.

Above the noise from the fire fighters, he heard the screech of two angry women. They stood on the boardwalk, on the fire side of the street. Both slovenly dressed in tattered satin fancy dresses that were too tight to be flattering and too old to impress. Sinclair saw that Rebecca's keeper was one of them. *What the heck is this about?* The last thing he needed was for her to draw attention to that house. He crossed the street and sidled closer to hear their words.

"You Devil's bitch, I know you set the fire."

"Don't you be calling me a bitch, you Satan's whore," screeched Rebecca's imprisoning madam, Stella Block. "I didn't have nothing to do with the damn fire."

"I don't believe you! Just this morning you were a screaming at me about stealing your customers. I can't help it that your old flea bag of a pig sty drove them to my place."

"My house don't have fleas and you better stop shouting that or I'll smack you silly!" Stella yelled, stepping closer to the other woman. "It ain't my fault you don't tend to your fires. Hell, I betcha you was brewing up some of that piss-beer you force on your customers. Probably set the fire your own damn self."

"Why, you slutty, filth monger, don't you be talking about my beer. Your rotgut is famous in these parts for sending men to the toilet."

At that point, both women charged each other, their hands curved into claws. The ruckus drew the crowd's attention away from the fire, which looked like it was coming under control. Soon there were cries in the nature of, "Get her, Martha!" or "Punch out her lights, Stella." Sinclair could tell both women were well known and not particularly liked since those yelling switched their goading to whichever woman seemed to weakening in her anger. Sinclair had to chuckle. It was, after all, an entertaining and free diversion for the spectators, most of whom wore the raggedly clothes and tired faces of the itinerant poor.

"Blessed are you who weep now, for you shall laugh," came the unbidden saying into his mind with the power of a blessing. He didn't wonder where that thought came from. Of course, he knew. He'd heard it often enough over the years. Damn, would his head ever be rid of the empty platitudes?

There was grumbling from the crowd as a policeman, his beehive helmet bobbing above the spectators' heads, officiously pushed his way forward. *Time to remove himself from sight* Sinclair thought and slipped between the whores standing in Stella's doorway. Once inside, he ran up the stairs to the second floor. There he unlocked the padlock and stepped inside. Making his way to the cot, his hand found the lantern in the dark and lit it. Setting it on the packing crate, he hauled the chair next to the cot and sat.

Rebecca's eyelids fluttered. No wonder, given the uproar outside. He stepped over to look at the boarded window. He'd been right. Even if she were able to stagger over to the window, she couldn't pull off the boards. He wasn't sure he could do it. The big nails were driven deep into the window frame.

A stirring at his side brought his attention back to her. She lay there, looking at him, her eyes wide with fright. "It's okay," he said. "There was a fire down the block but they have it out now."

"A fire?" she repeated and struggled to sit up.

He leaned over, putting an arm around her shoulders, he helped her to sit up until her back was against the wall, her legs stretched before her on the bed. With one hand she yanked on the thin shift the madam had given her, making sure it was pulled down to her knees. Her other hand held the lapels of jacket she always wore tight together across her bosom.

He averted his eyes as he said, "When I heard there was a fire, I came to check that you were alright."

"Thank you," she said softly. He started, ready to defend himself, and then realized she was being sincere--not sarcastic.

"You'll soon have company. I'll be bringing your sister to you." He watched emotions wash across her face—happiness, wariness, and finally, fear.

She raised her hand imploringly. "Please, don't bring Rachel here. Please let her be."

He shook his head, feeling unwelcome but genuine regret as he said, "I'm sorry, Rebecca, I have no choice in the matter. My boss is getting upset. I promised him. I've been paid."

"We'll pay you! You can give him the money back. Just don't take Rachel," she pleaded.

He leaned forward, reaching for her. She scooted away from him, scrunching up in the corner of the cot. "Don't worry, I was just going to take your lapel pin. You can just hand it to me if you'd rather."

Her trembling fingers opened the clasp of the enameled pin. Once loosened, she yanked it free and thrust it toward him, saying, "May you back into a pitch fork and grab a hot stove for support."

The venom used to say the words far exceeded the venom attached to their meaning. He couldn't help it. He laughed. For a minute her face blanked, then she turned her head away but not before he saw her lips twitch.

"I don't think I've ever heard such a utterly terrifying curse," he told her, still chuckling.

She turned around and gave him a faint smile. "It was one of my mother's. She taught us that ladies never use curse words but curses were alright." After a moment's silence she added, "It was the first one that came to mind."

Although Fong's slippered feet silently entered the room, his passing stirred the air and Sage woke up. "What time is it?" he asked.

"Near ten o'clock in the morning," Fong answered as he set a tray down on the small table in the windowed alcove.

Sage crawled out of bed, wrapped himself in a cotton robe and sat at the table. On the tray was a silver coffeepot, two cups, a pile of biscuits and a bowl of strawberry preserves. He poured the coffee into the cups and reached for a biscuit, saying, "I didn't get in until 6:30 this morning.

"I know," Fong said, taking the other seat at the table. For a moment he said nothing, his long face pale and lined with fatigue.

"Oh, cripes. I suppose you spent the night following me around," Sage said, before adding, "When will I ever learn to see you doing that?"

"Couple times, you knew but you did not honor knowing." Fong took a swallow of coffee and began spreading preserves onto the white fluff of Ida's buttermilk biscuits.

Sage chewed as he thought back and yes, there had been a couple times when he had the uncomfortable feeling of eyes staring at the back of his head. "Maybe I did, but when I turned around I couldn't see anyone."

Fong nodded. "That is the way it should be. Look is not enough. You should lay trap when that feeling happens."

"And just how do I do that?" he asked, aware he sounded exasperated, but then, who wouldn't be after less than four hours of sleep?

"That is for you to figure out. Every situation different," came another one of Fong's confusing answers. He didn't wait for Sage's response before changing the subject, saying, "What is happening with mission?"

Sage took a bite of biscuit and chewed as he tried to order his thoughts. "Well," he began, "as you know, the laundry workers are locked out. So, they are using the union hall building as their base of operations. Other unions are chipping in with money, food, clothing. Some of the women are out lining up temporary jobs for folks. And, the Trades Council is in the process of buying a steam laundry, one they can run as a union-owned cooperative.

"Unfortunately, the delivery drivers' union isn't supporting the women but that doesn't hurt them at this point. For one thing, there's no clean laundry to deliver and no sense in picking up dirty laundry that'll not get cleaned. Of course, if the Laundrymen's Association hires scabs to work in the laundries, then the delivery drivers' lack of support will become a problem for the laundry workers.

Fong was sipping his coffee to which he'd added way too much sugar for Sage's taste. His friend smiled and said, "Chinese laundry cousins make out like bandits." He flashed his toothy grin before adding, "Some of them are bandits. Brand new customers are paying much." Here Fong shrugged his shoulders as if to say, "But, who can blame them? Steam laundries been driving them out of business."

"Yes, the lockout must be a real windfall for them. Same with the two steam laundries that haven't joined the owners' association. Still, I don't know how long those two laundries will be able to keep operating." Sage told Fong about the mysterious withholding of chemicals from the U.S. Laundry.

"What I suspect is that Cobb and his cohorts have extorted the owner of the chemical company, telling him to either withhold chemicals or else face the consequence of no orders from the association members once the laundry dispute ends."

That information brought a headshake from Fong, "I am sure you are right. Laundry owners already prove they are mean men," he said before asking, "Do we know anymore about missing Rebecca Levy? Cousin say he watch close sister Rachel and Mrs. Clemens. He see no one following close, except maybe two times. At boarding house, he sit in back while Mr. Eich sit out front."

"Tell the cousins to keep a sharp lookout for a man wearing a bowler hat. I talked to a pencil seller that Eich discovered. That fellow said that, before Rebecca was taken, both Rebecca and Rachel were followed by a man wearing a bowler hat. He said the same man has since followed Rachel and Mother."

"Does bowler hat work for laundry owners?" Fong asked, leaning forward.

"I don't know, yet. I've been trying to figure that out. Thanks to Solomon I got a good look at the Farley fellow staying at the Portland Hotel. Thanks to Solomon's nephew and your cousins, the two men they found and have been following are two of Farley's operatives. Last night, I saw them meet Farley."

"Did men wear bowler hat?" Fong asked.

"Nope, one wore a cap and the other a fedora. No bowler hat on anyone. That means I still have to keep following Farley to see whether his third operative is our man with the bowler."

"You sure Rebecca Levy still in town?"

Sage shook his head feeling dread settle atop his shoulders. "No, Mr. Fong, I'm not sure. If a regular white slaver snatched her off the street, she may be long gone. Thanks to Solomon's porters we can be certain she wasn't taken away by train. Still, there was nothing to stop them from using a wagon or coach or worse, one of the hundreds of ships going in and out of the harbor. I'm beginning to think that our only hope lies in the idea that her kidnapping is connected to the laundry workers' dispute. If so, there's a chance that, once the fight's over, they'll let her go."

Fong's already narrow eyes, narrowed further as he said, "If that case, you think she still alive?"

Sage nodded but said, "Yes, if as you say, that is the case. Why would Cobb's hirelings murder a totally innocent girl? That's why Farley's third operative is so important. Fact is, I should check with the pencil seller today to see if he's seen the bowler man since I last spoke with him."

Sage held up a finger, "One more thing. When I visited the hygiene society lady, she said white slavers always move their captives far from the home town right away. Otherwise, there is too big a chance that the woman will escape and find help from friends and family. If they took Rebecca Levy from Portland, it would have been to either Seattle or San Francisco. We know she wasn't taken away by train. If the kidnapper is bowler hat man, he hasn't had enough time to steal her away in a wagon—not if he's the one who has been following Mother and Rachel around. If he put her aboard a ship, then we're lost because they'd just lock her in a cabin until she's at sea. I just wish bowler hats weren't the most popular damn hat in the city. There must be thousands of men wearing one."

"But if reason for kidnap is laundry worker problem, why he take sister?"

Sage heaved a sigh. "That is the one big question. It seems like they would have gone straight after Rachel. Her sister had nothing to do with the laundry. She works as a clerk in the Olds and King department store. I tell you, I am really worried about that. It's the one thing that says the kidnapping has nothing to do with the labor dispute—that Rebecca Levy is in the hands of white slavers."

"What is next step? How can I and cousins help?"

"I found out that the two operatives I saw last night are definitely posing as laundry delivery drivers. They seem to be sticking close to that union's president when they're not at a laundry. I suspect they are making sure he stays in the laundry association's pocket."

"What laundries they work at?"

"That's why I stayed out all night. Lucky for us both it was a warm night. 'Anyways,' as Mother would say, since you followed me the whole time, you will remember that I was outside their boarding house early this morning. Lucky for us, they left together. As you saw, one went inside the American Laundry. The other continued on to the Union Laundry and also went inside.

"I hung around and found out that the owners are taking advantage of the lockout to repair and move their equipment about. I suspect that once they've finished with those chores, they might hire scabs to run the laundries. If that happens, the union may have to surrender the fight. It's a terrible job in the worst conditions but laundry women still get paid more there than if they got some other women's job. Not that it is that much more money. It's still only about a third of what men get paid, even though many of those women are raising families on their own."

"How can cousins help?" Fong asked again.

"Your men are already keeping Rachel and Mae safe. But if they could also keep watch on those two fellows posing as delivery drivers that would be very helpful. You and Solomon already have men on the street looking for a brothel that might be doubling as Rebecca's prison and for a woman matching her description being marched down the street or onto a ship. Solomon's train porter friends are watching out for any woman who might be traveling under duress. I can't think what more we can do to find Rebecca."

Sage stood up, walked to his wardrobe and pulled out his businessman's walking suit. "As for me, I plan on sticking to Farley like a bear to honey. If we're lucky, he'll meet with Mister Bowler Hat and we'll know for sure that Rebecca's kidnapping has something to do with the laundry dispute. But first, I'm going to go buy me some more pencils."

❀ ❀ ❀

Mae and Rachel walked beneath already hot morning sun to the picket line outside Sparta Laundry. There were only a token five picketers. The union members decided that, during work hours, there were too few passersby for picketing to matter much. This was because the Willamette River's east bank, where it wasn't flooded marshland, housed lumber yards, warehouses, industrial plants, steam laundries, canneries, and workingmen's boarding houses. Most everybody in the area was hard at work by sun-up and off the streets until sundown. Still, walking the picket line meant strike benefits. So, there was no shortage of volunteers wanting to cover the three-hour picketing shifts.

Once they'd seen all was calm on the picket line, Mae and Rachel left to catch the trolley heading across the river to the union hall. There, a number of people milled about, most of them women with children. The corner kitchen was scenting the air with the smells of boiling soup and baking bread. Mae recognized the flour sacks and vegetable bags stacked up in a nearby corner. They'd come from Mozart's kitchen. Of course, that was a secret. Sage's money and Mozart's resources frequently lightened people's loads but always in secret. At least for now, hunger wouldn't be a problem. Still, it was early days. No telling how long the dispute would go on. Soon rent money would become the problem.

Mae rolled up her sleeves and took a place at the drain board to dry dishes. Other women in the hall were sorting clothes and various other donations, arranging them on rough planks that had been set atop wooden sawhorses. Small tables stood in two corners to provide for private conversation. Those sitting at the tables looked to be either being interviewed or doing the interviewing. Paper banners draped the wall behind the tables proclaimed, "Job, Rent and Utilities Support". A third table was empty but the sign tacked to the wall above it announced "Temporary Jobs".

Rachel was right. They had to get moving on finding temporary work for the locked out workers. Even a week without pay meant disaster for many of these single parent families. Even the single women would soon find themselves in dire straits. Mae envisioned landlords turning women and children out onto the streets with nowhere to go. Already the city had too many people sleeping beneath bridges, in doorways and anywhere else that offered a bit of shelter. Her lips twisted. She knew how it felt to be that poor.

"Hey now, Mae. Stop scaring yourself like some ninny afraid in the dark wood," she muttered to herself. As a distraction, she let her eyes search the room for Caroline. At last she saw the young woman sitting on a chair, a group of children on the floor around her. She was reading to them from a book, frequently pausing to show them the pictures. Mae had to admit Caroline, with her wide brown eyes and ready smile, looked like a kind, honest person. Unfortunately, Mae had learned the hard way that a friendly face could disguise a lying heart.

Near the end of the afternoon, when most of the laundry women had drifted out of the hall, she saw Caroline pinning her hat onto her curly black hair. Mae hurriedly thrust her dish towel at another woman and strode over to where Rachel was talking with some women sitting in a knitting circle. Drawing the union representative aside, Mae said, "I'm going to try to take care of that problem we discussed last night. I need to leave now to do it. You promise me you'll go right home and stay there? Our Chinese shadow and Mr. Eich will be watching over you but don't take any chances. Promise?"

Rachel hugged Mae around the shoulders as she said, "Yes, yes, Mae. I promise you that I will go straight home and stay there until you come. I still say you're going to find out Caroline's a true blue union supporter and loyal to these women."

"That may be but I have to prove it to myself," Mae said. She shoved her hat down on her head, gently patted Rachel's cheek and headed toward the outside door, exiting right behind Caroline.

Once she reached the sidewalk, Mae halted, looking up and down the street, until she spotted Caroline strolling south down the street. Mae began to follow. She was so fixated on not losing sight of the other woman that she didn't see her Chinese follower hesitate before he shrugged and began to follow her. She was, after all, Mr. Fong's very treasured friend. His departure left Rachel with just a single bodyguard, the Jewish ragpicker poet, Herman Eich.

TWENTY ONE

"You ordered me to get to know the other laundry foreman and make sure they are still loyal to the association." Sinclair knew he sounded irritated but didn't care. Part of him wanted the job to be done and over no matter how. "Now you're complaining because Rachel Levy is still around. I can't be in two places at once." Sinclair felt his face redden and his anger grew hotter than the provocation justified.

Across the table, Farley's face also flushed but he held on to his temper. Leaning forward he hissed, "Keep your voice down Sinclair, I wasn't casting blame. I just wanted to know if you'd made any progress." Farley's eyes were stony as he added, "But just remember who's paying you and show a bit of respect. You've been at this job for over two weeks and so far your results have fallen short of what's needed."

Sinclair heaved a sigh. "Sorry, Mr. Farley. I've never been mixed up in a labor dispute before and nothing is going right. Anyway, I did manage to corner most of the foremen one-on-one in various saloons last night and in cafes this morning. They're a mixed bunch, near as I can tell. Some of them have quite a bit of sympathy for the women and aren't afraid to say it."

"Do you think they're feeding information to the union?"

"Nah, not yet. I just think most of them feel like they're between a rock and a hard place, and need to complain a little about the pinch," Sinclair said. He felt suddenly wary of identifying exactly which foremen were uncomfortable. They were men struggling with their consciences and shouldn't be punished for it. That wouldn't be right, he told himself.

"What are they saying when they complain?"

Sinclair made the instant decision not to repeat the foremen's more colorful comments. Farley might parrot everything Sinclair said to Cobb and the other association members. That would only rile things up and make it harder for the two sides to iron out their differences. And it would definitely cost men their jobs. Where do my loyalties lie? he wondered.

To Farley he said, "Mostly they talk about how hard the women work, how miserable the working conditions are and how unfair it is they get paid less than half what the drivers are taking home, and one-third less than the men running the wash tubs."

"And what's your response to those complaints?" Farley's eyes had narrowed.

Maybe he thinks I'm developing sympathies he doesn't like, Sinclair thought and quickly said, "I figure they'll talk more freely if I act igno-rant. So, mostly I ask questions. A few times I suggested that maybe the men were paid more because they have families to support or because their work requires more strength."

"What was their response?"

"Some of them laughed. Said I didn't know what I was talking about. Others seemed to agree. A few are one hundred percent on the bosses' side. They only worry that they'll lose money if the plant repairs finish before the lockout ends. They're angry at the women for making a fuss."

Farley heaved a sigh. "Well, that sounds about par for the course. I'll need you to write me up two lists. One naming those fellows likely to turn traitor and the other listing those who've stayed loyal. Cobb's expecting it."

Sinclair nodded in agreement, hoping his face didn't reveal his thoughts. He hadn't slept the night before; partly because he worried Farley would ask for just such lists. Handing over lists like that would get some men fired. He found that he liked the men who sympathized with the women better than he liked those who were only out for themselves.

He didn't know what he was going to do. Back in his seminary days, he might have prayed over the decision. But he'd lost all faith in that route. Maybe the best course was to delay until he figured out what to do. Damn this job and all these moral dilemmas.

Farley put his coffee cup down and again leaned forward. "Now to the matter of Rachel Levy." Farley held up a hand as if to stop any protest. "I know that you were checking out the foremen, so I didn't expect you to do anything about her last night. But, Cobb is going to ask. You know that."

"It's gotten more complicated. Like I told you, that older woman, Mae Clemens, is sticking to her like a barnacle. And now, I am beginning to think there's also a ragpicker fellow standing guard. I've even wondered whether a Chinaman is guarding them except that is too ridiculous. It seems like, once the ladies are indoors, the ragpicker hangs around the front of their boarding house. I've seen him there late at night, hunkered down in a nearby doorway. Now that Chinaman, he walks right on past. Maybe he works and stays around there someplace. I'm sure it's just coincidence."

Farley didn't say anything, simply stared at Sinclair with pale dead eyes. Sinclair fiddled with a spoon, tapping it against the tablecloth. Taking a deep breath he finally said, "So, I figure the only way I can grab Rachel Levy is to lure her away from the Clemens woman and make sure that ragpicker isn't around when I do it. I've got this," he said, removing a woman's lapel pin from his pocket. He laid it on the table in the full light of the afternoon sun streaming through the veranda windows. It was finely crafted enamel—a tiny pink rose, its petal edges tinted red, attached to dark green leaves and golden stem. "When she sees this pin, she'll come running. It's her sister's."

Sage was hurrying. He'd gotten a message from Solomon to come to the Portland Hotel. Unfortunately, he'd been delayed by a delegation of businessmen who wanted to discuss holding their monthly meetings at Mozart's. Much as he resented the delay, he'd feigned deep appreciation for their business and exercised rigid patience as he made careful note of all their requirements before graciously departing. Gaining the street, he'd raced to the hotel, despite knowing it was probably too late.

Swiftly threading through a cluster of exiting guests, Sage caught a fleeting glimpse of a familiar face but couldn't place it. Probably one of Mozart's patrons. He saw so many people in the restaurant every day. And, besides, Portland's business community was relatively small. Walk downtown streets often enough and a man would see plenty of familiar faces.

Inside, Solomon was waiting for him at the entrance to the dining room. "Sorry John, you just missed them."

"Oh damn. I hurried but got trapped by a group of customers and couldn't get away without talking to them. It took much longer than it should have."

"Well, things are quiet here. How about you have yourself a coffee and a rest and I'll wander over for a chat?"

"Yah, sure," Sage responded, not for the first time mentally grumbling about the class and race prejudice that forced them to adopt such ruses just to carry on a simple conversation.

Once Sage again sat at the room's least desirable table by the kitchen door behind a palm, Solomon wandered over. "They were here just for coffee so they didn't stay long. It was Farley and another man I haven't seen before."

"Can you describe that other man?"

Solomon shut his deep brown eyes, transforming his face, with its high cheekbones, into a sculpted mask. Not for the first time, Sage saw traces of an Indian heritage in that burnished copper face. There'd been a lot of such mixing in the Carolina's where Solomon was from.

The brown eyes opened and Solomon said, "White fellow. About five feet ten inches tall, dark hair, straight nose, intelligence in the eyes. No mustache, nothing special or unique about him. Sorry, John. After I sent a runner for you, things got really busy with a minor disaster in the kitchen. By the time I returned to the dining room they were gone."

Both men were distracted by the sight of a waiter closing the restaurant doors to the lobby. The doors wouldn't open again until just before the supper hours began. Solomon glanced at the chair across from Sage, "Do you mind?" he said, even as he sat down.

Once the doors closed, their table wasn't visible from either lobby or veranda so the two of them could sit together like normal people. Solomon didn't have to worry about the wait staff or kitchen help tattling to his bosses about this breech in racial etiquette because he'd recruited every single one of them.

A waiter hurried over to pour his maitre'd boss a cup of coffee and received Solomon's thanks in return. Once the fellow left them alone, Sage said, "I've spent a couple of frustrating days, Angus. I was able to find the two operatives but that elusive third fellow seems to always disappear just before I get there."

Seeing Solomon's interest, Sage told him, "Right now, I'm trying to figure out whether Farley's third operative is the same man who's been following the union representative, Rachel Levy, and Mae Clemens. If so, is he the same fellow who was following Rebecca Levy before she got snatched? Because, if he is, that might mean Rebecca is still in Portland."

Solomon was nodding, clearly tracking the convoluted tale. Sage continued, "Yesterday, I met with a pencil seller who'd seen the man. He's a little bit slow in his thinking but completely honest and alert. He gave me good news and bad news. The good news is that he's seen that man almost every single day. That means, if he kidnapped Rebecca, she's probably still here in Portland. He hasn't had time to take her away to some other major city.

Regret lengthened Solomon's face. "I am so sorry John that I didn't notice more about the man. We're short-handed today so I couldn't ask one of the fellows to follow him."

Sage reached across the table to grip the other man's hand, "Believe me, Angus, I understand. Restaurants are always chaotic. Heck, look how long I took responding to your message. Well, I better go. I need to hit the streets again. It's about time for Farley's delivery driver operatives to get off work. They're working short hours during the lockout."

Their chairs scuffed quietly on the floor carpet as both stood. After shaking hands, Sage headed toward the door. Just as he reached it, he turned around. "Say, Angus. I don't suppose you noticed what kind of hat the stranger was wearing?"

Again, there was a pause as Solomon tried to recall. Smiling, he said, "Matter of fact, he wasn't wearing one when he came into the dining room. But, I'm pretty sure I saw him carrying a bowler."

Sage grinned and said, "Angus, you just might have made my day!"

"Ouch," Mae said and stuck her finger in her mouth. "Hidden straight pin," she responded to a woman's questioning look. They were sitting at a table with a group of other women, sorting a pile of donated clothing.

Mae studied the women, many of whom returned her gaze with a smile. Here she was, once again, with a group of women around a table. But this was so much better than the steam laundry's sorting table. That thought made her speak, "Sure is nice to be sitting instead of standing," she remarked.

"Sure is. And sure is nice these are clean, dry clothes instead of hot, wet, chemically ones," rejoined another.

"That's right," agreed another. "Look here, my hands have gone from lobster red to a lovely shade of possum-nose pink." The other women laughed as they nodded in agreement.

"I can't believe it's the middle of a summer day and I'm not thinking about fainting or throwing up from the heat," another offered somberly. Silence greeted that comment. Every woman there could remember when those worries were foremost in their minds.

"Has anyone else noticed the blessed quiet?" queried another woman who'd stayed silent up to that point. No sooner had she finished stating that thought than one of the toddlers galloping around the hall, let loose with a high piercing shriek that only very young girls could make. Everyone at the table burst into laughter with the gal who'd just spoken, laughing loudest.

Mae thought about how quickly women bonded when their hands were busy. Before today, she'd never met these women. They came from different laundries. Yet, they shared the same thoughts and laughed like women who'd been sugar-borrowing neighbors for years.

She also thought of how much she'd come to like Rachel. Looking around, she spied Rachel in a corner, talking quietly with Caroline. It was clear from the way the two women leaned toward each other that they shared a mutual liking. Heck, that was no surprise. They were the same age, both educated and intelligent. Matter of fact, she liked them both, too. The only difference was, she'd trust Rachel with her life. Caroline, well—knowing whether Caroline was trustworthy continued to be the problem.

Last night had provided no answers. Only more questions. After leaving the union hall, Caroline headed into northwest Portland with Mae following. Once there, she'd stepped into a cafe. Mae watched through the window as tea was served to her. Next, Caroline pulled a small notebook from her dress pocket and began writing. The young woman wrote steadily for a good ten minutes, then she'd finished her tea, pocketed her notebook and left the cafe.

Mae followed her for another three blocks until Caroline mounted the steps of a very well-maintained boarding house. It was too nice a place for a laundry worker's pay. Mae couldn't linger. She would have stuck out like a rooster comb on a duck had she tried to keep watch.

Another child's shout brought Mae's thoughts back to the union hall. She looked down at the shirt she'd been automatically folding. Good, she hadn't lost her touch. It looked perfectly tidy.

She gazed again at the two women in the corner. "Two more days and come hail or high water, I'm going to see what you've been writing in that little notebook of yours, if I have to snatch it right out of your hands," she vowed.

TWENTY TWO

"I'm sure I needn't remind you gentlemen that each of you must keep the faith," Cobb told them. The laundry association members were again at the Portland Hotel, meeting over supper in the small private dining room. Cobb studied each of their faces in turn, his eyes steely and expression stern. The eight men shifted uneasily but returned his look with solemn nods.

Cobb leaned forward, "I remind you of your commitment because my sources have given me a bit of unsettling information."

That pronouncement straightened postures around the table. Letting the tension build, Cobb pulled out a cigar, snipped its end and set it afire. His words followed the first smoky exhalation. "It seems one of you, here at this table, has been talking to the unions about selling your business to them for a union-run cooperative." There was a sharp intake of breath but Farley, sitting quietly in the corner, couldn't tell who'd been startled into taking it.

Cobb shoved his plate aside, stood, put his palms on the table and leaned forward, threat in every line of his body. "I don't have to tell you that such a sale would be gross act of treachery. A complete and utter betrayal of the solemn oath each one of you gave when we formed this association. A union-run laundry would take business away from us and, since profit would be less important, it could pay the employees more and still provide service at a lower cost."

Angry muttering broke out around the table. Cobb took advantage of it. "Whoever you are, you can see that the rest of us abhor this betrayal. If you sell to the unions, your name will be mud not only among those of us at this table but among those at every single table in polite society."

He sat, eased back in his chair and let the silence build until someone felt compelled to speak.

"How did you hear about this, Cobb? Is it more than a rumor?" asked Lewis Gillibrand. "I can't believe that any of the men sitting here tonight would do such a thing. Maybe it's the U.S. Laundry who is dickering with the unions. You know we put the kibosh on Finley getting chemicals. If he can't get chemicals, then he won't be able to take advantage of the lockout."

Cobb gave a short, irritated head shake. "It's only a matter of time before the U.S. Laundry ships chemicals down from Seattle. We've inconvenienced Finley and the shipping costs will dent his profits a bit but, no, it is not one of the two laundries who've refused to join the association. Unfortunately it is one of us, sitting at this table. Someone here is secretly talking to the unions."

Consternation lowered every brow with each man voicing adamant dismay and disgust. "One of them is a pretty damn good actor," Farley thought to himself. He, of course, knew Cobb's source since he'd been the one to carry the information to Cobb. It was the drivers' union president, L.D. Warder. Since the driver's union office was in the union building, Warder had picked up stray tidbits of information from unsuspecting attendees of the Federated Trades Council meeting.

Not everyone knew Warder was a traitor to the laundry workers, although he told Farley that fact would soon become public knowledge. Recently, the Council's chairman had given him an ultimatum: Warder would either support the laundry women or see the drivers' union kicked out of the Council. Warder was supposed to give his answer in the next few days.

Ryland McCarthy spoke up, changing the subject. "So, what are Farley's three operatives doing to assist us, anyway? I've seen neither hide nor hair of them. Exactly what are we getting for our money?"

Farley and Cobb exchanged glances before Cobb said in a controlled tone of voice that telegraphed his irritation, "Ryland, we told you before that the operatives are doing exactly what we need them to do. But, given that we now know there is a traitor in our midst, we are not going to say exactly what it is that they are doing."

McCarthy's face flushed with the effort of holding his tongue but he didn't press the issue. Instead, he asked another question. "It's been nearly a week since the lockout. I've got my drivers performing maintenance and a few other chores but I'm about to run out of busy work for them. Besides, it's costing me a bundle to keep their wages up when we're not bringing in laundry and making money." There was a quiet murmur of agreement as everyone's face swiveled toward Cobb.

This question didn't surprise Cobb because his tone was relaxed as he said, "One more week and we start hiring replacements. The ad will appear in next Wednesday's *Gazette*. We'll interview local folks Thursday and Friday for a start-up the following Monday. Additionally, Farley has already sent telegrams out to experienced strikebreakers he's worked with in the past. Acceptances are pouring in. A whole passel of the fellows should arrive by train the first of next week."

"Strikebreakers? Professional strikebreakers?" questioned Henry Teague, who ordinarily didn't speak at the meetings.

Cobb nodded. "Farley tells me there's lots of folks willing to travel and take the strikers' jobs. They either don't like unions or they like the excitement. Of course, we have to pay for their wages, travel and housing but, there is no question they know how to break through a picket line and keep the replacement workers on the job."

"I don't see why we have to pay for outsiders to come in. There's plenty of unemployed folks here in town who'll snap up the work, no questions asked. Why do we need replacement workers and professional strikebreakers?" said McCarthy.

"You're right, McCarthy. The majority of the replacements we hire will be local. They'll either be former employees willing to leave the union or else new employees desperate enough to cross the picket line. Once enough people take the jobs, the locked out employees will come crawling back to work. But, we need the professional strikebreakers to keep the replacement folks in line, tell us if we have spies in our midst and thump a few heads if the union members start threatening the replacements we hire."

The faces around the table were glum with McCarthy finally clearing his throat to express everyone's concern, "Professional strikebreakers won't know how to do laundry work. Neither will people right off the street. Customers aren't going to stick with us if we do a bad job or ruin their clothes."

Cobb had anticipated this question as well because he quickly responded, "Our customers might get irritated but they'll give us a second chance. They'll understand we're doing our best under difficult circumstances. We won't need to use the strikebreakers or unskilled workers all that long. Once it looks like they might permanently lose their jobs, those women will trample each other coming back to work for us," he predicted with a smirk.

He glanced at Farley who took it as his cue to offer additional reassurance. So, he stood up and stepped closer to the table. "Strikebreakers are key to putting an end to your union troubles. Once they're on site, leading replacement workers through the picket lines to fill those union workers' positions, you'll see the women crumble.

"Think about it. There are few jobs for women unless they have schooling and, most don't. The best they can find is house maid work. I've already given the local canneries a list of their names so they won't get hired there.

"We all know that steam laundries are right at the top when it comes to women's wages. Even so, you've kept your workers' wages low enough that they can't have saved anything. Without savings, they won't last long—they have kids who need to eat and have a roof over their heads. The single women adrift aren't in any better position. Most of them live paycheck to paycheck."

He glanced at the faces around the table, noting the men's fine suits and well-fed faces. Not one showed a smidgen of guilt upon hearing his words. He smiled to himself. That very absence of guilt is what kept him in business.

The previous night, for over an hour, he'd stood in the park, across the street from Lucinda's. Inside, lights blazed and piano notes drifted out the open window into the warm summer air. He thought it was Lucinda playing the piano. But he couldn't steel himself to climb the stairs and knock on her door. Couldn't face the chance of encountering her lover. He'd cursed himself for being a mooning calf, for being a coward and letting his mother and Rachel Levy down. Because at this point, they needed Lucinda's help. Despite their best efforts, neither Fong's men nor Solomon's had discovered where Rebecca Levy was imprisoned. They'd narrowed it down to near the rail yards but couldn't determine exactly which whorehouse.

So, this morning, dread accompanied him as he walked east across the Morrison Bridge. At the bridge's center, he paused. Below him the gray river flowed north, its current brushing against dock and warehouse pilings, ship hulls and the watery reeds of the eastside's marshland. Anchored sailing ships in the river's middle, waiting for a berth or the outgoing tide, rocked in the waves of passing paddlewheel tugboats pushing loaded barges. Overhead, gulls wheeled against the bright blue sky, scouting for eatables, impatience sharpening their cries.

Sage raised his eyes from the river. For once, a smoky haze didn't blanket the city. The light wind steadily ruffling the river's surface was carrying away kitchen smoke and, it being summer, no furnaces burned.

He sighed. He loved this city, despite its self-righteous attitude. In actual fact, it was no better than other cities of its size. On the surface it appeared staid and respectable, but corruption flourished behind its elegant doors and suffering roamed its streets. Still, Portland bubbled with a hopeful vigor that inspired good people, like Mary Harris with her social hygiene group. More and more people, mostly women, were eager to improve civic society. He didn't always agree with their approach but he applauded their desire to create more compassion in the world.

John Sagacity Adair, you are stalling, he silently chided. He tapped his fist on the rusted bridge railing feeling frustrated and angry because he still hadn't talked to Lucinda. If he delayed much longer, Mae Clemens would be very unhappy. As it was, she was certain to ask. Heaving a sigh, he turned toward the bridge's end. Might as well get it over.

The cafe occupied a small wood building squeezed between two faded warehouses. Fong's cousin lounged against the side of a horseless dray. Of course the Chinese man waited outside. He'd be unwelcome inside the cafe Nothing Sage could do about that. Just pay the man exceptionally well for his efforts and take comfort from the fact that Portland's Chinese were more adept than he was at ignoring the white man's idiocy.

Two hours earlier the cafe would have been crowded with people eating breakfast before work. Now, at eight o'clock, it was nearly empty so he quickly spotted Eich, Mae and Rachel sitting together in a wooden booth. Sage crossed the room to join them.

"Good morning!" he said, sliding onto the bench next to Eich and across the table from the women.

"Good morning to you, Mr. Adair," replied his mother. She hadn't told Rachel of their relationship and she was reminding him and Eich of that fact. "Have you any news?"

He nodded, saying, "I spoke with Leo and they have put out a solicitation for funds in the *Labor Press*. Unions and union members can now buy shares in the cooperative laundry. Each union on the Federated Trades Council has contributed sufficient funds to make the down payment. They expect to buy it next week.

"What about Rebecca?" Rachel asked, leaning forward. Her eyes were entreating and bleak above the dark smudges of sleepless nights. On the table, her hands clenched each other so hard that it seemed they were preventing her body from flying apart.

Guilt twanged through Sage as he shook his head, saying, "Nothing yet. But, I am expecting to hear something soon."

Rachel's eyes filled with tears and Mae put a hand over those clenched fingers and squeezed. "What about Lucinda? Did she agree to help?" Mae asked.

This was it. Sage glanced sideways at Eich and saw compassion soften the other man's bearded face. "I didn't get a chance to talk to her," he said, his voice dropping.

Mae's lips tightened. Good thing they were in a public place and Rachel didn't know Mae was his mother. That meant when she spoke, Mae's mild tone lacked the bite he knew she was suppressing. "It seems to me, you had better talk to her soon because, given our lack of success, she's now our best hope of finding Rebecca."

Sage nodded his agreement. He couldn't discuss Lucinda now. "I did get some news that sounds good," he said. "It looks like you might be right, Mrs. Clemens. The fellow who took Rebecca could be working for the laundry association. Also, someone may have seen him meeting with Cobb's henchman, James Farley. If it is him, he's been in Portland pretty continuously which means he didn't have time to take her out anywhere. That means she's still probably in Portland."

Rachel's face showed no relief. Instead, she said, "It's been thirteen days. How do you know he hasn't killed her? Or, sold her to a white slaver who has taken her away?" In the painful silence that followed, her tears spilled over.

❁   ❁   ❁

The morning air skimming across the river just a few blocks away sent a cooling relief from the building heat. The picketers steadfastly waved their signs while they paraded back and forth before the Sparta Laundry's closed doors.

"Good morning ladies, how are things going?" Rachel asked, as she handed out fresh breakfast rolls.

"Fair to middling," responded one of the women. Her tone was spritely but Mae noticed a tightness around her eyes. She presented a worrisome picture, picket sign in one hand, small toddler clinging to her other. She looked to be in her mid-twenties, with corn silk hair of pale yellow, tucked into a neat bun at the nape of her neck. Her dress was faded but clean and well-mended. The toddler at her knee was better dressed in jaunty red knee pants and a new-looking little white shirt.

"Maisie, are you keeping well? You have enough to eat, a roof over your head?" Rachel asked. She'd also picked up on the woman's worry.

The woman nodded, saying, "Aye, I'm paid up on rent till the end of the month. Folks have been bringing us food from the union hall so we're not going hungry. Davy here even got some new clothes from the donations." She smiled down at the little boy, flicked a stray hair away from his face and added, "Though, if Cobb keeps us locked out past month's end, I'm not sure what I'll do. My brother says we can move in with him," she reached down to stroke the towhead at her knee, "but his wife isn't keen on the idea. Not that I blame her. They've only got two rooms and there's already four of them living there."

Mae thought about her own tough times in the miners' shanty-towns. Sometimes, they'd lived three to a room. And there'd been hunger whenever the mine closed down. Such shutdowns were frequent either because of methane explosions or because the owners thought the miners needed to be taught a lesson. Those lean times, full of worry, were hardest on the mothers.

Rachel put her arm across the woman's shoulders. "Maisie, we're trying to get us all back to work. Things are looking hopeful. Just hang on a bit longer."

The woman smiled and said, "I will, Rachel. Like I said, our heads are still above water and the alligators ain't nipped at us yet."

A few more exchanges with the other women on the picket line and they'd left but not before Mae saw Rachel slipping folding money into Maisie's hand. Rachel was silent as they walked up the long ramp onto the bridge, the steady thud of their boots on the wooden boards sounding in matched cadence. Mid-span, Rachel touched Mae's forearm with just enough force to halt her steps. "Mae, I can't do this anymore," she said quietly, her eyes shiny with unshed tears.

Mae's heart sank. She glanced quickly around. Eich strolled ahead of them, nearing the bridge's end. Behind them, one of Fong's cousins paused to gaze down into the marshland along the river channel. The walkway was crowded, so Mae tugged Rachel toward the railing. There, they both turned to face the river.

Rachel looked downriver, her face bleak and lifeless. How the young woman had aged these past few weeks. "Tell me," Mae prodded.

"These poor women need someone who has hope, energy, who can give and not take. I can't, I just can't anymore. Rebecca . . . ." She didn't go on. She didn't need to. Sleeping in the same room with Rachel, Mae knew that most nights, Rachel tossed, turned, cried and slept little. When she did sleep, her body twitched and she whimpered in her throat. She knew what that kind of worry was like. She'd been in the same position too many times—her father first missing, found murdered, her son lost in a mine explosion, and too often, these days, it was Sage in danger. "We'll find Rebecca, I promise," Mae said with more confidence that she felt.

Rachel shook her head. "I know Mr. Miner is trying but I have to do something. I just don't have it in me to try to keep people's spirits up when my heart is so heavy with worry. I need to look for Rebecca. I'm going to start going to the whorehouses, asking questions. I have to."

She turned to look at Mae, her dark eyes burning, "Mae, you have to take my place with the women. Encourage them. They like you. They trust you."

Mae could only shake her head. "Rachel, I can't."

"But you can!" Rachel insisted, "You can do everything I do and probably better. I know you like to stay in the background but I need you to step forward, to take my place. Please."

"Rachel. There's a reason why I stay in the background. I can't tell you what it is. Please believe me, if I could, I would take your place. But I just can't do it. Surely, by now, you've figured out there's more to my life than working in a steam laundry." Mae nodded toward Eich and then toward the Chinese man at their rear both of whom were now feigning an interest in the river water far below.

Rachel sighed. "I figured there had to be something. You can't tell me what it is?"

"It's not mine to tell," Mae said, letting the regret show in her face.

Rachel nodded, accepting what Mae said though her shoulders sagged as she turned to again gaze downriver. "Okay, then," she said. "It will have to be Caroline. The women like her too. She's smart and well-spoken, and strong in her belief that the women deserve better lives."

Somehow, Mae wasn't surprised at Rachel's declaration. "Rachel, I know you don't want to hear this, but something just doesn't ring true where Caroline's concerned." Mae raised a hand to halt the protest that started from Rachel's mouth. "Yes, I know. I like her too. I want to trust her." She used a hand to turn the young woman away from the railing to face her. "You gave me three days to discover more about Caroline. I still have today and tomorrow left. Promise me you will wait two more days until you turn over the reins to her. If I haven't found out the answer by then, I'll stand behind you and behind her if you still want her to take over."

Rachel studied Mae's face, took a deep breath and nodded. "Okay then, you have until the day after tomorrow, then I am done until I find Rebecca."

TWENTY THREE

Cobb and Farley were leaning back in their chairs, puffing cigar smoke at the ceiling. "I bet you anything that Ryland is the traitor selling his laundry to the union," Cobb mused aloud. "He's been nothing but a weak sister since this whole thing started."

Farley nodded, saying, "I fear you might be right," when there was a timid knock on the half-open door.

"Come in!" barked Cobb.

The door swung further inward so a man could peek around its edge. "Ah, hello there Mr. Cobb, Mr. Farley. I was wondering if we might talk a bit."

Cobb straightened in his chair and smiled widely. "Why, hello there L.D. Glad to see you stopping by. I was planning on us getting together sometime today."

The man returned the greeting with a relieved smile as he stepped into the room and carefully shut door behind him. "Why, what is it you need, Mr. Cobb?" he asked as he removed his cap.

"L.D., take a seat," Cobb gestured toward a chair against the wall, "First, tell us why you're here."

"Well, sir. I thought I better report in. I've been keeping a close eye on the men like you asked. They don't much like having to walk past the picketers. I don't suppose there's a way you could chase them off? I mean, they're only a few women, after all."

Cobb and Farley exchanged glances, with Cobb's narrowed eyes signaling caution. "Well, L.D., we don't want to create a ruckus outside the laundries. It might draw the news reporters from that darn *Daily Journal.* That editor thinks he's going to be the 'voice of the working man'. Your men should just consider that walking through the picket line is one of the jobs we are paying them to perform."

L.D. frowned, "Well, sir. That's the other thing they're worried about. Most of them say the laundries are pretty much in tip-top shape. They done all the painting, moving, installing and cleaning and wonder if there will be work for them next week." L.D. was turning the cap in his hand, clearly nervous about asking the question.

"L.D., you can tell the drivers that the laundries will soon be back in business. Heck, we might even be able to get rid of the pickets. Things are afoot." Cobb said.

The drivers' union president relaxed, leaning forward on his chair. "Really? We're opening up soon? The lockout will be over? Why, that's great news."

Cobb raised a hand to dampen Warder's enthusiasm. "No, no. I didn't say the owners are ending the lockout. I just said the laundries will be up and running. That's all you are authorized to tell the men."

"Ah, well, okay," Warder said hesitantly. "But, I don't understand." Then his eyes widened. "Oh, you're planning on hiring scabs?"

That question turned Cobb's face stern, "L.D., we don't use that word," he admonished. "We call them 'replacement workers'. Good men and women who want to work an honest day for an honest day's wage."

This time it was Warder who raised a hand, "Oh, yes, sir. Sorry sir. Replacement workers. You think the women will give up once they see the replacement workers taking their jobs? And, the picketers will go away?"

This time a mirthless smile lifted the corners of Cobb's normally thin, straight mouth. "Some of the women will give up. As for the picketers, we've got some experts on union picket lines coming in. They know how to make things uncomfortable for people on picket lines."

Comprehension widened Warder's eyes, "Strikebreakers?" he asked. "I don't mean to tell you your business but the other unions will definitely get riled up if you bring in strikebreakers. After all, these are women. The men on the Federated Trade Council won't like it a bit."

Cobb's hand flicked away Warder's concern and he moved onto another topic. "L.D., you told us that the Council is negotiating to buy a laundry. Do you know which one, yet?"

Warder's head shake was rueful. "No, Mr. Cobb. The men are clamming up around me. That Rachel Levy appeared before the Council yesterday. She complained that I was stopping the drivers from supporting the women. Since then, I haven't heard a whisper. Though, I'm still asking around and I have some of my more trusted drivers keeping their ears open."

Cobb frowned. "L.D., we really need to know which laundry is trying to sell us out. We think it could be Ryland McCarthy's, American Laundry. The point is, L.D. a cooperative union laundry would be a blow to our plans."

Cobb leaned forward. "How's that second wagon you just bought working out? And, I hear your wife likes her new house."

Warder got the point. "Mr. Cobb, I'm mighty grateful for the extra money you've paid me and for your putting in a good word at the bank," Warder hurriedly said. "I swear I'm doing my level best to find out about that laundry sale. I'll try even harder," he promised.

Silence ensued following this declaration, only to be broken when Cobb said, "See that you do, L.D. See that you do."

Warder clambered to his feet. "Uh, well, I guess I better be getting back to work then," he mumbled and, when Cobb merely nodded, the driver's union president exited the office.

Farley squinted through his cigar smoke at the ceiling. "You didn't tell him that my two operatives are also trying to find out who is selling a laundry to the unions," he mused aloud.

Cobb gave a derisive snort. "Hell, no, I didn't tell him. You can't trust a man who'd betray his own. If he'll do it to them, he'll surely do it to you."

❀   ❀   ❀

"This is ridiculous," Sage said aloud. He was sitting alone on a park bench across from Lucinda's parlor house. He'd already delayed until the middle of the afternoon, telling himself that she got up late. That part was true but the time was long past for that excuse to hold water. He kept recalling the last time he'd seen her standing on those very steps, sunlight catching in her honey hair as she flung her arms around that same man he'd seen her with a year before. Of course, trying not to think about that scene made him think of it all the more. Rebecca, Rebecca, maybe if he said the missing woman's name enough he'd stop his wallowing and get on with it.

He stood up, strode across the single lane street, climbed the stairs, raised the brass knocker and let it fall with a clink. Lucinda's house, with its neat brick front and mansard roof, looked no different than the abodes of her well-to-do neighbors. They tolerated her sporting house next door. Of course her customers were among the city's most well-heeled and influential men. So, who could they complain to?

Elmira answered the door promptly. Her smooth, caramel face showed no surprise. Smiling, she said in her soft drawl, "I was a wondering how long you were going to stay out there in the park." Seeing chagrin change his face she added, "Miz Lucinda doesn't know you were sitting out there. I'll tell her you are here. You go sit yourself in the front parlor.

Sage entered the room, at first thinking nothing had changed in the year since he'd last entered the house. But, there was a difference. The gas jet sconces had been converted to electricity, with glass light globes replacing the gas chimneys. He turned at the sound of a rustle in the doorway. There she stood.

For a moment they simply looked at each other. Then her face stiffened and her voice was cool as she said, "Well, what a surprise. What brings you to our doorstep after such a long absence?"

Okay, so that's the way we're going to play it, he thought before saying, "And, how are you? Have you recovered from your arduous nursing duties in Prineville?"

She gestured him toward a sofa and took the chair across from him. There'd be no touching, no friendly greeting, then. "Well, seeing as how I got back over a month ago, I've had plenty of time to rest. Yourself? You are well? And, your mother?"

Only the last question seemed to carry any real warmth. Lucinda and Mae Clemens had forged a bond in days past such that each woman held the other in high regard. "We're both well," he said stiffly. "In fact, I am here at her behest."

For the first time, there was an unbending of Lucinda's reserve as she leaned forward. "Is she in trouble? Does she need help?" There was no feigning her concern as creases wrinkled her smooth brow and her eyes went from half lidded to fully open. All coolness banished.

So, she might not care all that much for me, but Mother is still high in her books. Ouch. "Yes, we both need your help, if you're willing," he said.

"Of course," she said. Was that bitterness or hurt that darkened her voice? She straightened and said, "What is going on? One of your missions I suppose." She was one of the few in Portland who knew Sage worked as an undercover operative for St. Alban. More than once, Lucinda had aided their social justice efforts.

Sage told her about Rebecca's kidnapping. "Despite Fong and Solomon's efforts, we haven't been able to locate the girl. We think she's being held prisoner. One of Solomon's people reported that, on the night Rebecca disappeared, a woman fitting her description was seen being "helped" down a street near the rail yards. If it was Rebecca, that might mean she is being kept in a bawdy house down there."

"And Mae thinks I can help how? It's not like I have much in common with the women running those establishments," she said, gesturing around a room that was very well-appointed and tasteful by anyone's standard.

Sage saw that Lucinda was slightly offended, but pushed on anyway. "We thought that you might be able to convince them that you were thinking of purchasing a second establishment to cater to a lower income cliental. Mae thought they'd be flattered by your interest and give you a tour of their places. Once you get a look, you might notice whether they had a room that was locked or they refused to show you. That way we can narrow down the number of houses where Rebecca might be.

"Good lord, there must be over 400 parlor houses in town. Just how many do you expect me to visit?" Despite this mild protest, Sage thought he saw a quickening of interest. Lucinda was always a game girl when it came to their intrigues.

"If we limit the search to those around the rail yard, we're only talking about six."

"How soon, would you need me to conduct these interviews?" she asked.

"Our fear is that they will transport her out of town. If that happens, she'll be lost to us. Maybe forever."

Lucinda was nodding as he spoke. "Alright, I'll do it," she said. "Tell Mae I will begin tomorrow. Have someone send me a list." She stood, signaling an end to their discussion. Seconds later he found himself standing on the front step with Elmira softly closing the front door behind him. Had that been pity in Elmira's eyes? Certainly they'd shone with more friendliness than did her mistress's cornflower blue ones.

❀ ❀ ❀

Mae's steps had the vigor born of desperation. She had only this afternoon and tomorrow to figure out exactly what Miss Caroline Stark was doing working in a steam laundry and positioning herself to become a leader in the labor dispute. She'd seen too many so-called labor leaders exposed as turncoats. There'd been that Irish fellow at the bridge carpenters' strike last fall. She hadn't met him but Sage said he'd been quite a charmer. Nearly led the men right into disastrous action. And then, of course, there'd been her own husband. That scoundrel was coming to mind too darn often lately.

Mae forced herself to focus on the woman who strode rapidly ahead, her shoulders purposefully squared. Obviously, this was no saunter home after a hard day of work. Caroline was definitely up to something. They were on Davis Street. Ahead, Caroline paused, seemed to extract a small watch from her dress pocket and after replacing it, doubled her pace. Obviously, she wasn't headed for a casual drink of tea or home to rest.

Fewer pedestrians and less traffic forced Mae to drop farther back. Finally, Caroline turned off to mount the stone steps of the St. Mary's Catholic Church. Once she'd entered through the big oak doors, Mae hurried forward. Slipping inside, she stood in vestibule, waiting for her eyes to adjust. It was dim inside the empty church, lit only by light filtering through the painted windows. Caroline was kneeling in the front pew, her head bowed. So, the girl was religious. Not surprising since Caroline always wore a gold cross—tucked into her dress so that only the chain showed when she was working but, otherwise, openly displayed on her dress front.

Humph, Mae thought. What am I supposed to think of this? If she's religious, does that mean she couldn't be a spy? Does seem less likely. But, Ma always said there were more hypocrites in church pews than there were fleas on a yard dog. Mae couldn't disagree.

A door opened and closed near the church's altar, the sound echoing high in the rafters. Caroline rose and moved into the aisle to greet the dark-haired priest who'd entered. The two exchanged a few words and then turned to cross the altar. Caroline glanced behind her down the aisle. This sent Mae dodging behind a big, fluted column. Seconds later, she peered around the column just in time to see the two of them disappear through the altar door which again shut with an echoing bang.

Mae left the church, chuckling to herself. "Maybelle Clemens, in all my days I never thought I'd see you skulking around a Catholic church like an egg-sucking hound." Mae wasn't a church goer but her mother had been, despite the hypocrites. She'd given her daughter respect for the church in earthly matters.

As Mae trudged the long miles back to the boarding house she pondered over what she had seen. Maybe the girl really was religious. But, why would the priest take her into his private office? Gloom settled over Mae like a dingy shawl so that she couldn't appreciate the bright blue of the early evening sky. One more day, that's all she had to find out exactly who Caroline Stark was and exactly what she was doing.

TWENTY FOUR

"You've got to eat and drink something," Sinclair told her. She mutely shook her head. "Come on," he coaxed, "it's not going to help anyone if you get sick."

His statement lifted the corner of her mouth and she looked directly at him, eyebrows raised, a tiny smile on her lips, "Well, I don't know, Mr. Kidnapper. Sounds like a good idea to me. Just how are you going to explain carrying a dying woman through the streets? I'm sure my sister has told the police I'm missing and they're looking for me. Someone will notice."

She had a point; he had to give her credit. He scratched his smooth chin. "Well, at least drink some water, Miss Levy. Your mouth's got to feel like the inside of a cotton boll."

She licked her lips, but shook her head when he offered a cup of water poured from the bedside pitcher. "No, thanks. I drink that and it's my head that feels like the inside of a cotton boll. I refuse to let you drug me anymore."

Sinclair set the cup down and considered the situation. If she didn't drink, she might get really sick. And, she was right. It would be darn hard to move her from this whorehouse to the ship if he had to carry her through the streets. The North End had a cop standing on practically every corner.

He studied her. She'd been cooped up in this room for over two weeks. They'd been hot days and she had to want a bath. Maybe they could make a deal.

"How about this," he proposed, "you drink the water and I'll see that you get a tub of water in here for a bath."

He saw her considering the offer. She raised her chin and looked down her nose at him."I will drink the water, but only if you go get me fresh water with no drugs in it and I get a bath and a clean, decent dress to wear instead of this skimpy shift."

She had moxie, this Rebecca, he'd give her that. "Where are you from?" he asked.

She blinked in surprise at the question but answered readily enough. "Rachel and I came here from Chicago. We had an aunt living here in Portland. When we arrived, we learned that she'd died of typhoid. We decided to stay. We didn't have any money to return to Chicago and no one there to return to. Our parents are dead. So, we both got jobs right away. We've been here about a year."

"Chicago? That's where I'm from," he said.

"Well, there's lots of different kinds to be found in Chicago," she commented drily.

He felt his face flush. To hide it, he stood. "Okay. I'll go fetch you a glass of pure water. And arrange for a tub and hot water to be brought up." He raised a finger, "And a clean, decent dress." She responded with a dignified nod.

He carefully locked the door behind him since he'd ordered Stella to leave Rebecca untied. Heading down the stairs, he'd heard women's voices in the front room of the house. Glancing through the archway, he noticed a well-dressed woman conversing with the house's madam. On the way back upstairs, carrying a full glass of unadulterated pump water, he paused to look at the woman in the parlor. She noticed, her cornflower blue eyes calmly examining him in return. He sent her a smile, not surprised at her interest. Women usually gave him a second look.

As Sinclair climbed the stairs he pondered why such a high-class woman would be sitting the parlor of one of the most rundown whorehouses in the city. Then he forgot her, his mind focusing instead on the dark-haired, dark-eyed woman waiting in the locked room at the top of the stairs. He'd told her his name was Paul but she insisted on calling him "Mr. Kidnapper".

"She's something else, that Rebecca Levy. She'll probably toss this water on me." he thought and smiled.

❋   ❋   ❋

It was a beautiful day. For the first time, it wasn't sweltering though the pleasure Sage felt carried a bit of regret as well. The recent heat wave was likely summer's last blast before the weather cooled into fall's crisp days. Fall was glorious with its colorful leaves, though after fall came the wet, dreary, gray winter. Sage shrugged off that thought, instead focusing on the fragrant summer roses and cheerful pedestrians who strolled with light steps beneath a cool, blue sky. Lucinda had sent for him. He couldn't tell if the ripples of excitement he felt came from the hope that she'd discovered where they were hiding Rebecca Levy or the anticipation of seeing Lucinda again. A combination of both, he decided.

The house was quiet. Likely everyone was out and about. Probably shopping since the women who worked in this parlor house were well-paid. This time, Elmira showed him into the small back parlor where he took a seat on the familiar red velvet settee. Gazing about, he saw that not much had changed in this room either. There was still the polished woodwork, subtly patterned wallpaper, small piano and tasteful, understated scattering of figurines and other whatnots. Thankfully, Lucinda didn't go in for the curio cabinets, draped tables and the other smothering touches considered fashionable these days. In fact, the only thing she'd changed in here was to exchange the gas lamp fixtures for incandescent electric bulbs. He wondered if, in the evening hours, the light made the room as white and glaring as he'd seen in other electrified establishments. Probably not. One of the things he admired about Lucinda was her balanced taste for both the elegant and the comfortable.

"No, Sage. Not much has changed. I've only been back in Portland a few months, though I do plan on making more changes than just the lighting," she said from where she stood in the archway.

She moved into the room, still continuing to talk. "When I was in Chicago, I spent some time with an architect, Frank Lloyd Wright. His houses are changing everything. He made me realize that this room, "she swept an arm, "is too fussy, the colors are too unnatural, the wallpaper annoying."

Sage had stood as she entered. He said honestly, "I've always considered this room one of the most attractive in town."

Lucinda dipped her head, acknowledging the compliment but said, "Maybe in this town but it is still too old-fashioned." She took the armchair across from him, gestured for him to retake his seat, tucked her long skirts close in and asked, "Do you want anything to drink?"

He shook his head, "Elmira already asked. I'm fine. What did you learn?"

Lucinda's smile faded as did the sparkle in her eyes. "I'm afraid I didn't learn anything at all. I went to the six houses. Of the six, four were interested in selling and let me look around. I saw nothing to indicate a girl was being held prisoner anywhere in the houses."

"What about the other two houses?" His spirits plunged at the thought of facing Rachel Levy and again telling her that Rebecca was still lost.

"Neither of the women wanted to sell, so they obviously didn't take me on a tour. I couldn't very well ask for one either."

Sage sat back, releasing his breath in a gust. "Damn, now what?"

Lucinda leaned forward, sympathy in her face. "At least you can eliminate the four houses. That means she might be in one of the other two."

"Yah, but how can we find out?"

"One of the houses down there caught fire a few days ago. A madam told me that everyone poured out into the street to watch the firemen. If everyone's in the street, maybe that would be enough distraction to let someone slip in the backdoor and take a look around."

"Well, I sure can't start a fire. That neighborhood's a tinderbox," Sage said thoughtfully. In the silence that followed, the mantle clock's ticking sounded loud.

Sage snapped his fingers, "That's it. I know exactly what we'll do." He jumped up, leaned over and kissed Lucinda firmly on the lips. She was too shocked to respond before he blurted, "You are absolutely brilliant, my girl," only to flush when he realized what he'd done.

"I mean, I'm sorry. I shouldn't have. I know you have a beau. I just got carried away. It's just the relief of figuring out what to do, you know."

She tilted her head, her forehead wrinkled. "What 'beau'?" she asked.

"That fellow from Chicago? I saw you with him." By this time, Sage had moved back to the settee.

"What do you mean, 'you saw me with him'?" Her face showed confusion.

"I saw you out front, on the stoop. You were kissing him."

"When?" she asked, still looking perplexed.

"In late July, the day after I got back from Prineville."

Lucinda sat back in her chair, the confusion gone, replaced with the clinched cheek. He knew that look well—she was feeling exasperated.

"You mean that you haven't come by these last six weeks because you saw me kissing a man on my front porch?"

"Well," he said and couldn't continue.

"John Sagacity Adair, you are the most annoying man I have ever met. I have been sitting here wondering why you were avoiding me. All these weeks." Pain shadowed her normally bright eyes as she relived those lost days.

"That means, ah, that maybe," Sage stuttered but she cut him off.

"That means I am so angry at you right now I'd like you to leave."

He looked at her in disbelief, but her chin was thrust forward and a very long, straight finger was stabbing toward the door.

"Um, okay," he said, scrambling to his feet. "I'll come back and let you know what happened—with Rebecca Levy, I mean."

She shook her head and kept pointing, "Out," she said loudly, as if he were a dog who'd tracked in mud.

When he reached the door, Elmira appeared with his hat and opened it for him. The last thing he heard coming from the parlor was Lucinda's voice saying, "Damned idjit."

He smiled. Whenever his mother called him an "idjit" it meant she was softening. Lucinda Collins was a lot like Mae Clemens.

"Shoot, this is my last day of trying to figure out what that Caroline gal is up to. Rachel's getting antsy and I promised her," Mae told herself as she put on her hat to follow Caroline out onto the late afternoon street. Once again Caroline headed toward Northwest Portland. So, it was either home or back to church, Mae surmised.

She was wrong. Caroline returned to the tea shop. When Mae peeked through the window, she noticed the young woman once again had her writing pad and pencil out. But this time, she was sitting at a big round table. Mae scooted away before being spotted. She took up a post halfway down the block, on someone's front steps, partly concealed by an overgrown bush that couldn't decide whether it was green or yellow.

As she watched, a few people entered the tea shop door. After twenty minutes, Mae got up to sneak another peek. This time Caroline had company at her table. There were three other young women sitting there, each with paper and pencil, each leaning earnestly across the table toward Caroline who was talking and gesturing emphatically, a fist pounding the palm of her hand.

Mae ducked out of sight and headed back to her steps to think. Those other young women didn't look like management spies. Maybe they were classmates of Caroline's. But how could Caroline be going to school? Before the lockout, she was working the same long days as the rest of the laundry women. A body was too tired to even think once that workday was done. And, since then, Caroline turned up faithfully every day, either at the picket line or the union hall.

Mae put her elbows on her knees and her chin in her hands. She thought best that way. Maybe, Caroline and her friends were studying some kind of Catholic thing on their off hours. That could be since Caroline always wore that small cross. Though Mae was raised Catholic, she'd never heard of any religious class like that. Darn it! Not a dad-burned thing about the girl made sense.

Mae squinted up at the brilliant blue sky. "Dagnabbit," she grumbled, "that fire hydrant will spout wings and fly before I figure out what that girl is up to. I'm tired of figuring. It's time to find out."

She rose from the steps, smoothed down her skirt, straightened her hat and strode to the tea shop door, a totally fake smile on her lips when she opened it.

TWENTY FIVE

Sinclair slipped between two houses to reach the street. Sure enough, that ragpicker was back at his post before the boarding house. It had been a long day—most of it spent waiting outside buildings. First, he'd lurked down the street from the Levy woman's boarding house until he'd seen her leave with Mae Clemens at her side. He'd followed them across the river to the union hall. So had the ragpicker and a Chinese man. Once the women entered the union hall, Sinclair loitered farther down the street for a number of hours.

Finally, he got lucky. In late afternoon, the Clemens woman left the union hall alone. The Chinese fellow started following her. That meant for the first time, only the ragpicker guarded the Levy woman. He'd followed as the ragpicker trailed her home, across the bridge, right up to her boarding house. Now the older fellow was in his usual spot, hunkered down beneath the low-hanging limbs of an ancient cedar. The good news was that the Chinese fellow was nowhere around. He was probably still following the Clemens woman. Sinclair's forehead wrinkled. Sure was an uncommon combination of folks. He shook off that thought. It was time to get down to business.

Patting his pocket, Sinclair confirmed he still had the envelope. He slipped away down the street. Half an hour later, he was back to peer once again around the house corner. Minutes later the young boy he'd just hired trotted up to the boarding house door and knocked. The door opened and the landlady took Sinclair's envelope inside.

Sinclair slipped down the street and across the ravine bridge. He made his way to a spot across the ravine from the boarding house. There he found what he'd hoped. The Chinese man was still absent from his usual post. If Rachel Levy believed the note, she'd soon be slipping outside and down into the ravine. Why wouldn't she believe it? His instructions had been clear and the enclosed proof irrefutable:

> I know where they are keeping your sister. If you want to see her, you must follow my instructions carefully. First, you must evade your watchers. I know who they are. Exit the back of your boarding house, go down into the ravine and follow it for a block. Then climb out and walk to Hawthorne Park at the corner Ninth and Hawthorne. Once there, go to the blue spruce tree. At its base, you will find a rock. Underneath that rock will be further instructions. If you are followed, you will never see your sister again. Just so you know I am serious, I have enclosed your sister's lapel pin, I am sure you will recognize it. You have just one hour to make it to the park.

He stood behind a bush, watching the boarding house and soon saw the back door open and Rachel slip outside. She was across the covered porch and heading down the rickety wooden staircase within seconds. He noticed that she hadn't even changed clothes. She must care a great deal for Rebecca.

He hadn't seen his own sisters since before he was expelled. Too ashamed to face them. His family's pride was boundless when he entered the religious life. These days, he was thinking about that seminary entirely too much. He could see Father Thomas looking at him with those sad old eyes and sorrowfully shaking his head. But the old man never lectured, being such a firm believer as he was in the presence of the "God Within"—a spiritual judge who answered a listening man's every moral question.

He clapped his hands over his ears, and then felt silly. "Shut the hell up, Sinclair. You've made your bed. Just lie in it and shut up," he muttered through gritted teeth.

Rachel reached the bottom of the ravine and began angling southward . She was right on course for the park. Sinclair started tracking her from the top of the bank. Once he was sure no one was following her, he sped ahead.

Fifteen minutes later she was in the park, running toward the solitary blue spruce. She picked up the rock, tossed it aside and unfolded the note he'd placed there. From his vantage point across the street from the park, he confirmed that her ragpicker guardian was nowhere in sight. She read the note and then raised her head to scan the park, obviously looking for its author.

Ducking behind a dust bin, he waited a few moments before rising up to peek across its top. He saw her run down Hawthorne toward the river. He'd written that she had to walk all the way to the North End. Told her he'd be watching her the whole time. That wasn't true of course. He'd be taking the trolley and arrive there long before she did.

It was dark when she showed up outside Stella Block's whorehouse. Sinclair was sitting in the saloon across the street drinking a beer and gazing out the window when she rounded the corner and mounted the single step. The door opened promptly at her knock and she quickly stepped inside. Sinclair heaved a sigh. He'd finally fulfilled his mission for Farley.

A few minutes later Stella stepped out onto her tiny stoop and quickly ducked back inside. Handing his empty mug to the barman, he put on his bowler and headed out into the street. As he crossed it, he tried to ignore the dread settling around his heart.

The warped whorehouse door opened promptly at his soft knock. Stella gave him a gap-toothed grin and held out her hand. As agreed, he dropped a twenty dollar Liberty gold piece onto her palm. Her fingers snapped shut like a crocodile's jaws. "It was easy as jack rolling a drunk," she told him. "Once I unlocked the door and she got a gander at her sister she was inside and across the room faster than poop through a chicken. Snapped that padlock shut and Billy Bob's your uncle—two birds in one room."

Her shrill cackle grated on his ears.

A bench stood in the hallway outside the offices housing what he'd come to think of as the "outraged ladies societies". Sage gratefully settled down to wait for the office to open at 9:00 a.m. His pocket watch said that was thirty-five minutes away. He was exhausted. He hadn't slept in the hours after Eich and Mae climbed to Mozart's third floor last night to tell him that Rachel was missing.

"I just don't understand it," Mae said. "Herman was outside the whole time. Someone must have climbed up the back while Fong's cousin was following me." Annoyance twisted her face. "Which he didn't have to do, I might add. I don't know why you insisted I needed protection."

This was the closest he'd seen his mother to panic, so Sage didn't take offense. "Ma, you know we weren't sure why the two of you were being followed. Maybe if you'd been alone you'd have been the one taken." He'd reached out and squeezed her hand where it lay on the table, He received a squeeze and apologetic smile in return. "Did anything in the room look like it was upset, like there'd been a struggle?"

Mae shook her head. "Nope, everything was neat as a pin, just like we'd left it. And, nobody in the house heard any noise. Sage, I just don't understand. If they'd used some kind of knockout drops how the heck could they get her down those rickety stairs out back, let alone carry her across that gully? It's steep and covered with shrubs and brambles."

Eich shifted in his seat, the rippling of his forehead signaling his distress. He'd lost the woman he'd been guarding. "I've been considering the events of this evening," he said slowly. "No one came to the boarding house after Miss Levy, except for a messenger boy who did not enter the building. It was only when Mae came running out that I had any indication Rachel was gone."

The three of them looked at each other. "Do you suppose he brought Rachel a note? One that made her sneak out of her own free will?" asked Sage.

Mae started to protest but Herman interrupted, "That is exactly what must have happened. That messenger must have brought her a note which compelled her to sneak out the back."

Then Mae saw it too. "Of course! They must have lured her away. Told her they'd take her to her sister but that she had to come alone. Go out through the back. That means they had to know Fong's man was following me," she said.

"Now they have both of them. But maybe that's okay. Two women should be easier to track and find than just one," Sage said thoughtfully.

"Especially, two women who look exactly alike. Though, we don't know what's been happening to Rebecca. She may look different now," Mae said.

Sage was nodding and then froze in mid nod. "What do you mean they 'look exactly alike'?" he asked.

Mae looked at him. "Why, identical twins always look alike," she said with a touch of asperity.

"What!" Sage roared. "Rachel and Rebecca are identical twins? Good Lord, why didn't you tell me?"

"I thought you knew. Really, Sage. You needn't get so het up." Mae sputtered, taken aback by Sage's reaction.

Sage put his elbows on the table, his head in his hands. He spoke quietly to the table between his two elbows. "If I had known they were twins I would have agreed with you and Eich that she was kidnapped because of the labor dispute." Sage looked up. "I would have focused all our resources on Farley and his operatives, on everyone connected with the laundry. I would have immediately believed that someone seized Rebecca by mistake, thinking he was snatching Rachel instead." There was no anger in his words, only regret.

Sage stood up and began pulling his John Miner outfit from the closet. "I'll head down to the North End. See if anyone's seen a woman matching Rachel's description. There are so many more men than women down there that a respectable woman stands out. I'll visit Solomon and talk to Fong. They'll get their fellows out tonight, to find out whether anyone has seen Rachel in the last four hours or so. After that, I'll find Farley's operatives and stick to them. Maybe they'll lead me to her. Even if the white slavers didn't kidnap the two, they may have them now. And, if the women are imprisoned in the North End somewhere, the whorehouses are still our best bet."

He laid a hand on his mother's shoulder, his face earnest. "Ma, please promise me that you'll go back to the boarding house and stay there. That you'll let Herman watch over you?"

Surprisingly, she agreed saying, "Well, I can't go places in the North End like you can. Besides I've got things to take care of tomorrow. The women's spirits will drop once they know Rachel is missing. I've got to spend the day meeting up with some of them."

For once, he thought she was being truthful and didn't intend to sneak around doing her own detecting.

He'd carried out his plans but failed to discover the Levy women's location. Fong's and Solomon's men had fanned out through the North End. There was one slim lead. One of Solomon's men was sure that a man working in a saloon kitchen had seen Rachel. The fellow was outside, smoking a cigarette, when he glimpsed a respectable-looking, dark haired woman, hurrying past the alley opening. She'd stuck in his mind because it was unusual to see someone like her in the North End so late in the evening.

Once again, this sighting of a dark-haired woman occurred close by the rail yards. So, on this very thin reed, all his hopes rested. And it was why he was waiting on the hard bench to talk to the Hygiene Society's leader. He had a plan to find the Levy women and was fairly confident that Mary Harris would agree to help.

"Caroline, this is what Rachel wanted," Mae insisted. The two women were meeting over coffee near the young woman's boarding house. Mae had waited outside the Catholic Church for Sunday services to end. When Caroline left the church Mae stepped to her side and led her to the café.

"I don't know Mae. It's too active a role for me to take. I'm already worried that my working at the union hall has compromised my integrity. If I become a leader, my objectivity will be questioned in the future. We can't risk that. We'll lose everything we've worked for." Caroline stared glumly into her coffee. Clearly she was unhappy about turning Mae down.

Mae was stumped. She understood the dilemma. Just like her, Caroline had a long range mission. Too much exposure would jeopardize Caroline's mission just like it would jeopardize her own. "Is there someone you could consult?"

Caroline fingered the cross at her neck. "I suppose I could ask my priest, Father O'Hara, at St. Mary's. Also, I better ask the women at the Consumers League."

"They both know about your work?" Mae queried.

"Oh, yes. Father O'Hara is an old family friend from Minnesota. He's the reason I am in Portland. He asked my sister to come here to teach at St. Mary's Academy. My folks wouldn't let her come unless I accompanied her. He's watching over the two of us." She smiled. "Says his job is to comply with my father's orders and ensure that we do not stray near the 'trough of temptation.' And, as for the Consumers League, they're the ones sponsoring our work."

Mae reached across the table and laid her hand upon the young woman's. "Caroline, I understand the dilemma. Believe me, I do. But the laundry women respect you, look up to you. Rachel's disappearance will frighten them and they'll lose heart unless you step in. Please explain that to Father O'Hara and the Consumers League people."

"I understand and I will go talk to them today. I can let you know, first thing tomorrow morning," she said before flashing a quick smile. "Who knows, maybe Rachel will turn up this evening or tomorrow morning."

"Yes, maybe she will," Mae echoed, though to her own ears, she didn't sound hopeful.

TWENTY SIX

Cobb and Farley sat at a small table in the corner of the Reception Saloon, one of the better establishments serving liquor late Sunday night. The light from the dangling electric bulbs shone on the white ceramic floor tiles and made the brass spittoons glitter.

"At last. Farley, I was beginning to think that man of yours would never deliver," Cobb smiled as he lifted his glass in a silent toast to his companion.

"Well part of it was our fault. We didn't know the Levy women were identical twins. Once we realized he'd taken the wrong sister he kept at it but, after the first snatch, Rachel Levy had three people guarding her around the clock."

"How is that Sinclair fellow performing these days?"

"He's made the necessary arrangements. He's had to pay extra to the whorehouse madam because she kept the two gals longer than expected. And, he's forked over a bit more money to the captain who agreed to delay his departure by five days, thank god. That means those two women will be headed downriver within the next thirty-six hours" Farley's expression turned thoughtful as he poured himself another shot of whiskey from the bottle on the table. "I don't think I'll use Sinclair again, though."

"Why's that?"

"Well, like I told you, he's been working as a panderer in Chicago's white slave trade. He came with very high recommendations. Everyone said he's the best when it comes to snatching gals with a minimum of fuss. But, I dunno. He acted hesitant when it came to the Levy women. It's taken too much of my time to keep him on track," Farley said.

"What is he, a secret union sympathizer?"

Farley shook his head emphatically. "Nope, I'm sure he's not. I checked on that before I hired him. But, I've been wondering. Maybe his background has become the problem." Farley fell silent.

"What do you mean man? How can pandering make it hard for him to grab those two women. You're not making sense." Cobb frowned and his lips twisted with irritation.

Holding up a hand, Farley said, "Wait a moment, Thaddeus. Like I told you before, his problem could be those years he spent in the seminary. I suspect it's those early teachings that are causing the problem. Regardless, I doubt that I'll hire him again. Once the gals have shipped out, he'll be on the next train back to Chicago."

This time it was Cobb who shook his head in the negative. "Sorry, old man, that won't work. I'm going to need him once the laundry gets up and running next week. Someone's got to play foreman until I can hire a genuine foreman who knows the business," Cobb said. "Do you still have him trying to discover who's selling a laundry to the unions?" Cobb asked.

"Yes. Sinclair's making friends among the other laundry foremen. So far neither he, nor my two operatives who are working as drivers, have discovered the name of the laundry. Whoever is planning to sell is keeping it very hush-hush."

"What about the strikebreakers? When are they arriving?"

"They'll be in town no later than Wednesday, three days from now. We'll use them to guard the laundries on Thursday and Friday when your applicants arrive for their interviews. The union women are going to see the ad and people going for interviews. Things might get rowdy on the picket line."

Cobb took a careful swallow of his whiskey before flashing Farley a humorless smile. "Just make sure your men behave if they see any reporters or photographers around. Otherwise, when things get rowdy, we'll just blame the women. Who's to prove different? The *Gazette* will make sure it's our story that's being told, not the women's."

"My men know how to act around a picket line. They've had lots of practice. Like I said, they're professionals. Is there anything else that needs doing?" Farley asked.

"Nope. We're all set except for finding out who is trying to sell his laundry to the unions. I expect our fellows will learn the answer to that in the next few days. Once we take care of that, we'll be sitting pretty. Those women won't know what hit them."

It was a quiet Sunday night because, the working poor who lived in the North End's cheap rooms needed to rest up for the week ahead. Those without employment would have already spent whatever spare change they'd scrounged. That left them with nothing better to do than settle down into a sleeping spot and be grateful for the warm, dry weather.

In the relative quiet Sage heard them approaching from two blocks away. Portland's Midnight Missionaries were on parade, their mostly female voices raised in a robust hymn as they strode forward, their torches held aloft like those of avenging angels. It presented quite a spectacle, even for a North End familiar with noisy Salvation Army bands and carousing sailors. He smiled. Damn lucky that Mary Harris and her friends so earnestly desired to rescue "wanton women" from those "Siamese twins of evil: liquor and lust."

While puzzling over how to sneak into the two whorehouses Lucinda had identified, Sage remembered the jail matron mentioning that the women of the Society for Social Hygiene were planning to launch a new tactic in their campaign to rescue Portland's fallen women. The tactic was one commonly employed by the Society's Chicago branch. It entailed singing hymns and sermonizing outside whorehouses, usually around midnight. Hence, in Chicago they were known by the nickname, "The Midnight Missionaries."

That information led him to visit Mary Harris. Upon hearing of his situation, she'd agreed to organize just such a mission. She was eager to help free innocent captives from a rail yard whorehouse. That led to him being stationed here, waiting for an opportunity to search the two houses while their inhabitants were distracted by the missionaries' rowdy crusade on their doorsteps.

About twenty-five crusaders halted in front of the first whorehouse. There were a few men in the parade but many more had gathered along the street to heckle. All fell silent as a wood fruit box was set down and mounted by a man wearing minister's garb. Turning toward the house, he began loudly exhorting the women inside. They immediately raised the windows to lean out above the street, their vividly painted faces expressing a mix of ridicule and shame.

> Oh Lord, we beseech thee to show mercy on those who are trapped within this house of perdition. Open the hearts of those waging their lives in sin, pestilence and degradation. Show them the light, let them know that they are loved and that we shall welcome them. Open their hearts, let them see the glorious salvation that is theirs. Oh women who are lost, step out of that house, out of a life spawned from the devil's cold, dead heart. Come out, you practitioners of wantonness even as your soul thirsts for God's love and forgiveness. Hear dear sisters, the voice of Lord God! Come out, I beg you. Come out and be embraced by God's love!

Sage doubted very much that the preacher's words would convert many of the women whose faces now showed at every window. But, the ruckus had done the trick. He was sure everyone inside was now at the front windows. He ran down the narrow space between the whorehouse and its neighbor, trying to avoid the broken glass and rusty tin cans. Lockjaw was a damned ugly way to die.

Reaching the back porch, he crept up the stairs only to nearly tumble back down them when a voice hissed, "Took you long enough."

"Dammit! You nearly scared the holy bejesus right out of me! What the hell are you doing here, anyway?"

Mae stepped from the shadows of the porch and said, "Two of us can search faster than one. In no time at all, the gals and their customers will tire of the entertainment you've arranged out front. That happens, you'll be caught sure as a mouse in a flour bin."

Sage couldn't argue. There wasn't time. Already he could hear those inside hollering back at the missionaries. "Come on then. You do the basement and I'll do the upstairs."

He eased open the back door and gestured her in, noticing that her skirt swung close against her legs. No petticoats then. She was ready to run if she had to.

Inside, the main floor was much as he expected, tawdry flocked wallpaper, threadbare velvet settees, a few cheap knickknacks—all calculated to give a surface appearance of Victorian luxury. At least the upstairs bedrooms had doors instead of mere curtains across their openings. Still, the place was only a single step above the cribs that fronted on many North End streets. All the bedroom doors stood wide open so he saw, at a glance, that the rooms were empty. He didn't bother with those at the front of the house since that was where everyone was gathered.

He stood in the hallway, frantically casting his eyes about. Spotting an attic trapdoor in the ceiling of the upstairs hallway, he grabbed a chair, raised the cover and stuck his head through the opening. Nothing. The attic was an open space of rafters and exposed floor joists. Vents at either end provided the space's only light and air.

He carefully dropped the cover back into place, dismounted the chair and returned it to its place inside the nearest room. Racing downstairs as quietly as possible he reached the ground floor and ran toward the back of the house. By the time he was back in the kitchen, he could hear windows slamming shut and people moving about. Obviously they'd grown tired of baiting the missionaries who were singing at the top of their voices.

Stepping out onto the back porch, he felt relief at the sight of his mother. "Whew, that was close," he whispered. "Find anything?"

At her head shake he said, "Come on, one more house to go." He didn't tell her that she'd been right. He couldn't have searched both upstairs and basement in time, though he did admit it to himself. There was a chance that the next house might prove more dangerous. Even so, he wasn't about to give her extra ammunition if he needed to ban her from entering next time. While Mae made her way to the back of the second whorehouse, Sage again entered the narrow passage between the buildings to reach the street. There he waited until he caught Mary Harris's eye. At his nod, she stepped forward to tug the preacher's sleeve. He stepped down from his box and began shepherding his singing flock down the street, his baritone voice singing loudly off-key.

Sage slipped onto the boardwalk, quickly strolling ahead of the parade to find a new place to position himself. Once again he waited until faces filled the front windows before slipping away and into the backyard where Mae stood concealed by a bush.

He reached for the back door knob but she stopped him with a hand on his forearm. "I checked," she whispered. "There is no cellar, I could see through a ground vent that it sits on pilings."

He paused. "Okay then, I can search the first and second floors myself. You can stay out here and keep watch. Give a whistle if you see anything.

Mae smiled sweetly and patted his cheek none too gently before she elbowed him aside, opened the door and stepped into the house. Sage sighed in exasperation but followed, leaving the door unlatched behind them.

They quickly looked into the back rooms on the first floor and found nothing. Upstairs, they entered a narrow hallway with six rooms opening off it, three on either side. Immediately, the door farthest from the front of the house grabbed their attention. An open padlock hasp dangled from it. They hurried down the hallway. Sage cautiously pushed the door inward, ready to fight if someone sprang at them. Nothing happened.

Stepping inside, they surveyed a small, bare room. Despite having a window, the room was unnaturally dim. Sage saw that the window curtain was covered by boards that had been nailed across it. That way the boards didn't show from the outside. Sage made out a single cot, a chair and a wooden crate beside the cot. Everything about the room said it was a prison cell.

Disappointment washed over him. This room proved nothing. "It's probably just the room where they always keep the new girls, feeding them liquor and drugs until they're too ashamed to run. I'll be sure Sergeant Hanke hears about it," he whispered. What he wanted in the worst way was to kick the chair and upend the cot.

Mae moved forward to lean across the cot before quickly standing upright. "Quick, Sage, get over here! Help me move this cot away from the wall. Quietly, so it doesn't scrape the floor."

He hesitated. Already there were yells and jibes sounding inside the house, clearly directed at the missionaries. Time was running out. "Ma, ..."

"Get over here, now!" she commanded in the voice she'd always used when she expected unquestioning obedience. She was already lifting the crate away from the cot as he moved to obey.

Together they moved the cot about two feet from the wall. She quickly sidled in. "Hand me a matchbox. Hurry," she hissed.

He pulled out his match box, handed it to her and she struck a match. Even in the feeble light, Sage could see there were scratches in the plaster just at the cot's edge—letters that spelled out, "Rebecca Levy."

Suddenly the noise inside the house increased. People were slamming the front windows shut. "Hurry, we're about to get caught," Sage warned. They quickly moved the cot and crate back into place. Seconds later they were rushing down the stairs, swinging around the newel post and racing for the kitchen. Behind them, an outraged male voice shouted "Hey! You! Stop!"

They sped up, charged through the kitchen and out the back door. "Run!" Sage urged unnecessarily. Mae's skirt was hiked well above her ankles and her boots were already pounding dirt as she ran into the dark field. Behind them the kitchen door slammed against the wall as someone charged out the door after them.

Mae gingerly twisted a brass door knob already warmed by the sun. Even so, every muscle in her body made a painful protest. "I'm getting way too old to race across the fields like a spring colt," she muttered as she stepped from the Monday morning heat into the cooler union hall.

Inside, the customary mix of female chatter and toddler shrieks sounded muted. The day before, Mae personally visited every woman who'd surfaced as the natural leader of her own laundry's group. She'd told each that Rachel Levy was missing, stressed that the absence was temporary, assured the woman that people were searching for Rachel and told them that Rachel would want the women to keep on fighting. They were all dismayed. More than one pointed out that Rebecca Levy had been missing for almost three weeks, despite the same people searching for her. Mae knew that telling them any different would be like telling a gopher to climb a tree. In the end though, all had agreed to try to keep the other women's spirits up.

"Hello, why's everyone so quiet?" she asked a bleak-faced woman listlessly sorting clothes at the donation table. In response, the woman silently handed her a newspaper. It was open to the help wanted ads. Below a "Help Wanted – Female" heading were at least seven different entries advertising for laundry workers. Mae's eye snagged on: "Wanted, neck band and body machine operator. Contact Sparta Laundry." Below that was the entry, "Wanted, laundry shaker, top wage. Contact Star Laundry. And so on down the column that made clear all nine of the association laundries were replacing their union workers.

So, two bits of bad news had hit the group this morning. Mae looked around the room at the subdued women. She shook off her own dispirited reaction. "Well," she said briskly and loud enough for all to hear,

"Looks like the laundries plan on opening up with scabs. What kind of laundry do you suppose they'll be delivering to their customers?"

"Nothing at all from union households," said one woman. "They voted Friday night to fine any union man whose household used the locked out laundries. They've been told to shift their business to the U.S. Laundry."

"Them scabs won't have no clue about how to do a proper job," asserted another woman to nods all around.

"My husband's a driver," said another woman, "He says only about half the drivers are going along with L.D. Warder. The rest are honoring our picket lines." Her back straightened as she said with pride, "And, my Harvey is one of 'em."

The sly query, "Wonder how much those traitors' tips will shrink once their customers get a gander at their spotty clothes?" brought out the smiles from most of the women.

Mae's shoulders relaxed as pride squeezed her heart. These women were sacrificing so much for each other and for future women. "Brave bonny lasses" her Irish ma would have called them. She breathed a sigh of relief as she watched them return to their tasks with lightened spirits and renewed vigor.

Sitting on a chair beside Caroline, Mae pulled up her skirt and studied her ankles. Both bore deep scratches that still smarted despite the healing salve she'd spread over them.

"Good heavens!" exclaimed Caroline, "What in the world happened to your legs?"

"Got into a tussle with a blackberry bramble last night," Mae said, before dropping her skirt and changing the subject. "What did your advisers say about you being our Rachel for a bit?"

"They said I can help the women here in the union hall, take on some of Rachel's duties and such but that I mustn't be seen as a union leader out in public."

"What's that mean you'll be doing?"

"Oh you know, say cheery things to the women and maybe organize who does what here in the hall and get the gals out talking to employers about temporary jobs. Set up speakers for the churches." Caroline's big dark eyes reflected a mix of regret that she couldn't do everything needed and fear that her meager offer would meet rejection.

Mae smiled as she reached over to pat the young woman's thigh. "Well, that's a fine start." She stood, shook out her skirt and added, "All right then, my girl. Let's get things a-goin.'"

TWENTY SEVEN

"Shhh, stop clanking them damn bottles." The two men were skulking through the North End, avoiding the busy streets and the gaslight flickering dimly before saloons and other, less respectable, establishments. It being a late Monday night, the streets were quieter, less populated. Absent were the weekend drunks with their roaring laughter and slurred shouts. It was late enough that the employed and those seeking work were resting, gathering their strength for the next morning. Even the shiftless and worthless were bedded down.

"Well, you should have wrapped 'em better in the towels," came the aggrieved response.

A forceful "Shhh," came again, followed by, "We were in a hurry, remember? Tonight's the best time to do this because nobody's around this late."

The other said nothing, leaving them to trudge quietly up the street, the scuff of their boots the only sound marking their passage.

Reaching a spot across from the laundry, they paused to assess their target.

"There's a light on inside. You sure no one's in there?"

"I'm sure. The laundry don't have no watchman and it's a Monday night, near midnight, for Christ's sake. Ain't nobody gonna be working in a steam laundry tonight. Besides, you don't hear no steam engine puffing away do you?"

"Wahl, I suppose it's quiet, sure enough. But, what about that there light?" Trepidation quivered in the whining question.

"He's one of those fellows who likes having the latest things. I expect he left one of them electric bulbs powered up to scare folks away. Can't really blame him, what with the lockout and all."

"So, what we gonna do?"

The other man looked searchingly up and down the street before responding, "Nobody's out and about right now. I'm going throw this here brick right through that big window over there. You be ready with the lit bottles. Once I've break it, you just toss them both in."

"I sure can't throw it through any hole from clear over here."

"My God, do I have to explain everything?" Receiving no answer, a terse explanation followed. "We're going to cross the street. I'm going to throw the brick. The glass is gonna break and you're going to heave in your burning bottles. Got that?"

At an answering, though hesitant nod, the two of them slunk across the street. After another quick glance in both directions, the one man heaved the brick. Everything went exactly as planned—the window broke and two burning bottles sailed in through the opening. What happened next was not according to plan. The explosion was a helluva lot bigger than it should have been. Luckily, they were a block away when it blew.

A metal bar propped the skylight open to a muggy night softly lit by cloudy moonlight. Sage sat on the polished wood floor mulling over his various failures. Despite more than a month of trying, he'd found no lever to use against Cobb's laundry owners' association. He couldn't even find a way to help the United States Laundry get its chemicals. Finley couldn't keep going much longer without them. Worst of all, Rebecca and Rachel Levy were both missing. Maybe they were already tied, drugged and bouncing out of town in the back of some wagon on their way to an horrific destiny. The elusive stranger in the bowler hat couldn't be found—he hadn't been seen since Rachel vanished. "Good clue, Sherlock," Sage muttered to himself.

This morning the situation had worsened. The laundries were going to open up with scab labor. What was coming next? Professional strikebreakers? He shuddered at the thought. How would those weary laundry women, many of them mothers of small children, faced down hard-hearted out-of-town professionals experienced in the art of breaking heads?

This is what it means to feel heavy of heart, he thought. It was a dragging, physical sensation in the center of his chest.

"Do not sit like lump of cold rice," came Fong's voice, quiet but startling in that Sage hadn't heard his friend enter Mozart's attic. "Stand up, do form. Let thoughts wash through like water through fish net."

Sage obeyed, unwound his legs and took the opening position directly behind Fong. They began moving, Fong's movements somehow combining both the gentleness of waving sea grass and, at the same time, the strength of the water that set that grass to swaying.

Sometimes during the exercise, Sage had sensed those two forces within himself but it was fleeting, as if his recognition chased both forces away. Fong, on the other hand, seemed to always move at the point of their balance.

Today his movements started out feeling totally unbalanced by the worries that wouldn't leave his head. Fong sensed Sage's problem. Upon reaching the end, he simply began all over and then did it a third time. Gradually, a sense of ease overcame the worries, calming their fervor until they flowed away like drifting leaves on a river's surface. Fong was right. The exercise worked, Sage realized, before letting even that thought go.

When they finally stopped moving, Fong turned around and smiled. "Feel better, now?" he asked.

"Exactly what I needed. Thank you," Sage said.

"We are ready to make plans, I think," Fong responded, pointing up towards the roof.

The two of them climbed the ladder and came out onto the flat, tarpapered roof. In one corner stood the pigeon coop, its inhabitants burbling sleepy objections at the disturbance. With a guilty start, Sage realized that he'd been neglecting his boxes of flowers. In this month's heat, he should have been watering them at least twice a day. The rooftop rain barrel had run dry. That meant carrying buckets of water up into the attic and then up the ladder onto the roof. He'd put it off to a point that he'd forgotten to do it. Sage squinted. All the plants looked healthy. The dim moonlight made their blooms colorless but they were there, along with leaves that seemed sturdy and without droop

"Who's been watering my plants?" he asked.

"Young Matthew volunteered. He comes up before going out to be a messenger and after lessons he has with me."

Matthew was the nephew of Mozart's cook, Ida. Now sixteen, he'd already been tested by the horror of his brother's gruesome death at the hands of a railroad bull and by the terror of later being accused of that bull's murder. Sage and his crew had saved the young boy by solving the mystery of the bull's death. Since then, Matthew had helped around the restaurant, used his safety bicycle to earn money delivering messages and in the spring, he'd joined their mission to save Teddy Roosevelt from assassination. Matthew was a very smart kid but also a very clumsy kid.

"You let him carry buckets of water across your attic and up the ladder?" Sage saw that as a real opportunity for a wet disaster.

"Ah, Matthew doing very good with snake and crane. Not graceful yet, but not so much like pup with big feet," Fong said, sitting down on the bench the two of them had hauled up onto the roof once the flower garden had begun to sprout springtime leaves.

Sage joined him on the bench. "I am starting to panic," he said.

"About two missing women?" Fong guessed.

"I don't even know if they're in town anymore. Once they snatched Rachel, I'm worried they shipped both women out."

Fong nodded somberly. "Maybe it is time to ask Farley operatives if they know anything. The cousins keep track of where those two are."

Sage looked up at the sky, noticing that cloud banks had moved in from the west. Idly he hoped that they would bring rain, or at least, some cooling. After a few days of cool it had turned hot once again. The unusually hot summer was getting on his nerves. He longed for the rinsing rain and the tang of autumn just as much as he'd longed for summer sunshine the prior spring. "So, you think we could corner those two tonight?" he asked.

"Yes, got message from cousin. The two men are out on town, going here and there. We could have a visit with them."

Sage snicked a sidewise glance at his friend, "You mean an underground talk?"

Even in the dark, his companion's eyes glittered when he answered by flashing his toothy grin of playful anticipation.

❀　❀　❀

Mae listened to the soft sounds the two men made while performing their attic exercise. Once that sound ceased, she hadn't heard them descend the stairs. That meant they had climbed onto the roof.

She hadn't stayed at the boarding house. Rachel's absence made the room there feel dead, cavernous. After hours of twitching around the room like a water drop on a hot cook stove, she'd had enough. Donning her hat and gathering up some of her things she slipped outside.

She saw Herman Eich hunkered down beneath a cedar tree across the street, his cart parked beside him. Even before she'd crossed the street, she set him to stirring. "Poor man, he's not been getting enough sleep." Herman had done his best but she'd let him down. She'd left Rachel alone, drawn off the Chinese guard leaving Herman to watch both sides of the boarding house. Of course he couldn't. All his efforts over the past weeks had been for nothing. Rachel had slipped from safety.

He was standing by the time she reached him. "Good evening Mae, did you come to keep me company?" he said, a smile parting his heavy beard.

She stepped closer to lay her hand alongside his face. "No Herman, dear. It's just that the empty room is giving me 'the crawlies,' as Sage used to say when he was a little fellow. I'm thinking I might as well go home. Once I'm in Mozart's I'll be safe as a tick on a stray sheep and you can sleep in your own bed for a change."

So the two of them, with Herman's cart in tow, trundled across the bridge toward downtown. In the middle of the span they paused. It had been quiet, with foot, trolley and wagon traffic absent. A nearly full moon, hidden by thin clouds, lent a soft glow to their faces and to their hands clasped together atop the railing. Mae's eyes stared at the outlines of the North End's buildings. Nearer, the black spars of anchored sailing ships silently swayed. Only the distant cries of drunken sailors making their way back to their shipboard berths, signaled that other people also roamed the night.

"'Tomorrow may be that day we've been hoping for.'" Herman said softly, almost to himself.

"One of those Jewish rabbi sayings?" she asked.

"Paraphrased, if you know what I mean," he'd answered with a chuckle.

"Rachel is Jewish," she said.

He gave a soft chuckle but merely said, "You just noticed?"

She used her other hand to lightly jab his shoulder. "Well, no I've always known that. I was just thinking about how brave Rachel is and how dedicated she is to making everyone's lives better."

"You wondered if our culture might have something to do with it?" he asked.

When she merely nodded, he said, "When Jesus said 'Love thy neighbor as thyself,' he was quoting Jewish law."

She looked at him and saw his lips twist ironically, "Of course, Jews are like everyone else: Christian, Buddhist, Jew, Hindu. All religions tell us to aim for the sun. If we're lucky, a few of us might hit the moon."

"Have you ever hit the moon, Herman?" she asked.

He turned and laid an arm across her shoulders, "Well, my gal, maybe one or two times I might have risen above the atmosphere. I can't lay claim to anything more," He tugged her away from the railing, saying, "Come on, dear gal. You need your rest."

He delivered her safe and sound to Mozart's kitchen door before wheeling his cart away, no doubt anticipating the comfort of his single cot inside his little shed.

Here she was, wide awake as a hoot owl. Standing in the alcove between her open windows, a slight cross breeze started up, cooling her brow and bringing her more alert. She stepped closer to the open window and stared down at the empty street three stories below. How many nights she'd stood in this spot, waiting for some sign of Sage, worried that his gallivanting had finally put an end to him? Now it was the thought of Rachel, held by some rascal, terrified over what would happen next, that wouldn't let her rest. At least, Rachel wasn't alone. Mae was sure of that. She was with her sister. That could be the only explanation. Someone lured Rachel from safety by promising she'd see her sister.

Two women, missing—held captive somewhere. They hadn't been taken out of town yet. Mae had to believe that. For sure, no one manhandled them onto a train. Angus Solomon's men would have seen and reported something like that. And, Fong's cousins were watching every street in the North End. No one had seen two women being led, carried or otherwise herded through the streets or onto a ship. Nor had anyone sighted a suspicious enclosed wagon or carriage. Fong said his cousins peered into every conveyance leaving the North End. When they couldn't see who was inside, they'd ran after it until they could.

At the same time, it is certain that whoever held the women planned to make them permanently disappear. After all, he'd kept Rebecca hidden all these weeks. The scoundrel had no way of knowing that so many people were searching for them. So, why hadn't he just kept Rachel in that room with Rebecca? Why had he moved them? And he must have moved them just hours before she and Sage had found Rebecca's name scratched into that wall.

Mae let her mind roam down the streets of the North End. Of course, they could have moved the women through the underground but there was no entrance to it from that boarding house because it had no basement. Besides, Fong's cousins were masters of the underground and he had some of them on the lookout for that very thing.

Mae shuddered. Dark, dirty, with spiders and the skittering of rats and mice, the underground was nearly as bad as she imagined a coal mine to be.

Pulling her thoughts out of the dark, she sent them sailing out over the North End's streets. She shivered, thinking of the open fields and weedy basements of burned out buildings. Being an older part of town, it had many more wooden structures that made fire a constant threat. Once a building burnt, it took a time for something else to rise in its place.

She shook her head violently. Of course Fong's cousins and Solomon's men would have searched all those places for the bodies of the two women. She let that fear go as well. No way those laundry association rascals wanted the scandal of a murdered union leader on their hands. Not when things were already going in their favor.

With a heavy sigh, Mae climbed into bed and closed her eyes though her thoughts continued to rove. She could smell the pee at alley ends, hear seagulls crying as they circled above a river mighty in its power and stinking from its slurry of sewage and trash.

Mae's eyes flew open and she sat up so fast it made her dizzy. Slinging her legs over the side of the bed, she quickly stood and crossed to her armoire. Shoving her laundry worker and Mozart's dresses aside, she found what she was looking for. Hurriedly she donned her shabbiest dress, a pair of cracked boots and flung a holey shawl across her shoulders. At the alcove table she scratched out a note to her son. Then she was gone, silently slipping down the stairs.

It was just an idea. She'd first check out her suspicion because she didn't want to get Sage's hopes up nor have him tell her it was hopeless. Besides, she admitted ruefully to herself, she didn't want Sage to steal her thunder if she was right.

Behind her up on the third floor, a gust of air blew in one window and out the other. A small white piece of paper lifted to ride it, following her out into the street.

TWENTY EIGHT

SHIFTING FOR BETTER BALANCE ATOP the wooden packing crate, Paul Sinclair carefully kept a firm grip on the nearly empty whiskey bottle. Tilting it up to take a slug, he noticed that starlight pinpricked the sky. The clouds were gone and so was the moon. It would be another hot day. He swiped a hand across his mouth and wiped it on his trousers. He knew that he looked like he'd slept in his clothes. As if he could sleep.

What the hell am I doing here, he wondered. Chicago was where he belonged, not in this dinky town with tree stumps dotting the pastures across the river. He returned his gaze to the small coastal steamer tugging against its anchor chain about fifty feet out from the wharf's edge. He imagined a tiny cabin, the two women packed together, maybe tied up. He hoped not tied up. No point in it. The captain's preparations would keep them secure. The cabin had a sturdy lock and a bolted porthole. He stared at that porthole. Was she staring back at him? He squinted, trying to see, but it didn't help.

Another swig and he commenced speaking, slurring his words but not caring. She couldn't hear him after all. "You'll be all right Miss Rebecca. Especially now that you have your sister with you. She's a tough one. That was a clever trick, he congratulated himself. She went right for it. She loves you, your sister does," he assured the invisible Rebecca.

They loved each other, those two gals. And he, damn him to hell, he'd used their love against them. It had been a simple, one-man job to move both women from the whorehouse to the ship. He'd simply moved them one at a time. First Rebecca, telling her she had to dress like a whore and walk beside him acting like his doxy. If she refused, gave warning or tried to run, he told her, the people in the whorehouse would kill Rachel. Rebecca had done as instructed, walking beside him dolled up like a tart, though anyone looking at her closely would have seen it was an act. There was a quality to her than couldn't be painted over.

Once Rebecca was securely onboard, he'd gone back to fetch Rachel who was definitely the more feisty sister. She too had performed as instructed though his forearm still ached where she'd dug her nails in while smiling sweetly at him.

He had to admire her spunk. She wasn't as gentle as Rebecca. In fact, she reminded him strongly of his sisters. His sisters. Once his sisters had loved him, too. Their shrieks and games in the summer evenings, their laughter when they'd ganged up on their spoiled baby brother. Still, all three had cried when he'd left for the seminary. But, they'd also been proud of him. His memory roamed across their faces. They were ten years older—probably married, maybe mothers by now.

A seagull squawked overhead, the sound jerking his eyes toward the river, back to the porthole. "I hope you get to be a mother, Rebecca. You'd be a good one. I can tell." Who was he kidding? Where she was going, Panama, she'd be lucky to survive—he'd seen the numbers. The men digging the canal were dropping like flies from malaria, yellow fever and who knew what else.

Yah, who was he kidding? Even if Rebecca managed to live, the other loathsome diseases would likely end any hope of her ever having children. That was the way of prostitution. That hygiene society had it right. Even if she did bear a child, it would likely be blind. He'd seen it happen. More than once.

Whoa, his damn bottle was empty. "I probably shouldn't be drinking to excess within your sight, Miss Rebecca. A gentleman doesn't do that. Hah! You know I'm not a gentleman. Though you're a lady, no doubt about that." He lifted the bottle to salute the porthole. "Yup, a real lady," he repeated forcefully as he threw the bottle into the river.

But he wasn't done confiding in the imagined Rebecca. "You know, I figured that once you were on your way so to speak, that I'd be on my way as well. I planned on heading back to Chicago, where I belong, leave this experience behind me. But 'ole Farley says I have to stay on a bit longer. Help Cobb see this god awful business through to the end or thereabouts. He wasn't exactly clear, our Mister Farley."

Sinclair leaned forward as if to impart a secret, even though the ship was far outside of hearing range. "I don't really like Farley. He's a cold hearted bastard with cold eyes and when you shake his hand, it's cold too. And it's not the weather. It's hot here. Not as muggy as Chicago, though. I don't miss that. Anyway, about Farley. I never took part in a labor fight before. Can't say I'll ever do it again. Don't like it. I used to think my grandma worked too hard on the farm. But those laundry ladies, they work even harder. It's a helluva job. Wouldn't wish it on my worst enemy."

Sinclair lifted his bowler from his head and dropped it on the crate beside him. For a bit, he was quiet, letting the river air cool his face and ruffle his hair. Heaving a sigh, he turned back toward the porthole. "Whiskey's gone. I'm going to have to. . ."

Wait. Had he heard a step? Holding his breath he looked north. Maybe it had been a rat. But, no. there was definitely a second step, this one closer. No rat then. He slid off the crate and crouched behind it. His eyes strained to see. There! A figure, stood at the corner of the building, not forty feet away.

It was a woman, he could tell because a skirt covered her legs. She stepped closer until she was just twenty feet away, staring out at the ship. He recognized that walk. He knew that profile. He'd been following it for weeks. "What the hell is she doing here?" he muttered, but he scrunched lower and froze in position until her boots moved off leaving the only the sound of wavelets slapping against the timbers beneath his feet.

Fong and Sage, dressed in working man's garb, slipped out of Mozart's. Once outside, they strode separately to the North End, keeping each other in sight the entire way. It wouldn't do to walk together. Many would notice, some might turn threatening.

At last they met up in the hallway of Fong's fraternal organization. There another man waited, no doubt he was one of Fong's so-called cousins. He spoke quickly in Chinese to Fong, who nodded then responded with a single word that sent the cousin out into the street.

"Come, we go," Fong said, gesturing to Sage. "Farley's two men met ten other men at train station and took them to hotel here in North End. Then all went to restaurant for dinner. After that, all men went to saloon. They are still in saloon. We go and try to bag our two." With that, Fong was out the door and on the street, setting off at a fast pace with Sage trailing behind.

Reaching the Slap Jack saloon, Fong stepped into the dark doorway of a job shark storefront while Sage opened the saloon's door and stepped inside. There was no mistaking the operatives' and their ten guests. The party took up an entire corner of the place and were so boisterous they drowned out every other sound in the place. It took Sage but a second to figure out exactly who the newcomers were.

The ten fellows from the train were strikebreakers, rather than management operatives like the original two. There was a difference. The strikebreakers were rougher men, big, with meaty hands. They telegraphed power, violence, and a low level of intelligence, exactly what would intimidate peaceful picketers. In contrast, the operatives exuded sneakiness, a characteristic essential to their function.

Sage cursed quietly as he waited for the beer he'd ordered. Then he picked up the drink and ambled over to an empty table near the rowdy group. Once seated, he made a show of sipping his beer and checking his cheap pocket watch every few minutes, as if he were waiting for someone who was late.

The men in the corner were so arrogantly drunk, they had to be incapable of suspicion. Their loud voices could be heard clearly by anyone in the room. "Woo hoo, sure is gonna be a mighty fine pleasure manhandling a bunch of women for a change," one chortled. "Any of them lookers?" a particularly ugly cuss asked one of Farley's operatives.

That fellow shook his head, saying, "Nah, mostly they're pale and stringy." Sage felt his blood surge. Any woman would be pale and stringy if she worked sixty hours a week in a steam laundry.

After the strikebreaker's initial outburst the talk around the table turned to bragging about past victories against union members and the pain they'd inflicted. Without having to feign disgust, Sage abruptly drained his glass, stood and left the saloon as if angry that his friend failed to show. Since he knew who the two operatives were, he wasn't about to sit there and listen to them crow. He'd rather wait outside with Fong.

An hour later, Farley's men stumbled out the saloon door and staggered toward their boarding house. Fong and Sage trailed behind. When the two came abreast of a dark alley opening they charged, moving as silent as twin sharks through water. Neither man put up much resistance because each one had left his coordination and reaction time back in Slap Jacks.

Without saying a word, Fong and Sage twisted the men's arms up behind their backs and shoved them toward the dead end of the alley. There, Fong held his captive in a one-handed grip while he rapped lightly on a plain door set into the brick building's wall. The door immediately opened to reveal a Chinese man standing on a stair landing. He silently pointed toward some descending wooden stairs.

Sage and Fong walked the men down the stairs, ignoring their grunts and squeals of pain. At the bottom was a wooden-walled storage room. It had a door opening into the larger basement beneath the building. Once the four of them shuffled across the threshold, they were in Portland's infamous underground.

As he stepped into the dusty dark, Sage experienced no surge of fear. It had taken some time but it seemed he had left behind his childhood fear of dark, underground spaces that he acquired in the Appalachian coal mine. After spending considerable time in Portland's underground, he'd managed to conquer his fear. Of course he wasn't fooling himself. Merely thinking of a cave or mine set him to twitching. .

The four of them shuffled through dust so dry it raised clouds in the air. Following the lantern held aloft by their Chinese guide they quickly reached the cell. It stood in a corner with brick walls on two sides. The two other sides were bounded by closely spaced iron bars, just like those found in the city jail. Days past, crimps used the cell to imprison shanghaied men before sending them on to their doom. Last year Sage wanted to destroy the cell but Fong talked him out of it. He'd promised that his cousins would make sure no shanghaier ever used it again.

Fong and Sage deposited their charges in the cell and slammed the iron door shut before the men understood what was happening. Sage and Fong stepped away, taking the lantern's light with them.

"I'm thinking they might be too drunk to answer any questions." Sage said.

"Maybe should try anyway. They not talk, we come back later," Fong responded.

Returning to stand before the cell, Sage told them, "You men want to be released, all you have to do is answer a few simple questions," He was careful to keep the light aimed at their eyes and away from his face. This was a kidnapping after all.

The smaller fellow seemed alert compared to the other bigger one who was sitting in the dust, his back against the brick wall, his mouth lax and gaping. "And exactly what are the questions?" asked the more alert one.

"First of all, do you know where Farley's keeping the Levy women?"

The fellow blinked. "Who?" he finally asked.

"Rebecca and Rachel Levy. Your boss has taken them. He's hiding them somewhere. We want to know where."

"Rachel Levy's that gal working at the Sparta Laundry, ain't she?" the fellow asked.

"That's right. She was kidnapped last Saturday night."

The fellow shook his head. "I don't know nothing about no kidnapping. Farley hired us to work with the drivers. He ain't said nothing about no kidnapping." The fellow's tone was emphatic and rang true.

Sage and Fong exchanged a glance. "Okay, then," Sage said. "How about the other fellow Farley hired? The one who wears the bowler hat all the time? What's his name? Where does he stay?"

The man sitting in the dirt stirred and struggled to straighten up. "Alfred," he slurred warningly.

"His name's Alfred?" Sage asked, amazed the man would be so compliant.

"Nah, my name's Alfred," the standing man said. "I don't remember nothing about any fellow in a bowler hat," he added. This time, there was a sly twist to his lips, accompanied by a narrowing and juddering glance of his eyes to one side. He was lying.

It being just hours before dawn, Sage was beyond tired and without patience. He looked at Fong and said, "I suggest we leave these fellows right here to think about their answers. Maybe come back in a day or two to see if their memories have improved."

Fong nodded and, without another word, he, Sage and the only light in the basement moved silently away from the cell, leaving the two captives behind in the pitch black dark.

Mae knew her boots were dragging but she didn't care. She'd started in the North End and walked the entire length of the waterfront. She trod down every dock access, studied every ship, trying to figure out which one might hold the Levy women. There'd been a lot of ships.

After all that walking, she realized that some ships could be eliminated based on distance alone. For example, it made no sense that they would have moved the two women all the way south, far from the North End. Too many chances someone would notice them during the move. And, Mr. Fong had assured her that not a single covered van, wagon or coach had left the North End without his cousins knowing who or what, was in it. That eliminated any ship south of Burnside Street, the North End's border.

Her footsteps slowed as she pondered the ships she'd seen berthed along the river north of Burnside, near the brothel where they'd kept Rachel. There'd been far fewer tied up along that stretch—six total. She sent her mind roaming across those six ships. Two were out because they were river boat tugs. A couple were huge ships in the midst of loading which meant they were busy hives of activity. So many people bustling about made them unlikely prisons for the two women. That left the remaining two. Which one could it be?

Mae let her mind still. Not trying to decide between the two, just letting her thoughts drift back and forth between them. Then a question came to her. One of the ships, a small coastal vessel, wasn't actually tied to the wharf. Instead, it had dropped an anchor out in the river. Why? There'd been room at the wharf, so why not tie up there? Besides, the boat was falling apart, its paint splotched, its mast rusty and stains were trailing down its cabin's side. She was no sailor and hadn't lived in a port city but a few years. Still, even she could see the ship's owner must not have money for upkeep. So, he needed money and might be tempted to do anything to get it. She realized one more thing. That small coastal steamer was the ship closest to the whorehouse where they'd imprisoned Rebecca. She took a deep breath as certainty took hold. That was the ship.

Minutes later she was at Mozart's kitchen door and soon on the third floor. She checked Sage's room. He wasn't there or in the attic. Going into her room, she noticed her note was gone. That meant he'd noticed she'd moved back from across the river and knew she gone to look at ships. All she had to do was scratch the name on a second note and he'd know where to find her. Quickly she scrawled "*Maggie Jane*," set her hairbrush atop the note and hurried back downstairs. She had to get back to that ship, keep an eye on it until Sage could get there with Fong and some men.

She slipped out the kitchen door, locking it behind her. As she moved rapidly down the empty street, Mae's mind traveled far ahead of her feet. That focused intent was why she failed to sense the other person who followed her onto the wharf—the person who suddenly yanked her back against his chest and slapped a wet, cold and stinky rag over her nose and mouth.

TWENTY NINE

"Good god, man. It's barely dawn," Cobb spluttered when he saw Farley standing on his doorstep. Gold was just beginning to shimmer at the eastern edge of an overcast sky.

"Sorry, Mr. Cobb but problems have sprung up since we last met. Problems I thought you should know about as soon as possible."

Cobb opened the door wider and gestured Farley inside. "Go into the parlor there, I'll be with you in a few minutes. I just have to pull on some clothes."

After Cobb left, Farley studied the room. It had that overdressed Victorian feel, all patterns, drapery and clutter. He couldn't live in the mess. He liked clean lines and open spaces. One of his clients lived in a new Frank Wright house and it was unlike anything Farley'd ever seen before. A man felt free walking through those rooms of glass, wood and light. If he ever built a home, that's the kind of house he wanted.

"So what's happened that's so damn bad you had to wake up my household?" Cobb was back, still wearing a bathrobe but now trousers covered his naked legs. His words were tough but his forehead wore deep creases of concern.

"First of all, someone set fire to the American Laundry late last night." Farley began.

"Oh, no. Did it burn down? Is it gone?" Cobb interrupted.

Farley held up a hand. "That's not the bad part. Ryland McCarthy was working inside when it burned. They found his body just a while ago in the ashes."

Cobb slumped against the back of his armchair. "Oh, that is bad news. Was it the union thugs? Did the police catch the ones who did it?"

"Well, no. They haven't arrested anyone but I did talk to the officer on the scene and steered him in the right direction."

"That was fast thinking. Who'd you tell him did it?" Cobb asked.

"A fellow who'd been sleeping in a doorway was telling folks he saw two figures throw something burning through the front window and then hightail it down the street. He said there was a big explosion right afterward. When I saw a policeman, I suggested the arsonists must have been the union president and one of his thugs, seeing how there was a labor lockout going on."

"An explosion? They used dynamite?"

"Nope, the fire chief said the place was full of gasoline cans. He hunted up one of the workers who told him that last night, just before the laundry closed, McCarthy took a gasoline delivery for his generator. They'd left the gas cans stacked in the laundry's front office. McCarthy planned to move the cans to the back first thing this morning. The fire chief thinks that when the arsonists heaved burning bottles through the window, they set off the gasoline cans inside. It made a huge explosion. People heard it from blocks away."

Farley fell silent. Cobb saw that the man was frowning and rubbing his hands. "What is it, what aren't you telling me?" Cobb demanded.

Farley looked up and said, "It's my two operatives, they're missing. They didn't come back to their boardinghouse all night. I looked in every saloon. Thought I'd send them snooping around, see if there was any activity at the Levy woman's boardinghouse. But, they weren't there. They're missing."

"Surely you don't think they had anything to do with the fire?" Anxiety shrilled Cobb's voice.

Farley hesitated, whooshed out a breath before saying, "That's just it. They told me that they suspected McCarthy was going to sell the American Laundry to the unions. And, I kind of supported their suspicion by saying he had seemed the fellow most resistant to the association's plans."

"Oh, my god. Do you think they're the ones who burned down McCarthy's laundry?" This time fear dropped Cobb's voice to a whisper.

Farley shrugged. "I surely hope not but I have to admit that was the first thought that came to my mind. That's why I went hunting for them right away. Now that the two of them seemed to have vanished it makes me think it's a real possibility. I'm sure whoever did it had no idea they'd cause an explosion, let alone a death. Since that's what happened, it would make sense that they would skedaddle out of town as fast as possible."

"What are we going to do?" Cobb asked as he lit a cigarette with shaking hands.

"I'm going to keep looking for them, quiet like. Check the stables to see if they rented horses last night. I know they didn't leave on any trains because none were running. If I find them, I'll ask if they did it. If they did, I'll make sure they get out of town."

Cobb was nodding eagerly. "Yes, yes. We can't be associated in any way with the fire. It would end the lockout, we'd have to cave. You did the right thing coming here, Farley. Thank you." He stood, ready to usher Farley to the door.

Farley stayed seated. "There is one other different complication that's come up," he said. "Sinclair caught that older woman, Mae, the one who was living with Rachel Levy, snooping around the ship where we have the two women stashed. He, ah, well, he . . . "

"Spit it out man! Don't tell me he killed her." Cobb sank back down onto the chair.

"No, no. He didn't hurt her but he did kidnap her."

"What! We now have three women on our hands that we need to get rid of?" Cobb's face flushed red. "This is turning into a nightmare. What are we going to do with her?"

"Sinclair dumped her in a row boat and took her out to the ship. She's locked up with the other two. I propose that we send her south as well."

Cobb was silent for a moment before clearing his throat to say hesitantly, "It's doubtful that your friends in San Francisco are going to be interested in paying her fare to Panama. She's a bit long in the tooth for whorehouse work."

Farley shrugged. "Once the ship crosses the Columbia River bar, do we really care what happens to any of them? We just need to be sure they can't come back to point their fingers at us."

"You mean at me or the association. You'll be long gone. Tell me that Sinclair didn't let them see his face. Tell me they have no way of knowing that it was my foreman who snatched them."

Farley said nothing, just pressed his lips together.

"Well, I guess that settles that. Either all three go the Panama or else . . ." Cobb left the sentence unfinished. He didn't need to finish his sentence out loud.

Sage hurriedly climbed the hidden staircase to Mozart's third floor. He couldn't remember ever being so tired. Pushing aside tapestry hiding the doorway, he stepped into the hallway only to freeze at the sight of a dark figure rushing toward him. He quickly spread his feet, bent his knees slightly to anchor himself before he realized it was Fong.

"Good grief, Mr. Fong. What is going on?"

"Mr. Eich just came to back door in kitchen. He say he is here to escort Miz Clemens to union hall. I come up here, no Miz Clemens. Her bed is rumpled but she is gone. Found this on her table." He handed Sage a note scrawled across a torn piece of paper. Only two words were there, *Maggie Jane*. Fong said, "Mister Eich and me are going to union hall to find this Maggie person. See if she knows where lady mother went."

Sage's scalp prickled, as if army ants were charging across it, just under the skin. "No, no, *Maggie Jane* isn't a person, it's a ship. That's why I was coming here, to get you. I think that the Levy women are being held on it."

"How do you know this, Mr. Sage?" Fong demanded.

"Because I just stumbled into two sailors who were yammering on about the fact they'd been waiting for two women to board their ship so it could set sail to San Francisco. They talked like the women were traveling against their will. I figured it has to be the Levy women."

"Where is *Maggie Jane* anchored?"

"That's just it, I don't know. I thought I'd head over to James Laidlaw's office. He'll know her berth and when the tide is going to turn."

Laidlaw was the British Consul in Portland. In that capacity he oversaw the British sailors and ships berthed in port. He made sure that the men signing on to British ships went willingly. He was an active enemy of the shanghaiers and the business men who profited from shanghaiing. The year prior, Laidlaw teamed up with Sage's group to put one particularly deadly shanghaier out of business. Laidlaw was someone Sage trusted, making him one of the few in the city who knew about Sage's undercover role.

"Yes, we all go out kitchen door. The restaurant still closed so not too many workers in kitchen. Quick, please. Mr. Eich waiting in alley. He very nervous," Fong said as he rushed toward the stairway that led down into Mozart's entrance hallway.

Sage followed on the heels of his friend. Soon the three of them were heading to Laidlaw's office three blocks away. Bursting in through the front door, they saw a line of men waiting before the counter. Fortunately, Laidlaw took one look at their faces and understood matters were urgent. He gestured them toward his office while telling his clerk he'd return to help in just a few minutes.

"What is it? Has something happened?" he asked once the door was shut.

"We think white slavers have three women. Mae Clemens is probably one of them. We think that they're taking the women down to 'Frisco on a coastal steamer called the *Maggie Jane*. We need to find out where that ship is tied up and when she's going to leave. You have that information, don't you, Mr. Laidlaw?"

Sage spoke in a rush but Laidlaw instantly grasped the situation. He pawed through papers on his desk until he found a list of some sort. Running his fingers down the column he settled on a spot, saying, "Here she is. The *Maggie Jane* is tied up at the Couch Street wharf." He plucked another piece of paper from the desk, studied it and said. "She was scheduled to leave this morning. If she's departing with the outgoing tide, she will have left nearly an hour ago."

"Christ," Sage swore and turned toward the door. As he flung it open he hurled a "Thank you" over his shoulder but didn't wait to hear Laidlaw's response. Fong and Eich were right behind him as he burst out onto the street.

Caroline stared open-mouthed at the big police sergeant who'd just burst into the union hall followed by a passel of men. "Someone's been ... been murdered?" she stuttered. "Who?" The silence in the hall was so profound that a dropping pin would have boomed. It seemed everyone was holding their breath.

"The fellow who owns the American Laundry, Ryland McCarthy," Hanke answered, glancing around the room as cries rang out. A few women began sobbing.

"I take it Mr. McCarthy wasn't hated, even though he locked you out?" he asked the room in general.

A woman pushed forward, her eyes wet with tears. "Mr. McCarthy weren't a bad man. Not like some of the others. I spoke to him, private-like. He wasn't happy to lock us out, he even apologized. He said he just felt he had no choice. That laundry association wudda run him outta business. "

Caroline could see the police sergeant considering the woman's words. Glancing around the room, he asked. "So, is Rachel Levy in the hall, here?"

Everyone shook their heads. Caroline wondered how the officer knew of Rachel but she only said, "No, we believe that she's been kidnapped. Rachel's been missing since last Sunday night."

Hanke's face didn't change but his blue eyes narrowed slightly. "Who's in charge here?" he finally asked. No one said anything until Caroline took a small step forward and said, "I guess that would be me for now."

Hanke gestured with his head toward the outer door. "Would you mind talking with me in private for a bit, Miss?"

Caroline dutifully followed Hanke through the doors once he told his men to stay in place and make sure no one left by another door. Outside on the sidewalk, he turned to Caroline. "Where's Mae Clemens?" he asked.

His question shocked her. How could he know about Mae too? She stuttered, "She, she was supposed to meet me early this morning at a cafe about a block from here. She never showed up. I thought maybe she'd forgotten and come on ahead to the hall, here. But, she wasn't here and the women say they haven't seen her." Caroline let the worry show in her voice.

Hanke's concern mirrored her own as he said, "I know she's been here every day. I've been keeping in touch with her folks. I counted on her to tell me the truth because she always does."

She stood quietly as the big policeman stared into an overcast sky that had finally brought relief from the heat. If the moisture in the air was any indication, they'd soon have rain. Thoughts were tumbling willy-nilly through Caroline's head.

"It's not like Mae to disappear without a word. And, she'd be the third woman we've lost in the last three weeks."

Hanke's gaze sharpened. "What do you mean, 'the third'? I thought it you said was just Mae and Rachel Levy who are missing."

Caroline shook her head. "No, the first woman who disappeared was Rachel Levy's sister Rebecca. That was over three weeks ago. Some of Mae's friends have been searching for her ever since. Then Rachel disappeared Saturday night and now Mae's gone this morning." Caroline couldn't help herself. Tears of frustration and fear welled up in her eyes. She blinked rapidly before dashing them away with the back of her hand. "I don't know what we're going to do now," she told the sergeant.

"I think you'd better come on down to the police station with me," Hanke told her. "It sounds like this whole situation needs some looking into."

THIRTY

"Forgive me." It was his litany, the phantom words silently sounding in his brain not once but a hundred times the last hour. Sinclair sucked in a deep, shuddering breath. It was over. He'd done it. No longer his problem, no longer his concern. That was the counter litany, one he had to force himself to silently repeat every time the guilt hit him.

Around him men shouted and produce wagons rattled as sun-tanned farmers drove onto the wharf, wagons sagging under crates of fruits and vegetables, all headed south aboard the small steam ship that slid into the berth once the *Maggie Jane* raised anchor and headed down river. He squinted, trying to identify the produce visible between the crate slats: apples, apricots, beets, carrots, the dark green of squash, all looking lush and fresh. He'd grown up in a farming community and couldn't shake the habit of gauging produce.

The ship they were loading must have a refrigerated hold. Rich land around here according to the fellows in the saloons. They'd claimed the dirt would grow anything, even a pencil. He didn't believe the bit about the pencil but from what he was seeing, it looked like everything else could thrive in the surrounding valleys.

Rebecca had said she and her sister grew up on a farm outside Chicago. Tropical Panama would seem so foreign to them. That Mae woman, she was older, not innocent like the sisters. Still, her toughness would be no match for the Canal sickness.

If she even made it that far. She was feisty. She'd planted a huge bruise atop his foot when she'd stomped on it. His shin had one too. Her scratches still hurt. In the end, though, she'd been no match for the chloroform.

His fingers fumbled around in his suit pocket until they found the amber glass vial with its tight glass stopper. Holding it up against the early morning light he tilted it, checking the line of the liquid's surface. Only about a quarter left. He pushed the stopper further down until he felt pain and noticed that his thumbnail had turned white.

Without this chemical, none of the women would be on the ship. He looked at the hand holding the vial, wishing it wasn't his. In sudden anger he raised his hand, bent his elbow and sent the vial arcing through the hot morning air. When it hit the water it sank, bobbed up and then quickly floated out of sight downriver, following the *Maggie Jane*. Too late for it to catch the ship. Probably wouldn't even end up at the same place. The ship would turn left and steam south along the coast. That bottle might float westward, all the way to China if it kept its air and wasn't busted up by a ship keel, drifting log, or other floating debris.

Panama. Once the plan had been set, he'd read a bit about Panama. He'd learned enough to know that there was a good chance that Rebecca or her sister could die there. For sure, if the Clemens woman made it that far, she wouldn't survive. It wasn't just the yellow fever. That sick engineer in the saloon, Copeland, had been accurate in his tale. The whole darn place was in an uproar. Columbia didn't want to sell France's half-built canal to the Americans. The governor and his buddies in the canal area did want to sell. Everyone thought they would try to secede from Columbia—civil war in other words. Just like Copeland predicted.

His mind's eye saw Rebecca fleeing as soldiers crashed through doors and distant cannons roared. She didn't deserve that kind of end. She . . . "God forgive me," his litany began again.

Sage ran, leaping around people and jumping curbs. He became aware that Eich was straining to keep up. "Herman, can you run and tell Sergeant Hanke what's going on? Fong and I will get to the wharf and see if the ship's still there. If it isn't, we'll be on our way to Astoria."

Eich merely nodded and peeled off, heading for the police station a few blocks away. Across the street Fong kept pace, breaking into a run at the same time Sage did. A closed coach rattled toward him from behind. He swiveled to look without slowing. Delicate designs adorned the door and side panels. This meant it was a private coach just as its unmarred paint said it was brand new. As it passed, a woman inside called out to the coach driver who immediately hauled back on the reins, the coach door flew open and a woman jumped out onto the sidewalk without waiting for the driver to dismount and lower the stairs. Reaching the sidewalk she turned and gestured impatiently to those still inside the vehicle. Five other women poured out.

Sage mentally cursed, trying to get around that gaggle of women would slow him down. He glanced at Fong and was surprised to see the other man crossing the street toward him and gesturing toward the women. Then Sage saw her—Lucinda.

Once their eyes met, she raised an arm, gestured that he should enter the coach and jumped back inside, leaving her companions to mill about on the sidewalk, cackling like hens shoved off their perches. Sage and Fong reached the coach simultaneously, clambered inside and slammed the doors shut. Sage shouted to the driver, "Couch St. Wharf, and hurry!" They moved forward with a jerk.

He turned toward Lucinda, "They've kidnapped Mae. She's on a ship bound for San Francisco and god knows where else." He quickly filled her in. When the coach reached the entrance to the wharf, Sage and Fong jumped out. Sage turned to tell Lucinda to stay in the coach but all he saw was her backside a moment before the door on the other side of the coach slammed shut. Turning toward the river he saw Fong and Lucinda hurrying away down the wood planks. He ran to catch up. Even as he did, he couldn't help but notice that the three of them were causing a stir among the men trucking crates in and out of the nearby warehouses. No wonder—they had to be an odd sight.

He'd caught up with them by the time they burst out onto the wharf. A ship was tied up at the wharf. A crowded gang plank bridged the gap as men hurriedly loaded produce crates aboard. He ran to the upriver end of the boat. His stomach plummeted. The script across its stern end proclaimed this was the *Lucky Abner*.

Fong and Lucinda caught his disappointment because both of their shoulders drooped. "Too late?" Fong asked.

Sage cast a glance around. The men now loading the ship wouldn't have been on the wharf until the *Abner* tied up. Then he spotted another man, slouched against some stacked crates. Beside him lay a bottle of whiskey. A bowler hat sat neatly on a neighboring crate. Abandoning his indolent posture and near empty bottle, the man's eyes narrowed and he slowly stood.

Sage didn't hesitate. He raced thirty feet and grabbed the man tightly by his shirt front, jerking him nearly off his feet. The man didn't resist. "How long ago did the *Maggie Jane* sail?" he demanded. "Where are they taking them?"

The man's hand reached up and pulled feebly at Sage's grip as he said, "She sailed over forty-five minutes ago. Much to my regret."

Sage let loose, noting that Lucinda and Fong both stood so that the fellow couldn't escape. "What do you mean?"

"I mean, I've been sitting here, hating myself for allowing them to take Rebecca, Rachel and Mae away. I'd give anything if there were a way to get them back. But the ship has sailed and I'm just one man."

Behind him, Lucinda said, "John, the coach. We have the coach."

Sage didn't have to think, he grabbed one of the man's arms and Fong the other. As fast as they could, they half-carried, half-drug the man toward the street and the waiting coach. Reaching it, Fong ran around the back to the other side to block any escape. He clambered aboard while Sage and Lucinda shoved the man inside, following him quickly and slamming the door shut. Lucinda shouted "Astoria! Hurry!" at the driver who hadn't moved from his perch. The coach jerked forward. They had barely rolled a block before Fong shouted, "Stop."

The coach halted and Fong stuck his head out the window to shout in Chinese at a man on the sidewalk who hurried over. There followed a quick exchange. Sage thought he caught the word "Hanke" in its midst. The man's face disappeared from the window as Fong sat back, hit the roof of the coach with his fist and shouted, "Go!" Once again, the coach jerked into action.

"Can we beat them to Astoria?" Sage asked no one in particular.

Fong said, "It depend on horses. Steamer will take one day. If we can find horses on way, we can maybe beat them."

"What about taking the Astoria Columbia River Railway? It leaves this morning in just a few minutes." Lucinda asked.

Sage was shaking his head even before her question ended. "The train will take too long. I rode that train once. It stops everywhere to let passengers on and off. It would take forever compared to this coach."

The man in the corner said calmly, "The captain said they should reach the Columbia River bar near sunset so he can cross during low tide. He's running with the outgoing tide and will be under steam. He's in a hurry to get away."

The three of them turned to look at him. There was no triumph in the man's face, only sad resignation. "Even if we get lucky and catch them, how can just four of us rescue them from a ship in the middle of the river?"

"So, Miss," Hanke began once Caroline was settled into a chair with a cup of hot tea at her elbow, "suppose you tell me exactly what is going on." As she opened up her mouth to speak, he raised a finger to halt her and added, "If it helps you to be more truthful, you should know that Mae Clemens is a very, very good friend of mine. I will do anything to make sure no harm comes to her."

For a second or two, Caroline could only blink. He watched her forehead wrinkle and her focus turn inward as she tried to understand that connection. Finally, she took a deep breath, fingered her cross and said, "I will trust you at your word" and began her explanation.

"So, for certain Rachel couldn't have had anything to do with the laundry fire since she was already missing, is that correct?" Hanke said. When she nodded, he asked, "What about the union president?"

"I honestly don't know. I would say that he does not seem like the type." She leaned forward, "Just exactly who told you union people were involved?"

Hanke flipped open a little pad of paper and ran a big finger down the page, stopping when he reached a scribble. "A bystander from out of town named James Farley said he saw a man and someone else running way. He said he thought it was a labor union president."

Caroline's snort of disbelief raised his head. He looked at her, "What?" he demanded.

"Farley's the union buster hired by the laundry association. I'd say that his 'witnessing' any such thing is highly suspect."

"Damn, I bet the police officer who took the information didn't bother to find out why Farley was in town." Hanke scooted his chair back and headed for the door and called, "Bingham, I need you!"

Caroline twisted in her chair in time to see a young police officer appear. "Bingham, go find that Farley chap you interviewed and bring him in. You and Clifford interview him. See if he confesses that he's a union buster for the laundry owners. If he doesn't, throw his butt into a cell."

Hanke returned and took his seat again. "Okay, that was helpful information. In just a minute I'll stir the troops and get them searching for Mae and those two other women. But, before I do, I want to know exactly what Miss Caroline Stark is doing in the middle of the laundry workers' dispute. I want the truth, please."

Caroline opened her mouth to speak but before she could say anything, there was a timid knock on the door frame and a fresh-faced young officer looked in to say, "There's a ragpicker fellow outside who says you're gonna wanna talk to him in person, personally. Says his name is Eich."

Hanke jumped up from his desk and disappeared out the door. He was back just minutes later. "Eich says they think Mae's on board a ship called the *Maggie Jane*."

"On a ship? But why would she want to . . ." Caroline began.

"Not willingly. Kidnapped." Hanke scowled as he tapped a pencil eraser on his desk. "I guess we better find out when that ship's going to sail and arrange a search of her."

Another timid knock on the doorframe interrupted them. Hanke scowled at the same young officer who said, "Sorry Sergeant, but now there's a Chink outside in the hallway. He's saying he has to talk to you, 'matter of life or death' is what he seems to be saying. It's hard to understand him with that accent."

Hanke looked at Caroline as if considering whether to send her out but then he shrugged and said, "Show him in."

The police officer left and soon returned with a Chinese man of twenty years or so. The fellow removed his tattered hat and stood before Hanke's desk, his face twisted in concentration. He didn't wait for Hanke to ask him to speak, "Mr. Fong. He say, 'Quick. Get to Astoria. Mae in trouble. For sure on ship, *Maggie Jane*. Big danger.'"

The accent was thick but Hanke understood the man because he leapt to his feet so fast that his chair hit the wall. Caroline, too, was on her feet instantly.

"I'm coming with you," she said in a tone that made clear she would argue and delay unless he agreed.

"Come on then. Hope you're up for a train ride." He also gestured to the Chinese man. "You, too. We might need your help."

Once outside the office, Hanke shouted, "Bingham!" only to get the response, "He's already left Sarge. You told him . . . ."

"Right, right," Hanke interrupted, "You come along then. Grab some men as we go. We're heading for union station. Run! We have to catch a train in the next ten minutes!"

As they stormed down the hallway, Hanke gestured toward an older man dressed in shabby clothes. To him Hanke said, "Come on, Herman. The *Maggie Jane* has already sailed!" As the four of them burst out the double doors and down the steep steps, Hanke grabbed Caroline's elbow. He began pulling her along as fast as her much shorter legs could travel.

THIRTY ONE

"It wasn't Ryland McCarthy," Farley announced without any exchange of greetings. Cobb looked up from his paperwork his face first puzzled then dismayed.

He threw his pencil onto the desk, where it hit and rolled off the edge. He didn't watch it roll off nor did he pick it up. "Who was it?"

"I just got word from my informer that the laundry sale was finalized about an hour ago. The Union Trade Council is celebrating and word got out." Farley caught Cobb's dead-eyed stare and added, "It was Henry Teague who sold us out."

Cobb jumped up, his chair banging against the wall behind him. "I should have known. That gutless snake never raised a single word of objection. At least Ryland had the guts to speak up." Anger reddened Cobb's face as he paced back and forth in the small office. "We have to call a meeting, discuss how we're going to react to a union-run cooperative laundry." He paused and stared at Farley, "How long until they'll be up and running?" he asked.

Farley shrugged. "My informant didn't know. And those two operatives of mine have completely disappeared. No one has seen them. I went to their hotel room and bribed my way into seeing their rooms. All their belongings are there. That makes me pretty sure that they had nothing to do with McCarthy's death. If they've done a scamper, they wouldn't have left everything behind. I'm thinking something bad has happened to them."

"Never mind about them. Did you get that loose end tied up? The women?"

Farley gave a hesitant nod. "I think so. I told Sinclair to get them aboard ship before tide change this morning. Problem is, I also told him to immediately report to me once the ship sailed with them on it. I've seen neither hide nor hair of him."

"What else can go wrong?" Cobb asked without expecting an answer. His hand fumbled for the chair arm and he carefully lowered himself onto its seat.

A knock sound on the office door and L.D. Warder slipped inside, carefully shutting the door behind him. "How come you guys are looking so glum?" The drivers' union president seemed to be twitching with either excitement or cheer. "I'd think you'd be celebrating!"

Cobb straightened, as if hope had suddenly infused his body. "What do you mean?" he demanded.

"Why, the laundry sale. It won't go through now that McCarthy's dead."

"You idiot!" Cobb shouted, finally giving vent to the anger that had been building. "The sale has already has gone through! Henry Teague sold them the Star Laundry this morning. Those union thugs are down there at their hall celebrating."

Color drained from Warder's face leaving it ashen. His knees buckled and he staggered, grabbing the wall with one hand to keep from collapsing. "But I heard you say . . . . It was Teague, not, not McCarthy?" he asked.

Horror contorted Cobb's face. For once he seemed speechless. Before words came to Cobb, Farley grabbed his hat from a neighboring chair, clapped it onto his head and stood. "That's it for me, gents. I don't want any part of a murder I had nothing to do with. I'm catching the next train out of here. Good luck." With that, Farley opened the door, stepped out and closed it softly behind himself.

In no time, the coach was rumbling along the dirt road that skirted the swampy morass of Guilds Lake north of the city. The coach was rolling at a trot. Since the glass windows wouldn't raise, Sage opened the side door and leaned out to consider the horses. They looked in fine fettle, heads up and manes flying. Slamming the door shut, he settled back onto the bench seat next to Sinclair. Lucinda sat across from

Sage, while Fong occupied the corner, across from the stranger, surveying all of them with heavy-lidded eyes.

"New coach?" Sage asked Lucinda.

She shrugged then smiled and answered, "Brand new. It was our first outing in it. The ladies are going to be upset with me."

"Since you're their boss, they're not likely to complain."

Her lips twisted in a faint smile but she said, "Maybe so. But they will be disappointed." Her regret was genuine. The realization came to him that everything was genuine about Lucinda.

Sage studied the interior of the vehicle to take his mind off the woman across from him. Tufted and buttoned leather covered the two seats with plenty of foot room between them. Glass insets filled each side opening to keep rain out. The coach's strong springs made for a smooth ride—as smooth as it could be on a rutted and potholed dirt road. Their fast pace had to be raising billows of dust.

He glanced to his side and saw that the stranger was staring at Lucinda, his eyes calculating. "Just who are you, Mister?" Sage's voice sounded harsh and overly loud despite the incessant road rattle.

That question tore the man's eyes away from Lucinda and he answered readily, "Name's Paul Sinclair. I'm out here from Chicago."

"What do you do in Chicago?" Sage's question made Sinclair stir uneasily and turn his face away, so that he was staring out the side window. When he turned back, all the life was gone from his face and his voice was dull as he said, "I'm a panderer, a white slaver, a seducer of innocent girls."

That candor took Sage off guard and in the pause that followed he looked toward Lucinda. She had stiffened and somehow withdrew from them all.

"What are you doing here in Portland?"

"I was hired by a man named James Farley to kidnap Rachel Levy."

Once again, the candor gave Sage pause then he said, "So, why are there three women aboard the *Maggie Jane* if Rachel Levy was your only target?"

Sinclair rolled his eyes to the ceiling, clearly exasperated with what had transpired. "I didn't know there were two sisters who were identical twins. I grabbed the wrong one, Rebecca. Then I tricked the second one, Rachel, to come to the aid of Rebecca."

Sinclair's voice seemed to soften when he said the name "Rebecca" but Sage couldn't think about that now. "So why did you grab Mae Clemens?"

"I did that early this morning. I panicked." He heaved a sigh. "She was snooping around the *Maggie Jane*. I was afraid she'd call for help before the steamer sailed. So, I grabbed her." He held out a hand that had been severely scratched as if demonstrating the task had not been easy.

Sage smiled but still asked, "Did you hurt her? Did you hurt Mrs. Clemens?"

Sinclair chuckled softly. "I only hurt her pride. She was mad as a wet hen, as my mother would say. Me, on the other hand, got scratched and stomped. I'll be limping for a week. She barely came to before she was telling me to take a long walk on a short log."

Lucinda snorted and even poker-faced Fong's lips twitched. "Where is the *Maggie Jane* taking them?"

"San Francisco. From there, they'll be taken to Panama to work in the houses there."

Lucinda gasped and, for the first time, she spoke to Sinclair in a voice raspy with anger, "You despicable, disgusting human being. They'll never survive working in a Panama whorehouse!"

Sage saw that her hands were balled into fists and quickly intervened to touch upon his greatest fear. "Mae Clemens is too old to be a prostitute."

Sinclair's face tightened and his lips formed a thin line. "That's why we have to intercept the *Maggie Jane* before she crosses the bar into the Pacific. I'm afraid the captain will just throw her overboard," he said.

Caroline settled onto the rail car's seat and for the first time relaxed. It had been a frantic run to the Union Station. What a picture they must have presented, the big Sergeant, towing her along by her elbow, a Chinese man running on her other side close enough to grab her other elbow should she stumble, the three of them trailed by four beehive helmeted policeman and the shabbily dressed older fellow. Lord knew what people on the street made of their odd little parade.

While Hanke talked with the engineer, she'd waited beside the huffing train engine with steam clouds billowing around her knees. It had been touch and go whether the engineer would comply with the sergeant's orders.

"This train has to go straight to Astoria, no stops," Hanke ordered as soon as the engineer appeared at the top of the iron-rung steps.

"I am sorry, sir. I am not authorized to take that action," the engineer spluttered in alarm.

"Three women have been kidnapped onto a ship. They're going to take them out into the ocean, maybe kill them by dumping them overboard. This train needs to beat that ship to Astoria so we can rescue them before it crosses the bar. There's not much time."

The engineer's brow wrinkled. He took his cap off to run stubby fingers through sparse hair. He turned toward his fireman who'd left off shoveling wood into the burner to listen. "Well, how about I find the station boss and get his okay?" he asked, turning back toward Hanke

The big police sergeant shook his head and raised both hands to halt the engineer's descent from the engine. "We don't have time. The ship sailed, under steam, over an hour ago. We need to leave right now!"

"But my passengers will raise a ruckus if we just blow past their stop. And what about all the folks at the stations waiting to board?"

"I'll go back and explain to the passengers once we are underway. And I'll have one of my men here explain to the station master so he can telegraph ahead to any waiting passengers and tell them what's going on. They can catch the next train, there's at least six a day." Caroline marveled at how rapidly the sergeant countered the engineer's objections.

The engineer straightened, squared his shoulders and turned to the fireman, "Better step up the pace there, Davy. We're going to be running real hot, straight through to Astoria. No stops." He saluted Hanke and returned to his controls.

Hanke's broad face broke into a smile. He gestured for one of his men to ride on the engine and said to another, "You run off and tell the station master what's going on. Make sure he telegraphs ahead to the stations. You telegraph the police chief in Astoria. Tell him about the coastal steamer and that we're heading his way." The fresh-faced young police officer nodded and ran off.

The engineer called down from his open window. "You better get yourselves aboard because this train's pulling out in one minute."

Hanke grabbed Caroline's elbow and they ran alongside the train to the first passenger car. Once they all climbed aboard, Hanke began his announcement. "Ladies and gentlemen, this train is now operating under the orders of the Portland Police Bureau. It will be proceeding directly to Astoria without stopping."

Gasps, cries and angry shouts greeted that pronouncement. Hanke held up a big palm to halt the outcry, saying, "Three decent women have been kidnapped by white slavers. They are on a boat heading downriver to Astoria. We need to get there ahead of them in time to arrange for their rescue."

Hanke's explanation triggered excited murmurs. Caroline knew there'd be no problem when one of the male passengers shouted out, "Well, what the heck are we doing sitting here? Let's get this goldarn train a-going." The other passengers' cheers echoed his sentiment.

And so it went in the next two cars, as the train rocketed down the tracks, taking the curves at speeds that caused Caroline to stagger in the aisle and grab for handholds.

Finally seated, Caroline studied her surroundings. Across the aisle, the older man had pulled a small book from his capacious coat pocket and was thumbing through it. She could have sworn it was a book of poetry from what she could see of the words' arrangement on the pages. He looked familiar. Then she had it. Without his cart, she hadn't recognized the ragpicker who'd been hanging around outside the laundry. Come to think of it, lately, he'd been outside the union hall as well. Who the heck was he? Why was he going with them?

As if feeling her eyes on him, the older man looked up. In those dark brown eyes she saw an intensity of worry but also the shine of kindness. He smiled gently and she returned the smile. Leaning across the aisle, he said softly in an accents she knew as belonging to New Yorkers, "How do you do, Miss Stark. My name is Herman Eich. I am a friend of Mae's and Sergeant Hanke's."

He reached out a gnarled hand and she shook it, noticing how rough and large it was. "Nice to meet you Mr. Eich. I surely hope that Mae's alright," she said.

For a moment, his brow furrowed. "That is my hope as well," he said before turning back to his book.

That conversation at an end, she turned her attention to the big police sergeant across from her. He seemed oblivious to his surroundings as he stared out the window. "Are you looking for something?" she asked. The question turned him to face her.

"Yup. I am thinking that Mae's other friends will be racing to Astoria along that road we can see whenever there's a break in the trees. I'm trying to spot their carriage."

"Are you going to get in trouble for commandeering this train?" she asked.

That question brought a smile to the broad, placid face. "Probably. Astoria's way outside my jurisdiction and the railroad company's going to raise holy hell. If we don't rescue those women, I probably need to think about becoming a farmer, again." Hanke's face was rueful before he shrugged off the worry. "On the other hand, if we do rescue them, folks will be so impressed that they might forget I broke a few rules to do it."

Hanke's eyes sharpened and Caroline found herself wriggling under that look. He gazed around the railcar which was only about half full. Gesturing to a collection of empty seats at the swaying car's rear, he said, "How about you and me move on back there where we'll have a little more privacy." She understood he intended it as neither a suggestion nor a question. She immediately stood and, using seat backs to keep her on her feet, she led the way.

Once seated again, Hanke focused his intent blue eyes on her face. "Okay, Miss Caroline Stark, suppose you explain exactly why you're hanging around the laundry workers. You needn't spare the details. We have plenty of time."

Caroline heaved a sigh. She should have known that this determined fellow wouldn't be distracted long from getting the answers he wanted. So, after taking a deep breath, she began to answer.

THIRTY TWO

When he reached the hotel's u-shaped driveway, hastily stuffed valise in hand, James Farley was disappointed to see other guests already taking the only hansom cab in sight.

"Wouldn't you know it," he muttered to himself. After pacing back and forth for a few minutes, fruitlessly hoping for another cab, Farley set off down the drive. He glanced at his pocket watch, "Thirty minutes to departure," he told himself both as a warning and a promise.

Farley tried not to break into a run. It would be too conspicuous and the police had no reason to suspect he was involved. Of course, he'd performed his share of skullduggery in the past. But when he pulled something off, he made damn sure the evidence disappeared. He should have known this whole operation was doomed to fail when Sinclair grabbed the wrong woman. Nothing went right after that. Not that it was Sinclair's fault. Who knew they were twins? That twit he was paying money to, probably knew. Just didn't think it was worth mentioning. And, why would he have said anything? It's not like Farley told the informer about their plans to kidnap Rachel Levy.

Women. He should have known this job would have problems. Damn women were scrappers and most of the operatives he used hesitated to lay a hand on them. That's why he'd hired Paul Sinclair. The Chicago man was supposed to be the best when it came to sweet-talking a woman into going wherever he wanted her to go. For sure,

Sinclair got that one laundry gal to blab but that had been the extent of his sweet-talking success. And the success had been short-lived since she'd clammed up right quick.

Farley irritably shifted his valise to his other hand and again looked for a cab on the street. All he saw were pedestrians and that electric trolley. Maybe he should grab a ride on that. It was heading the right direction. The trolley stopped at the corner and he hopped aboard, handing the conductor a few coins. "Keep the change," he told the uniformed man.

Once settled onto a wood slat seat, Farley mulled over his failure. "Where were those damned operatives, anyway? The last few days he'd been working blind. It wasn't like he could slink around, buying drinks for the drivers and wheedling information from them. That was the job of the two missing men.

Farley's face twisted in a sour smile. Old Cobb was going to have his hands full the next few days. He'd have to make his own deal with the strikebreakers. They were an unruly bunch. A bit too fond of head thumping, even women's heads. Liked to show they were tough. Without him there to control them he doubted they'd hold back just because the picketers were women.

The late morning heat was raising sweat on his brow. Farley glanced at his watch. He'd reach Union Station in another few minutes. That would give him fifteen minutes to buy his ticket and hop on the east-bound train. What could they trace back to him? He feverishly tried to remember all he'd done.

He'd had nothing to do with the fire and murder. But he'd been stupid. He was so sure that it wasn't his operatives that burnt the laundry down that he'd stepped in to push the police investigation in the right direction. All he'd done was draw attention to himself.

He was also clear on the kidnappings because he knew that the coastal steamer was long gone by now. It wasn't stopping until it reached 'Frisco. That hop-head Sinclair wouldn't say anything. In fact, once he realized Farley was gone, Sinclair would leave town.

The two operatives were a loose end if they ever turned up but he never asked them to do anything illegal. Nothing wrong with asking them to spend time with the delivery drivers to pick up bits of information.

By the time Farley climbed down from the trolley he felt reassured. He had nothing to worry about because he was just a few minutes away from leaving Portland, Oregon. He planned never to return. This was one job he wouldn't be bragging about.

Farley was standing in the ticket line, his valise at his feet, when someone tapped his shoulder. "Mr. Farley, isn't it?" said a somewhat familiar voice. Farley glanced around and was horrified to see the same police officer to whom he'd spoken at the laundry fire scene.

"Why, umm, it Officer Bingham isn't it?" he spluttered in surprise and fear as sweat popped out on his brow.

"That's right," said the police officer. "Are you leaving our city, then?"

"Yes, yes, business calls. I've enjoyed my stay but I've been summoned back to the home office," Farley said while silently cursing himself for sounding overly jolly.

"And what business might that be, Mr. Farley? My sergeant was a bit miffed that I forgot to ask you that question." The police officer's face communicated only polite interest in Farley's answer.

Farley mentally flailed about before finally saying, "Well, I hardly think my business should be of any interest but, that said, I was here in your fair city trying to locate an outlet for a line of parlor organs my company sells."

The police officer's eyebrow arched quizzically below the rim of his helmet. "And were you successful?"

Farley thought quickly. He couldn't think of the name of any establishment that might sell parlor organs. Why the hell had he picked something as unusual as parlor organs? If the plod asked any questions about organs he'd be fumbling for an answer. "Nope, no such luck. Afraid I'm heading back to Chicago an utter failure." He tried to shape his face into one of disappointment.

"Hmm," was the police officer's only response as he stood looking at Farley, who soon shifted uneasily beneath the gaze.

Then the officer's face hardened. "I'm afraid you'll have to come with me to the police station," he said, taking hold of Farley's elbow and drawing him out of line.

"What!" Farley spluttered. "I'll miss my train. It's leaving in just ten minutes!"

The officer nodded. "Yes, you certainly will miss your train."

"But, why? I've told you everything I know. I don't have anything else to tell you."

That answer caused the policeman to smile grimly and pull a little more forcefully on Farley's elbow. "Well, that's not exactly true, is it

Mr. Farley? We'll probably begin by discussing why you just lied to me about your business here in Portland and go on from there." The police officer gestured toward the floor. "You might want to pick up your valise and bring it along. You won't want to leave it here on the floor. Someone might steal it. We don't want to encourage crime, do we?"

Lucinda was staring out the coach window, her face softly lit by tree-dappled sunlight. She was lovely to look at with her honey-colored hair, cornflower blue eyes and curvaceous figure. Today she'd certainly dressed to impress. No one in either street or shop would have failed to admire her. But, he preferred seeing her without the face paint and wearing plain gingham. Whoa, don't go there he told himself. He turned his attention toward their prisoner, Paul Sinclair and was not happy to see the white slaver openly admiring Lucinda.

"Miss Collins, perhaps you would trade seats with me? That way I can keep a better eye on our guest here," he said, nodding toward Sinclair. "And, you won't have to ride facing backwards."

She smiled at him with what he took to be a hint of relief. No doubt she'd noticed Sinclair's interest. Sage saw with satisfaction that once they'd exchanged seats, she was careful to place her handbag between herself and Sinclair. Sinclair noticed as well because he sent Sage a knowing smile, dropped his bowler low over his forehead and settled back apparently intent on napping. Within minutes his mouth was slack and he was, to every appearance, sound asleep despite the coach's rocking. Sage looked at Fong and he too looked as if he'd left for a dream world.

When Sage looked back at Lucinda he was startled to see those bright eyes fixed on his face before she quickly looked away. He turned to stare outside at trees dusty from weeks of no rain. There was very little traffic on the road but that didn't help the driver avoid jolting in and out of ruts and potholes. While he wished they were making faster time, a tiny part of him wished this coach ride would last forever.

"Lucinda," he said softly.

She slowly turned her head from the window and simply looked at him. Her eyes were unguarded, open and waiting. He swallowed hard.

"Umm, how long have you had this coach?" was the best he could think to say.

Disappointment shadowed her eyes and the corner of her mouth quirked upward before she said matter-of-factly, "Just bought it last week. The ladies and I like to go on shopping outings during the day. I thought we'd even plan some country picnics."

Sage nodded politely along with her words even as he choked back the questions he really wanted to ask. "You probably never planned to go as far as Astoria today," he said. "I hope your coach and horses don't get damaged in this escapade," he added. His lips felt stiff as he mouthed the stilted words.

She sighed but agreed, "Yes, I never once considered driving to Astoria. As for the coach, the salesman assured me that it is 'top of the line'. Our little trip will be a good test of that guarantee."

"I expect you'll be selling it when you move back to Chicago. If so, I might be interested in buying it," Sage said finally turning toward the topic he dreaded.

His comment caused her smooth forehead to crinkle, "Move to Chicago?" she parroted. "Why would I move to Chicago?"

Before Sage could answer, there was a jolt, the coach tilted first right and skewed left before coming to an abrupt halt. The jolt sent Lucinda slamming forward into Sage who grabbed her and held on tight. Sinclair came awake as did Fong. An eye roll from Fong suggested he'd been listening to their conversation and was unimpressed with Sage's communication skills.

Their trailing dust quickly caught up to roil past the carriage which rocked a bit as the driver dismounted onto the dirt road. Seconds later soft cursing sounded outside. The man's grizzled face appeared in the door window. Sage leaned over, unlatched the door and swung it open.

The man took off his hat and wiped his brow with a kerchief. Slapping the hat back on his head, he said, "I'm sorry Miss Collins but we ain't a'goin nowhere. That big pothole back there done cracked our axle bad. It ain't safe to drive on her until it's been bound up."

Sage looked at Sinclair who sat upright in his corner. How could they keep the man a prisoner if they had to proceed afoot? Sinclair's lip twisted in a wry smile and he said, with an airy wave of his hand, "Don't worry about me. I've made my choice. If I can do anything to save Rebecca and the other two, I'll do it. I won't be running away. I'm done with hiding my head in the dirt."

Fong and Sage exchanged looks. Fong gave a what-the-hell shrug so Sage said, "Okay then, Sinclair. I'm going to take you at your word and not tie you up. But we'll be keeping an eye on you.

The four of them climbed down from the coach to stand beside it. Not a farmhouse was in sight. After the rattle and groan of the racing coach, the stillness laid heavy on the ears until the startled birds once again began to chirp and twitter.

Sage turned toward the coach driver who stood beside the coach, studying one of the big wheels and rubbing the back of his neck. "Where are we?" Sage asked.

The driver removed his hat, holding it in his rough hands. "'Bout three miles south of Scappoose. I'll take one of the horses and trot up there to fetch something to tie up that break so we can limp on into town. This coach won't be making Astoria today." The man looked down, clearly expecting an explosion of blame.

Lucinda merely patted his arm. The four of them looked at each other in consternation. "Maybe the four of us should ride the horses to Scappoose. We can send someone back with the repair material while we hire another vehicle to take us to Astoria," Sage said, scrambling to find a solution to the dilemma. No one had a better idea so they went to the front of the coach where the two horses were softly blowing, no doubt welcoming the halt.

"Stop!" commanded Fong in a loud voice. Everyone froze, watching as he turned toward the river. He pointed at the train tracks gleaming in the morning sunlight. "Maybe we catch train that is coming," he suggested. Sage strained to hear the rumble of an approaching train but heard only the horses blowing and the birds. Still, he trusted Fong. Seconds later they were running toward the tracks, following Fong. Lucinda ran close behind the Chinese man, the hem of her fancy dress hiked high above her shoe tops.

"There's no sense spilling tears as long as we've got hope," Mae admonished Rachel's sister whom she'd finally met. The young woman was thin and clearly weak from her long ordeal so Mae's tone was tenderly chiding. "You've done real good so far, Rebecca gal. Hadn't been for your scratchings on that whorehouse wall, we'd never have found you and your sister," she said and was gratified to see the girl's back stiffen and chin raise.

Mae took the few steps to the porthole. Outside the forest came down to the river's edge, where leafy trees, drooping willows and tall reeds shone green in the morning sun. She contemplated the porthole with its bolted window as she rubbed her shoulder. That scoundrel had pretty near yanked it out of its socket when shoving her inside this dinky cabin. She smiled wryly. He'd probably been getting even for the stomping she'd done on his foot and the gouge she'd likely made in his shin bone. She might have been woozy, but Fong's lessons had still worked. She hoped she'd get a chance to tell him. At least she'd been right, the sisters were captives on the *Maggie Jane*. She smiled again. Maybe this is what they meant when they said being proved right could be a "cold comfort".

She looked at the window bolts, then back out at the shore. The coastal steamer was sticking to the middle of the river. Even if they could somehow unbolt the window and slip out, they'd have to swim a great distance to shore. Too great. People were always dying in the Columbia from the cold water—even now during the hottest part of the summer. Besides, she was a darn poor swimmer at best. Growing up in Appalachia there hadn't been many swimming holes. Rocky creeks and tumbling rivers was how the water left the hollers.

She gave up on the window. Turning, she surveyed the cabin with a look. She didn't need more. There was barely room to turn around. Just two bunk beds hanging on the wall, a stained felt mattress rolled up against the wall and a chipped chamber pot shoved into the corner. Everything in sight was grimy and smelled of burning coal. They probably hadn't scrubbed it in decades. No doubt ticks, fleas and other vermin made cozy inside the mattresses.

The two sisters sat on the edge of the bottom bunk. Rachel was softly reassuring her sister but her voice turned determined when she looked at Mae and asked, "Okay Mae. What are we going to do? Sinclair told Rebecca that they are sending us to Panama. He wouldn't tell her why or what was going to happen once we got there. But we've heard stories. There's a real shortage of women." Though their eyes were big with worry, their proud faces were fierce.

"We'll die first," Rachel calmly vowed and her sister nodded in agreement.

Mae wasn't surprised to hear the resolve in Rachel's voice. The young woman had never faltered when leading the laundry women. Nor had she been anything but strong when the mangle mashed Debbie's hand.

The same when Sinclair fired her at the end of the workday. Even when her beloved sister had gone missing, Rachel hid her terror and carried on. Faltering just wasn't Rachel's style. That was reassuring. The last thing they needed was to fall apart, to turn too stunned by the situation to help themselves.

Mae glanced around. "Well, I don't suppose either of you have any matches?" The sisters shook their heads. "I guess we can't set this tub afire then." She looked up at the ceiling, less than two feet above her head. "How about something hard enough to break the porthole glass? If we got it open maybe we could signal someone on the riverbank? Shout for help before they could get in the door." Again the sisters offered only shakes of their heads.

Mae looked around again, rubbed her hands together and stepped the few feet over to the bunks. She gestured them to get up off the bunk bed and once they were standing, she flipped back the mattress covering the bottom bunk. "Good," she proclaimed, pointing at the flat metal slats serving as bed springs.

Grabbing hold of the upper bunk she hiked up her skirt, raised her foot and slammed it down onto one of the slats. It broke free of the frame and clattered onto the floor. Smiling with satisfaction she picked it up and showed it to the sisters. "A bit of work and we can turn these slats into decent pig pokers," she promised. "Anyone coming through that door is going to get a surprise. We'll overpower him and get ourselves up on deck." She wasn't sure what they could do once they were on deck, just trusting that a change in their situation would lead to an opportunity.

The two other women stepped forward, grabbed the upper bunk and stomped. Real anger powered those stomps. Soon the three of them were wrapping strips of torn blanket around one end of the slats to protect their hands should they be able to stab or brain their captors.

As they ripped, wrapped and tied, Mae talked about growing up in the Appalachian coal fields. "It was god awful hard and dangerous work for my dad and other men. It's bad now, but it was worse then. The mine owners refused to install emergency exits, fresh air pumping systems, or to make provision for safe shoring inside the mine. In Schuylkill County where I was raised, 566 miners were killed between the year I was born and my seventh birthday. And that don't account for the nearly 1,700 who were seriously injured."

"So the miners decided to form a union. Lickety-split the mine owners hired thugs who beat and killed. That made the miners mad and they decided to give the mine owners and thugs a taste of their own medicine. Of course, it only got worse. The mine owner's thugs murdered my ma's sister and her whole family. So, my ma and pa got involved. The men were working 12 hour days, six days a week, down in the mine.

My ma and the other women worked in the sorting shed but they were above ground and could travel around a bit. They carried secret messages. It was dangerous time. But folks felt they had to do some-thing. Otherwise they were nothing but slaves making other men rich. Terrible things happened to my pa and other men in that dirty old mining town. I got old enough, I tried to help."

She solemnly studied the two young women beside her. "You know, you two are carrying on for those miners and the coalfield women like my mother. There's always going to be men who'll use people up and throw them away like they're worth less than a year-old newspaper. It's up to us to stop them."

Turning from that somber topic, Mae told them a lively story involv-ing an ornery mule and nasty rooster chasing revenue agents. Soon, both sisters were chuckling as they sat upon the floor mattress with their homemade weapons between their knees. Even as Mae talked, the judder of the steamer's steel plates beneath them was a persistent reminder that they were traveling downriver toward the bottomless Pacific Ocean.

THIRTY THREE

As they reached the tracks, they heard the faint rumble of a westbound train from around the bend. "That train isn't going to stop for us," Sage said.

"Train will stop," Fong said and immediately began running up the tracks, away from the train.

"What are you doing?" Sage yelled after him.

"Need to make sure train has plenty room to stop," Fong called over his shoulder without slowing his pace. Lucinda understood before Sage did because once again she picked up her skirts and was running after Fong, Sage and Sinclair close behind.

Ahead, Fong stopped, turned around and raised his hands in the air, waving them wildly. Once the others reached him they too began waving. The train had just rounded the bend. Sage was alarmed to see it traveling at a very high rate of speed. Much faster than normal. "We may not have run far enough ahead," he said to Fong out of the corner of his mouth.

Fong looked grim as he nodded but he didn't move or stop waving. "We may have to jump," he said, flicking a glance toward Lucinda. Sage and Sinclair looked at each other, dropped their arms, grabbed Lucinda's elbows and lifted her to the side of the tracks.

She protested until Sage said, "You could trip over those skirts of yours."

Seconds later the metallic shriek of the braking train filled the summer air. The train engine's brass medallion grew rapidly in size as it bore down on them. Sage looking toward Fong. His friend had lowered his arms but remained calmly standing between the two rails, his knees slightly bent. Sage wondered if he planned to halt the train with a snake and crane move. The thought made him smile. Nah. Not even Fong could pull off a stunt like that.

Twenty feet from where they stood the train stopped, its stack huffing steam as if angry. Certainly the engineer was angry. He stuck his red face out the side window and shouted, "Get the hell off my tracks!"

Sage raised his voice in return, "We've got to get to Astoria, it's a matter of life or death." A beehive helmet appeared at the top of the iron rungs to the cab. Sage shouted, "Hey, Officer, are you with Sergeant Hanke?"

"Yes, sir, that I am. That's why you need to get off the tracks. We've got a rescue mission underway!"

By now they'd reached the side of the engine. Sage grinned as relief coursed through his body. "Well, Officer, we're with the Sergeant on that same mission."

The policeman was momentarily surprised but then gestured back along the train. "You all better hop aboard then. The Sergeant's back there with the passengers explaining why we aren't stopping until we get to the ocean."

The four of them ran alongside the engine toward the passenger railcars. When they reached the first door, it opened and Hanke looked out. "Glad you could make it," he shouted. Instead of lowering the steps he grabbed Lucinda's reaching hands and hefted her aboard. He did the same for the other three. Sage was last aboard, running alongside as the train started its slow roll up to speed.

Hanke led the four of them to the rear of the railcar. There sat Eich and a woman who worked in the laundry. Hanke gestured to the woman. "This here is Miss Caroline Stark. She's a friend of your mother and the Levy sisters."

Sage narrowed his eyes. He remembered that name and there had been some negative association with it. That's right. His mother had told him she liked the woman but was suspicious of her. He studied her but she didn't notice. Instead, she looked past him as her polite smile slid right off her face. "Mr. Sinclair, what are you doing here?" she demanded, standing up, her fists clenched. She turned to Hanke. "He works for the laundry owner," she told Hanke. "He probably had a hand in the kidnappings."

Hanke turned toward Sage, his normally placid face showing surprise, "Is that so, Mr. ah, Miner?" Since this was the first time they'd met during this particular operation, Hanke had to guess whether Sage was using his customary alias.

Sage gestured that Sinclair should take the bench seat next to the window so that he faced both Caroline and Hanke who also sat down. Sage sat next to Sinclair. Lucinda and Fong took seats across the aisle, facing Eich.

"Before we start with the explanations, Sergeant, suppose you tell me what Miss Stark is doing here?" Sage said. He saw the woman reach out a hand and lay it on the Sergeant's uniform sleeve. Hanke looked at her and she gave a little shake of her head.

Turning back to look at Sage with a steady gaze, Hanke said firmly, "Miss Stark is helping us with our inquiries. I had no choice but to bring her along."

"But," Sage began only to have Hanke interrupt.

"You must trust me on this," Hanke warned as he glanced toward Sinclair.

Sage clamped his lips shut. Trust he would because Hanke would have good reasons. Beneath the sergeant's calm and somewhat bovine placidity lurked a steel-trap mind and an excellent character-judging ability. Sage cleared his throat and said, "Well, then. Miss Stark is correct. Mr. Sinclair was working at the Sparta laundry and for the association of laundry owners. He's the fellow who kidnapped the Levy sisters and Mrs. Clemens. He's admitted as much."

Hanke's face didn't change expression but Sage saw a muscle in his jaw twitch. When he looked at Sinclair and spoke, his voice was calm. "Is that true, Mr. Sinclair? You're responsible for those women being on that coastal steamer heading downriver?"

Sinclair nodded and looked miserable. Hanke turned back to Sage and asked, "He's your prisoner, then?"

"Not exactly. We're keeping an eye on him, of course." Sage sent his eyes toward Fong who was clearly listening to the discussion. "To his credit Sinclair told us everything without us forcing him to talk and he volunteered to help in the rescue. It seems he's had a change of heart."

Hanke studied Sinclair for a few moments before saying, "Well, a change heart, huh? Suppose you tell me the whole story Mr. Sinclair?"

Sinclair took a deep breath and began talking. He told them everything. About working for Farley, who was working for the association's leader, Thaddeus Cobb. He told of accidently grabbing Rebecca Levy. How he'd kept Rebecca at the whorehouse. How he'd tricked Rachel into being captured. How he'd drugged and strong armed Mae onto the ship. He even pulled up his trouser to show them the purple shin bruise she'd given him. His display was met with grins from Fong, Eich, Lucinda, Sage and even Hanke.

Caroline Stark, who'd been staring daggers at Sinclair, was the first to speak. "Mr. Sinclair, I know Jesus says I should forgive but I must tell you, I will need to say countless Hail Mary's before forgiveness will enter my heart where you're concerned."

Sinclair hung his head, kept turning his bowler hat roundabout and said nothing.

"Well, we need to get on with the business of rescuing those women," Hanke said. Just then, the train's air whistle split the air and they all glanced out the window, startled to see that the train was entering a settlement.

"That'll be Scappoose," Hanke said. The seven of them froze, waiting to see if the train slowed for the station. It didn't. Instead, the platform whizzed by but not before they saw the station's telegraph operator standing at the platform's edge waving them onward. Ranged out on either side were the bypassed passengers, all of them aping his gesture and cheering.

"Good," said Hanke with a faint smile of satisfaction. "We shouldn't have any trouble from here on. It looks like the station master got word down the line."

Over the next two hours, the train rocketed through Scappoose, St. Helens, Rainier and Clatskanie. With each passing village, the crowd on the rail platform was larger. Clearly word of their rescue mission was spreading from the passengers to the settlements themselves. Meanwhile, the engineer was demonstrating his considerable skill. The railcar rattled and rocked more than any Sage had ever ridden, its brakes squealing as they approached a curve, sometimes taking it at a speed that nearly flung them off the tracks. He pondered the toll this hell-raising trip had to be taking on the engineer's nerves and the fireman's muscles. Mostly Sage craned his neck to look forward of the train, anxious to see Astoria's outskirts.

Everyone else seemed focused on that end as well because there was little conversation as they drew close to the river's end. Even Hanke grew grimmer with every passing mile. Finally Sage could stand it no longer. He gestured to the sergeant who rose and followed him out to the platform between the two cars. In a way, it was a relief to stand there in the open, the air flowing from the train's passage lifting Sage's hair. "What's going to happen when we reach Astoria?" he asked.

Hanke looked out at the scenery whipping past the windows. "I don't rightly know, Mr. Adair. If my officer was able to convince Chief Hunt to do as I asked, the town's police chief and reinforcements will meet us at the station. I've been thinking and I'm betting the *Maggie Jane* plans on steaming right past the town. If that's what she does, then we have to figure out how to stop her in the river. Steam ships can always maneuver; they don't need the wind. I don't know if we'll be able to stop her."

This was Sage's fear. Even if Astoria's police could commandeer a few fishing boats and their captains, how could they stop a bigger ship bent on steaming out into the Pacific Ocean? "Just a minute, we might be able to increase our rescue flotilla. Sage ducked inside the railcar, gestured to Fong who returned to the platform with his friend.

"Mr. Fong, we're wondering how we're going to stop that steam ship with just a few boats. Do you have any suggestions?"

Fong looked solemn. "I've been thinking about same thing. Once we get to Astoria, I will go find Chinese men. Some of them have boats. They will help."

"Good. Maybe we can slow the *Maggie Jane* enough to climb aboard her," Sage mused. Fong was nodding. "I have to find hatchet when we get to Astoria," he said.

Hanke and Sage looked at each other. They knew exactly what Fong meant.

The cabin's air was stale. Once the task of making weapons was over, the three women had given into exhaustion and the torpidity of heat. Mae and Rachel were sharing the floor mattress while Rebecca had climbed into the top bunk. A noise from outside woke them. It was the metal clank of an anchor lowering to the river bottom. The ship's mechanical rumbling ceased.

"They're stopping," Mae observed unnecessarily. Fear clutched her heart. Were they already at the ocean? She jumped up and stepped to the porthole. She saw the bright green of grasses and leaf trees, mixed with the dark green of firs along a wild shoreline. "They must plan on waiting here until the tide is right to cross the bar into the ocean. I've heard it is near impossible to get across when the tide is coming in," she said.

"I wish they'd left us with a jug of water," Rachel said quietly. "This heat sure makes me thirsty."

Mae smiled grimly at the thought they were surrounded by fresh water they couldn't reach. "Well, if we manage to break out of here, you may get to drink more fresh water than you'd like," she said.

Suddenly a flash of movement caught her eye. There, beyond the trees, she saw it again. It took a minute before she realized it was the train heading toward Astoria. She'd ridden that train with Herman on a day outing to Astoria. A memory she treasured. When Herman learned she'd never seen the Pacific Ocean he'd surprised her with two tickets and off they'd gone.

Mae felt a deep sadness crawl around her heart. She given up all thought of a man friend before meeting Herman Eich. Their's was a sweet, easy friendship, one that had become important to her. He'd blame himself if she didn't get out of this mess.

She didn't hold any illusions. Sinclair told the girls that they were going to Panama. When the steamer reached San Francisco, they'd transfer Rachel and Rebecca from the *Maggie Jane* onto a ship heading to Panama. Their feet wouldn't even touch solid ground. But, not her. Nobody would think it financially worthwhile to ship a tired, graying woman to Panama. Nor could the captain risk leaving her in San Francisco where she could point the finger straight at him. No, she'd have a different fate. Once they were on the ocean, they'd throw her overboard like a piece of garbage. Her eyes stung as she gazed at the lush green riverbank and the fir-clad ridge running high above it.

THIRTY FOUR

THE TRAIN CHUGGED INTO THE Astoria train station, its whistle shrieking. The engineer was probably relieved to reach the end of his hair-raising dash to the ocean. The platform was crowded with on-lookers but front and center stood Astoria's police force. Sage heard Hanke's sigh of relief.

Things happened quickly once they descended from the train. The po-lice chief stepped forward and shook Hanke's hand even as he pulled him toward the platform's end. Waiting there was a wagon with a police officer holding the reins of two eager horses. The men clambered into the wagon bed while Lucinda and Caroline were lifted onto the driver's bench.

As they rumbled away from the station the police chief shouted his information. "You made it in the nick of time. The tide is about to turn. We'll need to get our boats into the river without delay. I've got a number of fishing boats lined up." As Sage listened, he saw the Chinese man from Portland running alongside the river toward a cannery that stood on pilings in the water. He looked at Fong who said, "He's going to find Chinese boatmen. They will help too."

Sage looked out at the river. It flowed placidly along, its surface ripples sparkling in the afternoon sun. It was so wide. How could a few small boats possibly stop a determined steamer captain from getting past?

"What's the plan?" Hanke asked the police chief who replied, "We'll put out into the river in a long string. Form a blockade. I'll have a man with a rifle on every boat. We'll fire over their bow. What we really need is the *Commodore Perry*. She's a revenue service cutter that operates out of Warrington across the river. We were able to use our heliograph to signal the Warrington base but got the signal back that the *Perry* was out past the bar. They're sending someone up to the point with a signal heliograph but we don't know if the cutter will be close enough to see the signal. We can't count on it coming to the rescue."

"We don't have much time," Hanke said grimly. "We think we saw the *Maggie Jane* anchored about a mile upriver. If it was her, she'll be able to steam down here pretty quick to catch the tide."

The chief waved his hand at the other boats along the wharf. "We figured she'd lay up somewhere out of sight until tide change. That's why these boats have their steam up and are raring to go. Luckily your telegram came when they were still tied up, waiting for the change of tide. Normally, they'd already be out, waiting near the bar for the change. We don't want to intercept the *Maggie Jane* close to the bar, it's way too dangerous. We need to stop her a bit upriver.

Seven power boats were tied to the wharf, each with a man standing on the dock ready to untie it. The wagon drew to a halt and everyone jumped off. Sage grabbed Lucinda around the waist and swung her down. For just a moment they stood looking into each other's eyes, as though time had froze. Then, flashing her a devilish grin he said, "Looks like we're in it together once again. You be careful, you hear?" She didn't answer before they took off after the others, running down the long wharf to its far end.

The chief gestured the seven of them into the last boat. Hanke was first on board, he lifted Caroline down before turning to help Lucinda. Sage stepped forward, having a sudden need to tell her to stay ashore but the steel in her eyes shut him up. He'd seen that same look in his mother's eyes and knew better than to argue. The four men scrambled aboard without any help.

A patrolman stood at the helm. "Miska here was raised on fishing boats. He's our best helmsman. One of the best on the river." The chief nodded to a patrolman standing on the dock. He quickly loosened the tie lines and leapt into the boat as they pulled away from the wharf, the boat engine chugging. As they motored out into the current, Sage looked behind to see all the other boats being untied and following.

"Won't the captain of the *Maggie Jane* want to stop and pick up a bar pilot? I heard that the river bar can be highly dangerous," Sage said even as he stared upriver, hoping to spot the coastal steamer.

The chief's face was glum as he responded, "The bar's dangerous as all get out. Her captain would be a damn fool if he doesn't pick up a bar pilot. I looked at our records. It looks like the *Maggie Jane* has only crossed the bar once, when she first came up the Columbia. So the captain might be unaware of the danger. Since it's summer, he probably thinks the bar will be calm."

Seeing six pairs of eyes staring questioningly at him, the chief went on to explain. "Three forces work against you when crossing the bar. The shallow water, the wind blowing in from the south and the fast river current. The wind is steady, not too bad today but it still can cause a problem because even a light wind makes the waves stronger and bigger. The water flow is the real danger. When those big Pacific waves hit the shallow bar, it's just like they're hitting a wall. Like what happens when big waves hit the beach, except you got the river current pushing at those waves from underneath. So you got the top of the wave pushing up river while the river is pushing the wave bottom out to sea. That creates a strong undertow. The water turns terrible swirly but you can't always see that on days like today. If the pilot doesn't know how to approach the bar, that undertow can yank the stern under the waves while the top of the waves push the boat right over, end-over-end."

The six of them looked at each other, fear on every face. What chance would the three women have if the ship went under? They must be locked in a cabin. On the train ride, Sinclair had told them his opinion of the steamer captain's skill. He wouldn't know how to handle a perilous situation.

Sage said to the chief, "From what I know of him, the captain is a reckless drunk. He's not going to stop for a pilot."

The chief nodded. "Yup, that's what I figured. Any fellow who would kidnap three women has to be darn short on common sense. We've got to hope he's smart enough to heave to when he sees an armada of boats blocking his way. The danger is that he'll try to run over the top of us. If he does that, someone's going to get hurt."

By now they were well out into the harbor, nearing the river channel. The chief glanced over his shoulder and then straightened. "I'll be darned," he exclaimed. "It looks like the whole Chinese fishing fleet is chasing after us."

Sure enough, a smallish power boat was pulling out into the current. Trailing after it, were about eight small wooden boats, attached to the power boat by a long line. A single man sat in each boat, his oars out of the water as the bigger boat towed him along.

"Wonder if they mean to help?" the chief said as he turned to look at Fong, "Is this your doing, Mister?" he asked Fong.

"Yes, Chief. I sent request for them to help. Very happy to see they respond to request," Fong said quietly.

"That's mighty good of them. I hope they are careful. The *Maggie Jane* could run right over the top of those small boats of theirs and not even feel a bump. This here boat might be big enough to stove her in, but she'd crush those little boats like beetles underfoot."

Sage heard the exchange but his eyes were straining to see upriver. A ship's prow was visible, now that they were nearing the channel's middle. He couldn't tell whether the ship was anchored or moving.

Seeing the direction of Sage's gaze, the chief turned to stare upriver. "Looks like we made it just in time," he noted. "If that's the *Maggie Jane* she's underway or will be shortly, that's a heap of smoke coming from her stack."

※　※　※

"This is it. We've got to act. I'd hoped we'd be rescued by now but it looks like rescue is up to us." Mae turned from them and began gouging at the door with her metal slat. "We're moving again. That means the tide is turning and we're about to cross the bar. Once that happens, all is lost." She said this without pausing her attack. "Are you ready?" she asked over her shoulder.

Their eyes are as wide as an outhouse owl's on a moonless night, Mae thought. She just prayed they'd have the courage to smack a sailor's head while he was tussling with her. She checked. Good, their slats were hidden behind their skirts.

Outside in the corridor, rattling sounded. Mae didn't pause, just kept up her gouging. The door slammed open, she jumped away, stumbling back against the bunk. After quick glance at the young women, the angry sailor advanced on Mae, reaching out for the hand holding the slat. "You give that to me, or I'll knock your damn block off," he roared at Mae who was now crawling onto the mattress bunk hoping her knee wouldn't shove the mattress through the gap they'd made in the slats. She kept a firm grasp on her own slat. As the man grabbed her ankle, she awkwardly swung the slat at him, hitting his arm as best she could. Probably felt like a tap to him, she thought as she fought against the fear that the two women had turned too paralyzed to act.

Suddenly, he released her ankle and slid to the floor, his eyes momentarily dumbfounded before they closed. Behind and looming over him, their slats raised for more blows, were Rachel and Rebecca. The latter nudged the man with her boot. "Do you think we killed him?" she asked. "I hit him hard as I could."

Mae scrambled off the bunk, kneeling down to put a hand to the man's neck. "Naw," she said. "His heart's beating steady. While I fish through his pockets for anything helpful, you two take those strips we made and tie his feet and hands. We'll need to gag him too. Be quick about it. I think he's already coming to. Sailors have hard heads."

The two sisters moved quickly. By the time Mae had finished searching the man's pockets, they had his hands and feet tightly bound and were ready to gag him. That done, the three women stood looking down at their captive. "Never knew you could knock someone out hitting them in the back of the head," Rachel commented in a dry voice.

"Well, as a friend of mine pointed out, a knocked out man can't hurt you. He showed me where to hit," said Mae.

"What do we do next? Sneak onto the deck, jump off and swim for it?" asked Rebecca, adding, "I'm not much good at swimming."

Mae shook her head vigorously. "No, no. We can't swim, it's too far and too cold." She didn't tell them about the young man who'd died the last year doing that very thing in this same exact spot. Nor of the long nights when she'd sat beside his grieving widow. Instead, she smiled grimly and said, "We're going to do something they don't expect. We're going to figure out how to disable this ship. If she can't run, she can't cross the bar into the ocean. That'll buy us time."

Mae crossed the room and quietly opened the door to the companionway. She stuck her head out and then turned to the other two. "It's clear. Come on," she whispered. Once outside, she quickly pulled the door shut and locked it using the unconscious sailor's key. "As long as that fellow in there doesn't make someone come running, they won't know there's a problem." She pocketed the key. "Even if they figure that out, it will take them awhile to get the door open."

She gestured to their right. "That way's the deck so we better head the other direction," she said, turning left. Moving down the companionway, they opened every door, looking for the ladders that went down into the bowels of the ship. That's where they'd find the steam boiler and the engine.

THIRTY FIVE

"It's her! It's the *Maggie Jane*!" shouted Paul Sinclair who was leaning far out over the boat's rail on the upriver side.

If he wasn't more careful Sinclair was going to end up in the river, which was already growing choppy from the tidal turn. Sage grabbed the man's waistband and yanked him back. "You fall in and we'll have to rescue you instead of the women. Have a care, man."

Behind them the police chief stood in the boat's stern, using big arm gestures to point at the oncoming coastal steamer. The flotilla of power boats adjusted their course to one that would intercept. The only exception was the single boat towing the small crafts of the Chinese fishermen. That boat seemed to be heading to a point between the bar and the rescue boats. Evidently they're making themselves the last line of offense, Sage thought to himself. As Sage watched the tow lines dropped free of the towing boat and the Chinese fishermen dropped their oars into the water. It would be hard for them to maintain their positions.

Sage turned back toward the *Maggie Jane*. She didn't look seaworthy enough to make an ocean run to San Francisco. Mid ships, she rode exceedingly low—her deck no more than five feet above the water. Her stern was stubby while her bow was long and narrow. One third of the deck supported a low house punctured by portholes and a few doorways. Atop that housing structure, near its front end, was a wheel house with a smoke funnel rising skyward at its rear. Every part of the boat looked like it was long overdue for a scrape and paint job. She definitely fit the definition of what was commonly called a "rust bucket".

He turned to Sinclair who was also staring at the ship. "They're locked up on which side of the ship?" he asked.

"Port side, the side closest to us," Sinclair told him. "Third porthole back from the bow end."

Minutes later, their boat halted right in front of the oncoming ship. The police chief, resplendent in his official uniform, picked up a megaphone and his voice boomed, "Ahoy, captain of the *Maggie Jane*! Shut down your engine and prepare to be boarded."

Sage watched as the *Maggie Jane's* crew began running to and fro. His blood froze when many of them ran toward the cabin housing. Were they going to throw the women overboard? He swiftly bent down and untied his shoes. When Sinclair saw what Sage was doing, he did the same. Sage frantically searched the deck around him for something that would float since he wasn't much of a swimmer.

The *Maggie Jane*, instead of stopping, sped up as even more smoke belched from its stack. It began to change course, clearly intending to dodge their boat. Sage heard the police chief shout an order and a rifle shot rang out, followed by a wooden splinter flying off the *Maggie Jane's* nearest rail. That shot had the effect of driving the coastal steamer's crew off the deck. Sage couldn't see how shooting was going to help. The crew could just hide inside. The ship was still picking up speed.

By now the other boats in the rescue flotilla had formed a semi-circle in front of the fleeing ship. But that tactic failed to stop the ship's forward momentum. It charged directly at one of the small boats forcing it to quickly reverse away. The *Maggie Jane* powered past the last of their boats and was free. Only the frail shells of the Chinese fishermen's boats floated between the *Maggie Jane* and the open sea.

The boat Sage was on gave chase. In no time at all it was within a hundred feet of the *Maggie Jane's* stern. Sage, Sinclair and Fong ran to the bow. Fong too had shed his shoes and was dropping his trousers as well. Sinclair and Sage stripped down to their underwear. Only then did Sage notice Lucinda standing at the railing, a few feet away; her whole body stretched forward as if urging their boat to move faster. He stepped over, hugged her tightly and returned to his post.

As they moved up on the *Maggie Jane's* side, Sage could see forward to the Chinese fishing skiffs. When the big boat got closer, he saw the skiffs part and the man in each one stand. Each held a hatchet, machete, big knife or some other big weapon. As the *Maggie Jane* rushed by, the men leapt for her midship railing, one hand grasping the rail and the other a weapon as their feet scrabbled to propel them upward. They were boarding the boat. Their invasion took but seconds.

Sage's mouth flew open and he turned toward Fong who shrugged and said, "China Sea full of pirates. Sometimes have to take back stolen boat."

Sage turned toward the police chief. "Can you move us closer to the ship?" The chief nodded and their own boat surged forward. Obviously, the chief approved of a pirate approach to their problem. He and the other officers on board joined them at the rail. Two of the officers clutched lines in their hands, ready to leap aboard the *Maggie Jane* and tie it to their boat.

Everyone, except Lucinda, Caroline, Eich and the pilot, crowded the railing nearest the ship they were overtaking. When their boat came close enough to rub hulls, they all leapt over the tiny gap. Sage landed awkwardly but quickly regained his footing. As he did so, he saw that the weapon-wielding Chinese had a couple of the *Maggie Jane's* crew backed up against a packing crate on the deck. He and Sinclair didn't hesitate. Like a well-matched pair of horses they turned and ran toward the housing.

They reached the first open doorway and plunged through only to be driven back when a pistol roared and bullets splintered the walls beside their heads. They ducked outside. "You hauled the women aboard. Is there another way in?" Sage asked Sinclair. The man shook his head. "Anyone in the corridor has a clear shot at anyone who enters from the outside.

"Let's go look through the porthole. Make sure they're in the cabin," Sage said. Sinclair nodded and led the way, crouching low and moving fast. A few more shots rang out but no bullets hit them. Finally, Sinclair cautiously raised his head to look through a porthole. He had to shield his eyes from the reflection, the positioning making him a clear target for anyone inside with a gun. He stood motionless, his hands cupping the side of his face and then he dropped back down. "They're not there!" he cried, panic shrilling his voice. "There's someone lying on the floor but it's a man." He clutched at Sage's arm. "Where are they?" he demanded.

Sage glanced over his shoulder. Hanke, the police chief and his men were helping the Chinese fishermen round up the crew and corral them on deck. He turned back to Sinclair, "You know, we haven't a single weapon between us."

Before Sinclair could respond, the deck underfoot gave a great shudder that was followed by a roar and then an explosion powerful enough to knock both of them onto their butts. Sage was the first to recover. "Quick, the boiler's blown. They'll be distracted!" Saying no more, Sage scuttled through a companionway door on his hands and feet. He heard Sinclair following. No shots sounded. Sage flung open a nearby door. An empty kitchen. He kept going.

Midway down the corridor a door swung open and a man stepped into the corridor. He was big and in his hand was a old shotgun, its twin barrels aimed straight at them. The gun didn't waiver as the man said, "I suggest you gentlemen back out of here immediately. If you don't, I will blow you both to smithereens.

"We just want the three women. That's all. Where are they?" Sage said in a voice he hoped sounded calm.

There was a metallic crack as the man pulled back on the shotguns hammer. Sage sensed Sinclair moving up closer beside him. Sage put his hand out to hold Sinclair back and froze. A cloud of smoke was working its way down the corridor from behind the man. A small figure with bare feet and legs was inching down the corridor within the smoke. Sage hoped Sinclair's face wouldn't betray Fong's approach. He could hear distant shouts of men and felt the deck beneath his feet list to one side. He kept his eyes on the man even as he fought to keep his balance. "Captain, you don't' have to do this. We just want the women."

"Ha! Do you really think I can just sail away? The damn boiler just blew. The *Maggie* is dead in the water. At least I'll have the pleasure of taking some of you with me." He raised the barrels and jammed the weapon against his shoulder.

Fong leapt around the man and shoved the barrels up just as they discharged. The shotgun slid along the tilting floor toward Sage, even as bits of wood rained down from the corridor ceiling. Two seconds later, the man was on his knees, his arm twisted behind his back, his mouth wide open in a cry of pain.

Sage picked up the shotgun and walked toward Fong and the man. "Where the heck did you come from?" he asked his friend.

Fong grinned toothily as he answered, "Cabin house have two sides and more than one door."

"You didn't see the women anywhere did you? We can't find them," Sage said just as the ship lurched abruptly before beginning a scary side-to-side roll.

"No, but maybe staying here is not good idea."

Sinclair brushed past him to fling the remaining doors open, calling at the top of his voice, "Rebecca, Rebecca!" The terror in his voice answered any question Sage had about where Sinclair's feelings lay. When he reached a locked door, Sinclair raised his foot and kicked the lock so hard that the door flew open. Rushing inside, he was soon dragging a man from the room, one bound hand and foot.

Sage smiled. "Don't worry, that looks like Mae's handiwork. I bet she had something to do with the boiler blowing as well."

"Having those damn women aboard cursed the ship," muttered the captain who now lay face down on the floor, his arm still twisted behind his back in Fong's strong grip. It had to be getting difficult for Fong to keep holding the man because the ship was violently rolling from side to side.

"Can you get him out on the deck?' Sage asked his friend.

"No problem. Upsy-daisy," said Fong to the captain who immediately began squeaking as Fong encouraged him to stand by wrenching his arm upward.

Sage turned to Sinclair, "Come on. If Mae blew that boiler I bet they're hiding somewhere outside. Reaching the deck, Sage ran to the rail and saw that police chief's boat had pulled about a hundred yards away. As he grappled with that situation, he saw the chief raise the megaphone. "Ahoy, you on the *Maggie Jane*! We had to stand off. Your ship is sinking and we're at the bar. Try to get into a lifeboat and launch. We'll do our best to pick you up."

Sage searched the railing of the other boat. He saw Lucinda, Caroline and Eich but not the three missing women. He whirled toward Sinclair, "Come on, they're still here. We've got to find them!" By now the ship was canting, side to side, broadside to the river flow and the ocean waves. No doubt they'd reached that place where the river collided with the ocean.

Seeing no lifeboat nor people on the forward deck, they both turned and raced toward the stern. They arrived just in time to see three women struggling to free a lifeboat tied to a rack. Greatly relieved, Sage raced to help with the lines. "Really, mother," he said under his breath when he reached her, "You do manage to get yourself in a pickle now and again. I really, really wish you wouldn't."

She turned to him, a wide grin on her face but all she said was, "It took you long enough to get here. Though really, Sage, you could have at least taken the time to pull on your britches."

As they freed the small boat it got away from them, crashing onto the deck and then slamming against the railing with another of the ship's violent rolls. Sage saw that the waves were now at least six feet high. He wondered whether the eight of them could fit into the small lifeboat, let alone keep it afloat in such a turbulent froth. It looked impossible.

He again fought to keep upright as the *Maggie Jane* leaned into the side of a wave and wallowed to its crest. There he was startled to see a large ship bearing down on them. Just before the wave dropped them out of sight, an air horn blasted.

"Good grief, what was that? Is that a gigantic whale sounding? What next?" Mae asked, her voice fearful for the first time. She hadn't seen the approaching boat.

"Don't worry. I think it's a revenue cutter, the *Commodore Perry*, coming to our rescue," Sage told her. At his urging, the five of them abandoned the stern and ran for the bow just in time to see a line harpooning from the cutter onto the bow of the *Maggie Jane*. Fortunately, Fong was there to catch the line and tie it off around a deck stanchion.

As the cutter swept past the line tightened and the cutter tugged the *Maggie Jane*'s bow upriver. Moving at a glacial pace, the cutter towed the foundering *Maggie Jane* out of the bar's roiling waters.

Sage glanced around. He saw only the bound sailor lying on the deck. "Where's the captain?" he asked Fong who sat on the deck, his hand gripping the tow line as if he feared it would vanish if he let go of it.

Fong shrugged. "We came on deck, just as cutter start to pass by. I had to run grab line so had to let captain loose. He took one look at cutter and decided to go swimming."

It took a second for Fong's meaning to penetrate. Sage ran to the railing, searching the heaving water for some sign of the man. He saw nothing but rolling swells of angry green water.

THIRTY SIX

Unquestionably, the Levy sisters were the guests of honor as they sat side by side at the head of the table. Prior to the gathering, Mae had obtained their promise to keep secret that John Miner's real name was John Adair and that he owned Mozart's Table. The key players in their adventure were all there—Sage, Mae, Fong Kam Tong, Lucinda Collins, Herman Eich, Angus Solomon, Sergeant Hanke as well as Caroline Stark.

It was a Monday night in early September. The summer's heat wave was just a bad memory. Mozart's was closed for the night though Ida was still cooking dinner for the ten people sitting at the big table they'd created by pushing tables together.

We're as merry as Robin Hood's men, Sage thought as he circled the table with a bottle of wine. Sitting down he said, "Well, I'd like to toast our wrapping up of recent events." They all raised their glasses and voices in return.

At Sage's nod, Rachel started off by detailing the outcome of the labor dispute. "Once Thaddeus Cobb left town, the association quickly fell apart. I think most of them were ashamed that they let Cobb lead them so far astray. We ended up winning our nine-hour days, a nickle more an hour and back pay for the two weeks they locked us out."

"What's going to happen with the union's steam laundry cooperative?" asked Mae.

"The Trade Council is going to get it up and running. They say that want to make sure our wins are permanent before they sell their "ace in a hole" as they like to put it."

"Rachel has some other news," Rebecca said. "She's probably too shy to tell you but, she's going to take over as president of the laundry workers' union. The international union was so pleased with our outcome that they hired the president away. The gals voted for Rachel to fill his position. She'll be the only female union president in the state." That information brought forth cheers and toasts which set Rachel to blushing mightily.

"Exactly what's going to happen to Cobb and Farley?" Sage asked Hanke once the congratulatory noise died down.

"Mr. Farley's got a bunch of important friends in Washington D.C. Still, Sinclair's testimony against him might hold up. Problem is, none of the ladies here, ever saw Farley. He's going to say it was Sinclair's plan from beginning to end and that he knew nothing.

"As for Cobb, we'd like to talk to him but his wife says he was suddenly called back east to assist a sick relative." That brought snorts of derision. Hanke continued once they'd quieted, "Cobb will probably say the same thing. His problem is that he hired Sinclair and Sinclair is confessing everything. I suspect our Mr. Cobb might stay away a long time." Everyone around the table clapped.

"Surely, Warder's not going to go free after killing Ryland McCarthy," Solomon exclaimed. "Not to mention nearly setting fire to the entire North End."

Hanke took a sip of wine, set it down carefully and said, "Farley tried to trade his information about Warder for his own freedom. He wasn't too clever. He should have hired one of your lawyers, Adair. Anyway, he signed a statement saying Warder started the fire that killed McCarthy. Once Warder saw that statement, he admitted to everything.

"The prosecutor says he's not going for the death penalty because Warder didn't know there was someone inside the laundry. But, for sure, Warder and his confederate will be spending quite a few years in the Salem penitentiary.

Solomon cleared his throat. "I feel like I'm a bit of an interloper at this celebration since I wasn't much help in finding the ladies."

They all protested, assuring him that was not the case. Sage spoke for them when he said, "Thanks to you we were able to find Farley and his operatives right off the bat. Most importantly, it was your man who spotted Rebecca here, being hustled down the street near the rail yards. That's how we knew to look there. Lastly, thanks to your railroad porters, we didn't have to keep an eye on the trains. That way we were able to narrow the search."

Mae cleared her throat to ask, "What about Paul Sinclair? What's going to happen to him?"

Rachel said, "Rebecca should answer that question because she's stayed in touch with him."

Blushing red, Rebecca said, "He's already down at the penitentiary. He pled guilty and received a sentence of a year and a day for kidnapping us. Thanks to Sergeant Hanke, the judge said his subsequent efforts to save us were a mitigating factor. Also, Paul says that, when he's released, he intends to work with the Society for Social Hygiene. Mr. Adair got that lady, Mrs. Harris, to tell the judge that the Society would be happy to accept Paul's help and that she believed his offer is sincere."

"Tell them the rest," Rachel goaded.

Still blushing Rebecca told them that all three of Sinclair's sisters were already on a train coming from Ohio. They intended to visit Paul in the penitentiary and she added softly, "They say they are looking forward to meeting me." This declaration brought forth teasing whistles which only heightened the poor girl's color.

Caroline Stark, who'd not spoken up to that point, now spoke. Sage thought she did so, in part, to rescue Rebecca. "Since you have promised to keep what I tell you confidential, I will tell you that as Mae rightly suspected," she sent a sweet smile in Mae's direction, "I was working at the steam laundry under false pretences. In truth, my training is as a social worker which is a relatively new field of science.

"In that capacity I am currently working for the Consumer's Union which has me conducting an undercover survey of women's working conditions here in Portland. Three other women are also doing the same thing in the other traditionally female occupations. Mae discovered us meeting to discuss our project and I had to tell her what I was doing but made her promise to keep it secret."

Caroline paused to look earnestly into each face. "Our purpose in gathering and publishing this data is to use it to push the Oregon legislature into adopting legislation that sets minimum hourly wages and maximum working hours for women. Our proposed law will also create a state agency to oversee compliance. Once we accomplish that, we'll move on to the task of enacting the same conditions for men."

She turned toward Rachel saying, "I hope you understand that I couldn't confide in you. We have to be extremely careful to ensure that the employers don't learn what we're doing and take steps to head us off at the pass."

Rachel stood up, walked around the table to Caroline and hugged the young social worker around the shoulders. "Don't you feel bad about it, Caroline. I would have done the same thing. Thank you so much for what you're trying to accomplish," she said before returning to her seat.

Caroline looked pleased and leaned forward to tell them something additional. "I have found the experience so enriching that I intend to continue working on labor issues for the rest of my life. After spending many hours talking to my priest advisor, Father O'Hara, I will be doing so as a nun in the order of the Sisters of the Holy Names Jesus and Mary."

That announcement elicited gasps of surprise from everyone but Hanke. He just looked sad. Sage caught his eye and raised an eyebrow. Hanke nodded slightly and then shrugged. Obviously, Caroline had already shared that bit of information with the Sergeant. Sage could imagine why, given the man's disappointed face.

The subject changed again when Mae looked at Fong and asked, "Whatever happened to Farley's two operatives that you and Sage penned up down there in the underground?"

Fong's normally impassive face looked stunned. Mae half rose from her chair, "Don't tell me you forgot and left them there!" Then she caught the twinkle in Fong's eyes. "Pshaw, you devil!"

Sage was sure she would have slugged Fong in the arm if he'd been closer.

Fong grinned at her. "Not to worry Mae Clemens. Next day, after we get back from Astoria boat rides, Mr. Adair gave them fifty dollars and train tickets. They left town lickety-split."

Sage's forehead wrinkled. First Fong was saying "upsy daisy" and now he was coming up with "lickety-split." It was like he had suddenly decided to adopt American jargon with a vengeance. Sage studied his friend and concluded he wasn't too sure he liked that idea.

Silence settled over the table until it was broken by Mae saying, "Well, I for one, intend to never, ever, set foot in a steam laundry again. Not even if its work hours drop to three. That's definitely a young woman's job."

"Oh, I forgot to tell you," Rachel jumped in. "You remember, Debbie, the woman whose hand was amputated after it she caught it in the mangle? Well, her sister said that some older fellow turned up at Debbie's door and gave her three thousand dollars cash. He wouldn't tell her why he was giving it to her or who it was coming from. She tried to give it back but he just shuffled away. She's going to buy a big house so she can rent out rooms."

Eich shifted uncomfortably in his chair and shot a quick glance at Sage who winked in return. Eich had reported that, when Debbie realized it wasn't a mistake and she could keep the money, she just stood in her doorway and sobbed.

Mae swallowed wine and then said thoughtfully, "I've been thinking about how sometimes life works like one of those mangles. It squeezes us together into the same time and place and that always changes us. Here we are, sitting around this table laughing together like lifelong friends when just a few months ago most of us didn't know each other existed. What we've gone through together has changed each one of us."

Rebecca straightened and leaned forward eagerly. "I think I know exactly what you mean. Paul, I mean Mr. Sinclair," her face again flushed crimson at the stumble, "he says he's glad about what happened. He says he's a different man."

Rachel said, "I sure felt like I was being fed into a mangle. When Rebecca went missing, I would have given that contraption both my arms to have her back." She reached over and patted her sister's hand. "But, now, I guess I like the outcome of being squeezed like that. I have Rebecca, we have a win for the laundry workers, and I have a new job I am excited about."

Eich apparently also wanted to follow-up on Mae's mangle comment because he said, "Certainly, Paul Sinclair and the rest of us learned much this last month. We know now, just how far some bosses will go to retain power. We learned how important mutual aid and support is for those seeking economic justice. Just look at us, who would have thought such a diverse group of people, could accomplish so much?"

He raised his glass to Mae saying, "So, Mae is right. The mangle that is life has melded us together, tested us in unexpected ways, and has made us stronger." His summation brought forth other raised glasses and "hear-hears."

His mother's mangle theory was spot on of course, Sage thought. Poor Debbie lost a hand and that for sure mangled her life. As for the rest of them, circumstances had, indeed, squished them together, bad with the good, innocent with the guilty, such that all their lives were permanently altered.

But, instead of speaking those thoughts, he said with a grin, "Sounds to me like you've all had a bit too much wine to drink what with all this late night philosophizing."

Mae got a laugh from the group when she delivered the expected punch to his shoulder. It didn't hurt as much as usual.

He looked across the table at Lucinda. She was smiling only at him, her eyes alight with a warmth he hadn't seen in a long, long, time.

The End

Historical Notes

Story Background – Laundry Workers' Dispute

1. The working conditions this story describes were taken directly from contemporaneous reports. Heat, steam, standing, exposure to chemicals and loss of limbs were the hardships faced by the steam laundries' primarily female workforce.

2. A labor dispute, involving Portland's steam laundry women in 1903, inspired this story. The women sought both the nine-hour, six-day workweek and a miniscule wage raise. For the sake of the storyline this book ends with a win for the steam laundry women. In actual fact, the employer association lockout of 1903 ended with the steam laundry workers caving in. So, to them it must have seemed to have been a loss. In the long run, however, it wasn't. Their plight triggered public debate over what were reasonable working hours and wages for women working in steam laundries. Their fight set in motion a change that would significantly impact Oregon and other workers across the country. In 1913, the legislature mandated both nine-hour work days for steam laundry workers and a higher minimum wage.

3. There was a United States Laundry, managed by a man named James Finley. I used his name in the story because he deserves recognition for trying to do the right thing. He voluntarily agreed to reduce the work hours to nine. He also went one step

further and wrote an opinion piece for the *Labor Press* in which he stated that he believed the reduction in hours was the humane and moral thing to do.

4. Finley also refused to join the Laundryman's Association or lockout his steam laundry workers. In retaliation, the Association members put pressure on the local chemical supplier until that business refused to provide chemicals to the United States laundry. As stated in the story, while that chemical business could afford to lose one laundry customer, it could not afford to lose all the laundries represented by the Association. Eventually, Finley succumbed to the association's pressure and the United States Laundry reinstituted a ten-hour workday and joined the Association. That association had a strong leader. The character of Thaddeus Cobb is modeled after that real life scoundrel.

5. The Portland Federated Trade Council did, in fact, solicit funds for a cooperative laundry that eventually began operating the next year. They encountered a number of difficulties which could be attributed to the Association putting pressure on suppliers.

6. The laundry drivers union, led by its president, officially supported the employers. Nearly half of the union's drivers however, refused to cross the picket lines during the lockout. The union president was not involved in arson or murder. Nor is there evidence that he accepted bribes from the employers. His union was, however, expelled from the Federated Trades Council and assigned partial blame for the laundry workers' failure to win the dispute.

7. The tale of Mae's dastardly husband is based on the horrific labor disputes that took place in the Appalacian coal fields. Strikers and labor organizers were frequently jailed, transported to remote places and told never to return. Not infrequently, they were also killed. Subsequent to the time period in this story, a number of Portland's female cannery strikers were jailed. Although there is no evidence that women strikers and organizers were murdered or transported out of Portland, it is not inconceivable that they could have been targeted for white slavery.

8. The character of James Farley is based on a real life person of
    the same name who was hired by the laundrymen's association
    to end the labor dispute. The actions subscribed to him in the
    book, were based on stories told by a former management spy.
    He called himself GT-99 and wrote a book called *Twenty Years
    a Labor Spy*. He quoted his Farley-like boss as saying this about
    strike breakers:

    > "If your man is highly intelligent he will use discretion.
    > But highly intelligent men are not working as strike-break-
    > ers. Highly intelligent men are . . . not loafing around wait-
    > ing for a strike to start . . . . All finks [another term for
    > strikebreaker] are about the same, which means they are
    > terrible. They're worse than anyone outside the business
    > has any idea of. No decent workman will take a job as a
    > fink; so you get the other kind. He'll cheat and steal and
    > lie from the minute he comes to the job until he leaves."

9. Also taken directly from history is the description of the interna-
    tional politics behind the U.S. taking over of the Panama canal,
    as well as the U.S. railroad corporations' efforts to stop the canal
    construction. Also accurate is the description of the horrific toll
    that building the canal took on workers' lives and health.

Union and Consumers League Efforts To
Create Economic Justice

10. Oregon's labor unions were quick to recognize the plight of the
    women who worked in the steam laundries. In 1902 the state-
    wide union convention took place with 77 unions attending.
    The Shirt Waist and Laundry Workers union sent four represen-
    tatives, two of whom were women. This first state-wide union
    convention adopted a three-point platform to govern their ac-
    tivities in the coming years. The points were as follows: a) Stop
    bad legislation and support good legislation; b) Stop child labor
    for those under 15 years of age; and, c) Work for an 8-hour day.

11. Shortly after the first state union convention, the labor unions
    successfully lobbied for legislation limiting women's hours of

work to ten hours. This was the country's first statute limiting work hours. The law, however, failed to include an effective enforcement component and so it largely went unenforced.

12. The Consumers' League was a leader in advocating for better working conditions. That organization and labor unions made a deliberate choice to first seek better working conditions and wages for women before pursuing the same rights for all workers. It was reported that this decision was the result of meetings between the female head of the National Consumers' League, Florence Kelley, and John L. Lewis, the then-powerful head of the Miners' Union.

13. Some suffragettes at the time disagreed with the "women first" approach. This is because the initial and winning argument used was that women were the "weaker sex" and needed "protection." Today, some of the suffragettes' successors criticize the decision to employ this tactic on the ground that it created a legal difference between men and women that hurt the cause for women's equal rights in the long term.

Legal Ramifications of Social Welfare Advocacy

14. In a 1903 test case, *Mueller v. Oregon*, a laundry owner challenged Oregon's first minimum hours law all the way to the U.S. Supreme Court. His lawyers argued that Oregon lacked authority to interfere with the employers' freedom of contract by dictating working conditions to employers. Louis Brandeis, later a U.S. Supreme Court justice, argued that states had the right to implement such laws based on research showing the law was necessary for the greater good of the community's welfare.

15. Brandeis's winning argument was precedence setting. It created a legal principle that endures to this day: We, the people can enact laws for the good of the community even if those laws overrule an individual's rights. This legal principle was subsequently relied upon by Thurgood Marshall when he successfully argued the landmark school desegregation case, *Brown vs. the Board of Education.*

16. After writing this book I discovered that, in 1902, the Oregon Supreme Court upheld a jury decision in favor of a woman whose hand had been severely burned and crushed in a Troy Laundry mangle. *Stager v. Troy Laundry*. In that case, the jury found that the employer had not provided properly installed safety equipment.

17. At some point after the events in this story, the Oregon legislators prohibited the use of strikebreakers with the current statute stating: "No employer shall knowingly utilize any professional strikebreaker to replace an employee involved in a strike or lockout, for the duration of that strike or lockout."

Character Background- Caroline Gleason

18. The character of Caroline Stark is loosely based on Caroline Gleason, a young Catholic social worker who traveled from Minnesota to Portland. The real Caroline, however, came to Portland around 1908, five years after the setting of this story.

19. At the behest of the Oregon Consumers League, Gleason and other young women worked undercover collecting data on women's working conditions in Portland. They found steam laundry work to be the most physically taxing and debilitating. They also noted the gross discrepancy in wages between the women and men working in the industry. Finally, their data exploded the myth that women laundry workers entered employment to earn "pin money". Instead, their data established that most female workers were either supporting households or single women "adrift" without alternative support.

20. Caroline Gleason was representative of the young women who had the desire and means to attend college at the turn of the century. Social work was a new discipline that had its origin in the gross economic inequality created by the industrial revolution. It attracted young women who sought higher education in something other than teaching. In the United States, it manifested itself in the work of Jane Addams and the settlement house movement. Educationally, it focused on the gathering

of data in a scientific manner. In the years that followed, this scientific data gathering, frequently carried out by women, resulted in numerous pieces of legislation intended to improve society.

21. Caroline Gleason completed her undercover work and generated a pamphlet setting forth the data she and her female colleagues compiled about working conditions for women. The pamphlet was presented to the Oregon legislature in 1913 and was so persuasive that the legislators unanimously passed laws setting forth wage minimums and hour maximums for women workers. Moreover, the legislation included the creation of an enforcement agency. Caroline Gleason was subsequently appointed its first director. It is not an exaggeration to state that a woman was responsible for the first enforceable wage and hour laws in the United States.

22. Shortly after achieving legislative success, Caroline Gleason became a nun in the order of Sisters of the Holy Names Jesus and Mary. As Sister Miriam Theresa, she worked as a university professor and lifelong national advocate in the field of labor management relations and workplace justice. She was highly regarded and respected throughout her life. Senator Wayne Morse said "Her work was the foundation ultimately for the development of a Federal Fair Labor Standards Act."

Character Background – Rachel Levy, Paul Sinclair, Sergeant Hanke and Others

23. In this story Rachel Levy serves as a stand-in for the many Jewish American women who played a central role in the American labor movement even before the early 1900s. As stated by Alice Kessler-Harris in her article, *The American Labor Movement,* Jewish American women:

> "... [B]rought to trade unions their sensibilities about
> the organizing process and encouraged labor to support
> government regulation to protect women in the workforce.
> As Jews who emerged from a left-wing cultural tradition,

> they nurtured a commitment to social justice, which would develop into what is often called 'social unionism'. From their position as an ethnic and religious minority, as well as from their position as women, they helped to shape the direction of the mainstream labor movement."

24. Hanke's frustration at the police department's low wages and manpower shortage mirrors reports in news articles at the time. As a consequence, the raid on the saloon was lifted directly from the news of the day. This includes the fact that the police chief had to summon the officers in the middle of the night, keeping the target from them until it was too late for one of them to alert the saloon owners.

25. The story models the character of Paul Sinclair after a real person of that name and follows the life story that he related subsequent to his arrest. At the age of fourteen the real Paul Sinclair ran away from his small Midwest town. He soon became the lover of a Chicago madam and her trusted right hand man. Later, after the authorities returned him home, he graduated from high school and entered a protestant seminary. He was expelled just a few months before graduating from that seminary. At that point, he became an opium addict and eventually worked as a skilled white slavery procurer in Chicago.

26. The story bases the transformation of the fictional Paul Sinclair on the transformation undergone by real Sinclair after he was arrested for his white slavery activities. Following that arrest, Sinclair turned remorseful about his actions toward women. Upon his release from jail and, for the rest of his life, he worked with those striving to eradicate prostitution. There is no historical evidence, however, that he ever visited Portland.

27. At the century's beginning, many newspapers printed horror stories about white slavery. An Oregonian article reported that a Portland woman escaped from a locked room, claiming that her captor had force-fed her alcohol, opium and tobacco in an attempt to turn her into a prostitute. The man was charged and convicted. Another Portland woman was reported to have been abducted from a St. John's trolley stop and shipped to China as a white slave.

28. There was a social hygiene society in Portland. There is no evidence, however, that it adopted midnight missionary tactic that was pioneered by the Chicago Society and used elsewhere in the country.

29. The owner of Olds and Kings department store did break from tradition and decide that a five and one-half day week was a long enough workweek for his female clerks. He took an ad out in the *Labor Press* to make that announcement. The ad also encouraged other store owners to shorten their employees' weekly work hours.

Columbia River Bar-Revenue Cutter and Coastal Steamer

30. The Columbia River Bar is three miles wide and six miles long, though it narrows to just six hundred yards wide. It is considered one of the most treacherous river mouths in the world. The story accurately explains the reason for this. Large vessels always use a bar pilot to navigate its waters. Over the years, the Bar has claimed more than 2000 ships and 700 lives. One of the worst disasters was in 1961 when three coastguard rescue boats and five crewmen were lost in a rescue attempt. Because of its danger, it is home to the only school in the United State that teaches rough weather and rough surf rescue operations. One of the training maneuvers used has the crew rolling and then righting their boat in the midst of the Bar's roiling waters.

31. The United States revenue cutter, *Commodore Perry*, moved into service at the mouth of the Columbia in January 1903. The *Perry*, commissioned in 1884, was a 165-foot iron-hulled, single screw vessel. In 1904, the *Perry* attempted to cross the Bar and rescue two foundering ships. The Bar proved impassable and the two ships sank. In later years the revenue cutter service was combined with the rescue service to become today's U.S. Coast Guard Service.

32. The description of the coastal steamer in the book, the *Maggie Jane*, is based on a photograph of circa 1900 coastal steamer. The photo showed that the gunwale of the loaded vessel rode

perilously close to the water. This fact made it possible for the Chinese men in the story to scale the sides and board the ship. In the early 1900's hundreds of coastal steamers transported crops, manufactured goods, lumber and passengers between the Pacific Coast ports of the United States, Canada and Mexico.

For a short bibliography and photos, please visit:
www.yamhillpress.net.

AUTHOR'S NOTE

Wʜɪʟᴇ ᴡʀɪᴛɪɴɢ ᴛʜᴇ Sᴀɢᴇ Aᴅᴀɪʀ Historical Mystery series I have encountered a number of unexpected coincidences. *Dry Rot* is about a carpenters' strike for the eight-hour day. Only after the book was completed did I learn just such a strike had taken place during the same time period as in the book. And, like in the story, the carpenters won the strike.

For the book, *Black Drop*, I researched President Roosevelt's Portland parade route and settled on a specific location for an assassination attempt. Only after the book was finished did I learn that, in that exact same location, on the exact same day, the police arrested a man for charging at the president. It was the only such incident occurring during his visit.

With this book, the coincidence was even more peculiar. After finishing the book and settling on the title, *The Mangle*, I Googled it to see if there was any other book with that same title. I didn't find one. What I did find was a scientific article describing a theory its author calls "the mangle". The theory describes a process that is similar to what Mae talks about in the story's wrap-up. She noted that their individual lives had undergone a process that changed and joined them all—just as if they'd gone through a laundry mangle together. The scientific mangle theory hypothesizes that scientific discovery and advancement is the product of a process that mangles together the participants' culture, personal bias, technology, history and happenstance to yield a new scientific "truth". Subsequent theorists have applied "the mangle" theory to a variety of fields, including social work and cultural anthropology. It remains a viable theory.

ABOUT THE AUTHOR

S. L. Stoner is a native of the Pacific Northwest who has worked as a citizen change agent and as a labor union and civil rights attorney for many years.

ACKNOWLEDGMENTS

Once again, I want to start by thanking the readers of this series. Their enthusiasm and support has encouraged Sage to keep fighting the good fight. I hope his adventure stories return the favor by encouraging their individual efforts to make the world a better place.

To the extent this series accurately reflects history, that is due to those who have done their best to preserve the past. In particular, I want to thank the staff of the Oregon Historical Society, the Multnomah County Library and Sisters of the Holy Names of Jesus and Mary, Holy Names Heritage Center Library. Also important to this work was a book written by Julia Allen, entitled *Passionate Commitment.* This book tells the true story of two women of the early 1900's who, like the real life Sister Miriam Theresa, dedicated their lives and social work education to the endless task of improving the lives of their fellow humans.

This book in the series received special reviewing assistance from Claudine Paris, Lane Poncy, Anna Johnson, Caroline Miller and George Slanina. Many heartfelt thanks to each of them. That said, any remaining errors are solely my own.

A special thank also goes to KBOO radio's Labor Radio show which has given the series exposure and an ear. And finally, as always, I must acknowledge my husband George Slanina whose unwavering support, kindness and always pithy, right-on observations continue to make this series possible. One can never acknowledge great husbands too often or too much.

Black Drop

In this ripping yarn, President Theodore Roosevelt has left Washington D.C., embarking on his historic train trip through the American West. Little does know that assassination awaits him in Portland, Oregon. The words of a dying prostitute warn Sage Adair and his allies that they will be blamed for Roosevelt's murder. Since life is never simple, Sage also learns of young boys who need rescuing from a fate worse than death. As the presidential train and the boys' doom rush ever closer, every crucial answer remains elusive. Who is enslaving the boys? Who plans to kill the president? Can either tragedy be stopped?

Dead Line

Sage Adair encounters murder and mayhem midst the sagebrush and pine trees of Central Oregon's high desert. This captivating land of big skies, golden light and deadly secrets is the home of hardy and hard people–some of whom intend to kill him.

Request for Pre-Publication Notice

If you would like to receive notice of the publication dates of the seventh Sage Adair historical mystery novel, please complete and return the form below or contact Yamhill Press at www.yamhillpress.net.

Your Name: ______________________________

Street Address: ______________________________

City: __________ State: ____________ Zip: ________

E-mail Address: ______________________________

Yamhill Press
P. O. Box 42348
Portland, OR 97242
www.yamhillpress.net

NOTES